BLIND IMPACT

A GABRIEL WOLFE THRILLER

ANDY MASLEN

TYTON PRESS

CHAPTER 1

The call Kasym Drezna had been waiting for came in at 10.30. He went out onto the balcony of the hotel suite to answer his phone. The stars reflected in the screen matched the white headlights streaming along the road beneath him into the centre of Stockholm.

"It's Erik. The Bryant women are here. They just asked for a car to take them back to the hotel. The Birger Jarl on Tulegatan. You know it?"

"No, I don't know it, you idiot. And it doesn't matter, does it? That's what satnav's for."

"Oh, no. Sorry. How long shall I tell them?"

Kasym checked his watch. "Fifteen minutes. Give them a drink on the house."

"OK. Text me when you arrive and I'll bring them out."

"No. Elsbeta will come in and get them. Just keep them happy. Oh, and Erik?"

"Yes?"

"Pack up some food for me. I haven't eaten today."

He ended the call and went back inside.

"Elsbeta! Get your jacket, we're leaving."

The woman he'd shouted for came out of one of the bedrooms. She was dressed in a smart, black trouser suit. Only a careful observer would have noticed that she wore combat boots under the well-cut trousers, or that the space under her left armpit was bulkier than that on the right. Together, they took the lift down to the parking garage. He thumbed the door-unlock button and pointed at a big black saloon flashing its indicators behind a square concrete pillar edged in black-and-yellow hazard tape. Clearly, the tape was insufficient warning for the hotel's guests: it was rubbed away on the edge, and replaced with scrapes of blue, red and black automotive paint. He gave her the chunky black key for the Mercedes.

"You drive," he said. "They're at Gro Restaurang. Waiting for a car to take them to The Birger Jarl on Tulegatan. Think we could manage that?"

Elsbeta settled herself in the driver's seat and pressed a button marked "2" by her left thigh. They sat, not talking, as electric motors inside the seat brought it closer to the steering wheel, raised it by four inches, tilted the backrest more upright, and performed a half-dozen other movements, accompanied by a conversation of whirrs, hums and buzzes from inside the thickly padded leather.

"Are we ready now?" he asked.

"It's not my fault you're built like a giant," she said. "I want to be comfortable."

She selected Drive and rolled the car around the pillar and along the rows of expensive German and Swedish cars, then left the car park via the ramp that took them out onto Råsta Strandväg. The car was virtually silent inside. She spoke.

"When we get there, I'll bring them out. Are they both going in the back with you?"

"It's best, I think. Easier to watch them. I don't want any funny business, grabbing the steering wheel."

They drove to the restaurant without further conversation. Elsbeta was a good driver. Careful, nothing flashy. She slowed early for red lights and waved people out in front of her. Sometimes it drove Kasym crazy, but tonight it felt right. Appropriate. Luxury limousine drivers didn't power-slide round corners like those stupid American cop shows, or streak away from traffic lights leaving trails of black on the road surface. The fact that she could do all those things was helpful, but tonight he felt the need for calm.

He looked out the side window as Stockholm rolled by. Such affluence. Such ease. These people didn't know what they had. Back home the only cars like the one he was riding in were owned by the men at the very top of Government. Or men like him, he supposed. But here, in social democratic Sweden, they were everywhere. Perhaps not the top models like this one, but plenty of BMWs, Mercedes and Volvos for the common man.

"We're here."

Elsbeta's short sentence roused him from his musings on the inequalities life dealt to different people, different countries. He fished out his phone and sent an even shorter sentence to the Maître D'.

Outside.

He turned to Elsbeta.

"Go."

She opened the door and walked up to the front door of the restaurant. He watched her disappear inside, then got out, moved to the rear seats and squashed himself down on the extreme right of the soft, sculpted seat. God, those fat-arsed Germans loved their comfort. From the outside, the darkened glass would give no hint of his presence.

Then he saw them. Two western women. English women. Coming out ahead of Elsbeta, who had even found a cap with a shiny, black plastic peak from somewhere. She was smiling broadly and extending her arm towards the rear of the car. He noted with approval the foil-wrapped package in her other hand. Erik was nothing if not obedient.

He evaluated the two women. The older one, Sarah Bryant: the wife. Elegant, middle-aged, maybe late forties, early fifties. Blonde hair tied back away from her ears. Tanned skin. Light make-up. Grey skirt and cardigan. High heels. Bad for running. The younger woman, Chloe: the daughter. Still well-dressed, but not formal like her mother. Tall. Tight jeans, red leather biker jacket. Baseball boots. The women were laughing and talking. He watched as they drew closer to the car door.

Elsbeta moved in front of the daughter and opened the door. The young woman slid in, looking out at her mother. By the time she bumped into Kasym's hip, it was too late.

He pulled her across and clamped his hand over her mouth. Elsbeta pushed the mother, not too hard, but hard enough to unbalance her so that she stumbled off the kerb and fell into the back of the Mercedes. The door slammed behind her and in another two seconds, Elsbeta had arrived in the driver's seat and they were pulling away.

As often happens when you catch people out, Sarah Bryant had said nothing, done nothing. Chloe was quicker on the uptake and was writhing and kicking out.

Then Sarah Bryant found her voice.

"What are you doing? Leave her alone."

Kasym needed to take decisive action to silence her and to end the struggles of the daughter, who was now kicking out at the back of the driver's seat, threatening to unsettle Elsbeta.

He reached inside the jacket of his suit and withdrew a long-bladed knife. Keeping his left hand around the young woman's mouth he brought it into her eyeline, where it caught the orangey-yellow glow of the passing streetlamps. The move worked. It usually did. She became completely still. The mother stared, open-mouthed, at the blade. It had a very narrow tip, and glinted viciously along its stone-whetted edge.

Slowly, so that his intent should not be misinterpreted, he uncurled his palm and freed the girl's face from his grip.

She gasped and sobbed in one drawn out, halting exhalation.

Before either woman could speak, Kasym began his prepared words.

"Please listen and say nothing. Not until the end. Then you may ask questions. We are kidnapping you."

Sarah Bryant caught her breath at the word and clutched her daughter's left hand. She glanced down at the chrome door handle.

"Please don't bother. Child locks," he said. "We do not intend, at this point, to harm you, but you must behave yourselves. This is a delicate business, and we have some travelling to do tonight. We need you to encourage your husband to carry out certain actions for us. When he has done as we ask, and we have achieved our objectives, we will let you go. We will even drive you to the airport and give you first-class tickets back to London. But please know this. If you do not behave as required, I shall kill you. In war, one must be prepared to take difficult decisions. Perform unpleasant duties. You would think women would always be safe, but, sadly, it is not so. Now. Question time."

The mother had been rendered speechless by his monologue, but the daughter was less scared. Brave girl. He liked her spirit.

"What war? What actions is Dad supposed to do for you? Why are you doing this? Who are you people?"

"My name is Kasym. Your driver tonight is Elsbeta. We are Chechens. We have our own resources - money, guns - but we need outside assistance from time to time. Your father will be assisting us."

"How? He runs a publicly-owned pharmaceutical company. He's not a banker. He can't just give you money to buy guns or whatever."

Kasym grunted his approval at her smarts.

"We have someone on our payroll at your father's company, in the R&D department. He has a . . ." he paused briefly, ". . . a fondness for young girls. *Very* young girls. We discovered this, and now he is our inside man at Dreyer Pharma. He is making certain modifications to a drug your father's company is working on. For the British Royal Air Force. Then there is a very evil man in Moscow called Oleg Abramov. He is what you would call an oligarch, though this is a polite word for an ex-KGB commander who gets fat by stealing state assets. We heard he plans to buy this drug and sell it to the Russian Government. We cannot allow that to happen." *And after telling you this, I'm afraid your freedom won't happen either.*

The mother had regained her composure and asked the next question.

"Promise you won't hurt us? Promise! Chloe is only twenty-five. She has her whole life in front of her."

"Dear lady," he said. "You have only to cooperate and everything will be fine."

"And where did you learn English? If you're really a Chechen."

"I know, amazing isn't it? A savage terrorist from a place you couldn't even point to on a map, able to speak the Queen's English. I learnt while at university. UMIST. You know it?"

"University of Manchester Institute of Technology," Chloe said. "I studied at the University of Manchester."

"Coincidences, eh? Such an amazing thing. I studied aerospace engineering there. Plenty of time to pick up the lingo. Your Radio 4. Very educational."

Elsbeta spoke. "We're here."

They had pulled up outside the Birger Jarl Hotel.

"Ladies," Kasym said. "Your room number, please."

"It's a suite," Sarah said. "749."

"Very good. A suite. So, Elsbeta will go inside and fetch you some things. We will stay here and get to know each other a little better. Keycard please."

Ten minutes later, Elsbeta exited the hotel's front door carrying two weekend bags. The thumps as she dropped them into the boot were barely audible inside the soundproofed cabin, felt, rather than heard. Then she was back inside the car, and they were pulling away into the traffic on Tulegatan.

"Where are you taking us?" Chloe asked.

"All in good time, young lady," Kasym said.

"And all this. This is for your cause, is it?" Chloe asked. "You're, what, nationalists? Separatists? You want to get out from under Russian control, is that it?"

"You are a clever young lady," Kasym said. "Yes. No doubt they don't teach Chechen history in your English private schools, and I will spare you the details. But let us just say that I have no love for Russians, and nor do my countrymen."

"Actually, I do know some history. You fought in the war for independence?"

"I fought in many wars. I even fought for the Russians in Afghanistan against the Mujahideen. It was . . . expedient. Then, yes, in 1994, against the Russians for a free Chechnya, and once more in 1999. Now I fight once again to free my country from the yoke of the oppressor. I would not expect you to understand, as a child of a great colonial power, but Chechens were not born to be slaves to the Soviets, or the Russians."

The car swung right at a roundabout, leaving Birger Jarlsgatan for the 277. It wasn't the most direct route, but safer. They had to wait while a blue and white city bus pulled past them, its rubber concertina joint flexing as the double-length vehicle negotiated the tight turn.

Without warning, Sarah Bryant leapt forward from her seat and clawed wildly at the back of Elsbeta's head, tearing out a hank of her dirty-blonde hair.

"You take us back right now! Take us back!"

The car swerved as Elsbeta yelped in pain and swung her free hand behind her, landing a glancing blow on Sarah's cheek.

"Shit! You bitch. You could have killed us all. Kasym, do something or I'll stop the car at the next junction and deal with her myself."

As if the effort of attacking Elsbeta had exhausted her, Sarah sank back against the seat and sobbed quietly, her face covered by her hands.

Chloe was sitting upright, tense, arms crossed, sandwiched between mother and kidnapper. Kasym leant across her body and pinched her mother's chin between his strong thumb and forefinger. He wore a heavy gold ring on the third finger of his hand set with a red carved seal. A dragon, it looked like.

He breathed in, then out again, clenching his jaw. It would not do to let these English women see the other side of his character. For now, the courteous kidnapper was the trump card.

"My dear Mrs Bryant," he said. "Please do not be aggressive to Elsbeta. She was assaulted by Russian troops in our capital city, Grozny. It left her with a horror of violence. Will you promise me that? Please?"

Sarah Bryant lifted her head and glared at him.

"Fine. But if you hurt as much as a hair on Chloe's head, I will kill you."

"Oh, I have no doubt you would try. Which is why we must all agree to get along peaceably. We have a long trip ahead of us, and I do not want to have to restrain you beyond the bare minimum necessary to prevent your escape."

"What do you mean, 'a long trip'? Aren't we staying in Stockholm?"

"Tell me something," Kasym said. "Have you ever visited Estonia?"

"Estonia? No, of course we haven't been to Estonia!" Sarah Bryant said. Her eyes widened and she reared back away from Kasym.

"Why 'of course'? The Baltic States are very beautiful countries. Friendly people, lots of money now. Ideal tourist destinations. You agree, don't you, Elsbeta?"

"Tallinn is Estonia's capital and cultural hub. Its walled, cobblestoned Old Town is home to many cafes and shops. Kiek in de Kök, a fifteenth-century defensive tower, guards the city centre like a sentinel." She paused. "Wikipedia."

Kasym grinned at them, showing a row of mottled teeth.

"We will put you up somewhere nice, and you can learn all about the history and culture of this fine city."

"Mum," Chloe said. "Leave it for now. Think about Dad. He's going to be worried."

Kasym approved of the younger woman's tone, and her suggestion. The father would need to be contacted. But not until he had the women safely in Tallinn. For now, they could keep their counsel.

Elsbeta stuck to the speed limit. Kasym didn't want any attention from the police, even though he was a skilled corrupter of underpaid public officials. Keeping his knife in plain view, he looked out of the window, thinking about the Swedes and their designer shops and upmarket restaurants. So much affluence in the West. So much freedom. So much softness, too. Try this little stunt with a couple of Chechen women and you'd likely end up eating your own balls instead of succeeding in the kidnap. He checked his watch: 11.15. Dukka and Makhmad should be tied up at the jetty by now, the boat fuelled and provisioned for the trip. They'd reckoned on a trip of perhaps 12 to 15 hours depending on wind and currents, which meant they'd be at the dock in Tallinn at about two o'clock the following afternoon.

Something caught his eye through the windscreen. A flashing blue light. Elsbeta was already braking. She said a single word.

"Police."

CHAPTER 2

The taxi dropped Gabriel Wolfe and Annie Frears outside the National Portrait Gallery on Charing Cross Road, just north of Trafalgar Square. Gabriel squinted as a shaft of sunlight pierced gathering rain clouds and temporarily blinded him. He paid the driver, then turned to the gallery door with Annie squeezing his arm and chattering about the exhibition of photographs they'd come to see. As they were about to go in, a wizened man approached them. He wore a filthy cream and blue anorak, and had one tooth in his upper jaw and sunken cheeks where the rest had fallen out. He stank of piss and booze, and clutched a handful of copies of *The Big Issue* magazine.

"Excuse me, sir," he said to Gabriel, in a cockney accent rasping with cigarette smoke. "Would you care to purchase a copy of possibly the worst magazine in the whole world?"

The owners of this thin publication sold by homeless people would probably not approve of their salesman's unorthodox technique.

"Er, no thanks. Not after that pitch."

"Well, in that case, 'ow about a donation for a moderately amusing beggar?"

Gabriel laughed and gave the man a pound.

As he and Annie entered the gallery, it started to rain.

Three miles north, Dain Zulfikah was making his penultimate delivery: 200 litres of chemicals to a big commercial laundry in Islington. He dumped the last of the ten-litre cartons in a humid storeroom with a slosh and a thud, and got his docket signed by the manager. Then he swung himself back into the cab of his truck, slammed it into first with a metallic gnashing from the gearbox, and lurched into the traffic. One more drop, and then home for lunch and maybe a quick tumble with the beautiful Amira, his wife of three months. Dain drove in a hurry, speeding towards amber traffic lights, cutting up slow-witted car drivers and frightening over-eager pedestrians back onto the kerb with a sharp blast on the twin air horns he'd retrofitted to the truck. The transport manager had turned a blind eye to this unauthorised modification in exchange for some of Dain's weed. "Best skunk in Peckham," Dain had said at the time.

Gabriel and Annie entered the gloom of the gallery's lobby. After checking in their bags, they headed for the stairs and the sign announcing a new exhibition by Annie's brother, Lazarus.

Annie stopped at a poster. The young man staring off to the side wore a dusty combat helmet, canvas strap dangling at his chin. He looked too young to be wearing it, as if he'd been snapped while playing soldiers.

"Look! There he is. He's only twenty-two and Magnum have invited him to join. Can you believe that? You know who they are, don't you?"

"War photographers," Gabriel said.

"Not just war, but yes. They've been everywhere. Laz is in the same group who had Henri Cartier-Bresson and Robert Capa. It's the big league."

Laz had won his Magnum entry ticket with a series of wrenching pictures of civilian victims of American drone strikes in Afghanistan. This exhibition marked a departure from his war reporting. It was titled, simply, "Angels", and was the result of a three-month trip to the US when Laz had ridden with a chapter of the Hells Angels. Gabriel had met some members of this organised crime gang not long before the exhibition had opened. The experience had not left him eager to renew his acquaintance, even through photographs. But Annie had persuaded him in bed one morning, pushing her tousled hair out of her eyes and pouting in a way she knew Gabriel found hard to resist. They weren't in a relationship, according to her. She'd used the phrase "friends with benefits" which he'd never heard before. Apparently, it meant shopping, hanging out and sex, but "definitely not anything serious". That worked for Gabriel. Commitment was a hard word for him, and as he had no intention of settling down, the arrangement suited him perfectly.

* * *

"Out my way, loser!" Dain yelled over the drum and bass pounding from the truck's stereo as he tailgated an electrically-powered city car. The little vehicle veered into the bus lane to let him through, a tinny beep from its horn letting him know of the owner's disapproval. Holborn was slow and Dain was impatient. Reaching the crossroads where Southampton Row and Kingsway join, he raced for the dregs of the amber light to make it across and into High Holborn, scattering a crowd of office workers and tourists mooching across the pedestrian crossing on the far side of the junction.

He peeled off to the left down Monmouth Street, stabbing the brake pedal and swearing as a taxi swung into the curb in front of him to pick up a fare whistling for a ride. Then he found himself enjoying an unexpectedly empty stretch of road that took him barrelling south towards St Martin's Lane, Cranbourn Street, and then Charing Cross Road, heading for Trafalgar Square. He reached for his phone as he visualised Amira's generous hips and rounded bottom, and spoke into the mic.

"Call Amira."

* * *

In the gallery, Gabriel and Annie stood before the first of several whitewashed walls hung with 50 cm-square black-and-white portraits. Seven hard faces stared out at them. Starting at the right, they stared back. The first man had a tattoo of a death's head on his right cheekbone. His eyes looked like ball bearings.

"He looks bad, Gabe," Annie said.

"He probably is," Gabriel said.

"Oh God, look at him," she said, pointing to the next man along.

The face above the leather waistcoat with a Flint Chapter patch was pockmarked from acne, and weirdly pale. Odd for someone who spent his life on a bike.

As Annie stared into the fat man's fleshy face, Gabriel looked around the room. There were a few twentysomethings with notebooks and heavy-framed glasses who he assumed were photography students; a middle-aged couple who looked like they had been aiming for the Titians and Caravaggios in the National Gallery round the corner and been waylaid by a mischievous tour guide; and a guard in a cheap navy-blue uniform with half-hearted silver badging, slumped on a plastic chair against the far wall and picking something out of his left ear.

"Gabriel, look at this one," Annie said. "He gives me the creeps."

Gabriel turned to look at the portrait. As he took in the scar bisecting the man's ruined eye, and the shiny, gold, canine tooth winking out at him, he felt a tingling in his fingertips. His breathing became fast and shallow and the room seemed to recede around him. Sweat broke out on his brow, his palms, and under his shirt. He knew this man. His name was Davis Meeks. Gabriel had met him, twice, on his last mission. First at his clubhouse in Flint, Michigan, then at the farm belonging to a South African arms dealer named Bart Venter. Neither man was now alive.

Then the face of Davis Meeks spoke to him, right out of the portrait.

"I'm coming for you, boy. Like I said the last time. Gonna put you down like a dog."

Gabriel's body flooded with adrenaline. He started hyperventilating, and his pulse rate jerked upwards.

An immense tide of fear broke over the internal barriers he'd erected so carefully over the years to protect his psyche. As Davis Meeks leered down at him, Gabriel's arms and legs began trembling violently. He turned away from Annie, who was still engrossed by the Hells Angel's wickedly disfigured countenance.

Not now. Please. Meeks is dead. This isn't real.

Gabriel looked over at the seated guard. But now the man wore the face of Mickey "Smudge" Smith – an SAS Trooper Gabriel had left, dead, in a Mozambican jungle, his body pinned to a tree by machetes through both palms. The guard looked up and smiled. His dark brown skin was shining. The smile widened until the skin at the corners of his mouth split and blood started flowing down onto the white collar of his shirt.

"Smudge?" Gabriel said, heart racing now. "Is that you?"

The guard spoke.

"How could it be me, Boss? You left me behind after we took out Abel N'Tolo. Couldn't survive this, now could I?"

He looked beseechingly at Gabriel as the whole lower part of his face splintered into bloody shards and fell into his lap.

Gabriel shouted "No!" and ran from the gallery towards the main doors.

* * *

Driving down Charing Cross Road, Dain was enjoying the call with his wife.

"Why don't you wear your birthday present? ... Oh, you would,

would you? Well we'll have to see about that, won't we ... God you're a dirty tart!"

He didn't notice the cycle messenger a few feet in front of his front bumper. Her Lycra and carbon-fibre gear might have looked good, but afforded little protection from a three-tonne delivery truck.

"Shit!"

He dropped the phone and swerved at the last possible second, hearing her curses flash by the open passenger window as he crossed the white lines down the centre of the road to avoid her. The island placed in the road by Westminster Council to bracket the pedestrian crossing rushed at him. No option but to skirt it on the wrong side of the road. God was smiling on him at that moment: either Him or whoever set the timing programme for the traffic lights at the exit from Trafalgar Square. They changed to red, halting the cars, bikes and vans, and giving him a free run around the traffic island and back onto his side of the road.

Even without its load, the truck was an unwieldy vehicle, and its designers had never intended it to take corners as viciously as Dain was forcing it to now. Up ahead, at the red lights, three bikers revved their machines impatiently, the sound carrying in the still air. He didn't want to be facing them in a head-on: the company's insurers would kick up a fuss and his job would go down the toilet just like that.

He passed the crossing island and wrenched the wheel over hard to the left, dimly registering the black-haired man racing from the plate glass doors to his right. The truck skidded, its tyres unable to grip the greasy road surface under so much lateral force. The rear end slewed around and mounted the pavement.

The bang was loud inside the truck's cabin.

Dain slammed on the brakes, cut the engine and leapt from the cab.

Lying on his back, bleeding from a gash on his scalp, was a man in a dark suit. His eyes were closed.

Dain pushed through the circle of onlookers taking video on phones.

"Get out the way! Call an ambulance!"

Dain bent over the prone figure on the pavement, kneeling carefully to avoid the blood pooling underneath his head, and checked his pulse. Then he leant closer still and felt the cool whisper of breath on his cheek.

"OK, he's alive. Stand back. Give him some air."

Minutes later, a siren's wail made everyone look round, then Gabriel was being lifted onto a gurney and pushed quickly but carefully into the interior of the ambulance. Annie jumped in beside him, batting away the paramedic who tried to restrain her from cradling Gabriel's bleeding head.

"Leave me alone!" she said. "He needs me."

"What him need is a hospital, my love," the woman said, her soft Jamaican cadences at odds with the harsh lighting and stainless steel inside the cramped space. "You can ride here, but please, sit yourself over there so we can do our work. What's his name?"

"Gabe. I mean, Gabriel. Please, is he going to be all right?"

"He's had a nasty bump, love. We'll get him to St Thomas' and the doctors can look after him."

CHAPTER 3

Kasym leaned forward.

"Be calm. There's been an accident. Just be who you're supposed to be – a chauffeur with three important passengers. Talk them round."

He turned to the two women in the back seat.

"You will stay silent and Elsbeta or I will do any talking that needs to be done. You might feel that you can signal with your eyes, or scream for help, and they will save your lives." He shook his head. "One word and we will kill them. Then you. We are fighting for our homeland. The lives of two Englishwomen and a couple of Swedish cops do not even make the scales tremble."

Elsbeta brought the car to a smooth stop a couple of yards away from the traffic police officer standing behind the blue and white Saab that half-blocked the road. She pressed the switch to lower the window. The blond policeman leaned down and spoke some words of Swedish. Elsbeta gave him a blank, uncomprehending look and shrugged.

"British?" he asked.

She flashed him a wide, toothy smile.

"Estonian. Sorry."

"It's OK," he continued, switching seamlessly into English. "Sorry to hold you up. There was a hit and run. Did you see a red van passing you in that direction?" He pointed back behind the car, the way they had come.

"Sure, yes we did. On Lidingövägen. Going like a bat out of hell. All over the road."

"Excellent. Thank you." He glanced into the back of the car. "Good evening, folks. Sorry to disturb your journey."

"That's perfectly OK, officer," Kasym said. "Just taking my cousin and her daughter to the ferry terminal."

"OK. Enough room in the back there for the three of you?"

"Ha! It's OK. We like to sit in the back. Road safety statistics show it's five times safer for a passenger than sitting up front."

"You got that right. You wouldn't want to see what we see on a Saturday night after the bars close. Have a good night."

"Good night officer," Kasym said with a gracious smile. He could feel Chloe's arm muscles tense against his side and pushed his left elbow firmly but slowly into her ribs. Just a reminder to play it by the rules. Her arm softened. Then the policeman was back in his car and driving off, siren wailing in the night.

After that, they encountered no further interruptions, and five minutes later they were pulling off the main road and onto a feeder road to the ferry terminal. They drove the whole length of Frihamnsgatan, then pulled up in the lee of a huge blue corrugated steel shed. A warehouse of some kind.

"We're going to get out now," Kasym said. "Our friends Makhmad and Dukka are waiting for us down there." He pointed towards the water. "We have a very nice motor boat for the trip. There are berths for you both so you can get some sleep. Please don't think of running or screaming. The only people round here this time of night are truckers sleeping in their cabs, and they'll just assume it's a couple of disgruntled whores."

To emphasise his point, he pulled back the flap of his suit jacket. Tucked into his belt was his second-favourite pistol, a Makarov he'd pulled from the shaking hand of a teenaged Russian soldier in Grozny before knifing him in the gut. He'd felt bad for a moment, killing the kid, but he'd probably have gone on to rape a few more Chechens so no sleep lost. The gun wasn't as accurate or as well made as Kasym's Glock 17, but it symbolised the struggle. It symbolised the victory.

The women looked disorientated. They'd be docile enough. And Elsbeta could always administer a couple of sisterly slaps if they showed signs of skittishness. Somehow, violence was always more disturbing when it came from a woman. In Elsbeta's case, it was a fact at least thirty Russian troops had become acquainted with, to their great misfortune.

Outside, the temperature had dropped. He didn't really mind the cold, but the two women were shivering. Probably more shock than anything else.

"Come on," he said. "I can hear the boat."

Together, he and Elsbeta herded the two women towards the concrete barrier separating the access road from the water. He carried both holdalls so the three women could travel ahead of him. They stepped over the low moulded blocks of concrete to see a sleek white cabin cruiser, its motor burbling as it bobbed on the incoming tide. A name, 'Anja', was painted in neat, black script on the prow. At the wheel stood a tall man with long, untidy black hair and a bushy black beard: Makhmad. Standing on the foredeck, holding out his hand, was a shorter, fatter man: Dukka. The three men were former comrades in arms, fighting against the Russians. Now they ran a number of "lines of business" as they liked to call them: extortion, protection rackets, kidnapping and assassinations. All to fund ongoing actions against the hated Russian authorities.

Before they climbed down onto the boat, Kasym put out a restraining hand on Sarah Bryant's forearm.

"A moment," he said. "Your phone. Please."

He held out his calloused hand.

Watched her as she looked at his outstretched fingers.

Registered her look of surprise, the mouth dropping open involuntarily.

The first and middle fingers were missing their top joints. The skin closing the wounds was puckered, like tiny pursed mouths.

"Not very pretty, are they?" he said. "I was captured for a while in Afghanistan. This was just the start of what those savages had planned for me. But Dukka – who you will meet in just a minute – he rescued me. Shot them down like dogs. Then removed every single finger and toe and stuffed their mouths with them. He is not someone to cross. Just a friendly warning. Now. Your phones."

He twitched his fingers upwards a couple of times. Sarah Bryant reached into her handbag and pulled out her phone, a sleek silver model – something bespoke, he'd not seen one before – and dropped it into his palm. Without waiting to be asked, Chloe placed hers, a Samsung in a turquoise silicone case, on top of her mother's.

He pocketed the phones. "Thank you. Now, let's get onboard."

Kasym was glad to see his crew. He'd operated outside Eastern Europe several times, but preferred the familiar territory of home. Similar culture, similar languages, better food, more drinking than in the prissy, health-conscious West. And always a good living to be made for a man prepared to be entrepreneurial and violent in equal measures. As he got down onto the deck and handed the women's bags to Dukka, he sighed happily and hugged the round man tightly, kissing him on each cheek.

"Dukka! I'm glad to see you. Those Swedes and their herrings. I thought I was going to turn into a fish if we had to stay there another night!"

"Come below, Boss. I got some steaks cooking. And cold beers." Then, as if noticing the women for the first time, he jerked his chin. "What you want to do with them?"

"Show them their berths. And the heads. Give them food, drink. Make them comfortable." Then, loud enough for the women to hear, and in English this time. "And if they try anything funny, use your knife."

"Sure, Boss. Ha! I'll slit them like fish. Flopping on the deck. You got it!"

Dukka was simple, but loyal. He'd saved Kasym's life on three occasions, and Kasym felt a powerful love for the squat, smiling man. And for his innocent joy in despatching Russians or anyone else Kasym asked him to.

He opened the door to the cabin.

"Kasym!" the tall man at the wheel roared. "I thought you'd decided to move here permanently. Those Swedish girls, eh? You could spend your life fucking them and not get tired."

"No way my friend. After a month, you'd feel like you were eating cakes and pastries all the time. No meat on them. Give me a good strong Chechen girl any time. You have a course laid in for Tallinn?"

"Say the word, my Captain."

"OK. Let's go. I'm tired of this fucking country."

While the women slept, Kasym briefed his team on their next steps.

"Elsbeta, when we get to Tallinn, you and Dukka take them to the safe house. Get them settled. Then go out and buy some food and a newspaper. Dukka, you stay with them. Makhmad and I have some rents to collect."

"Boss?" It was Dukka. Loyal, faithful Dukka. Kasym smiled at him. Like an overgrown child, only with the strength of a bull and a temper to match.

"What is it?"

"Supposing, I mean, those women. If they try anything. What you want me to do with 'em? Like a slap or something. Maybe more?"

The big man's wide open eyes pleaded, as if he were half afraid of angering the boss and half desperate to please him.

"No. Don't hurt them. They will be quiet, I promise you. I'll have Elsbeta give them their instructions. You just need to watch them."

"Like a hawk!"

Kasym leaned across the table and patted the big man on the back of his huge hairy paw.

"Yes, Dukka. Like a hawk. You remember, we used to watch them at home, in the forest?"

"Oh, yes, Boss. Beautiful, weren't they? So high. We wanted to fly like them too."

"We did. And one day we will, I promise. But for now, we need those women alive and well so that's your job, my friend."

They finished their steaks, drank some beers and, apart from Makhmad, settled down on the thin cushions to grab such sleep as they could manage, as the big motor cruiser powered east, through the Baltic Sea towards the Gulf of Finland.

CHAPTER 4

Gabriel's coma, caused by the collision with Dain Zulfikah's delivery truck, then maintained by his doctors, lasted for nineteen days.

He sat up in bed and immediately wished he hadn't. Fireworks exploded in his head, sending pink and white stars fizzling around the periphery of his vision and igniting a charge in his skull that made him groan from the pain. He sank back onto the pillow. Maybe a less abrupt recce would be more sensible. He inched his head to the left. There was a big sash window, through which he could see an expanse of striped lawn, dotted with benches. Some of the benches had men sitting on them. Men with odd, glistening limbs that twinkled in the sun. Men crying, and being comforted by nurses. Men playing chess, gripping the black and white pieces with two fingers, or between their toes.

He turned to his right.

In the next bed, a man lay, staring up at the ceiling. His face was badly bruised and scraped, and half his hair was shaved away. A long wound bisecting his scalp was closed with dozens of black, spidery stitches. He was humming a tune. Gabriel recognised it. It was the theme from an old war film.

"Hey," Gabriel croaked. "Where are we?"

The man stopped humming, mid-bar. He turned his head

towards Gabriel. His pale-blue eyes were wide open but they didn't focus on Gabriel's.

"Audley Grange."

"Audley Grange? But that's military. I was in London. How the hell did I get here?"

"How did any of us get here? One minute you're flying at 10,000 feet, the next you think your cockpit's full of talking spiders and then you go blind. Just like poor old Eddie."

"Jesus! Is that what happened to you?"

The man sighed. "I remember it like it was yesterday."

* * *

Squadron Leader Tom Ainsley smiles as he pulls the throttle lever on his Typhoon all the way back. He glances left, then right. He flicks the switch to light the afterburners and whoops with delight as the additional thrust kicks him hard in the back. Climbing vertically, he checks the instruments: everything is fine. Christ! I'm a lucky guy, he thinks. He looks behind him, at the chequerboard fields receding into a fine-grained mosaic of green, brown and yellow. Up beyond 3,000 feet he shoots, into the untried zone. He can feel Gulliver, or thinks he can, coursing through his bloodstream. Tom popped the two blue and green tablets half an hour before take-off and now someone has lit the afterburners in his brain, too.

He looks to his left and sees the curvature of the Earth. Every detail is etched with a fine point: he can identify individual trees and buildings over what must be forty or fifty miles. The air mixture being fed through his mask smells wonderful, like strawberry ice cream. The engines are singing to him. Tom can feel individual synapses firing in his brain, their microscopic bursts of chemicals leaping the gaps between the nerve fibres and transmitting his wishes from mind to controls instantaneously. Now he thinks about it, the plane is anticipating his will, adjusting bearing, speed and trim at the precise moment he begins evaluating the correction.

Tom nudges the control stick and sends the jet into a sharp turn to port, then back the other way, rolling over a wingtip. The jet flips up into a tight reverse loop before barrel-rolling out of it and resuming its climb.

At 7,500 feet, Tom feels something clambering out of his right boot and pattering around the outside of his olive-green flight suit. He looks down at his lap. A spider sits there: its fat, brown body is as big as the palm of his hand and covered in black and red hairs. Its eight eyes are looking up at him. They are the red, white and blue roundels painted on the wings of his plane.

Tom dismisses it. You don't get spiders in the cockpits of fighter jets. Anyway, he's in the mood for some fun.

"Time for more aerobaticals my chums, my mates, my pearly gates, let's see . . . what can we show the boffins? I know, an inside-out stall turn. Here we go, my gorgeous, look lively."

The second spider is harder to ignore. He is holding its tawny body in his hand instead of the control stick. As he screams, other spiders show themselves, swarming out from under the ejector seat and skittering their way into the sleeves of his flight suit.

Tom screams some more. The spiders have long, amber-coloured fangs. The biting doesn't hurt but he can't feel the controls any more.

When his vision snaps off like a dead TV set he moans with despair and tries to reach his eyes, but his hands are too heavy and they hang uselessly between his legs.

The Typhoon twirls towards the ground. Tom sees nothing, but he hears the spiders forcing their way into his brain and laughing at him.

"Pancakes for tea, Tom," they giggle.

He finds some deeply-hidden reserve of strength and pulls the black and yellow ejector seat release handle between his thighs. Then the lights go out.

* * *

"I totally forgot my training. Every single page of the manual turned to vapour. Didn't panic. Didn't choke. Took my flight helmet off at some point. Then some little part of me got clear-headed enough to eject. I went sideways. Hit a copse while the rockets were still firing, hence the mess I made of my face."

Then he started weeping. Fat, translucent tears rolled sideways out of his eyes and into the neck of his pyjama jacket.

"And I'm blind. They say it's temporary but that that's just the MO trying to keep my spirits up. I'm never going to see again. Never going to fly again."

"But what happened? It sounds like you were tripping. You weren't on anything were you?"

Gabriel knew from his days in the SAS that drugs and soldiering – or flying – just didn't mix. You'd be out on a dishonourable discharge if they caught you with so much as an oversized Rizla paper in your kit.

"Of course not! I dreamed of flying since I was a kid making Airfix kits in my bedroom. That's how come I got onto the Typhoon Programme. Look," he said, leaning awkwardly across the gap between the beds, "keep this to yourself, but we were recruited onto a drugs trial. Totally hush-hush. Performance-boosting meds you take thirty minutes before take-off."

"And you think this was a side-effect?"

"I don't know. We'd tried them groundside for months in prep. All kinds of test rigs, static line parachute jumps, sensory deprivation chambers. Christ, we popped so many of the damn things we used to rattle. But they were so good. I used to zone in playing Tetris and just fry the damn thing. A mate halved his reaction time. Halved! That's just not possible, normally. It would mean whole seconds in a dogfight. Life, instead of death."

This speech seemed to exhaust the man and he levered himself back onto his pillows and resumed humming. His sightless eyes remained open.

The room had two other beds, but they were empty. Gabriel tried to sit up again. He was rewarded with another starburst, but the pain was a little less this time. He twisted around and saw what he was looking for. A red button set in a cream plastic surround. Above it, in white capitals pressed out of blue plastic tape, a single word: CALL. He pressed it hard and left his thumb there for a count of ten.

The door hissed open on damped hinges. A plump young woman in nurse's whites and rubber clogs strode into the room. Her hair was the colour of polished copper. Her face was set in a frown, but she smiled when she saw Gabriel sitting up in bed.

"Was it yourself who pressed the call button?" she asked, her accent a lilting melody from somewhere in Ireland.

"Sorry. I just, this is all a bit confusing. He said this is Audley Grange. Is that right?"

"It is. And do we know why we're here?"

"*We* were in London at the National Portrait Gallery. We had to get some fresh air. Next thing we know, we're lying here with an axe buried in our skull."

The nurse sat on the end of Gabriel's bed, tutting at his sarcasm. She smoothed out a crease she'd pulled in the blanket as her weight settled onto the mattress. She spoke softly, as if to a child worried about monsters under the bed.

"First of all, do you know your name?"

"Gabriel Wolfe. The Prime Minister is . . ."

She laughed. "No need for that. You had a bad concussion and a fractured skull. The ambulance took you to St Thomas' and when we heard about what happened, we whisked you up here to lovely Warwickshire. You've been in a coma, my love."

"What? How long for? And why am I here? I mean, on whose authority?"

"You've a lot of questions. I'm going to leave someone else to answer them. He'll be here directly once I tell him you're awake. But it wasn't just fresh air you wanted in that gallery, was it?"

"What do you mean? It was hot in there, I was wearing a suit. I just felt . . . off."

The nurse smiled, a little sorrowfully. "Annie told us you were staring around you like you were having a night terror. Then you ran out of the gallery and practically fell under the wheels of a truck. It's a miracle you're not dead, so it is," she said, crossing herself. "Now, you sit tight, young man. I'm going back to the nurses' station to make a call."

Gabriel lay back against the pillows, massaging his temples, trying to stop any more charges detonating in his brain. He focused on his breathing the way his childhood tutor Zhao Xi had taught him in Hong Kong. "Slow, like the tide turning," Master Zhao had said, patiently, as the teenage boy in front of him had huffed and puffed. Now, he felt the muscles each side of his neck start to unclench. The anxiety squirrelling around in his stomach started to fade, and he felt a delicious calm settling on him like a cool sheet on a summer night. What had happened, really? He'd seen the portrait of Davis Meeks. Then he'd seen Mickey "Smudge" Smith, carrying the fatal wounds he'd sustained in a botched operation in the African jungle.

Gabriel's superiors hadn't thought of it in those terms, of course. They'd judged the mission a success. Yes, Trooper Smith's death was unfortunate, his unrecovered body, regrettable; but the leader of a bloodthirsty militia was dead and his plans secured. They'd wanted to decorate Gabriel for the action, but he'd told them he would refuse to accept any medals. That was when the nightmares had started, and he'd resigned his commission not long afterwards.

Now he was back in the protective bosom of the Army. Audley Grange was the specialist hospital for all British and Commonwealth veterans of conflicts, domestic and foreign, stretching from Belfast to Bosnia, Zambia to Zagreb. The men he'd seen outside wore the latest prosthetic limbs, developed specifically to deal with the traumatic injuries inflicted by IEDs in the Middle East. And psychiatric care was always on hand for any serving or former soldier who woke up one day afraid to go out, or to climb outside of a bottle.

His reverie was interrupted as the door swung open again. He recognised the man who entered. He was in mufti – tan trousers, a forest green V-necked jumper and open-neck white shirt.

"Sir! I—"

"Now, now. None of that 'Sir' business. You're on civvy street now and I'm quite happy with Don."

The speaker was Gabriel's former commanding officer.

"OK, Don. Please can you tell me what's going on?"

"I've been here for a couple of days. Waiting to do just that. Are you up for a tootle round the grounds?"

"My head's not so good but sure, why not?"

"Wait there. Just going to liberate a chair."

Webster left the room and returned a few minutes later pushing a wheelchair.

"Hop in. I know you were mobile troop, but if the old bonce is giving you gyp, probably better to let me drive."

Gabriel swung his legs over the side of the bed and half dropped, half levered himself down onto the black vinyl seat of the wheelchair.

CHAPTER 5

"Boss! We're here!" It was Makhmad, calling from the cabin.

Kasym knuckled his eyes to get the sleep out of them, and stumbled forward to see where they were.

Ahead, he could see the lights of Tallinn. Red and green navigation beacons marked the official entry channel to the port, but they weren't using them. With their shallow draught and unorthodox cargo, they motored on a virtually closed throttle up to a private dock behind some blocks of flats well to the west of the customs officers, police, dockers, ships' crews, fishermen, crane drivers, truckers, foot passengers, tourists, locals and all the other opportunities for their hostages to cause trouble.

While Makhmad held the boat steady a foot or two from the ridged concrete wall of the dock, Kasym and Elsbeta flipped the blue plastic fenders over the rail to cushion the boat's side. Then he leapt across the two-foot gap to the quay, and began tying the bow rope to an iron bollard worn smooth by centuries of use. Dukka joined him, tying up at the stern. With the boat secure, Makhmad cut the big diesel engines, the only sound now the slapping of the water trapped in the gap between the side of the boat and the dock.

It was 2.15 in the afternoon. Nobody about. Perfect for getting the women from the boat to the house. Kasym went below. Sarah and

Chloe were talking in low voices. As he entered their cabin they stopped immediately and clutched each other's hands. Kasym noticed their knuckles were white.

"Welcome to Tallinn, ladies. Now, if you will go before me, we can get you onto dry land."

He ushered them in front of him with one arm held wide, and watched as the younger woman climbed the short ladder ahead of him. Then the mother. He resisted the urge to help her up the narrow steps with a steadying hand on her hip. Once everyone was standing on the weedy, cracked pavement, bags at their feet, Kasym pointed to an archway that led straight through a block of flats facing the water.

"Through there. Elsbeta and Dukka, you go first. Ladies, you next. Makhmad and I will come last."

He hefted the bags, and the ill-assorted party made their way across the dusty road to the arch. Beyond, there were masses of young trees in full leaf. Whatever else Estonia had managed since throwing off its Soviet-forged shackles, it had not yet succumbed to the squalid commercialisation that always seemed to follow. The road on which he'd acquired the house was so full of trees it resembled a track through a forest campsite more than a housing estate.

He stopped at a red front door, identical to all the others save for a white number 10, painted to the left of the door on the sand-coloured bricks. Kasym looked left and right. Down the street a couple of little kids were playing in the dust with a rudimentary trolley filled with dolls. The girl, obviously in charge of her younger brother, looked up at him and smiled. He waved back. Then he unlocked the door and pointed.

"Inside, please," he said.

They walked into the house. The hall was narrow, with three doors leading off it. Dumping the bags, he opened the first door, for all the world as if he were an estate agent and his hostages were potential buyers.

"Living room. You have a TV, VCR – sorry, out-of-date technology, I know, but this is Estonia now, not Sweden. There are playing cards, even board games. Look, Monopoly. The perfect symbol of everything the Soviets hated."

From the sitting room, he led them into a smaller room empty save for a rowing machine and a set of dumbbells.

"I'm afraid while you are our guests, we cannot permit you to leave the house. You can keep fit in here."

The women were mute. They were still holding hands. He noticed a look on their faces he had seen before. Realisation. Their faces were slack, mouths downturned, eyes blank. This was really happening, the expression said. He didn't mind. It made them easier to handle, docile. Handing out rewards for good behaviour later would seem the act of a saint.

He took them through to the kitchen. It was basic, but equipped with oven, fridge, microwave and sink, so enough to live with quite comfortably for weeks, or months, as needed. Through the kitchen window, they looked out onto a small patch of garden. Vegetables grew there. Tall tangles of scarlet-flowered runner beans twined up pyramids of bamboo canes; courgettes spread their hairy leaves like umbrellas over the swelling emerald cylinders and splashy yellow flowers; tomatoes grew along the chain-link fence at the rear of the plot, heavy trusses of red and yellow fruit drooping to the ground.

Kasym pointed.

"Plenty of fresh fruit and vegetables, you see. No problem with your five a day!"

Elsbeta laughed. A girlish sound, even after everything she had been through, that always made Kasym smile.

"Yes, we must keep you healthy," she said. "Can't send you back home with scurvy, can we?"

"OK, that's enough," Kasym said. "Elsbeta, take them upstairs. You have a room to share, ladies. Have a wash. Get changed. Then I want you down here in one hour."

When Elsbeta returned, he repeated his orders from the boat.

"Elsbeta, get food and a paper. *Eesti Päevaleht* or *Äripäev*. Make sure it's today's edition. Dukka, you are on guard here. I have their phones, so they can't create too much mischief. There are knives in the kitchen but I put a lock on the drawer. Any trouble, a little tap only. Got that?"

"Sure, Boss. Be nice but a little tap if they're naughty girls. Got it."

"OK. Makhmad. We have some money to collect from that casino downtown. Everyone, we meet back here at four."

Kasym and Makhmad walked round to the back of the house. A battered Peugeot hatchback sat under a lime tree, its roof and bonnet spattered with droplets of the tree's sticky sap that had attracted pollen and road dust, forming a thin velvet coating the soft beige colour of ground ginger. Kasym unlocked the car, and the two big men squeezed their frames into the front seats. With a wheezy cough, the little car's engine came to life. Lacking Elsbeta's finesse behind the wheel, Kasym muscled the gear lever into first and took off down the tree-lined road, turning right and heading for Tallinn's tourist area in the Old Town.

Ten minutes later, having parked the Peugeot in a side street amongst a gaggle of mopeds, he and Makhmad entered Casino Festival by the plain steel back door, the one reserved for staff. It was too early for the place to be open, and in the light provided by half a dozen halogen spots they could see a man vigorously swabbing the floor with a mop whose shaggy head matched his own straggly blond locks.

They approached him silently. He raised his head only when the toe of Kasym's boot blocked the progress of his mop. He was wearing headphones under his hair. Kasym reached forward with his damaged left hand and pulled the little earbuds out.

"Hey! Don't mess with my music, man," the blond cleaner said. Then he registered the size and facial expressions of the two men facing him. "Oh. I mean, who are you looking for?"

Makhmad spoke.

"Tell Pete, Kasym and Makhmad are here for the rent." Then he clipped the young man round the ear with a flat, hard palm that rotated his head on his scrawny neck.

The cleaning guy retreated swiftly into the gloom behind the bar, disappearing through a scarred door.

They waited.

Thirty seconds passed, during which time Kasym and Makhmad did nothing, said nothing. Then the door swung open again and a thin, greasy-haired man in a denim waistcoat and fake leather jeans came through. He looked at them: Kasym first, then Makhmad. Coughed. Ran his hand over the bald spot at the back of his head, just in front of the place where his ponytail started.

"Oh, hey, Kasym. I heard you were away."

CHAPTER 6

Outside, Gabriel and Don meandered along gravelled paths set in beautiful gardens planted with flowers and shrubs in fiery summer hues. Gabriel recognised some from his own sprawling cottage garden.

"Why am I here, Don?" Gabriel asked again.

"You know as well as I do that you were always entitled to ask for help here, whether or not you were still serving. There's a standing instruction posted with every hospital in the UK that if an ex-serviceman or woman gets admitted, they notify us. If they're from the Regiment, they come straight through to my personal email, bypassing everyone." He sighed and came around the front of the wheelchair, squatting down so his grey eyes were level with Gabriel's brown ones. "You didn't just trip on a kerb, Gabriel. I spoke to your lady-friend, Annie? You had a full-blown panic attack and nearly got yourself killed. Want to tell me what that's all about?"

"It was nothing, really. I just felt a bit overheated in there. Probably wearing too many layers."

"And the truck? Forget our Green Cross Code, did we?"

"He was on the wrong side of the road. Must have been. Otherwise I'd have seen him."

Don got to his feet and walked round to the back of the chair again. Started pushing.

"You'll be signed off fit again in a while, with some paracetamol for the headache. Apparently they have degrees of coma – something called the Glasgow Coma Scale. You were between a two and a three – not the worst. They'll tell you to report to your local doctor's surgery to have the stitches out of your head in a week or two. But I'm telling you to think about what's happening on the inside. Been having flashbacks, by any chance? Nightmares? Fearfulness? Bursts of anger?"

Gabriel pushed away the image of Smudge Smith and his fractured face.

"I'm fine. Really. Can we go inside, please? My head's splitting."

Don turned the wheelchair gently and pushed Gabriel back inside, up a ramp, along the corridor and into the room he shared with the blond pilot. A sour silence persisted between the two men. They both knew Gabriel was lying, and neither had the desire to pick the scab covering the wound that provoked the deceit.

"Look. Get yourself better. Get back home. And think about what I said. There are people here, good people who can help you. One call is all it takes. Take this." He held a small rectangular card with simple, black script embossed on one side. "It's not my work card, it's my personal one. For friends. When you need me, call that number. I promise you, I'll be ready to help whenever you do."

Gabriel felt a sudden, overwhelming urge to cry. He fought back the tears and tried to swallow the lump in his throat. Eyes glistening, he took the card and muttered a gruff, "thanks".

Don smiled, turned on his heel, and was gone.

"Is that you, mate?" the pilot said. "Listen, there's something I think you should hear."

Gabriel wheeled himself closer to the pilot's bedside. Then he changed direction and headed for the window, which he pulled closed. Something about the way the man spoke made him feel the need for greater privacy. He looked at the man's face. He was no more than twenty-four or five – the Royal Air Force was still doing its best work with the young. If you could ignore the scabs and scratches, and the bare scrape of scalp furrowed with that long crawling line of stitches, he was handsome. The sightless eyes were a light brown, fringed with long lashes. Odd to be able to look so closely at someone without their looking back at you.

"My name's Gabriel, by the way. Sorry not to introduce myself before." Gabriel took the pilot's hand in his and they shook, awkwardly.

"Tom. Former Squadron Leader Tom Ainsley." The way he said "Former" carried equal parts of despair and venom.

"So, tell me. What happened?"

Tom pulled himself upright and orientated himself to the sound of Gabriel's voice. His neck muscles strained with the effort and pushed the pyjama jacket's collar open. They seemed thick and out of proportion to the rest of him. The effect of battling extreme G-forces every day, Gabriel supposed.

"There were five of us on the programme. They called it Project Gulliver. Supposed to make us giants surrounded by Lilliputians. God knows how long it took them to dream that one up. Me, Mark Willis, Josh Harrison, Eddie Hepper and Shiona Webb."

"Shiona? I thought . . ."

"You're a bit out of touch, then, aren't you? The RAF has been training women for fast jets for years. Well, not years, but they're up there. And they're bloody good. Calmer than the guys, the best of them."

"Sorry. We didn't have girls in the SAS. Carry on."

Tom's demeanour changed as soon as the three initials left Gabriel's lips.

"SAS? You guys are the best. Three years ago, my squadron was flying attack missions off a US aircraft carrier. We were embedded with the US Marine Corps. Afghanistan. It meant we could support the Yanks, but the politicians got to say there were no British forces active there. Technically we were American forces. Can you believe that?"

Gabriel thought back to the conclusion of his last mission. To the casual way the Home Secretary had admitted to extrajudicial killings to clean up after an operation on British soil. Oh, he could believe anything of politicians.

"Easily," he said. "Go on."

"One of our pilots was shot down by an surface-to-air missile. It was a group of SAS guys who went out to rescue him. Where was I? Oh, yes. Sorry. My head's a lot better, but I still keep tuning out. I'm not being funny, but we five were the best pilots in the RAF. Consistently aced all flight exercises, varied combat experience, more kills, better test scores. It's just how it was. One day, I was summoned to see my CO and he just tells me I'm going to Oxfordshire. RAF Brize Norton. You know it?"

"Yes. We flew out of there a couple of times on C-130Js."

"So, we're gathered in a little briefing room on those really hard chairs with the thin blue cushions, and in walks our CO and this woman in a suit. Real ball-breaker, too. You could tell just by the look of her. Blonde hair tied back, red lipstick, black stilettos. And rimless glasses." Tom shuddered. "They always give me the creeps. Don't know why. Just those thin bits of glass floating in front of your eyes. Anyway, she's working with the RAF on secondment from this drugs company, Dreyer Pharma. The CO introduces her as their Head of Communications, one Dr Nicola Morrison. The CO nods, and she gives us this spiel about a new performance-enhancing drug they're developing. Not just for pilots. Anyone in an elite role. Wouldn't be surprised if they were trialling it on a few of your guys as well. She runs us through some of the details, but it's all neurotransmitters and synaptic firing rates, and you know what those boffins are like. You start drifting off and thinking about flying or whatever keeps you looking interested.

"Then the CO gets up. Tells us even though we're the best five pilots, even we can't exploit the Typhoon's full potential. You know about that?"

Gabriel shook his head. Then cursed himself inwardly as another lightning bolt of pain crackled through his skull. "No, only that it's our latest plane and probably had about a million percent overrun on the MOD cost projections."

Tom laughed. A good, healthy sound. It was the first time Gabriel had seen him smile since he'd woken up in the next-door bed.

"Only a million? More like a zillion. I won't bore you with the physics but, basically, until the Typhoon, plane designers tried to make jets super-stable. You could take your hands off the controls and they'd happily fly in a straight line till you nudged the stick. They wanted to fly straight. But it meant you had to work harder to take them off their true line. So in a dogfight, they're stiff, you know? That slows you down, gives your enemy longer to get you in their sights.

"The Typhoon's different. They designed it to be unstable. You let go of the stick, it's going to flip, roll, tumble, it's totally random, like a bucking bronco trying to throw you off. But if you can master it, it's beautiful. It's so fast, turns on a sixpence. You spend most of your energy keeping it steady, but when you want it to change direction, it's . . . it's like an extension of your mind."

"So why the drug company? If it's so responsive, I mean."

"Because we were still getting caught out. We were good, don't get me wrong. I said we were the best, and that's true. How can I explain it? You like cars?"

"I have a Maserati at home. Does that qualify?"

"Wow. I guess you found a job that pays better than soldiering, then."

"Actually it was from an inheritance. My parents both died a few years ago."

"I'm sorry. Shouldn't have assumed. How did it happen?"

Gabriel took a deep breath. He'd never told anyone about the circumstances of his parents' deaths. But sitting here with a blind and battered air force pilot in a hospital full of maimed and traumatised brothers and sisters, it felt like the right time.

CHAPTER 7

"Yes. You heard right. I was away," Kasym said. "And guess what? Now I'm back. You owe me a month's rent. Which, let me see, comes to ten thousand euros."

"Yeah, well, see, here's the thing. Business has been really quiet. You know, we got raided, on account of that little poker game we had going in the back. Plus, I don't know, the Germans have been staying away. There's a new club on Roseni, been taking our regulars. So, what I'm saying is, we're a little short this month. Like, I can maybe give you five but, honestly, we're bleeding here, Kasym. Really. I mean there's nothing I can do to make it up. You gotta see that, man."

Kasym smiled, then rubbed his chin. "I understand. Competition's a fact of life, right. I mean, we all wanted freedom, right? Capitalism? So there's a bit of give and take in the market, I understand that. I'm not some communist fossil from the bad old days, huh?"

The greasy-haired man smiled. His shoulders dropped a couple of inches, and he leaned forward to clap Kasym on the shoulder.

"Oh, man, I'm glad you understand. I'll make it up next month. We're going to get some girls in here, you know? Pole dancers? The guys go crazy for that shit. Stuffing bank notes in their panties. We'll clean up."

Kasym nodded at Makhmad.

Makhmad's right hand shot out. He caught Pete round the throat and squeezed hard. Pete's eyes bulged as the oxygen to his brain was summarily choked off.

Kasym closed the distance between him and Pete to just a few inches. Leaned closer still until the tip of his bulbous nose was a finger's width from the club owner's sharp-edged beak.

Shouting was for low-grade thugs. He had people who would shout if he wanted them to, but Kasym always favoured whispering. It ramped up the fear factor. "Get your pole dancers if you want to. There are plenty of Russian tarts who'll strip off for a few euros more than they can make cleaning offices. But right now? You go to your office and you bring me ten thousand euros. Either that, or you put your right hand out on the bar over there and let Makhmad take one of these . . ." he held his left hand in front of the man's goggling eyes and waggled the stumpy fingers, ". . . as the shortfall."

He nodded again. Makhmad let the man go. Clutching his throat and coughing, he retreated behind the bar to the door to the office. Half a minute later, he reappeared clutching a bundle of multi-coloured notes. Shaking, he counted them out in front of Kasym.

"Look, Kasym, I'm sorry. I was out of line. We'll do some advertising, bring in the punters again. Here's your money."

Kasym swept up the notes and stuffed them into his jacket pocket without taking his eyes from Pete's.

"Good. Very good. You know, this is a nice place, Pete. You do good business here. I know that young Lithuanian chick you have holed up in your flat is expensive to keep. Maybe you felt you needed to skim something off the top to buy her nice things."

Pete shook his head vigorously.

"No, Kasym, it's nothing like that, really. I . . ."

Kasym touched his index finger to Pete's lips.

"Shh, my friend. You buy her perfume, maybe? A nice designer dress or two? I understand. A man's got to protect his investment, hasn't he? But that goes for both of us. So here's how we're going to leave things between us. Next month, I'm going to swing by the

Casino and you're going to have my money all ready to go. The usual ten thousand plus a little extra, say two thousand, as a fine for fucking with me today. That will settle things between us, and we can go on together as business partners. Or, maybe you feel these terms are unfair. In which case, I will send Dukka round and let the two of you . . . renegotiate . . . the terms of our agreement."

"No!" Pete said, whitening, pulling on his ponytail like it was a bell rope. "No need for that. It's all fine. Come whenever you like next month. I'll have your money."

"Good boy. Now, how about a little drink on the house, hmm? Makhmad and I have had a long and demanding day."

* * *

Back at the house, Kasym set up the sitting room for filming. He placed the copy of *Eesti Päevaleht* on the seat of one of the two hard chairs facing the window. The script he'd laboured over, printed in block capitals on a sheet of ruled paper ripped from his A4 notepad, lay on top of the newspaper. The camcorder, a high-end model with an extendible mic covered with a fluffy grey shield, stood ready on its tripod.

"Go and fetch them, Dukka," he said.

"Sure, Boss."

He reappeared with the two hostages a few minutes later, pushing and prodding Sarah Bryant in the small of the back to ensure she was tightly grouped with her daughter. Easier to kill the enemy when they were close together.

Kasym looked them up and down. Taut muscles around the eyes betrayed their fear but these women had themselves under control. No screaming, or beseeching to be let go. No shaking or weeping. Strong. He admired that in a woman.

"Sit, please," he said, pointing at the chairs. Sarah Bryant took the chair nearest the door, Chloe, the one with the newspaper and script. She picked up the slim bundle before she sat, turned the paper over in her hands, glanced at the script, then back at Kasym.

"You want to film us. Is that it? Making an appeal to Dad? The paper's to show we're alive?"

"As of now, yes. It will reassure your father that we are treating you well. Now, shall we begin? I'm afraid we cannot offer lighting or make-up, but you both look fine as you are."

"What do you want us to do?"

"First you both say hello. Then Chloe, you will read the words I have written for you. Please do not mention our location. We will simply do another take. Just like in Hollywood."

Behind him, Makhmad snickered. Elsbeta and Dukka looked on impassively. Elsbeta, because she had seen it all before. Dukka, because he looked at everything with great interest but without a great deal of excitement.

It was a hot day, and a light breeze inflated the dingy grey net curtain from time to time, bringing with it the scent of lime blossom from the trees outside in the street.

Kasym clapped his hands loudly, making the two women start.

"Let's begin." He stood behind the camcorder, thumbed the power button and waited a few seconds while the electronics inside the silver case woke up. Then he pressed the record button and spoke. "Mrs Bryant, you first."

Through the viewfinder, Kasym watched as the Englishwoman prepared herself to speak. She straightened in her chair and pulled her shoulders back. She brushed her tawny hair behind her ears with both hands and began to speak in a calm, clear voice.

"Darling. Please don't worry. These people have kidnapped me and Chloe, but they are treating us well. Just be strong. I love you."

She looked sideways at her daughter.

"Hi Dad. We were in Stockholm and now—" She stopped as Kasym waved an admonitory finger at her beneath the lens of the camcorder. "OK, so these people have kidnapped us. Mum and I are fine. Just do what they say. I love you Dad."

Then she looked down at the newspaper in her lap. Held it up under her chin. Kasym zoomed in on the masthead. Panned a little to the left of the black and red type blaring the newspaper's name to focus on the date. Then zoomed out again. Beneath the lens he pointed down, signalling for Chloe to drop the newspaper. She placed it on her lap and picked up the script.

"So, I guess you know from the paper that we're alive today. Now I'm going to read out a speech they've written."

She cleared her throat and shook her head a couple of times.

"Every nation should be free to govern itself. Its people should have the same basic human rights as all other peoples. This is true for Chechnya. This is true for the Chechen people. Think back, Mr Bryant, to the days of the British Empire. How many millions did you squash down, beat, torture or kill to preserve your own dominion over half the planet? Britain saw the error of its ways and freed its former colonies, but today, right now, there are other empires who do not see why they should follow Britain's example. For us, for the Chechen people, that oppressor is Russia."

Chloe paused and looked up from the script into the camera. The breeze caught a wisp of her hair and blew it across her mouth where it stuck to her lip. She picked it off and resumed reading.

"We intend to free our country from Russia's stranglehold. But to do that, we need funds. We do not ask you for money directly, but you are a powerful man. You can help us. We understand that there is to be an official investigation into Project Gulliver. Make sure it finds nothing wrong. That is all you need do to secure the continuing wellbeing and eventual safe return of your wife and daughter. Needless to say, any involvement of the police or security services will result in an adverse outcome for your family. Perhaps you doubt our sincerity, Mr Bryant. I will send you a token of our commitment to a free Chechnya."

Kasym leaned away from the camcorder and turned to Elsbeta. He nodded, then returned to the viewfinder.

Casually, as if she were stretching her legs, she walked in front of the camera, pausing to retrieve a balaclava from a pocket and pull it down over her head. She squatted down beside Chloe Bryant on her left side. She reached up and brushed back the young woman's hair, revealing a thin, silver wire earring with a small diamond dangling from it on a second loop. She fingered it gently, flicking it with the tip of her forefinger.

Chloe whipped her head round and glared at Elsbeta.

"Don't touch it! Dad gave them to me for my twenty-first."

Elsbeta said nothing. Instead she gripped Chloe's jaw with her left hand and pushed her head around so that her left ear was facing the lens. Then, using her right hand, she squeezed the loop of wire between her thumb and the knuckle of her index finger until her thumbnail whitened, and tensed her right arm. She looked at the lens. From behind it, Kasym nodded again.

Chloe's shriek of pain was loud but quick. Her hand flew to her ear, then, reflexively, she pulled it away to stare at her reddened palm.

"You bitch!" she shouted. "Fuck you!"

Sarah Bryant took charge, surprising Kasym.

"Get me some ice and a clean towel. Do you have a first aid kit? Well, do you?"

Nobody moved. They were waiting for him. He reflected that the English lived up to their reputation for being calm in a crisis. They'd faced down their own would-be oppressors nearly eighty years ago; now it was the turn of the Chechens.

He turned off the camcorder then nodded to Elsbeta, who was watching him closely. She fetched ice from the freezer and clean towels from a drawer in the kitchen. Makhmad disappeared and came back a few minutes later bearing a small red plastic box with a white cross on the lid. The girl was in pain, but she wasn't crying. He admired that. The mother was pinching the torn earlobe between thumb and forefinger and murmuring reassurance to her daughter.

"It'll be all right, darling. Do you remember Rachel Jackson? She caught her earring in the strap of her riding helmet last year. Did exactly the same thing. It healed up perfectly. Hardly even a scar."

"She didn't have some fucking terrorist pull it out though, did she, Mum?"

The mother looked over at Kasym. She knew he'd heard and the worry showed in the tight crinkles fanning out from the corners of her eyes.

"Don't worry, Mrs Bryant," Kasym said. "Your daughter is brave, a fighter. In Chechen, we have a word for women like her: nanaćökҕalom. It translates loosely as 'she-tiger'. Teeth, claws, plenty of strength, plenty of courage. We admire them. Now, take care of her. We have some work to do. Dukka. You stay here. Guard them. Same rules as before."

"Sure, boss. Only, can't I come with you this time? I'm not just a babysitter, you know. I got these."

He adopted a caricatured bodybuilder pose, standing straight and jacking his arms up so that his biceps threatened to burst the sleeves of his cheap white shirt.

"I know, Dukka. And next time someone needs a little lesson, I'll bring you along as the teacher. But for now, you're the prison guard, OK?"

Dukka dropped his arms and the corners of his mouth simultaneously.

"OK, Boss. I'm the prison guard." He turned to the two women. "And nobody gets past Dukka."

"Good boy. Now, you two, come with me."

Leaving the kitchen, which had temporarily become a dressing station, Kasym, Elsbeta and Makhmad walked outside to the car.

They got in, Kasym in the front with Makhmad, Elsbeta in the back.

"Right, we've got what we need to really put pressure on Bryant."

* * *

Having left Elsbeta and Makhmad in the Old Town, Kasym arrived back at the house carrying two bulging Maxima supermarket carrier bags. He dumped them on the pine table in the kitchen. Chloe and Sarah were in the sitting room, playing cards under the watchful eye of Dukka.

"I am sorry to interrupt your card game, ladies" he said. "But I need your help in the kitchen. If you don't mind."

He gestured wide-armed towards the door and waited for the two women to put their cards down and precede him into the kitchen.

"Tonight, I will cook for you. Elsbeta and Makhmad are attending to some business for me so it will just be the four of us. We will have a Chechen speciality. You like lamb?"

They nodded. He'd noticed they preferred to keep silent around him. Well, perhaps some good home cooking and wine would make them more talkative. He emptied the bags. White onions tumbled across the tabletop, followed by long, red Romano peppers, a couple of heads of garlic, and a crinkled deep-green sheaf of what he called black cabbage. He lined up three bottles of Estonian wine, two red, one white, and a dozen lamb chops, still smelling of the butcher's shop and bearing inch-thick rinds of creamy fat.

"Mrs Bryant, perhaps you would trim the fat from the chops. Save it though. It's good for frying. Chloe, please would you chop the onions? Not too fine, leave something for us to taste."

He unlocked the drawer containing the kitchen knives and handed them out. He caught the look that flashed between mother and daughter.

"May I ask you both a question?" he asked. He decided to wait for a spoken answer this time. He counted and looked the women in the eye in turn. He reached six before Sarah Bryant spoke.

"Of course you can ask us a question. You are in charge, after all."

"Have you ever used a knife on anything with a pulse?" Kasym asked.

CHAPTER 8

As Gabriel began to unload the story of his parents, he wondered whether he would cry. He hadn't when the two police officers had turned up at his door, sombre-faced and overly respectful. Perching on the edge of a leather sofa in his white-painted living room, the older of the two cops, a woman detective inspector, had informed him that there had been an accident. He could feel a lump in the back of his throat, but he decided it didn't matter. Here, surrounded by so many people who'd lost friends, comrades or parts of their minds and bodies, his own loss felt like an admission ticket.

"Dad was really fit. He played tennis every day, nearly. Walked the dogs. And he sailed. He had a stroke and died when they were out on the boat. He always said to me he wanted to go doing something he loved, so I try to believe he wouldn't have minded. But he was young. Too young, really. Not even seventy."

"I'm really sorry,' Tom said. "Strokes are bad. Like a sniper bullet."

"Yes, they can be. But this wasn't such a bad one. He could have recovered if they'd got to him in time."

"What happened?"

"My Mum was on the boat with him. But . . ." Gabriel sighed deeply. "Something happened after I joined the Army, back in Hong Kong where they were living. It undid her and she started drinking.

When Dad had his stroke, she was passed out downstairs. He died with his wife just five feet away from him. She must have come upstairs when she sobered up, and found him. She left a note. The Coastguard found her body in the water. Another boat reported her."

"So you lost them both in one day." Then Tom smacked himself hard on the forehead. "Sorry, statement of the bleeding obvious."

"It's OK. Thanks for even asking. It wasn't Mum's fault, not really. This spoilt rich kid in HK she was tutoring didn't get into university. Knew his parents would blow their stacks so he made up this accusation about Mum. That she'd behaved . . ."

He stopped. Felt the heat of his tears on his cheeks. He sat there, in the wheelchair and sobbed. Tom did very little. Just waited. Put a hand out and patted Gabriel's shoulder, left it there until the heaving subsided into stillness.

"Oh, God, sorry. Didn't know that was going to happen," Gabriel said.

"Stay here a little longer and you'll hear a lot of guys crying louder and longer. Nobody minds. The shrinks say it's cathartic."

Gabriel cleared his throat and swiped the soft cotton of his sleeve across his eyes.

"You were asking me about cars?"

"Yes. So imagine driving your Maserati flat out, but you're sitting on the front lip of the bonnet. Now imagine those Italian engineers had reworked the aerodynamics so it got skittish at anything faster than fifty. And taken the self-centring out of the steering. And put you on a test track covered in water and diesel."

"OK. Doing that. Not enjoying it."

"Good. That's what flying a Typhoon's like."

"But that sounds like a nightmare."

"It is. Until you master it. Then it's just a sublime moment. Those crates will do whatever you want. It's like telepathy. Flip, roll, climb, dive: you think it, and it happens. But they knew – we knew – there was more we could do if we could somehow speed up our thought processes."

"And that's where Dreyer Pharma came in?"

"With their 'Viagra for the brain' as the R&D woman put it, yes."

"What was it like? Did it work?"

"Yes. It worked. I told you. We were already the sharpest pencils in the box. Then we got sharper. They ran so many tests on us, I swear there are astronauts who had less done to them than us. So, the time comes for the first flight test. Nothing complicated. Just take a Hawk jet trainer up to 3,000 feet, couple of laps of the base, then back home for tea and a biscuit.

"We all did it, nothing to report, Sir. It was amazing, you could see for miles, sense tiny shifts in air currents. Then, they wanted to prove the drug. Eddie won the lottery to go first. Climbed into a Typhoon with instructions to take it up to 30,000 feet, play around, have some fun, come back down, and get plugged into the science-woman's laptop and have his brain downloaded for analysis."

As Tom recounted his story, Gabriel looked out of the window again. A wind had sprung up, and the trees at the edge of the gardens were swaying at their tips. A bird of prey of some kind, a kestrel maybe, was beating its way against the air currents, being pursued by five crows.

"He went up fine," Tom said. "We watched from the airfield with binoculars. He was showing off, basically, doing stuff that shouldn't have even been possible. Then something went wrong. He didn't pull out of a stall turn. The damn thing just fell out of the sky. We were screaming for him to eject but he didn't. Eddie hit the ground at probably two hundred miles an hour. Nothing left but a crater and some pieces of tin.

"Here's the thing. They wouldn't play us the recording from his mic. He was wired for sound and was supposed to talk the whole time. Let them know what was going on in his head, his muscles. How he felt. So Shiona and I, we broke into the control room in the middle of the night. Had to dodge the Rock Apes too."

"Rock Apes?"

"RAF Regiment. You know, the Military Police. MPs."

"Sorry. Go on."

"We played the recording. It wasn't hard to find on the computer.

Stupid civilians think everything is safe because it's on base. Eddie was fine, initially. Reporting on the controls, the plane's responses, his reactions, saying how smooth everything felt. How he was plugged in to the avionics. Then the weirdness started. He began singing. Old Beatles numbers. Then he started screaming about snakes. He was shouting 'Get away from me!' over and over again. Then the static when he hit the ground."

"What did they do? They must have investigated, surely?"

"I don't know. Project Gulliver got iced for a couple of weeks, and the four of us went back to our squadrons. But then we were summoned again. They told us the company had redesigned the drug, and identified a rogue molecular bond that had screwed up Eddie's perceptions. I was selected next, a week ago. Same thing happened. Fine up to about 10,000 feet then whammed with this total, flop-sweat fear. Thought my lap was covered in giant spiders. They were everywhere. Now I'm here. So, look. I heard Don – he your old CO? – I heard him telling you you'd be out of here in a little while. So I want you to do something for me."

Revolted by the idea of giant spiders in his lap, or even normal-sized ones, Gabriel pulled a face, wrinkling his nose and pulling his mouth down in a frown of disgust. "What? Anything."

Tom gripped Gabriel's arm and squeezed, hard.

"I want you to find out what's going on inside that drugs trial. Because now there's just Mark, Josh and Shiona, and I don't want to lose anyone else. There's a lot at stake for the RAF and Dreyer Pharma. And I'll give you pounds to peanuts the MOD's got its grubby little paws in this business too, somehow. Do you know what's coming up in a month's time? The Farnborough Airshow. They're pushing for a big demo of the Typhoon and the RAF's superior flying abilities. Probably a PR stunt to flog some hardware, or the drug itself for all I know. Shiona's been given the job. Women fighter pilots are like gold for the image of the air force. I want to see her again." He paused. "If I can. I don't want to hear on the radio about another 'tragic accident'."

Gabriel thought back to the kestrel being mobbed by the big, black scavengers. About his mother, bullied into alcoholism. And about people who were poisoning young fighter pilots until they killed themselves. He unclenched his fists and let his breath out.

"Leave it with me."

CHAPTER 9

Sarah Bryant looked at Kasym with eyes narrowed, defiant.

"No. Of course we haven't stabbed anyone."

"I didn't think so. I, on the other hand, have. Many times. Sticking a knife into a person – even into an animal – takes commitment and a certain amount of skill. Blind hatred on its own is not enough. Please don't imagine that you can use one of those on me. I'll disarm you, then I'll be forced to punish you. And I have both the commitment and the skill. Your ear is healing nicely, Chloe, by the way. Now, let's begin, shall we?"

While the two women trimmed, peeled and sliced, Kasym halved and deseeded some ridged, irregular tomatoes from the garden. Then he sliced the tops off the peppers and deftly twirled the point of his long cook's knife around the stalks before pulling them free with a soft pop, bringing most of the pith and seeds with them.

Soon, the kitchen was full of the sizzle and spit of onions frying in aromatic lamb fat. The meat was browning separately in a little flour seasoned with salt and black pepper. Kasym mixed everything in a large saucepan with a blackened underside, along with a bottle of the red wine, a small handful of fresh thyme, rosemary and oregano, and the chopped tomatoes. Last, he added a pinch of brown sugar, a handful of black olives and a splash of red wine vinegar before sealing the pan with a heavy lid and turning the gas down low.

He opened a second bottle of the red wine and poured three glasses.

"Please," he said. "Let us put this unpleasantness between us aside for a while."

He picked up a glass and pushed the remaining two by their bases towards the women. Sarah Bryant took one, but Chloe just glared at him, her mouth compressing into a thin, lipless line.

"I don't drink," she said.

Her mother's hand hovered over the glass nearest to her, stopped in its progress by her daughter's words, but she seemed to decide a drink was worth her daughter's disapproval. She picked up her glass. As she did so, Kasym raised his and clinked it against hers.

"A toast," he said. "Chloe, you would honour me by joining us?"

Sarah looked at her daughter, who had crossed her arms over her chest.

"Come on, darling, please. Just a sip. It will relax you."

"Oh, yeah, Mum. Because I really need to relax right now. Sure, why not. Let's get pissed with the fucking kidnappers."

"Chloe Bryant!"

"Ladies," Kasym said, lowering and softening his voice. "It is just a simple toast. No need for an argument."

He knew that proposing the toast would act like a magnet, pulling them into his orbit just as surely as the offer of a handshake to a man.

Chloe picked up the glass in front of her and both she and her mother waited for Kasym's next words.

"To, freedom. Ours, and yours."

Sarah replied. "To freedom." They all drank, then Sarah's eyes widened.

"That is really, extremely good. What is it?"

"I thought you might like it," Kasym said. "It is a local wine, made just outside Tallinn. Many wine critics rate it as highly as some Australian or Chilean cabernets."

"What is this, *Come Dine with Me and My Hostages*?" Chloe asked.

"For God's sake, Mum, can't you see what he's doing? Haven't you ever heard of Stockholm Syndrome? Ironic, given where they took us. He wants us to get comfortable around him and his knife-wielding mates, and then we'll start accepting his worldview and before you know it, there's a photo on Twitter of me pointing a gun at some bank clerk in Moscow. I've got news for you. Both of you. Not. Going. To. Happen." Chloe got up abruptly, jogging the edge of the table with her hip and spilling wine from the three glasses. "I'm going upstairs."

* * *

After dinner, Kasym left Dukka in charge once again. He left the house by the front door and walked to the corner. Elsbeta and Makhmad were waiting.

"Makhmad, take the film and the earring to the courier office. Tell them it's express. No return address on the package," Kasym said. He turned to Elsbeta. "You and I are going to collect the van. It's time to move."

"OK," she said, always a woman of few words. As Makhmad trotted off back towards the Peugeot, Kasym and Elsbeta walked shoulder to shoulder down the street. The guy they were buying the truck from lived about a mile away. His neighbourhood wasn't the best in Estonia, and the truck was in all likelihood somebody else's legal property. But he had it, and the key, and that was good enough. After twenty minutes' brisk walk, they turned down a side street. The suburban avenue gradually changed into a treeless strip of cracked concrete and Soviet-era blocks of flats, and it was clear no happy families of prosperous middle-class Tallinnites lived here. Rubbish blew in eddies where walls of concrete blocks intersected, and the only cars parked on the street were cheap Fiats or Nissans with out-of-date licence discs or busted aerials. They made another turn into a street lined with bars and a couple of strip clubs.

"He's down here on the left," Kasym said. "After the Top Hat. You have the money?"

Instead of answering him, she flicked her hand out and tapped his thigh with the tips of her fingers, the old signal. Trouble.

Kasym looked left and right and saw what she'd already noticed. The few drinkers on the street had vanished. But the street ahead wasn't empty. Ahead, standing like a row of bollards from one pavement to the other, were six men. Six big men. All dressed the same: black leather zip-up jackets, faded denim jeans.

The men closed up a little and one stepped ahead of the others. He was as tall as Kasym, but not so heavily built. Only ever one spokesman, Kasym thought. Two lieutenants, three makeweights. Standard formation for gang enforcers from Marseilles to Tblisi. He and Elsbeta moved a little further apart, maybe a yard or so. They kept walking, a little slower than before, but still moving towards the men.

"You Chechens have been talking to the wrong people," the lead man said. "Paying visits to establishments already under our protection. We've had the word out for you. Just got a call from a friend. So now you're retiring."

Always the stumbling speeches in English, Kasym reflected. Globalisation was a wonderful thing, but intimidation was always preferable in one's mother tongue. No matter. It wouldn't have worked in Estonian either. He didn't really have time for a conversation. The lieutenants and the makeweights were still relaxed, expecting the dialogue and the threats to go on for a while longer. Big mistake.

Kasym considered his options. He knew Elsbeta would be doing the same. His Makarov was tucked down the back of his waistband. If he went for it, the men, employees of a business rival, would in all probability blow the two of them away in a hail of bullets. No. They had to let them believe they'd already won. Put them at their ease. Besides, he had other weapons. He faked a stumble and, as he turned side on to them, slid his right hand into his trouser pocket. Good, they hadn't noticed anything. The cold brass felt reassuring as he slid his thick fingers into the four holes of the knuckleduster and closed his fist around the fat handle.

Next to him, Elsbeta put her hands above her head, then let them drop to the bun of hair pinned to the back of her head. Together they walked on, until they were within three yards of the line of men.

Kasym stopped.

And he waited, scanning along the row of muscle. Taking in the differing physiques, the telltale bulges beneath the jackets, the hands lingering near belts or pockets.

He felt a fleeting sadness. How many widows? How many children about to lose fathers?

"Now!" he said.

Elsbeta pulled the flick-knife from her bun, where she'd poked it before setting off to collect the truck. She rushed at the spokesman, yelling an old Chechen war cry. Surprised by the full-frontal attack, he stepped back instinctively, swearing.

"Kurat sa tšetšeeni lits!"

He went for the gun at his waist. Too late. Too late by far. She closed the gap in less than a second and swept the opened knife up and across his face, opening a deep gash from his jawbone to his eyebrow. The man screamed in pain as blood spurted from the wound, blinding him.

"No!" she shouted. "This Chechen bitch says, fuck *you*!"

The others were busily spreading out and pulling out guns, knives, coshes and in one case, a baseball bat. Kasym charged to the left of the staggering leader, elbowing him in the face as he barrelled past. Chaos would prevent them getting a clear shot at him or Elsbeta. Out came the knuckleduster, doubling the weight of the fist that clenched it, and turning it from a formidable weapon into a lethal one. The two lieutenants were the next priority. One, a tall, blond guy with a crewcut and the eyes of a stone killer, cocked his baseball bat then swung it at Kasym's head. He was an easy target, and Kasym slowed his approach a fraction before rearing back to let the aluminium bat whistle harmlessly past his face. His own attack was less showy, but brutally effective. No backswing or flashy roundhouse; he just punched upward in a vicious uppercut that broke the man's jaw. Thanks to the brass knuckles, he felt nothing but a minor jarring. Only fools had fistfights without protection. As his adversary crumpled, he caught him across the side of the face with another heavy blow. The curved metal rings, half an inch across and with edges milled to wickedly precise right angles, lifted a long flap of skin from the plane of the man's cheek, deep enough to reveal his teeth through the rent in his stubbled flesh.

Beside him, Elsbeta stumbled. One of the Estonians had caught her a glancing blow with his cosh, something short, fat and made of black leather. Filled, no doubt with lead-shot, coins or ball-bearings. It was four on two, and those were odds that made Kasym happy. He kicked the man with the cosh, hard, in the side of his knee. The snap as the bones broke brought a smile to his lips.

"Yes!" he shouted. "Come on, Elsbeta. Let's finish these dogs."

He elbowed the man in the throat as he went down on his good knee bringing forth a gargled choking sound. In went the knuckleduster, popping an eye from its socket. The choking became a coughing scream that cut off abruptly as Elsbeta leaned down and cut his throat.

A huge bang bounced off the alley walls. Kasym and Elsbeta whirled round.

One of the others, a makeweight, had pulled an ancient revolver from his jacket pocket. It smoked in his hand and from the shake at the muzzle it was clear this man was out of his depth. The round had gone wide, and as he fumbled the hammer back, Kasym rushed at him and smashed his brass-clad fist down on the man's forearm. A double-snap this time: radius and ulna both fractured. The gun fell from his useless right hand, and before he had time to think about another weapon, Kasym's boot lifted him off the ground as it connected with his groin. A thin cry escaped his lips, and Kasym left him writhing on the ground.

Now it was two on two. Game over, as far as the two Chechens were concerned. These barely counted as odds at all. Hardly ten seconds had passed, and already the Estonians had seen four of their number cut down. They turned to run. Elsbeta gave chase. Kasym considered calling her back, but then just shrugged. It was Elsbeta.

Better to try calling off a pack of wolves. She was fast. They were slow. Big men who'd never thought much about the advantages of speed. The trailing man went down in a comical stagger. Elsbeta simply tripped him with a tap to his trailing foot. His head made a dull smack on the cobbles, and he lay still. Without breaking step, she raced off in pursuit of the remaining man. Her next move made Kasym gasp in admiration. He'd seen it before, in Chechnya, in 2000, as she brought down a bulky Russian infantryman on the outskirts of a burning village.

She dived forwards as if for a rugby tackle, and sliced her blade hard against the back of his right thigh, just above the knee. The triple pops as his hamstrings separated were audible all the way back up the alley. Down he went, just as the Russian had done all those years ago. Elsbeta was on top of him before he hit the ground. She rolled him onto his back and pushed her face close to his.

"No," she said. "*You* are retiring. The Chechen bitch says so."

Then she slit his throat. Blood burst out from his pallid neck, and she stepped smartly back to avoid getting covered.

People were watching from behind shuttered windows and doorways veiled with swinging aluminium chains. It didn't matter. Bar owners and club managers didn't really care who ran the district. They knew better than to complain or, worse still, involve the police. Just pay your rent and offer free drinks, or lap dances, and everything would be OK.

"Nearly finished," Elsbeta said, panting, as she rejoined Kasym outside a video arcade called London Popstar.

Now there was no risk of an extended firefight, she reached inside her jacket and drew her own pistol, a Beretta 92FS. The Italian-made semi-automatic was fitted with a dull, black cylindrical suppressor. She stepped over the still-groaning man whose ruined groin was the result of Kasym's steel-toe-capped work boot.

She approached the former spokesman for the Estonians, stood over him, extended her right arm downwards and shot him through the face.

The sound was like a telephone directory being slammed onto

the floor, but not the devastatingly loud bang made by an unsuppressed weapon.

She moved to the next man, kicked a knife from his hand, aimed and fired another shot.

Three more times she repeated the simple action, until the cobbles were speckled with bone fragments and brain tissue, and ran freely with the Estonians' blood. Then she marched over to the sixth man, whose eyes were wide with terror, the bright-blue irises floating in a sea of white.

He put his arms out to her, palms upwards, like a saint about to be martyred in some old church painting.

"Please," he said. "I have children. Three. Girls. Please don't leave them without a father."

Elsbeta's expression crumpled into a snarl as if someone had screwed up her face from the inside, pulling all the muscles into some point centred just above the bridge of her nose. Her lips were drawn back and she bared her teeth.

"Do they know what you do for a living? You piece of shit. Do they?" This last question was shouted and Elsbeta jammed the end of the suppressor in between the man's quivering lips. "I was one of three sisters. Do you know that? Men like you raped my sisters. Killed my sisters. They raped me too. But I killed them. So fuck you, Mr Good-Daddy. And fuck your children, too."

The man flinched and the acrid stink of urine suddenly filled the air.

"No, Elsbeta!" Kasym said, placing a hand on her gun arm and pressing down hard enough to move the barrel of the pistol downwards, so that it scraped across the man's lower incisors and pulled his lip down in a grotesque parody of a pout. "Wait. He can be our messenger."

"Yes, yes, anything. I'll carry a message for you," the man said, smiling now, anxious to please, desperate to justify his reprieve. "To Yuri, yes? Our boss?"

"Yes. To Yuri," Kasym said, kneeling down by the man's side and looking into his eyes. "Here's what he's going to learn from you. One, you do not fuck with Chechens. Two, if you do fuck with Chechens, you need to send more men . . ."

"Three?"

"Three, if you send more men to fuck with Chechens, better make sure they're better at fighting than you six."

Kasym held the man's gaze and reached behind him, hand open. He closed his fingers round the object Elsbeta placed in his palm. He got to his feet, brushed the road dirt from his trousers, then extended his arm and shot the man through both knees. His scream bounced off the walls of the bars and strip clubs, but it might as well have been echoing through a forest for all the good it did him. Kasym and Elsbeta looked around. The street was still empty. The revellers knew better than to take pictures on their phones or stand around gawking. In this part of Tallinn, you kept your nose in your drink and waited it out.

"Come on," Kasym said. "Let's get what we came for and get the fuck out of here."

CHAPTER 10

Kasym and Elsbeta crossed the street, and Kasym pressed a grimy button next to a steel-shuttered door between a strip club and a check-cashing joint. They waited for half a minute, looking around, before the metallic sound of bolts scraping back focused their attention on the door again. It opened a crack, and a single pale blue eye was visible in the slit of street light.

"Hello, Ferdy," Kasym said.

"Oh, it's you," a gravelly voice said.

The door was pushed to again, then it opened inwards. Kasym and Elsbeta stepped inside the gloomy hallway while the stocky occupant slammed and bolted the door. They followed him down the passageway and out into a concrete yard surrounded on three sides by ramshackle sheds roofed with corrugated iron. Piles of tyres framed a double-width, steel-gated exit like sentries. Taking up most of the space in the yard was a delivery truck, cab for three up front, panelled loadspace behind. It was hard to tell the exact colour in the yellow glow from the sodium street lamp outside the gate, but if pressed, Kasym would have said shit brown.

Kasym pulled a wad of cash from the inside pocket of his jacket, then Elsbeta tugged on his sleeve and pointed at a shadowy recess under the rippled metal roofing. A low, sinuous shape shrouded in thin grey plastic seemed to be hunkering down amongst the welding rigs, tool trolleys and oil cans.

"What's that?" she asked Ferdy.

"That? Nothing. An old wreck, that's all. Must send it to the scrap heap one of these days. It's cluttering up the yard. I need the space."

Perhaps realising he was saying too much, he zipped his lip.

"Oh, yeah?" she said. "You cover all your wrecks with plastic? Can I have a look?"

Kasym caught the reluctance in the guy's stance and the way he kept easing over to block Elsbeta's view.

"Come on, Ferdy," he said. "We've got plenty of time to inspect the truck and give you your money. Why don't you show us what you're hiding under the wrapping paper?"

The man sighed, defeated. "OK, OK. We're taking care of it for a guy who owns a couple of the nightclubs here. Yuri Volkov. Big, big wheel in the Russian Mafia, you know? But just a quick look, OK? This guy? He's like my best customer. No offence, Kasym, just business, you know?"

"Sure, we know, don't we Elsbeta? Just business. Everything's just business nowadays. We understand that." He gave Ferdy a broad grin, revealing those stained teeth again.

Ferdinand Tarvas was known throughout Tallinn. Anyone who stood close to either side of the line dividing law-abiding Estonians from those who'd relieve them of a portion of their wealth would know him as "Ferdy Motors". He took hold of the front edge of the shimmering plastic sheet and slowly, reverently, drew it back.

"1974 Porsche 911 2.7 RS," he said. "Martini Racing colours, all matching numbers. It's a classic. Only one in the Baltic States. Hell, only one in Europe full stop, as far as I know."

Elsbeta ran her fingertips along the blue, red and black stripes painted on the car's silver bonnet and flanks.

"Is it worth much?" she said.

Ferdy became loquacious, always happier talking about metal than people. Never inquiring too deeply into his customers' sources of finance, just their ability to pay.

"Worth much? Car like this? You're talking a million euros, easy. See, they make replicas now, just rebody an eighties car, tune up the engine a little, give it the correct paint, but this little beauty's an original. Story is my client got it from . . ."

The squeal of metal on metal stopped him mid-sentence.

"No, no! What the fuck? Stop doing that! Oh, Jesus and all the saints, you crazy fucking bitch!"

Elsbeta stopped walking midway from the sloped nose of the Porsche to its flaring haunches. The tip of her knife rested on the pristine paintwork, at the end of a gleaming, silver groove she'd just carved into its flank.

She closed the gap between herself and Ferdy in one quick movement, bringing the point of her blade to within a centimetre of his left eye.

"Yes. You are right. I am one crazy fucking bitch. And your Russian," she spat out this last word, "client just sent six men to kill me and Kasym here. But guess what? I'm breathing. Kasym, he's breathing. The goons back there? Not breathing. Now, I was in the middle of something. Can I continue?"

"Sure, OK, I mean, whatever, but Yuri, he loves this car, so you know, it's going to be, I mean, are you sure you want this because he's done some very bad things to people over the years."

She pulled back a step, lowered the blade, looked him in the eye.

"Ooh, bad things. I'm scared, OK, I get it. Big, bad Russian gangster. Let him come after us. I would really, really like that."

She turned away from him and, as Kasym and Ferdy looked on, reared back then kicked out with her right foot. Her heel, reinforced with a steel band around the back, punched into the thin metal of the Porsche's door, leaving a crumpled depression marked with the boot's tread pattern. She looked around her, caught a glimpse of something hanging from a hook on the wall of one of the sheds and went over to lift it down.

She swung the length of heavy chain experimentally, then whirled it around her head and brought it down with a scraping clang on the car's roof.

Ferdy Motors actually cried out at this and started forward, but Kasym laid a restraining hand on his arm. He wished Elsbeta hadn't started in on the car. It would raise their profile even more than the fight just had. A man like Volkov might be prepared to write off the loss of six goons as a cost of doing business, but those mafia and their status symbols, well, that was a matter of personal pride.

"Better let her finish it," Kasym said, sighing. "You don't want to get between Elsbeta and, well, whatever Elsbeta wants, basically." *Because she has some anger issues that I, for one, don't want go anywhere near.*

Round went the chain and down it smacked again, cracking the windscreen, leaving it starred and opaque. She dragged it down the bonnet, scarring it with herringbone furrows of steel and undercoat that showed through the white, red and blue paintjob like hard-frozen soil through winter frost.

Then, as if she'd simply become bored by the vandalism, Elsbeta slung the chain over the roof and walk back over to Kasym and Ferdy, breathing heavily and smiling broadly, her eyes glittering.

"I hope your client has insurance. Or you do," she said, brushing her hands together.

Ferdy had temporarily lost the power of speech. He was no doubt wondering which option was best – quitting Tallinn immediately with whatever liquid assets he could scrape together into a bag, or toughing it out with Yuri Volkov. Kasym guessed he'd be on a ferry by midnight.

He grabbed the man by the lapels, pushed his face into the other man's.

"Looks like you're going to be needing all the cash you can lay your hands on. I've got three thousand euros for you right here, for the truck, remember?"

"Oh, Jesus, Kasym, OK, the truck, yeah, three thousand. My God. I'm dead, you know that?"

"I do know that. And if I learn that you've told Yuri I bought the truck, you will wish you *were* dead."

Ferdy's lower jaw was trembling and for a moment, Kasym

thought the guy was going to start crying. No spine, these Estonians. Good to go when the sun was shining on them, but you wouldn't want them at your back when the storm clouds gathered, that's for sure. He pulled the envelope full of cash and pressed it into Ferdy's clammy palm, folded his fingers around the packet as if otherwise it might flop out of the man's limp grip.

"Keys?"

Ferdy looked at him blankly.

"For the truck. Where are they?"

"Oh, OK, yeah. They're in the ignition." Ferdy flopped his hand out in a half-hearted salesman's welcome wave for the new owner of the vehicle he'd just shifted.

"Good. Thanks, Ferdy. See you around some time. Come on, Elsbeta, you drive."

They swung themselves up into the cab, which was surprisingly clean for one of Ferdy's knocked-off rides. Even had a pine air freshener hanging from an air vent control knob on the dashboard.

Elsbeta twisted the key in the ignition, and the truck's asthmatic diesel motor coughed and wheezed into life, releasing a belch of oily grey smoke from the exhaust pipes. Kasym looked down at Ferdy and then pointed at the yard gates, mouthing the word, "open". Ferdy slouched over to a control panel set into a wall and listlessly poked a green button. With a rattle and a clank, the doors shuddered then slid back on greased rails. As soon as the gap between them was wide enough, Elsbeta engaged first gear and carefully, as always, manoeuvred the truck out of Ferdy's yard and onto the back street beyond.

* * *

The following day, Ferdy stood, trembling, in front of his client. The man facing him was fifty-seven, but through a careful regime of diet and exercise he had maintained the physique of a man thirty years his junior. He was wearing silver satin shorts, supple, white leather boots, their high tops laced tight around his ankles and calves, and blue boxing gloves. Beads of sweat stood out on his forehead, and his muscular torso was slick with it. His hair was white and cut short; it stood up in spikes. He had stepped down from the ring to address Ferdy face to face. Behind him, a burly trainer with a towel draped across his massive bull-like shoulders tended to a bleeding boxer, whose nose now pointed in two different directions at once.

"What did you want, Ferdy? You know I don't like to interrupt my workouts."

Instead of speaking, Ferdy began to cry. Tears dribbled along the creases etched deep into his cheeks, lined prematurely through years of smoking cheap, high-tar cigarettes. One of the two men flanking him spoke in his place.

"He says he's got some bad news, Yuri. Wouldn't tell us. Said he had to deliver it to you in person."

"So what is it my friend?" Volkov said, laying a gloved hand on the other man's shoulder. "What was so important that you stopped my exercising and wouldn't talk to Adnan or Mikhail?" He bopped him lightly on the nose with the other glove. "Come on, man, better spit it out now you're here."

"Jesus, Yuri, it's your Porsche. It wasn't my fault. I thought they were just going to pay for a truck I found for them and go. But the woman, she's crazy. I was going to try to stop her but he, he said to let her do it or it'd be the worse for me. Said he'd kill me."

Yuri Volkov frowned at the mention of his car. One of the perks of his business activities in Tallinn was that he could afford the finer things, from the Patek Philippe watch currently nestling on a folded blue towel on a nearby bench, to the Porsche 2.7 RS he'd taken in payment for a debt from a competitor back in Moscow.

He moved his face closer until he could smell the stink of fear coming off Ferdy Motors in waves.

"What happened to the Porsche? Who was the woman? And who," he prodded him, harder this time, on the end of his bulbous nose, "was the man with her?"

Ferdy motors drew in a deep ragged breath. "The car is damaged. Badly. Bodywork. Glass. It's going to take a lot of work. The woman,

Jesus, she was strong. Hoisted a length of Grade 40 galvanised steel chain like it was string. She's called Elsbeta. I don't know her surname. The man is called . . ."

"Kasym Drezna."

"Yes, but how did you know?"

Volkov grinned, a mirthless expression that showed neat, even, white teeth. "The woman, blonde, yes? Face her mother wouldn't kiss?"

Ferdy nodded.

"Her name is Elsbeta Daspireva," Volkov continued. "We've come across her before. She left five of my guys dead in the street right outside your workshop, I'm surprised you didn't slip in the blood on your way here. She works with Drezna. She's his Number Two. That Chechen scumbag has been throwing his weight around all over my operating territories these last few years. I never dreamed he'd have the balls to bring it to me in this way."

"That's right!" Ferdy said, his hunched shoulders dropping and his face regaining a little colour in the cheeks. "Those Chechens have been muscling in on legitimate businesses in Tallinn big time. They forced me to watch, Yuri. What could I do?"

Volkov sighed. "Take your clothes off."

"What?" Ferdy's eyes widened and deep ridges appeared in his forehead as his eyebrows shot up to his hairline.

"I said, take your clothes off. Then put some shorts on," he gestured with a big bunched leather fist at a rack of spare boxing gear in a corner. "When you've done that, join me up there." This time Volkov pointed to the ring, with its bloodstained canvas floor.

The two minders, Adnan and Mikhail, who'd accompanied Ferdy into the gym looked at each other and grinned.

A few minutes later, a trembling Ferdy Motors climbed awkwardly through the ropes and stood cringing in a pair of borrowed red satin boxing shorts, his gloved hands dangling by his sides. Volkov faced him, light on the balls of his feet, hands punching the flat faces of his gloves together with a smack.

"It wasn't my fault, Yuri," Ferdy said. "She'd have knifed me. Or he would. They're Chechens, you said so yourself. You know what those people are like."

Volkov looked sad, his mouth turned down and his eyes dull. "I do. And I agree. It wasn't your fault. But the car was in your care. I trusted you to look after it for me. Now it's damaged. You see, I have a reputation in Tallinn to maintain. What will everyone think if the word got out? 'Ferdy Motors let some crazy Chechen bitch smash up Yuri Volkov's car and all he got was a reprimand.' That, my friend, would not be good for business. So, we'll fight, yes? Settle this like men. Three rounds, three minutes each. Adnan can ring the bell. Honour satisfied one way or another."

The taller of the two minders consulted his watch and rang the bell.

Volkov danced towards Ferdy on the balls of his feet. As if still expecting the bout to be called off, Ferdy just stood there, flat-footed, his hands dangling by his sides, watching as Volkov drew closer. Two quick jabs from Volkov's left glove snapped Ferdy's head back on his neck and he staggered to maintain his balance. Volkov came at him again. More jabs. Then, as Ferdy appeared to grasp the situation properly for the first time and raise his gloves, Volkov smashed a hard right into his nose. The snap was audible, and Volkov noted with approval the flinches from Adnan and Mikhail. Blood running freely from the cut on the bridge of his nose, and out of his rapidly clogging nostrils, Ferdy attempted to back away, his eyes wide and pleading, but Volkov was out to make a point, and to work off some of the anger he felt at knowing his prized racing Porsche had been defiled by that Chechen cunt. Time to deal with her later, but for now, Ferdy needed to pay his debt.

"Come on, Ferdy," he called across the ring. "You'll never land a blow if you cower on the ropes the whole time."

Ferdy had clearly given up any thoughts of landing a blow. He stayed back, gloves up and covering his rapidly swelling face. Volkov skipped over to him and began belabouring him in his soft midsection, driving the wind out of him. As the pounding blows stole his breath, Ferdy dropped his guard. Volkov took a half-step back and then launched a vicious, driving uppercut that connected with the point of the younger man's jaw. Without a gumshield to clamp his jaws on, Ferdy's mouth was a dangerous place, full of sharp, pointed and grinding surfaces. The blow drove his incisors together through the tip of his tongue; the triangular gobbet of greyish-pink flesh flopped down onto the canvas. Volkov delivered a swinging roundhouse punch catching his opponent as he sagged to his knees; it landed on Ferdy's left temple, knocking him out.

"Clean that up," Volkov barked to Adnan and Mikhail, then went off to take a hot shower. The Chechens would pay dearly for messing with Yuri Volkov.

CHAPTER 11

In a building on a business park near Reading, in England, two days after Ferdy's bout with Volkov, a man dressed in a handmade suit stood looking out of a full-height plate glass window. As CEO, he had a beautiful office on the top floor. He stared down at the manicured gardens and artfully meandering gravel paths that snaked around a manmade lake. In his hand, he cradled a plain water glass half-full of whisky. His hand was shaking, causing the surface of the brown liquid to ripple and shimmer. He kept running his hand through his prematurely greying hair. He thought back to the call he'd taken two days earlier. How it had started this nightmare.

The trip to Stockholm was supposed to be a bonding trip for mother and daughter while Chloe was deciding which job offer to accept after university. She was beyond bright. A starred double first in computer science and electronic engineering. Recruited while still an undergraduate onto her professor's post-graduate artificial intelligence research group. A Masters in quantum computing at twenty-five. Now she had management consultancies, foreign universities, government departments and global electronics companies fighting each other to hire her. Then came the phone call at the weekend. He'd been at his tennis club. Knocking up. Made his excuses, ignoring the frowns and eye-rolling of his partners. They knew his job was demanding and made allowances on account of his stunning serve.

A man's voice had come on the line. Remarkably clear signal, he'd thought at the time. His voice was rough, with an East European accent, or maybe Russian; he spoke English well. The words were still fresh in his mind. He replayed them now.

"Mr Bryant. I admire your wife greatly. She has great courage. And your daughter, too. Such a bright young woman. Such lovely long fingers."

"Who is this?"

"My name is not important to you. My associates and I have invited your wife and your daughter to stay with us for a while. Under our protection, you might say. A package is on its way to you that will confirm my account."

"What do you mean? What have you done with them? What do you want?"

Bryant could feel his pulse thumping in his ears. He'd heard stories of chief executives hiring security and ex-military types as chauffeurs, but had always dismissed it as hubris. Now he felt scared and wished he'd done the same.

"You are a very powerful man. You run a successful pharmaceuticals company with a new and exciting military aviation contract, no?"

"How did you know about that?"

Bryant looked over at his doubles partner, who was tapping his watch and pointing at the court. Bryant shrugged and held up a couple of fingers.

"It doesn't matter. Listen, I know you want to get back to your tennis match so I will keep this brief. After the recent unfortunate events with the Typhoon test flights, your Ministry of Defence has begun an inquiry. You will see to it that they discover nothing amiss. I don't care how. It is in your interests. And those of your wife and daughter. And no police. That would really not be a good idea."

Bryant could feel a heavy squirming in his guts. His lungs were sucking air in and out too fast. He felt light-headed.

"How did you know I was playing tennis?"

"Relax, Mr Bryant. I could hear balls being struck in the background. Like Wimbledon, you know. Pok! Pok!"

"Please don't hurt them."

"Oh, we will try very hard not to hurt them. We Chechens have a sense of honour. And of family. We do not hurt women. Unless we have to."

"Chechens? Oh, Jesus."

"What? Do you think we are savages? They are our guests, but we need you to do as we say to keep them safe from harm. Once the investigation has concluded that Gulliver is safe, you will ensure there are no further high-altitude tests until the Farnborough Airshow. After the drug is demonstrated at Farnborough, you will have your womenfolk back."

The line went dead.

Bryant had stood transfixed, the phone clamped to his ear. Pleading a stomach upset, he dashed for his car and sped home at twice the legal limit.

* * *

Looking down at the landscaping around his office building, trying to squash the fear down with gulps of whisky, Bryant remembered the moment the couriered package had arrived two days earlier. Jill, his secretary, had entered his office carrying it before her like a bomb.

"I've just signed for this, James," she'd said. "It's odd, no sender's address, just yours, here at Dreyer."

The package had contained a cardboard box, about four inches by six, maybe one inch deep. It sat, now, on his desk. The lid lay to one side, his name, position, company and address printed on a generic white label.

A rectangular pad of white nylon foam lay beside the lid. It matched a similar pad that lined the box. Sitting together in the centre of the pad were a micro videocassette and a piece of jewellery. It was a single earring. Silver wire fashioned in two interlocking loops, with a small diamond suspended in a delicate mount from the smaller of the two. The larger loop was crusted with dried blood, and the white pad was stained red.

There was no note accompanying the box. There didn't need to be.

Bryant stared over at the box then walked back to his desk. He stretched out a finger and gently prodded the earring. A flake of dried blood adhered to his fingertip and he stifled a sob. He replaced the lid and slid the box into the drawer on his right.

He drained the glass and slumped into his chair. The air cylinder supporting the seat hissed as his weight pushed it down hard. He stabbed a button on the desk-phone.

"Jill, please would you have Nicola come up?"

While he waited for his Communications Director, he rearranged his pen and pad, straightened the wireless keyboard, aligned everything with the edge of the desk.

He jumped when the intercom buzzed.

"Nicola's here, James. Shall I send her in?"

"Yes, please. And then no calls or visitors for the rest of the day. You can go now, Jill."

"If you're sure?"

"Yes! Go." He rubbed his face. "Sorry, Jill. I'm just a little tired today. It's OK – just go home. I'll see you tomorrow."

The door opened, and Nicola Morrison walked in. She sat facing Bryant and waited for him to speak.

He looked up from his doodle – a precise series of interlocking cubes, shaded to look three-dimensional.

"I need that MOD investigation to go away. Our shareholders are putting pressure on me. Last quarter's results were not great, as you know. They're getting twitchy."

She straightened in her chair, pulled the hem of her skirt down towards her knees. Then she adjusted her rimless glasses, pushing them higher on the bridge of her nose.

"You know they lost a pilot. Nearly two. I'm not sure what you think I can do – we can do – to stop a MOD investigation. But I'll happily work with you on anything you think will fly. No pun intended."

"Look. It's simple. We created a drug that seems to be turning fighter pilots into acid-heads before they go blind and crash. Now I want you to help me squash an investigation that will see Dreyer Pharma, and all the thousands of jobs and mortgages that depend on it – yours and mine included – go down the toilet." His voice was loud, even in the large airy office.

Nicola poked at the nosepiece of her glasses again. "Since Arjun recruited that team from the contract research organisation, that's when we started having the problems with the molecular bonds. Are you sure we can't put the heat on them and get out from under? I know Project Gulliver means a lot to you, but we have other drugs in the pipeline we could focus on."

"No!" He leaned forward and slapped his palm on the polished wooden surface of the desk. The noise and the pain in his hand shocked him, and he began thinking about Sarah and Chloe. *Please, God, I hope you're all right, both of you. I couldn't bear to lose you.*

He looked up at Nicola, who was frowning at him. How long had he been gone? He continued with his speech.

"The researchers stay. They're not the problem. Please don't make me doubt your loyalty to the company, Nicola. Not now. We get this back on track and there are going to be the kind of bonuses handed out that mean you could give it all up and live off the interest for the rest of your life."

"Fine. They can stay. But I still think it's odd, the way they just happened along just after we won the contract. I mean, how many CROs are there in Ukraine anyway?"

Bryant was sweating. He stared at the leather blotter on his desk. *Please don't hurt them. Please send them back to me whole, and alive.* He realised Nicola was talking.

". . . and I suppose if we create some shadow protocols and duplicate data records, we can palm them off on the investigators to show it was an issue of inventory mismanagement. Some of the Phase Two tablets got assigned to the pilots instead of the Phase Threes.

We'll have to cull a few managers in distribution and logistics control, to look like we're getting our house in order, but that will probably do it. Maybe client relations could lose a couple of mid-level heads too, for added impact."

"Just answer me this. Can we keep a lid on it and keep Gulliver going?"

"Yes. I think so. We might even be able to create enough of a smokescreen to shift the blame onto pilot error. Maybe they doubled-up their dosage. There was that incident a few years ago, remember? Those US pilots had enough speed in their systems to fly without planes. Killed those Canadian observers, babbling into their radios about enemy spies, the whole time. Believe me, there are plenty of high-ups in the MOD who want this to go ahead. There are a couple of procurement people in the Ministry who are, shall we say, predisposed to look favourably on our position. Tell me, do we still have that summer house on Grand Cayman?"

CHAPTER 12

While the majority of Tallinn's inhabitants slept on, Kasym woke at dawn. Somewhere off in the distance, a mournful, two-tone blast from a train horn told him at least some other people were already at work. He washed and shaved in cold water, relishing the sharp little pains as his razor sliced through the tough bristles on his cheeks. Then he went to rouse the others. Makhmad and Elsbeta came to their doors on his first knock, fully dressed and ready to move.

Dukka was another story. When Kasym entered his curtained room, all he could see was a vast hump under the bedclothes. The big man was a child in some ways and hated to leave any part of himself exposed when he was sleeping. The blankets and sheets were rising and falling in time with Dukka's breathing, and the room smelled of farts and sweat – Dukka's signature blend. Kasym reached down to the head-end of the twisted bundle of bed linen and gave the lump there a hard prod.

"Hey, Fatso! Wakey-wakey. We've got goods to move to Tartu. So if you want any breakfast to pad out that skinny little frame of yours, get up and get ready." He was smiling as he uttered these words, and Dukka could tell.

"Fuck off! Sleepin'."

"Now, you big ox. I'm sending Elsbeta in here in two minutes unless you present yourself for duty."

"Fine, fine. Bloody tyrant that you are. No need for blondie and her lover's arms. I'll be down."

Kasym's final port of call along the upstairs hallway was the women's bedroom. He stood a moment, listening at the closed door. Faint snoring. The girl perhaps.

He knocked quietly, but firmly, three times.

"Mrs Bryant. Chloe. It's time to rise and shine."

Silence. The snoring had stopped.

He knocked again.

"It's Kasym, my ladies. Morning has broken. Did you hear me?"

"Yes, we heard you," Chloe shouted through the door.

"Cover yourselves, please, I have to come in," he said, then counted to three and pushed the door open.

The women were lying still in their single beds, both with the covers pulled up to their necks. Although the younger woman had a defiant jut to her chin, the two sets of wide eyes betrayed their owners' nervousness.

"Please come down for breakfast; we have a long drive ahead of us."

"Suppose we just lie here?" Chloe said.

"Then we will manhandle you – that is the word, I believe – into the truck in your night things, which will not be very dignified. Now, please, get dressed and come downstairs."

So it was, ten minutes later, that this odd group of people sat around the plain kitchen table, or stood in the corners of the room, munching croissants with thick, black cherry jam, and drinking strong coffee. Conversation was sparse. Elsbeta and Makhmad stood to one side, muttering to each other in Chechen. Dukka was too busy cramming the warm pastries into his mouth, a rain of buttery brown flakes littering his belly.

Sarah and Chloe Bryant sat silently, eating the croissants spread with the sour-sweet jam, quickly but daintily, Kasym thought. Amazing how these Englishwomen would maintain their cool even in the most extreme of situations. He imagined women just like these two, sitting astride elephants as they toured their plantations in India or Ceylon, as they liked to call the country everyone now knew as Sri Lanka. They had the ease of empire in them, the casual assumption that the rest of the world was grateful to have them in charge, just like the Russians in Chechnya. Well, maybe not for too much longer. He wiped a splodge of jam off his lip with a thumb and then clapped his hands together.

"Ladies and gentlemen, it's time to go. Now, Mrs Bryant, Chloe, a word of advice, if you'll permit me." He waited for a sign of acknowledgement, much as a parent waits for a child to establish eye contact. The mother was quick to comply but, as usual, the daughter took her own sweet time. That was all right – she was still angry about her ear. It probably did still hurt, but not as badly as the sorts of injuries they could have inflicted. Eventually, Chloe looked at him, eyes glaring from under her fringe. "Thank you. We are transferring you to a new location in another town. It's good: more space for you. For this purpose, we have bought a truck. I'm afraid the accommodation in the back is primitive, but we have fitted it with a couple of mattresses and some cushions for your backs. You may feel, as we leave Tallinn, that this is your moment to make a run for it. Or perhaps to raise a hue and cry from inside the truck. Bang on the sides perhaps, scream for help. That would be unwise. Running? You would have to be faster than Elsbeta. She is swift, and she is apt to become irritable. As to noise from the truck, we don't intend to shackle or gag you, but I am perfectly willing to adopt those measures if it will keep you quiet until we reach safer ground. So, the choice is yours. I know which way I'd vote. Shall we?"

Kasym gestured to the door. The Bryant women stood together and trooped out past him, keeping as far from his body as they could as they went through the door. Elsbeta escorted them outside to the truck while Dukka retrieved their bags from upstairs.

"Makhmad, you and Dukka take the Peugeot. Pick up supplies. Meet us there as soon as you can."

"OK, Kasym. One other thing, are we going to make another video do you think?"

"I don't know. I think it depends on what we hear from England. Bring the equipment anyway, just in case."

Outside, the street was empty. The people who lived in this part of Tallinn had comfortable white-collar jobs – no need for these accountants and middle-managers to be heading to work at dawn. The windows of the neighbouring houses were all curtained or shuttered. The residents slept on for the last precious hour or so, dreaming of a new car, a new TV, or a new lover. No need for any of them to dream of freedom; that was theirs already. Kasym swiped a hand across his brow. With that butcher sitting in the Kremlin, whetting his knives and whistling Russian folk songs, they should be having fucking nightmares. One slash of his arm, and Estonia could be bleeding into the Baltic like a pig with its throat slit. Rain was falling, cold and sharp, despite the summer. He yanked open the rear doors of the truck. They swung back silently – how Ferdy Motors loved his grease guns – revealing the basic-but-comfortable accommodation he'd arranged for his hostages: an old but clean double mattress, a battery-powered storm-lamp made of hard grey plastic, and a bright-orange bucket with a lid, for emergencies.

He spoke to the two women, in a tone he hoped was kind but firm.

"Mrs Bryant, Chloe, please, get in."

He offered his hand to Sarah Bryant. She looked at the inside of the truck, then at Kasym.

"It's a bit high. I need some help."

She placed her hands flat on the floor of the load compartment and then bent up her left knee as if mounting a horse. Kasym laced his thick fingers together and placed this cradle under her shin. Without waiting, he lifted her and felt her muscles push off his hands as she bounced a couple of times on the road with her free foot then sprang, balletic, into the truck.

"Thank you," she said, "Chloe, darling, come on, you next."

"Fine, but I don't need any help from you," she said to Kasym. She placed both hands flat on the floor and boosted herself in, getting one knee up first then the other before jumping to her feet and turning round quickly to look down at her captors.

"Where are you taking us?" she said.

Looking up at her, at her blazing eyes, her long blonde hair, her slim build, Kasym wondered whether his own daughter would have emerged from the chrysalis of childhood into a young woman with as much fight in her as this one.

"A place of safety. You don't need to know more."

"How long is it going to take? There's no food in here. Or water."

"No, there isn't. We have the refreshments up front. Maybe we'll stop once we're out of Tallinn and share them with you. Behave yourself and we'll see."

"Well, can I least have my phone? It's got music on it."

"I don't see why not. One second."

Kasym called out. "Elsbeta, bring me the girl's phone." He smiled pleasantly at Chloe. No teeth, gentle eyes. An indulgent father's smile.

Elsbeta appeared at his side holding out Chloe's phone in its turquoise case, a spark of spring colour in this grey dawn. He took it from her.

Chloe's eyes lit up as she looked at the phone and she reached down from her lofty position. Kasym held it out of her reach, peeled the case off the phone and stuffed the wriggling sheet of silicone into his jacket pocket. Then, with small economical movements, he removed the plastic back to the phone and flipped out the battery with his thumbnail. He slid out the SIM card, replaced the battery and put the phone back together. The tiny sliver of electronics, Chloe's lifeline to the outside world, joined the case in his pocket. Kasym felt for the girl as her expression dulled into passive acceptance. Had she really thought he would hand her a working phone just like that? The optimism of youth, maybe, coupled with a casual assumption that her elders were as unable to grasp the intricacies of technology as an ass walking round inside a water mill.

He held the phone out to her.

"Here you are. Enjoy your music."

Then, with a smile, he slammed the doors of the truck together and swung the fastener across and down to lock them in.

Inside the cab, he looked straight ahead.

"Let's go," he said.

Elsbeta started the engine, put on the windscreen wipers to clear the rain, and coaxed the gear lever into first. Then, with a rattle from the still-cold engine, they moved off, away from the safe house, towards the next phase of the operation.

The drive to the scrapyard would take three hours, Kasym had calculated. Three-and-a-half with a stop. He had coffee in flasks, and rough sandwiches, and had always intended to share them with the Bryant women. The little threat to leave them inside the back of the truck was merely an attempt to keep the daughter in line. He figured he wouldn't have much trouble from the mother.

As Elsbeta negotiated the traffic, which was starting to thicken, Kasym spoke.

"Do you think Tarbosy and his crew of geniuses can fool the management at Dreyer long enough?"

"Sure they will," she said, taking her eyes off the road for a second to look across at him. "We just have to keep Bryant on track and any investigators at bay until Farnborough. Then boom – drug discredited, Abramov in the shit with the Kremlin, and we make our move on him and his empire."

"And you're sure the Russians will cut off his support?"

"Listen, Kasha," she said, her voice softening as she used her pet name for him, "our intelligence is solid. Makhmad spoke to Artur in Moscow less than a week ago. Abramov has been boasting all over the place how his under-the-table deal with Dreyer is going to bring air superiority back to Mother Russia. It's in the papers and on State TV, for God's sake. He's staked his reputation – and all his holdings – on this bet. When it explodes over the British countryside in front of the world's defence industries in a couple of weeks' time, Abramov won't be able to take a piss within ten kilometres of the Kremlin without someone trying to shoot his balls off."

She laid her hand on his thigh and patted him. At her touch, he relaxed. She was right, of course. All they had to do was deflect the MOD inquiry. Piece of cake. Well, not cake. Not exactly. He felt for his knife through the leather of his jacket and ran his finger along the handle.

Out of Tallinn, the road wound through beautiful countryside, its vibrant green clothing emerging into full summer colour. Kasym stared out of the windscreen, lulled by the monotony, half asleep. He was thinking of a school he'd once visited with friends in a place called Beslan. As they'd arrived, the sound of children's laughter had filled the air. The young women who'd taught them were fair-haired and so pretty. Then he started. Elsbeta was braking.

"What is it?" he said.

"Nothing. I need coffee, and it's your turn to drive for a while. We should check in the back, too."

She pulled off the main road down a wooded lane that led to a picnic area, though there were no other vehicles parked. The rain that was wetting Tallinn's commuters had abated and out here, it was a fine summer's day. Sun streamed down through the branches of the massive oak trees that shaded the rough grassy circle, split into narrow shafts of pale-green light. The truck bumped across some tractor ruts leading to a field gate then, with a greasy cough, the engine fell silent.

They got out and stretched, joints popping and cracking. While Kasym unscrewed the flasks of coffee and unwrapped the sandwiches – garlic sausage in thick slices of rye bread – Elsbeta rounded the truck to check on their hostages. She stepped back as she threw the doors wide, but there was no need, Kasym noticed. No screaming harpy emerged, fingers clawing at Elsbeta's eyes. Instead, he saw her extend her hand into the truck and then, courteously, help Sarah Bryant to descend. Sarah stretched too, then approached him.

"Is that coffee?" she said, nodding at the flasks he'd set down on a rough wooden bench.

"It is. I can't vouch for the quality, but would you like some all the same?"

"Yes please. I don't know if Chloe will," she said, looking back to the truck. "You know, she's a little . . ."

"Fierce? As I said to you before, it is an admirable quality in a woman. I regret that we have been forced to take these steps Mrs Bryant, but in a year or so, this will be merely a story you tell your dinner guests. For us, it is part of a long, long struggle. If Chloe wishes to hate me, that is her prerogative. I will not hold it against her."

Elsbeta returned from the truck.

"She says she's staying there. Fine, she can listen to music and piss in the bucket for all I care. Coffee, please."

The three of them stood around in a tight little group, sipping coffee and munching the big peasant sandwiches, for all the world as if they were travelling to a country market with a load of fruit and vegetables to sell and had decided to take a break on the way.

As they were finishing their food and draining their enamelled mugs of the coffee, a pheasant scraped out a cry of alarm in the neighbouring field and its wings clapped the air as the ungainly bird sought safety in a tree at the field edge. Kasym looked round sharply, then ran to the back of the truck.

"Fuck! She's bolted."

Without waiting for any further instructions, Elsbeta sprinted for the gate and vaulted it like an Olympic steeplechaser, barely touching the top rail with her hand. She landed in long grass on the far side of the gate, stumbled, then regained her balance and was running through the waving barley, away from the truck and after Chloe Bryant.

Kasym ran back to Sarah Bryant, who was looking at him coldly.

"You planned this, did you?" he said. "Wait for a stop then she runs because she's young and fit?"

"What, did you think we'd just be your docile prisoners, you bastard?" She spat at him. "You're kidnappers, murderers, and I don't care what you're fighting for. You ripped her earring out to scare

James. Chloe ran for her county till she went to university. She'll be long gone by now."

Her eyes were flashing as she delivered this impassioned speech and at one level Kasym was impressed.

Then he hit her, hard, across the face.

CHAPTER 13

Gabriel left Audley Grange after an interminable round of observation and tests. The red-haired Irish nurse had clearly been assigned to look after him personally. Her name was Niamh.

"You pronounce it 'Neeve'," she'd said, when he'd looked inquiringly at her after reading her name badge.

Niamh asked him to accompany her on walks and to play cards with her. He suspected she had been briefed by one of the head-shrinkers to get him to open up, and he didn't blame her for doing her job. The morning after his conversation with Don Webster, he was sitting at a shaded picnic bench by a lake with Niamh, playing gin rummy.

"What was on at the gallery?" she asked him, as she picked up a three of spades from the discard pile.

"What? Oh. It was photographs. You know, portraits. Well, it would be, wouldn't it, at the National Portrait Gallery. Hardly likely to be landscapes."

He picked a card from the deck and discarded it straight away.

"I had a quick look," Niamh said. "On their website. Hells Angels. Not a very pretty bunch for portraits, were they?" She selected a card from the deck. Kept it and threw out an ace of hearts.

"I don't know. Can't really say I took much notice. I only went because it was Annie's little brother who shot them." He picked up the ace of hearts.

"So, it wouldn't have been something you saw that set you off, then?"

"No! Look, can we just play, please? I can't concentrate with you interrogating me like this." He knew he'd overreacted, but the memory of that ugly scarred face was overlaid with another, more distant tableau. One in which the face's owner and four of his friends hadn't been standing around getting their pictures taken by Lazarus Frears. There'd been another kind of shooting altogether on that particular day. He wiped his hand across his forehead. It came away wet.

"Sorry," she said. "I shouldn't have pushed you. Oh, but one more thing."

"What is it?"

She flipped the card she was holding face-up on the discards pile and fanned the remaining seven cards out on the table between them.

"Gin."

Their shared laughter broke the tension that threatened to cloud the temporary friendship that had sprung up between them. Gabriel knew enough about the so-called Florence Nightingale effect not to fall in love with his nurse, but she was good looking and had a lovely smile, and he didn't want anything to spoil their easiness with each other.

The following day, the doctor in charge of his case signed him off. Her name badge said 'Norton', but at their first meeting she'd asked him to call her Gail.

"I'd be more comfortable with Doctor Norton," he'd said at the time, with a grin. "Doesn't pay to get too friendly with the MO. They might want to start sticking needles into you." They'd compromised on 'Doc'.

Now it was she who was speaking as she handed a prescription to him.

"This is a just a little bit stronger than paracetamol", she said, "if you need it." Then she leaned across the desk and placed her hand across his wrist. "I know you don't want to talk about what triggered your little episode in London. And that's fine. It's your decision. But I want you to promise me one thing. If you change your mind, or if life starts getting a little hard to handle, come and see me. Post-Traumatic Stress Disorder is nothing to be ashamed of, you know."

Gabriel lips tightened then relaxed.

"That's not what's wrong with me, Doc, but OK, I promise. On one condition."

She smiled. "And that would be what, exactly?"

"If you ever find yourself in Wiltshire you'll look me up and come for tea."

"I think I could manage that. So, we have a deal?"

"We do. And thanks. For everything. You are amazing. All of you, I mean." Gabriel half-rose from his chair then frowned and sat back down again. "Actually there is one last question I want to ask you."

"Ask away."

"The guy I was sharing a room with, Tom Ainsley. Can you tell me what caused his hallucinations? He said he thought his cockpit was full of giant spiders." He suppressed a shudder as he said this. He'd never had a problem with jungle warfare, except for the bloody spiders.

She pressed her lips together. "You know I can't discuss another patient with you, Gabriel. Even if I wanted to. There are medical ethics, and military rules, not to mention my Hippocratic Oath."

"But if I asked you something, and you said nothing, and I decided that meant I was on the right track, that wouldn't be in breach of your code of practice, would it?"

Now she was frowning. "Look, I appreciate you want to help Tom. Poor boy's been through a lot. But this is really too much."

"Please. I promised him. Just one question."

She paused for a long time before she answered. Time enough to notice the small muscle firing involuntarily under her right eye.

"One question. That's it."

Gabriel looked her squarely in the eye. OK. Time to deliver the line you've been practising and refining for the last day or so.

"If I were to contact a certain pharmaceutical company and make some inoffensive enquiries about their work with the RAF, would I be wasting my time?"

She looked down at her prescription pad.

Then back up at Gabriel.

She said nothing.

"Thanks, Doc" he said. He rose and offered her his hand. They shook, briefly, and then he left.

He sat in the common room – a warm space full of leather armchairs, with a table tennis table, and a big plasma TV on one wall – and called Annie. The distant burr made him realise how easily you could get used to life in an institution. Especially one as comforting and compassionate as Audley Grange. He looked around him. The men sharing the space with him were all damaged in one way or another. They were young, fit-looking guys for the most part; only one appeared to be older than forty. But each man had a distinctive feature that would draw stares "out there", as one Royal Marine had called it in conversation over breakfast, nodding his head at the windows, and the world beyond the landscaped parkland.

The physical injuries were the easiest to spot. Gabriel had seen plenty of guys airlifted back to field hospitals with horrific injuries. Limbs missing, torsos split open by IEDs or bullets. Faces obliterated by blast trauma or shrapnel. Here they were again, sitting around playing cards, watching TV or just shooting the breeze about life and its ups and downs. The blood had stopped jetting, the guts had been neatly packed back into bellies, the faces repaired as best as the plastic surgeons were able, the limbs mended, pinned or removed altogether. But the memories of the firefights, the roadside explosions, the hand-to-hand fighting when the ammunition ran out – they weren't so easy to shift. And for another group of casualties, it was the memories themselves that had brought their possessors to Audley Grange. Maybe voluntarily, after one too many fights in a pub, arrests for domestic violence or a kind word from a sponsor at an AA meeting. Maybe compulsorily, as part of a court order or sentencing from a sympathetic magistrate or Crown Court judge.

They were the ones with whom Gabriel could identify. He'd served his time, first in the Parachute Regiment, then in the SAS, without sustaining any serious injuries in combat. But when he'd left a member of his patrol dead on the squelching floor of a jungle in Mozambique, it had undone something inside him. He didn't use the four initials that doctors – and even the general public – now bandied around with such abandon: PTSD. They scared him. Whenever the flashbacks or the nightmares got too much, he could take off the rough edge of his terror with a glass of something cold.

But now he was surrounded by men who looked physically undamaged, yet whose behaviour betrayed the mental turmoil that threatened to destroy them from the inside. Saddest of all was a young kid, only nineteen. His name was Mark and he looked like he should be working as a primary school teacher. He had soft blond curls, china-blue eyes and such a light beard he could probably get away with shaving one day in three. Gabriel had talked to him in the grounds for half an hour or so the previous day.

Mark had been an infantryman with the Irish Guards, a private. On an operation in Afghanistan, he'd been part of a platoon that fought its way into a village against heavy fire from insurgents. There had been solid intelligence from an interpreter that there were women and children held captive by the Taliban. The last enemy fighter down, they'd begun to search the low, whitewashed houses looking for the hostages. It had been Mark's misfortune to find them. He'd kicked in the door to a low, single-storey building – a village hall of some kind – to be confronted by a scene that made even the battle-hardened, thirty-five-year-old sergeant who followed him in retch and stagger back into the sunlight.

Mark had not vomited, or run. Instead, he walked into the midst of the carnage and sat down among the newly dead, letting the blood soak into his uniform. To remove him, the two men who arrived next had to first prise a dead toddler from his arms and then carry him bodily out to the truck. His limbs had locked so that he appeared to be floating cross-legged between them. Wherever his eyes were focusing, it wasn't on the buildings of the village, nor on the faces of his comrades. Somewhere beyond the far distant mountains, possibly, where men who could do those things to women and children burned eternally.

Now he lived at Audley Grange, walking endless circuits of the gardens or talking in a low, affectless voice to a psychiatrist whose job it was to bring this teenaged boy-man some peace.

Gabriel shook his head violently, then winced at the burst of pain that flared behind his eyes. Time to go home.

Annie picked up.

* * *

Annie was practical as well as beautiful. She brought Gabriel a soft leather weekend bag packed with clothes.

"I didn't know what you'd feel like, so I brought you a selection," she said.

Back in his room, empty now that Tom had been transferred to a newly free single, he unzipped the soft, navy leather bag. He rummaged through the garments, noticing how she'd folded or rolled everything, right down to his underwear.

"This is really kind of you," he said. "I mean it."

"Oh, for Goodness sake, did you really think I'd not come?"

"No. But that doesn't mean it's any less kind of you. And I know you talked to the doctors and brought me some stuff when I was admitted."

She took his hands out of the bag and clutched them to her chest.

"Look at me, for a minute, will you?" she said. "We may not be boyfriend and girlfriend, but I love you. Properly. The way friends do. No angle, no passive aggression. Just the good old-fashioned kind. And that means here I am and I'm happy to be here. So stop being such a dick and choose some clothes out so I can get you home."

He did look at her. Into her green eyes, flecked with brown. Noticed the web of tiny lines radiating out from their corners. At her lips, wide and full. He pulled her close and kissed her. She softened in his arms and kissed him back, opening her mouth and letting their tongue tips touch in a gentle dance.

He was still wearing pyjamas and a dressing gown, so she pulled the free end of the braided cord around his waist and opened the front of his gown, slid her hand inside the trousers and gripped him firmly.

"Someone's feeling better," she breathed in his ear. "Want to do something about . . . this?" giving him a squeeze.

He looked over his shoulder. The door was closed. He nodded.

In bed, Annie lay on her side and backed into him, lifting her leg and reaching down to bring him inside her. Their lovemaking was fast, urgent, the risk of discovery an additional thrill. When they came, seconds apart, they stifled their cries before bursting out laughing.

"Oh, my good Christ," Annie said. "Have we just broken the rules?"

"Probably all of them. Fraternising with a civilian in a military facility. Engaging in PT while improperly attired. Misuse of Army property. We'll be lucky if we're not up on a fizzer before the CO."

"I have no idea what you're talking about, but it doesn't sound good. Come on, let's get dressed and let's get out of here. I want a drink and some chips."

On the drive down to Salisbury, Annie was in a more serious mood.

"Do you want to tell me what happened in the National Portrait Gallery?"

"Nothing. I said. It was hot, I needed some air. Maybe I got a bit overheated but that's it."

"But you were staring at that security guard like, I don't know, he was a ghost or a devil or something. And you completely blanked me when I asked you what was wrong. Just before you yelled out," she cleared her throat, "and ran outside and under the wheels of a lorry."

"I didn't run under the wheels. I hit the side, and he was on the wrong side of the road, anyway. Maybe he's the one you should be interrogating. Anyway, look. Something happened at Audley Grange. I might need your help."

Annie pursed her lips and stared straight ahead.

"What?" Clearly not happy and Gabriel knew she'd want to return to the subject of his accident again. Not now, though.

"That room I was in. I shared it with this young pilot. According to him, he was a real flying ace. Old school. He told me something that I want to investigate."

"What was it?"

"Just something to do with his last flight. I can't tell you more, I'm sorry. But I need some help with some background. In your firm, is there someone who could dig up a bit of background on a pharmaceuticals company for me?"

"We're headhunters, of course there is. I've got a couple of interns champing at the bit for something meaningful to do. What do you need?"

"Well, anything really. They're called Dreyer Pharma. Have you heard of them?"

"Who hasn't? They were a startup after a few senior execs jumped ship from one of the big boys five years ago. Specialising in a new technology called pharmaco-neurostimulation."

"Viagra for the brain."

Annie flicked her head round to look at him. "What was that?"

"Nothing. But these drugs they make, they give you sharper mental abilities, that sort of thing?"

"Exactly. And guess which executive search firm found them their new chief exec?"

"Hmm, let me think about that for a nanosecond. Lainey Evencroft?"

"Not just us, darling. Me! I found him for them after the launch partners cashed out and went off to buy yachts."

"So you can help me out then?"

"What do you want? A full briefing, financials, key personnel, location, marketing, drug pipeline?"

Gabriel blinked. "You can get all that?"

"I'll have one of the Jennifers do it."

"The Jennifers?"

"That's what we call them. Eager beavers just down from uni with a burning desire to work in the city, and enough of Mummy and Daddy's cash propping up their rent not to have to worry about a salary."

"Well, in that case, yes please. And Annie?"

"What?"

"Thanks."

"It's nothing. They'd only be photocopying CVs otherwise."

"No. I mean, you know, for fetching me from Audley Grange and getting me there in the first place."

"Don't be a dick. Who else was going to come and get you? Plus it wasn't me who got you there."

"No?" Gabriel realised he'd not asked anyone at the hospital what had happened in the aftermath of his accident. Don Webster had been vague on the details. "Who did then?"

"Oh, it was weird. I rode in the back of the ambulance with you and they took you to St Thomas' Hospital. The A&E was rammed with people, but they whisked you straight through on that trolley thing. I came with you as far as I could, but they made me wait when they X-rayed you. Then they took you from there into surgery. While you were there, this man just appeared. Tall, grey hair, big nose."

"That was my old CO, Don Webster."

"Yes, he said he knew you. He went to talk to the doctor in charge and then, when you came out of the operating theatre all patched up, he told me they were moving you to Audley Grange. He told me to bring you a change of clothes and your shaving kit."

"Did he say how he knew I was there?"

"He said they had an arrangement with the NHS. If any ex-serviceman comes in, they get a call, or a text or something."

"And how long did it take before he appeared? In A&E, I mean?"

"I don't know, about twenty minutes, something like that. Why?"

"It just seems a little quick. I mean, the Army's great at reacting fast in combat, but the bureaucracy side of things, well, let's just say I've seen snails move faster."

"I think they just look after their own. It's all that Help for Heroes stuff isn't it? If they left someone in a plain old NHS hospital, the media would have a field day. 'Our brave boy left to sleep. In a corridor!'"

"Maybe." Gabriel looked out of the window. His brain was turning slower than normal, probably the effect of the painkillers. They were making him a bit fuzzy like a vinyl album when there's dust on the needle.

Outside Annie's air-conditioned Audi TT, it looked hot. The fields were full of ripening cereal crops. He rested his forehead against the cool glass. Closed his eyes. Something was going on inside Dreyer Pharma. He could feel it. He needed to get close. Inside, preferably.

"Shit!" Annie said, swerving half into the hard shoulder. "Hey, you cock-bollocks, get off your fucking phone! Wanker!"

Gabriel marveled once again at Annie's rich and inventive way with Anglo-Saxon. Her cursing sounded all the more transgressive for being uttered in her finishing school accent. Ahead of them, a gleaming black BMW was signalling left to leave the A34 at the next junction. The driver, visible through the rear window, was gesticulating. Not an obscene gesture, just waving his hand around.

"What happened?"

"That fuckwit was on the phone, I could tell as he drew level. Hands-free, little law-abiding twat, but just gassing away. Then he cut me up. Tosser!"

"That's what I love about you, Annie. That sweet ladylike manner of yours."

"You didn't seem to mind my rough talk an hour ago, did you?" she said, winking at him without looking away from the road.

"Mind it? Why do you think I like you so much? You're like one of the boys."

"Ooh, you cheeky fucker." She punched him hard on the thigh. "What does that make you then? A little bit bi-curious, if you were doing it with one of the boys?"

"Me? Yeah, I'm all over the place, hadn't you heard? Maybe that's the real reason they wanted me in Audley Grange."

Annie was silent. No riposte or further sweary insults. Gabriel looked over. She was crying. Blinking the tears away and letting them roll down her face.

"Hey, what's up? Why the waterworks? I'm fine, really I am." Gabriel reached across and gave Annie's thigh a gentle squeeze.

"You could have been killed. I heard the bang from inside the gallery. Now all you do is joke about it. Maybe you do need to talk to someone. You know, someone professional."

Gabriel thought about Don Webster. His personal card. He turned back to Annie, brushed the tear trickling down her left cheek away with the pad of his thumb.

"I think you might be right. I'll make a call first thing in the morning."

CHAPTER 14

Sprawled in the rust-red Estonian dirt, Sarah pressed her hand to her cheek, which was flushing scarlet as blood rushed to the site of the insult. Her eyes were shining, but she was holding the tears back. Impressive, again.

"Fuck you," was all she said. Then she got to her feet and stalked back to the truck.

Five minutes had gone by, and there was still no sign of Elsbeta. Perhaps the Bryant woman's confidence in her daughter's athletic ability was well founded. That would be a problem. A huge problem. They had people they could call on, but they'd still have to get to the Bryant girl before she found a phone or a lift or, God forbid, the police. Maybe they should cut and run. They could keep Bryant on the hook with dead hostages just as much as with live ones. At least until he asked to speak to his wife or daughter. He took out his knife and held it into one of the shafts of lights spearing down through the bright-green canopy. Sunlight danced along its edge and he sighed. He hated killing women. But then, a shout. It was Elsbeta.

"Kasym, a little help?"

He slammed the truck doors closed and threw the latch across, then climbed the gate and set off through the narrow slot Elsbeta had smashed into the stiff stalks of barley. He only needed to jog about twenty metres before he came face to face with Elsbeta. She was holding Chloe Bryant in a very effective armlock with one hand, but the girl was struggling to get free. He walked up to them and delivered another open-handed blow. The girl gasped and tears spurted from her eyes. He shoved his face into hers, so close he could smell her sweat.

"I was just about to send your mother to her ancestors before coming after you. We would have put you down a well or fed you to the dogs and carried on with our struggle regardless. Pull a stunt like that again and I will. Understand?" He barked the last word so loudly she flinched, and raised her free hand to wipe his spittle of her cheek.

"Yes," she said, so quietly he could barely hear her.

Kasym turned to Elsbeta. "Get her back in the truck, I think it's time to press on."

Elsbeta practically threw Chloe Bryant up and into the back of the truck and within a minute, they were back on the motorway.

After another couple of hours, Kasym pulled off and took a narrow single-lane road, little more than a track, really. The truck bumbled and jounced along the broken tarmac. He let the cracked, black plastic steering wheel slip and slide through his fingers, keeping the wheels facing broadly in the right direction and letting the potholes, alternating to left and right, do the rest. They were full of water from recent rains and reflected the sky like dozens of earthbound mirrors until the truck's heavy wheels shattered them and sent sprays of water, now clouded with red mud, into the air.

He noticed Elsbeta had clenched her jaw.

"These shit Estonian roads'll have your fillings out," he said. Then laughed. "Whereas, of course, our fine Chechen roads are like driving on glass, no?"

She allowed a tight-lipped smile at that one. A victory. Small, but a victory, nonetheless. Then she pointed through the windscreen, over to the right.

"Over there," she said. 'Look."

He half-stood, raising himself off his seat far enough to see over the hawthorn hedge on Elsbeta's side while keeping his right heel braced on the floor to maintain pressure on the accelerator pedal.

"I see it."

"It" was a curious monument. A pile of ten or twelve wrecked cars, stacked floorpan-to-roof as if by a monstrous toddler. Kasym turned a corner and slowed the truck to a stop at a pair of massive steel gates, the tops of the metal uprights split into vicious tridents, burred with jagged barbs of steel along their edges. Beyond the gates was a sprawling ten-acre plot, the front of which was occupied by a scrapyard. The yard had been abandoned by the previous owner some years back and acquired for a pittance by Kasym from the man's children. With its sprawl of derelict land beyond the cluster of buildings in the centre, and its warren of narrow walkways and dead ends piled high with the burnt, stripped and mangled vehicles, it had served him well as a part-time armoury, forward operating base and occasional body dump. Heavy plant was scattered across the facility, including a compactor, an industrial incinerator, a couple of cranes and a backhoe.

Kasym got out and hooked a bunch of keys on a length of bright silvery chain from his trouser pocket. The grinding squeak as he turned the old-fashioned key was answered by a skittering noise made by thirty-two claws scrabbling for grip on the uneven surface of the yard floor. Two huge dogs hurtled down a canyon of more stacked cars towards the gates, their lips drawn back from their teeth, but emitting no sound at all. They were black and brown with white throats and thick, fluffy coats, like huskies.

When they saw who was attempting to break into their territory, they calmed down. The sharp ridges of stiff hair along their necks and spines flattened. Their ears flopped over. Their lips descended to cover their armoury of incisors, canines and carnassial teeth. Skidding to a stop just inches from the gate, they waited, both heads cocked to the left, as Kasym finished with the lock and pushed the gates round until he could sink long steel bolts into holes drilled in the concrete.

"Away, dogs," he said, loudly, but not roughly, pointing at a hut at the far end of the canyon. They turned immediately and padded back the way they had come, tails wagging, perfectly in step.

Then he turned and waved Elsbeta to drive in. She had taken his seat while he was unlocking the gate. Once the truck was completely inside the boundary of the yard, Kasym relocked the gates and walked to the back of the truck, just as Elsbeta killed the engine. The motor's timing was off and it continued to fire sporadically for another fifteen or twenty seconds, jolting and coughing, as Kasym pulled the rear doors open and released the women from the back of the truck. Elsbeta jumped down from the cab and was taking no chances this time. She stood, legs apart, some distance back, Beretta drawn and hanging loosely in her right hand. The silence was only interrupted by the odd bird singing and a distant, mournful train klaxon.

Sarah and Chloe Bryant rolled their hips round in circles, stretched and yawned, trying to get their circulation working properly again. He watched them as they surveyed their surroundings. It was not a pretty sight. Three prefabricated cabins, little more than a collection of reinforced and connected boxes, huddled together at one end of the yard. The steel sides, measuring thirty feet by ten, were painted in flat blues and reds, and could never have been attractive, even when new and clean. Now, they were scabbed with black, yellow and brown lichen that gave the painted surface a diseased look. A long, green stain had spread down one wall where a gutter joint had given way, and the windows, long uncleaned, had taken on a greyish cast. The steel bars across the frames removed even the slightest idea of windows as a building's eyes.

"Welcome to your new quarters," Kasym said. "More spacious than the last place and considerably harder to escape from." He looked at Chloe as he said this, but she avoided meeting his gaze. "Let me give you the guided tour. Again." Once they were all inside the central box, he locked the door, a steel-reinforced slab of softwood, behind him. "Follow me."

Elsbeta prodded Chloe hard in the back with the muzzle of the Beretta.

"No more Miss Nice Guy, eh?" Chloe said, scowling.

Kasym couldn't help but admire the girl, although he felt sure what he had planned would put an end to any lingering friendliness from the mother.

"You ladies have your accommodation through there," he said, pointing to an open door at the end of the dimly lit cabin.

All four of them stood in the next box along the chain. There was a double bed, a modern construction of grey-painted metal frame, and a second, single, bed pushed against a wall. That still left space for a couple of cardboard hanging wardrobes with the words "Global Move Tartu" stencilled in black on their doors.

"There is a kitchen, a living room, even a laundry room. We'll bring you some books. If you're good," Kasym said. "We'll leave you to get yourselves settled in. I'll come back with your bags in a moment. One last thing. If you're wondering about another escape attempt, please stand by the window there and look into the yard."

Elsbeta had disappeared while he was speaking. A few moments later they saw her striding across the yard to a barn in the far corner. When she re-emerged, she was leading the two dogs on rope leashes. One was pulling; Elsbeta dealt it a sharp smack across the snout and shouted something that caused the big animal to stop dead, flatten its ears and tuck its tail out of sight between its legs. *Always the alpha bitch, our Elsbeta. Best do what she says or take what's coming to you.*

She bent to the dogs' collars and unsnapped the trigger clips connecting the leashes. They bounded away from her, running in circles around the yard, pissing up against walls, posts, concrete horse troughs, anything that would take a message that said, "our territory, stay away". Then she looked in at the three people staring out at her and waved.

"Those are Zelim and Shamil. They are brothers," Kasym said. "They are named for Chechen national heroes. A friend of ours bred them from Basenjis and Japanese Akitas. They don't bark, but they are fierce. Some local druggies decided to climb over the fence a year ago. Big mistake. We had to run what was left of the bodies through a wood chipper. While I am gone, they will protect you from further incursions. I suppose they might also deter you from wandering, but that will have to be your choice. In any case, we'll be locking you in, and Elsbeta will be staying behind, so I suggest you just sit this out and wait until we have what we need from your husband, Mrs Bryant."

"James will do what you want. Please, no more violence. Just get whatever it is you need then let us go."

"I very much hope we'll be able to do just that. I very much hope so. Now, if you'll excuse me, I have matters I must attend to."

He left, closing the door behind him, and descended the stairs to where Elsbeta was waiting for him.

"I'm off to meet the others," he said. "I want an update on what's happening in England. Any trouble, you know what to do."

Elsbeta nodded with a smile, looking over in the direction of the wood chipper.

Kasym drove the truck back the way they'd come for fifty miles, then pulled off on a slip road marked with a sign featuring a crossed knife and fork. The café was filled with cigarette smoke. Kasym drew a great breath deep down into his lungs. Bliss. Even though he had given up smoking some years earlier, he still loved that heady aroma of cheap, high-tar cigarettes. And here, on the road between Tallinn and Tartu, they were the favoured style among the truckers and farmers who comprised the clientele of this particular roadhouse. The Bon Jovi playing on the jukebox, and the Lamborghini and Manchester United posters on the walls, couldn't disguise its utilitarian design or its roots in state-ordered provisioning of hungry and thirsty workers. Kasym noted with approval a scarred and battered AK-47 assault rifle hanging above the bar. Below it, a wooden plaque bore an engraved brass plate reading, "6 September 1991 – FREE again" The Baltic states had achieved independence from the hated Soviets decades ago, but Chechnya still had the bear's claws in its back. Maybe not for too much longer.

Makhmad and Dukka were already waiting for him. Dukka's round face broke into a childlike grin as he saw Kasym, and he jumped to his feet, waving one pudgy hand.

"Boss. Over here!"

A dozen heads popped up like rabbits in a meadow at this sudden explosion of noise. Makhmad scowled at his friend's childlike display of enthusiasm and pulled him back down to his seat. Around them, the mountainous truckers and wiry farmers slowly returned to their coffee and their conversations, which now probably included unflattering references to foreigners disturbing their peace.

Coffees ordered from the skinny, pale waitress, the three Chechens got down to business.

"So, tell me," Kasym said. "What's happening in England?"

"It's what we expected," Makhmad replied. "The Ministry of Defence has launched an enquiry. Our friends in London say the British Government still wants the trial and demonstration at Farnborough to go ahead. They want the drug to be safe, and they want their pilots ramped up to the hilt with it. Powerful people are pushing for a clean bill of health. And once it's proven, there are channels they'll use to exploit it commercially – under the radar you might say. That's where Abramov comes in with his dirty money and his connections. He's told them he can funnel the drug to Ukrainian separatists to give them an edge over the Russians. It's the other way round, of course, but they don't know that."

"Which is good news, Boss, isn't it?" said Dukka. "I mean, we still get to nail Abramov?"

"In time, Dukka, yes, in time. But first, we have to make damn sure that inquiry finds nothing that will cause them to shut down Gulliver."

Makhmad took a sip of his coffee, then centred it in front of him on the scratched red plastic tabletop. He spoke.

"So we put more pressure on Bryant. I think we should send him another video. Another present from his daughter."

Kasym sighed. "I agree. He's ours as long as he believes his womenfolk are alive. And Western plastic surgeons are geniuses at reconstruction."

* * *

Leaving Makhmad and Dukka to drive back to the scrapyard in the truck, Kasym climbed into the Peugeot and started the engine. There was someone he needed to speak to in Tallinn about the next phase of the plan. With Bryant under pressure, the British end of the operation was holding up well. Now to meet a man whose organisation made the Corleone family look like missionaries.

Ninety minutes later, he pulled up in a back street in the city centre. He walked for half a mile to a brightly lit avenue thronging with youngsters out for a good night. Boys and girls, sometimes girls and girls or boys and boys. By the prophet, the world had changed. Even free, Chechnya would never descend to this level of depravity; he'd see to it, one way or another. Though he had no political ambitions of his own beyond independence, he still felt he'd be able to exert a degree of influence over whichever self-serving bunch of "patriots" got to rule a free Chechnya. As he went to pass them, one of these brightly dressed couples swayed and fell against him, giggling. He bunched his right hand, but then forced himself to relax again. He was here for business, not pleasure.

Ahead, he saw the sign for the bar he was looking for: red and white neon spelled out the words "Uncle Sam's". *Pathetic. You exchange serfdom under the Soviets for enslavement to American culture.* He pushed open the door and was enveloped in a cloud of cheap-smelling aftershave, perfume and beer fumes. The music was overpowering, and he couldn't see much through the darkness, punctuated as it was by strobing pink and green spotlights. He shouldered his way through the brightly dressed customers and was trying to catch the bartender's eye when a hand seized his left forearm in a tight grip. He spun round to his left to see the man he had come to meet.

The man inclined his head – "follow me" – and released Kasym's arm. Which was probably wise. He headed away from the bar and pointed above the heads of the bar customers to a door marked Private, set between American movie posters: *Independence Day* and *Ghostbusters*. Kasym followed him, elbowing a few people out of the way for good measure. Beyond the door was a dimly lit hallway where the sound levels dropped to a burble. A door stood open to his right, and he went through it. The room was decked out with all the trappings of a corporate CEO's lair, or at least one as imagined by a violent Moscow-based gangster obsessed with the 1980s: a bank of dark blue steel filing cabinets; a glass-topped chrome coffee table surrounded by low-slung, white leather and chrome armchairs; a drinks cabinet open to reveal a clutch of high-end spirits and cut-glass tumblers; a gleaming, silver Mac on the blond wood desk; even an aquarium, in whose limpid water swam small striped fish, like postage stamps from somewhere in Africa.

The man stood in front of the desk, right hand extended. They shook, then he returned to sit in a black leather swivel chair. Kasym took a matching chair facing him across the expanse of beech or whatever it was, noting as he sat that this chair didn't rotate. He stood again and pulled the chair back until he could stretch his long legs out in front of him. He toyed with the idea of putting his crossed feet up on the desk, but then parked that particular piece of provocation.

Instead, he looked closely at the man he come back to Tallinn to meet. He was the head of a Russian Mafia operating group, a former Russian special forces soldier – *Spetsnaz* – a murderer, rapist and committer of war crimes. Not that anyone would form that impression from his appearance. Media executive, they might say. Or football manager. Industrialist, even. He was average. Mid-grey business suit, white shirt open at the collar. Average height, average weight, average looks, short, silver-grey hair. No scars on that pale face. No break to that short stubby nose. But there was something behind those average pale-blue eyes. Something distinctively not average. A capacity for ferocity. For violence. It came through in the gaze. Kasym had seen it many times before. He'd even wondered what, precisely, it was that led one to back away from certain people when they looked at you. Elsbeta had it; this man in front of him had it. Whatever it was, it made small men piss themselves, and big men get ready for a beating, in one direction or the other. He stared back.

They had yet to exchange a word, but now the man spoke.

"Kasym Drezna. The Butcher of Beslan. Delighted to make your acquaintance. We do business at last."

He smiled, but it was a predator's grin. A show of teeth, not humour.

"Ruslan Gregorovich. Torturer of innocents. How are you keeping?"

The man behind the desk narrowed his eyes and inhaled deeply through his flaring nostrils before letting the air out in an explosive laugh.

"'Torturer of innocents'! I like that. Though if you call those peasants innocents, you don't know much about life in the Russian countryside. In any case, they should have known better than to rat me out to the authorities. What's a few less alcoholics in Russia anyway? She has millions more to fill their place. So, now the pleasantries are out of the way, tell me the news."

"We are making ready to move on Abramov. The Gulliver drug will be demonstrated at the Farnborough Airshow in a few weeks' time. Abramov will be in the audience with a few of his friends. He will be expecting to see the fruits of his investment. Instead? Boom!" Kasym smacked the desk with the flat of his hand. "With a bit of luck, the plane will crash right into the VIP stand, and he will be obliterated without us needing to use a single bullet. Either way, when the Typhoon hits the ground, so does Abramov's standing with his masters in the Kremlin. Then you and I will move in on his business interests and carve them up between us as agreed."

Gregorovich smiled a doglike smile, revealing big, yellow teeth, the points of the canines extending fractionally below the upper incisors.

"As agreed," he said. "And if he survives Farnborough, you will carve up Abramov yourself, hey?"

Kasym nodded, his mouth set in a thin, humourless smile.

"After what he did to my family? I will use a very small, but very sharp knife."

"Ah, you Chechens are all the same. Family, always family. What did he do anyway? Evict them from some housing estate he owns?"

"No. Before all this 'new Russia' bullshit he was KGB. You know that about him, I'm sure?"

Gregorovich nodded, unscrewing the cap on a bottle of Grey Goose vodka. He motioned at the thick-bottomed cut glass tumblers he'd taken from the cocktail cabinet, tilting the neck of the bottle towards Kasym and raising his eyebrows.

"Please," Kasym said. Then, "Grey Goose? Not Russian?"

"That rotgut? I'd rather drink my own piss. No, my friend, one of the advantages of my position," he swept his hand around the office, "is that I get to drink better hooch than we did in the bad old days."

"In those bad old days, Abramov commanded a specialist unit with the army. They went into Grozny first in '99. Old men castrated in the street. Old women – and young – gang-raped by teenage soldiers. Babies gutted and hung from lampposts like fucking dolls. My wife and daughter suffered before they were shot like dogs. So yes, Abramov has it coming to him – at the point of my knife."

"Then let us drink to his downfall and his death."

Kasym liked his business partner scarcely more than Abramov, but needs must, so he clinked his heavy tumbler against Gregorovich's, and knocked back the smooth imported vodka. The spirit coursing down his throat gave out a deep warmth, though it was silky compared to the Chechen-made firewater he was used to. As it hit his belly, the fumes in his nose left a lingering smell of aniseed and black pepper.

CHAPTER 15

After Annie left, promising a full report on Dreyer in a couple of days' time, Gabriel felt twitchy, unable to settle. The stitches in the back of his head were itching, and he couldn't concentrate on the book he was reading.

He shook his head, then headed upstairs for a shower. As he undressed, a pale lilac and brown carton fell out of his trouser pocket. It contained the painkillers given to him by Doctor Norton: Tramadol. He read the tightly folded leaflet inside the packet. Worked his way down the long list of side effects, from dizziness and diarrhoea to anxiety and itching. He decided he'd be happier, and safer, with a known quantity. Something that came in a slope-shouldered green glass bottle.

After the shower, he put on some clean jeans and a grey T-shirt and went barefoot down to the kitchen.

First, he needed music. He found what he wanted on his hard drive. As Jimi Hendrix played the plaintive opening bars of *Little Wing*, he pulled open the fridge door, then slammed it as he realised he had nothing fresh to work with. Some dried chillies and a few slugs of olive oil went into the wok, followed by a squirt from a new tube of garlic paste and packet of vacuum-packed noodles. Finally a splash of soy sauce, Chinese rice wine and lime juice. As the steam rose above the hob, he chucked in a handful of coriander leaves fresh from the garden and scraped the whole lot into a bowl. Then he poured himself another large glass of white Burgundy, and took wine and food to the table.

Hendrix was soloing, soaring somewhere in outer space, as Gabriel sucked in the slippery noodles and washed them down with mouthfuls of the cold, white wine.

"Tell me, Squadron Leader Tom," he said out loud. "Who fucked around inside your head? And did they know what would happen to you . . . and to Eddie Hepper? The snakes and spiders and everything? Because I am going to find out. Just watch me."

CHAPTER 16

High above Eastern Europe, on a great circle route that took it directly over the Baltic States of Lithuania, Latvia and Estonia, a US Navy Lockheed EP-3 spy plane was completing a sweep. Its four million dollars' worth of digital surveillance hardware and software were crunching terabytes of data from smartphones, social media feeds, websites, chatrooms, short and long-wave radio transmissions, GPS pings, walkie-talkies, CB radio sets and encrypted military radio communications.

The senior comms analyst onboard was Petty Officer First Class Maria Damasio. She was running a standard spectrum-sweep analysis or "Triple-Ess-Ay" in the lingo of her trade. The computers did all the sorting and sifting, cleaning up some signals, boosting others, but it was Maria's job to let the data run through her fingers, feeling for nuggets that might mean more than just random squeaks or blips. There! There it was again. A regular three-beat signal from some kind of GPS-enabled smartphone app. Two things bothered her about the signal, which was metronomic in its regularity.

First, she'd never come across a signal with this electromagnetic signature before. It wasn't civilian and it wasn't military, or not in her experience, which was ten years and growing. Second, smartphone apps didn't do this in the first place. They weren't powerful enough for a start. And where was the need? You wanted to know where your friends were, you wanted to find a hook-up in a one or two mile radius of the bar you were in. You didn't want, or need, to send a signal that would radiate out from your phone to the edge of the troposphere.

Yet here it was. *Beep-beep-beep . . . beep-beep-beep . . . beep-beep-beep.* Packed in amongst the ones and zeroes was enough positional data to get a fix on the transmitter. She ran a back-find algorithm and tapped her bitten nails rapidly on the edge of her keyboard. A dialog box opened in her screen.

Latitude: 58°22'35" N
Longitude: 26°43'27" E

A GPS reference. She tapped another key and the digits were replaced by decimal degrees.

Latitude: 58.3806200
Longitude: 26.7250900

Estonia.

She swivelled her padded leather chair round and pulled her headphones off, scratching through her short red hair to her itchy scalp where the cans had pressed down on her head.

"Mike?" she called. "I'm picking up some very strange shit over Estonia. Can you ask the pilot to take another pass, a thirty-klick radius holding pattern over these coordinates?" She pointed at her screen and waited for Chief Petty Officer Mike Rollings, her boss, to squeeze his ample frame between the chairs of the other four analysts staring intently at their monitors and join her.

"What is it?" he asked, when he arrived and began to peer over her shoulder at her screen.

"I'm picking up a strange GPS ping from somewhere in the southeast of Estonia. It's coming from a smartphone, that's what the rig's telling me, but something's off. For a start, why does a smartphone user have an app that's capable of reaching us all the way up here anyway? For Christ's sake, are they trying to talk to their granny on a space station?"

He frowned and scratched his chin, then looked down at her.

"I'll call it in to Ray, ask him for a twenty-minute hold."

As Mike went forward to talk to the pilot, Maria bent over her keyboard again. Her fingers flashed across the keys. The screen launched new windows that overlapped each other, closed others down, brought up frequency spectrum analysers, mapped coordinates, and finally started beaming pictures from the ground centring on the map reference still chittering away in its high-energy beam of ones and zeroes from the surface of the planet.

It was a cluster of buildings in a 10.1-acre site, surrounded by a fence or an enclosing barrier of some kind. Lots of dead metal, cold, no heat signature, all over the shop. There was a truck of some kind parked near the buildings. Maria flicked a switch. Any living organisms would show up as white figures on the screen. She held her breath as the image flickered then stabilised in front of her. In the enclosed area outside the buildings she could see two small blobs moving in random patterns around the perimeter. Quadrupeds. Guard dogs? In the largest building, she could see two people in full outline, close together. Lying down. In a separate room she could see two more people, one standing, one sitting. As she watched, a second vehicle drew up next to the truck and a couple more people emerged. They went inside the occupied building and joined the two upright figures. They embraced, coalescing into larger indistinct blobs before parting and resuming more recognisable human forms.

The big plane banked to port, and Maria watched as the signal strength indicator on her monitor ticked up another couple of notches. Someone in that building had a real dope smartphone. Finding out who was above her pay grade.

Mike came back.

"Ray's happy to fly a holding pattern for twenty minutes, then we have to continue on up to the Arctic Circle. What in God's name is that?"

"I don't know. Could be something, could be nothing. Could be a student hangout, could be a couple of hostages and four captors. What do you want to do?"

"Call it in. Hand it over to the NSA. And Maria?"

"Yes, Mike?"

"Good job."

* * *

In a small, windowless room at CIA headquarters in Langley, Fairfax County, Virginia, 4,300 miles to the west of the Lockheed EP-3 and 26,000 feet closer to sea level, a classified email dropped into the inbox of Deputy Chief Intelligence Analyst Cory Miller. She'd been about to head out to grab a deli sandwich and a coffee, and swore under her breath. Nevertheless, she returned to her desk and clicked the email.

"Hmm," was all she said, though she did raise her eyebrows a quarter-inch. Which for Cory, the department's best poker player by a country mile, was a sign she thought this was interesting. Very interesting.

"First my BLT-on-rye and a doppio espresso. Then take a look at Sparky there," she said out loud, even though the office was empty but for her and a stuffed honey badger. The honey badger was the team's unofficial mascot. *Personal decorative items are forbidden within the precincts of the intel dept. excepting a maximum of two photographs of close family members,* stated the departmental manual. But they all ignored it. The honey badger was reputedly the bravest animal in all of Africa. Would take on lions for a laugh, apparently. They liked to think Harold reflected their own do-or-die philosophy, even though their battlefield was composed of pixels not pinewoods, desks not deserts.

When Cory returned to her desk, already munching on her BLT – the doppio was long gone – she took another look at the email. It was from a colleague at the NSA.

Subject line: Inter-agency intel-share

Message: *Unidentified GPS location ping from civilian smartphone over Estonia.* Plus the coordinates. OK, this was worth kicking upstairs, and maybe they'd decide to alert the nearest field office. She didn't know if they had bodies on the ground in Estonia, but they did in Scandinavia, and that was right next door.

CHAPTER 17

The following morning, Gabriel called the number on the slim wafer of white card tucked into his wallet. After a couple of rings, the phone was answered.

"Don Webster."

"Don. It's Gabriel. I want to find out what happened to the pilot I was rooming with at Audley Grange. Somehow I've developed this feeling my stay there wasn't just part of the Army's aftercare service. Am I right?"

There was a pause, during which Gabriel could hear his old boss breathing slowly through his nose, mumbling a characteristic "hmm-mm-hmm" as he marshalled his thoughts.

"Confession time. I've had my eye on you for a while for a bit of freelance work. I was going to make contact anyway, then you had your little incident outside the NPG and, well, it seemed like I could help you and me at the same time."

Gabriel's stomach flipped like he was about to ask a girl for a date, or jump out of a plane for a HALO – a high altitude, low opening parachute infiltration. It was a while since he'd felt it: the signal his body sent him when there was action in the wind.

"What kind of freelance work?"

"Well, I heard on the grapevine you were setting up in business for yourself as a security consultant. I'm running a discreet little department that works on sensitive cross-border security operations."

"What, *Mission Impossible*, you mean?" Gabriel thought he was going to laugh or get a bollocking, one or the other. In the event, Webster showed his hand.

"Let's cut all the Ministry bullshit about discretion and sensitivity. There are some really evil bastards out there, and they're either too clever, too connected or too well-protected for the regular cops-and-robbers brigade to get close to them. Drug cartels, traffickers, off-grid militias, common-or-garden terrorists, you know the type. I have the thoroughly enjoyable job of bringing them to justice. And note, I say 'to justice' not 'into custody'. I have a pretty open brief and some amazingly powerful friends of my own."

"Sorry, Don, the work?"

"Oh, yes, forgive me. I don't often get to tell people about what I do. Crapping on about 'a job in government admin' makes me want to cry into my drink sometimes. Let's play a quick word association game. Ready?"

"Ready."

"Chechens."

"Moscow theatre siege."

"Good man. Yes, eight hundred and fifty hostages taken in a Moscow theatre in October 2002, by fifty tooled-up Chechens. Russian Special Forces gassed them with an aerosolised version of Fentanyl or a derivative, then shot the lot."

"What's Fentanyl?"

"Pray you never need to find out. It's a powerful opiate. Related to morphine. Our guys with their legs blown off by IEDS? More often than not, the medics will shoot them full of it. The gas killed a hundred and thirty hostages too, unfortunately. Trouble is, as well as killing pain, it depresses respiratory function. They fell over in positions where their airways were constricted and simply suffocated. After Moscow, there was the Beslan school massacre in September 2004. The numbers were even worse. Eleven hundred hostages, including nearly eight hundred kids, of whom three hundred and eighty-five were killed."

"Jesus!" Gabriel said, trying not to visualise nearly four hundred dead civilians.

"Jesus indeed. Basically, you've got your standard separatist-cum-freedom-fighters-cum-psycho-bloody-terrorists, depending on where your sympathies lie. Think IRA without the charm. There's a bunch of them, we think, meddling in Dreyer's R&D operation. We found out too late to save the pilots, but we're all over it like a rash now. Now add in a power-hungry ex-KGB oligarch called Oleg Abramov who's trying to buy the Gulliver technology to sell to Ukraine – still with me?"

"Just about."

". . . and you have the mother of all geopolitical clusterfucks, pardon my French. Into which I and my jolly band of cutthroats will jump with both ballet slippers, stop the Chechens and their friends at Dreyer Pharma killing any more British pilots, prevent Abramov getting his mucky paws on the drug, and generally keep the world spinning more or less evenly on its axis. And I'd like you to help."

"Well, as long as that's all, I'm in."

Webster laughed, a warm, relaxed sound that made Gabriel suddenly long to be back in uniform. "I hoped you'd say that."

"But one question. If you know that these Chechens are in bed with Dreyer Pharma, why not just send in Special Branch or MI5 to arrest them all and shut down the trial?"

"Good question. We could do that, but the trouble is the drug was performing amazingly well in the clinical trials and the ground-based test phases. We need the edge that Gulliver will deliver for Typhoon pilots. So we want Dreyer going full steam ahead on the final stages of development, just not with whatever hold the Chechens have over them. Plus, we wouldn't be entirely averse to Abramov brokering a deal with the Ukrainians. Strictly between us, of course, but the PM would be delighted if they could give the Russians a bit of a bloody nose, get them to wind their necks in. All this Russian self-confidence and empire-building is bad for business."

"So, you want me to, do what, exactly?"

"Come and see me tomorrow. I work out of a military base, can't stand all those stuffed shirts in Whitehall. Head for MOD Rothford in Essex. Go to the main gate and say you're there to see me. They'll direct you. By the way, you still driving that Italian knicker-loosener?"

"The Maserati? Yes. Why?"

"Nothing. Just old man envy."

Gabriel laughed. "OK, so what time do you want me?"

"Get here as soon as you can, we've a lot to get through."

CHAPTER 18

Staring out of his window, James Bryant thought back to the meeting he'd had with Dreyer's Head of R&D four months earlier. Jill had ushered in Dr Arjun Pandatta to discuss a new team of scientists he was hiring to work on Project Gulliver. They had the missing piece of the puzzle, Pandatta said.

The scientists had delivered. Or so it had appeared. Everything went perfectly on the ground-level and low-fly tests. Until that poor pilot went crazy in a Typhoon and flew it into the ground. It was a miracle the second man had survived his own crash. Now Bryant was in shit so deep he couldn't see how he was ever going to get out.

The view across the landscaped grounds of the business park, and on to the Berkshire countryside beyond, would normally afford him some serenity amid the pressures of running a global pharmaceuticals company. But on this particular afternoon, it did nothing to release the tension compressing his rib cage. He'd received another call. And another package.

The caller was the same man who'd made contact the first time.

"The MOD inquiry is over. You did well. Farnborough is only a couple of weeks away now. Do nothing, say nothing to anyone. Let the demonstration flight go ahead as planned . . . with Gulliver. I will know if you have cheated, and I will delight in bringing the lives of your womenfolk to an end. You will receive another package very soon. Pay close attention to its contents and think about their implications. Goodbye, Mr Bryant."

The outer envelope and inner box were identical to the first package. He'd opened it with trembling fingers. There was no videotape this time. Just a small folded parcel of white cotton, like something torn from a sheet. He'd eased the corners apart with his fingertips and spread the three-inch square of fabric open like a flower to be pressed.

Nestled in the centre of the cotton was a piece of flesh. Not large – perhaps half an inch on the cut edge. It was an earlobe. His daughter's earlobe. He knew this because it bore a jewelled, silver hoop that matched the one in his desk drawer.

CHAPTER 19

Gabriel was up, showered, shaved and dressed by six-thirty. No suit for his meeting with Don; jeans, white shirt and a navy V-necked jumper with his driving shoes would be fine for the man's no-standing-on-ceremony style. Back in the Regiment, they'd all chosen their own uniforms. As long as they conformed broadly to military ideas of appropriate dress, they were free to select any and all items according to their own personal taste. Some of the guys had adopted piratical touches like bandanas and cutoff jackets. Others bought stuff in the US, off their Delta Force counterparts, or on the grey market all soldiers knew how to tap into. Extra ammunition belts were a popular item. So were additional personal weapons, from butterfly knives to coils of piano wire. Anything obviously flashy or customised was simultaneously admired and derided with the exclamation, "Very Gucci, mate".

At seven o'clock, Gabriel pulled out onto the main road and pointed the Maserati's wide-mouthed grille north, aiming for the A303 and then the M3 and M25 motorways that would take him round London and then onto the M11 due east towards Rothford, in the Essex countryside. His stomach was filled with butterflies, flittering around and trying to escape, and for once, he didn't quell the restless insects with breathing exercises or focused meditation techniques. He let them fly, enjoying the anticipation of action. It felt good to be on his way to see his old CO again. Good to be going after the bad guys again. He drove fast, but more-or-less legally for four and a half hours, stopping twice for coffee, and pulled up at the main gate of MOD Rothford at 11.03 a.m.

There were two soldiers in standard camouflage chatting at the door of the gatehouse, SA-80 assault rifles held diagonally across their bodies. One looked like he could stand to lose a few pounds, Gabriel reflected, as he brought the car to a stop and killed the engine. As the slimmer of the two soldiers walked towards the car, he got out to stretch his legs and to meet the guy. An old habit, but he always liked to meet people eye-to-eye. That proved difficult as he was five foot nine, and the man walking towards him looked like he'd been eating three Weetabix for his breakfast since he was a boy and had forgotten to stop growing.

"You here to see Colonel Webster, Sir?"

"Yes, that's right. Good call."

"Wasn't really too hard, Sir." The man's sun-weathered face cracked into a grin. "He told us you drove a flash Italian motor and to be honest, we don't really get that kind of vehicle through these gates."

After getting his mugshot taken by a civilian security guard working the computer in the gatehouse, and a pass issued, Gabriel came back outside to get directions to Don Webster's office. Then he was back behind the wheel and thumbing the engine start button. The soldiers called out to him to "give it some", so he obliged with a few blats of the big engine, startling a murder of crows out of a tree growing on the camp perimeter, and gaining a thumbs-up from the two guards before he nosed the car forward, over the clunking steel teeth of the one-way traffic treadles.

No matter where in the world he'd traveled, there was something about military bases that rendered them all the same. Architecture, he mused, signs in military abbreviations, or maybe it was the chain-link fencing one kept glimpsing through trees or bushes. He rolled along at the specified twenty miles per hour – no sense pissing off the

MPs or making a show of his ostentatiously expensive car among the four- or five-year-old Fords, Nissans and Fiats clustered in the mess and barracks car parks.

Ahead, he saw the sign he was looking for: *Admin Offices – Spec. Ops.* He turned into the side road that led towards the centre of the base from the perimeter road. Montgomery Drive, it was called, a tribute to one of Britain's military geniuses and, Gabriel thought, another shortarse like himself. He nosed the car into a visitor's parking slot and got out of the car for the second time.

Ask a civilian what sort of sounds you'd hear on an army base and they'd probably say, "gunfire", "shouting" or "boots". They'd no doubt be surprised to stand next to Gabriel and hear nothing. There was occasional chattering of a pair of magpies high in a beech tree, but mainly just silence. The shooting and shouting happened far away from where any random civilian delivering bread or coming to interview the CO would stray. He locked the car and turned to walk into the building and track down Don. He needn't have worried. The man himself was striding towards him, smiling broadly, hand extended.

"Hello, Old Sport. Good to see you up on your feet. Come on, I've got a lot to tell you. We'll get a brew on, too. Though I have to confess, I have a secretary now, so no cooking fires in the middle of the carpet."

They shook hands, and Gabriel felt himself relax another notch as he grasped his former commanding officer's dry, hard palm in his own.

He followed Don down a blue-carpeted corridor lined with office doors labelled with an alphabet soup of initials, the doors bracketing large-scale photographs in aluminium frames. In one, a British soldier in desert camouflage was preparing to fire an RPG – a rocket-propelled grenade – while hundreds of large-calibre brass cartridges rained down on him from an unseen source, probably a helicopter firing its mini-gun. The cartridges were frozen in mid-air, captured by a superfast shutter speed, so that it appeared to the observer that they could have reached out and plucked one from the swarm. In another, a blue Ford Sierra saloon was caught at the moment when a bomb underneath it was detonated by a remote-controlled robot. The windows were bulging, cracks already widening into fissures all over the glass. Doors and roof were bursting outwards, tearing into lethal shards of razor-edged pressed steel. This one was for demonstration purposes. Gabriel had sat in others just like it in Belfast, observing suspected terrorists in ill-lit neighbourhoods and wondering whether a sharp-eyed teenager was about to blow their cover and call down a shitstorm of local aggression onto him and his patrol.

Don interrupted his scrutiny of the photo.

"Here we are. Home sweet home. For my sins."

The door sign read, OC – Spec. Ops. D. Webster.

"No 'Colonel' Don? The lads on the gate seemed to think you were still in harness."

"Oh, for PR reasons we find the rank works better, but strictly speaking I'm just a lowly Mister these days. Don't even get to run about with a shooter. Just a desk jockey."

"How does that suit you?"

"Come in and I'll tell you," Don said with a warm smile, the crows' feet round his eyes deepening to small crevasses.

* * *

As he took in the office, Gabriel let out an involuntary whistle of appreciation. It was big and, by Army standards, sumptuously appointed. A long rectangle big enough for a solid-looking wooden desk and chair, two chairs for visitors facing it, plus a leather sofa with a couple of matching armchairs, and a coffee table. Then there was the connecting door that led to another office – the secretary's, Gabriel assumed. The walls were hung with a variety of prints and photographs. The centrepiece, hanging behind Don's desk, was a large square photograph of Don shaking hands with the Queen, who was smiling broadly as if she'd just heard a good joke. Perhaps she had. Don was grinning at her and the way his eyes were twinkling suggested to Gabriel that he may well have shared one of his legendary 'bombs' with Her Majesty.

Gabriel pointed to the photo.

"She seems to be in a good mood."

Don turned to look. "She was. We'd just helped her out with a mucky little bit of family business. One of her idiot nephews had managed to get himself into a scrape with some very well-connected Arab gentlemen in an Abu Dhabi nightclub, and we had to exfiltrate him pronto. That was taken at a private party a week later. She's got a wicked sense of humour, too. Told me the filthiest joke I've ever heard. Coffee?"

"Please."

Don walked to the connecting door where a woman with fans of smile lines round her eyes, and bejewelled spectacles dangling from a gold-coloured chain round her neck was talking to a female sergeant. The young, black NCO snapped to attention as she saw Don. Clearly, his lack of official rank or uniform was no impediment to a level of respect normally only accorded to serving officers or top ministers.

"Sorry to interrupt, Sue," he said to the smiley woman. "When you've a moment, do you think you could rustle up some refreshments for us. Coffee and maybe some biscuits if you can scrounge any?"

"Of course, Don," she said. "Chocolate digestives all right?"

"Magic, thanks. As you were, Sergeant," he said to the other woman. "I'm a civilian, remember? You stand any straighter and you'll snap something important."

She stood easy again, but the set of her shoulders told Gabriel she'd enjoyed the subtle praise from a man she'd have read about if she'd ever picked up a book about the Regiment.

Don closed the door and gestured for Gabriel to sit opposite him at the desk. He looked steadily at him for a couple of seconds.

"Thanks for coming to see me. I wasn't sure you were going to call, you know."

"But then you'd have called me, wouldn't you?"

"I would, yes. So you saw through my kind offer to get you help?"

"It was something Annie said. About how quickly you turned up at St Thomas' after I was admitted. It seemed much too quick. And what you told her about watching out for ex-servicemen going gaga. There are thousands of us. Tens of thousands. That's just too big a number for me to get personal service."

"You're not just an ex-squaddie though, are you? You're ex-Regiment. I was your CO. You were decorated for conspicuous gallantry."

Gabriel thought back to the medal ceremony. He'd been awarded the Military Cross after he disabled a Russian T-55 tank that was preparing to obliterate a dozen or more civilians in Bosnia. The PM's hand had been sweaty and warm. Gabriel had smiled and mouthed the appropriate pleasantries, then stuck the medal in its box at the back of his wardrobe and never taken it out again. He'd lost friends on that mission. Any one of them would have done what he'd done. It was a team effort. But the public needed their heroes, and the Army needed its ways of motivating its people. So. Medals.

"I'm still not buying it. Why don't you tell me what's really going on, sir?"

Don sighed and reached into a drawer for a thick pale-green folder, stuffed with papers.

"OK, I guess if you weren't as bright as you are, we wouldn't want your help in the first place. I should have known you'd work things out on your own."

"So tell me. What's going on?"

"How's your Russian? You were a very capable linguist as I remember."

"*Moy russkiy khoroshiy, drug. Nemnogo rzhaviy, no menya ponimayut.*"

"Impressive. Although you could have just called me a superannuated old fart for all I know. Translation please."

"I said, 'My Russian is good, my friend. Maybe a bit rusty, but enough to get by.'"

"Excellent fellow. It may come in handy where you're going.

While you were staying at Audley Grange, you talked to Tom Ainsley, right?"

Gabriel nodded. "He was blinded by some experimental drug. He asked me to do some digging. I'd already decided to before you gave me your card."

"We know something's up at Dreyer Pharma. I've had a couple of chaps . . ."

There was a firm knock at the door and Don paused. "Come!"

The secretary appeared bearing a tray loaded with a chrome-and-glass, two-pint cafetière, cups, saucers, milk jug and sugar bowl, plus a white plate stacked with chocolate biscuits.

"Where would you like it?" she said.

"Here, let me take it, Sue. Thank you. You're a star."

Coffees poured, Don resumed his briefing.

"As I was saying, I had a couple of my chaps have a poke around their systems through the back door, but it's all locked down pretty tight."

Gabriel frowned, and took a swig of the coffee, which was excellent. Hot, strong and with a nutty edge that made him think of Christmas.

"Could we just back up a little, please? Who are these 'chaps' and what, exactly, are you doing these days? I would like to have a vague idea of what I'm getting myself into here. I mean, what is this 'department' you talked about on the phone? MI5? Special Branch? Department of Black Helicopters and Memory Wiping?"

Don leaned back in his chair, cradling his coffee.

"I run a little outfit devoted to counterterrorism involving particularly sensitive considerations."

"You want to watch it, Don," Gabriel said with a grin, "You're picking up a nasty case of civil-servantitis!"

The older man licked the tip of his right index finger and drew a vertical mark in the air.

"Got me! Sorry. You spend enough time around the men from the ministry, and you find dead children turn into collateral damage and bombed hospitals become munitions targeting error-tolerance."

"Don't worry, I used to have a job in advertising. If ever there was an industry devoted to paid bullshitting, it's that one. So these 'particularly sensitive considerations'. Would they, perchance, extend to blind, hallucinating fighter pilots?"

"In one. That's why my colleagues and I were asked to lend a hand. As you may know, the Farnborough Airshow will be upon us shortly. We believe a person or persons unknown, but a Chechen national, wants to sabotage the Typhoon display. Naturally, that's not going to be allowed to happen. But we'd like to follow the strands of the web back to their point of origin rather than just shut the whole thing down. Which we could do, by the way."

"So you think the spider's at Dreyer?" Gabriel said, leaning forward across the desk. "And you want me to help you catch it?"

It was Don's turn to pause while he sipped his coffee.

"I know your skill-set, and now you're a private contractor, it's perfect for my needs."

"You've been doing your background checks, then."

"It wasn't hard. A few calls to some friends here and across the pond, and I had it all on my desk in a couple of hours. You did some nice work with our friends at the Department of Defense, didn't you? That coup business."

Gabriel inclined his head, thinking back to a black female agent named Lauren Stevens-Klimczak with a penchant for brightly coloured trouser suits. "But why couldn't you send me an email, like normal people do?"

"Oh, I intended to. But thanks to your . . . episode . . . at the National Portrait Gallery I had a perfect way to get you into Audley Grange without arousing suspicion. We don't know who knows what, so the more you're under the radar the better."

Gabriel's mind was whirring away, putting pieces of the puzzle together.

"Hallucinations. That sounds like LSD. Could Gulliver have been contaminated somehow?"

"That's what I want you to find out. We do know they've been using amphetamines for the cognitive enhancer aspect – Benzedrine, which flyboys have been popping since Korea. And if you pop too much, it can lead to euphoria and then paranoia."

"But the hallucinations and the blindness have you stumped. Which is where I come in?"

"Yes. I want to know what's going on so we can keep Gulliver on the table without killing anyone else. Well, anyone we like, obviously. So I want you to make an approach to their CEO."

Gabriel had already decided that he was going to take the job, whatever it was. His fledgling security consulting business would remain just that unless he started getting work, and if Don Webster was the client, he'd pretty much go anywhere and do anything he asked. But there was friendship, and there was business. And this was business.

"May I raise an ugly subject, Don?" he said, reaching for a biscuit.

"You mean money? Nothing ugly about money, Gabriel. A man's got to eat. You don't think I'm sitting behind this desk out of the goodness of my heart, do you? I'll see you're well paid for your expertise and your time. Two grand a day plus expenses sound good to you?"

Gabriel failed to restrain a smile. He'd been about to ask for half that amount.

"More than fine. But I'm happy to take it," he added quickly, before Don could pull the offer off the table and replace it with something smaller.

"Good," Don said. "I'd love to be able to pay you more, but that's my ceiling set by the bean counters in Whitehall. There are IT guys mending laptops who get as much, so please don't feel guilty."

"So I approach the CEO of Dreyer Pharma. Then what?"

"Just introduce yourself and your services as a corporate troubleshooter. I have a strong hunch he needs you, so we'll just fly a kite in front of him. If he grabs the string, fine. If not, well, we can start laying the old NatSec argument on him."

Gabriel finished his coffee. "Assuming he takes the bait, then what?"

"I think that's rather down to you. We know something's going on down there, so he's bound to be at the heart of it. Take him out for dinner, get him drunk, whatever you think will get him to open up. Once we have some decent intelligence, we can plan our next steps."

"Just to recap then," Gabriel said, and began counting points off on his fingers, "you know something's going on at Dreyer Pharma, and their experimental drug. It's Chechen terrorists. I need to prise the reason from the CEO, then the men in black rush in and kill everyone. That about it?"

"More or less. Although the PM is rather keener on our having at least a few warm bodies to parade in front of the media before we try them and fling them into the Tower for the rest of their lives."

"Great. Count me in. I'll start on it as soon as I'm home."

Don smiled. "Excellent. Now, why don't we go for a quick tour round, then can I offer you an early lunch in the Officers' Mess?"

* * *

Over huge plates of freshly fried fish and chips, complete with mushy peas and mugs of tea, the two men talked of other days, other missions. As he inhaled the sharp tang of vinegar vaporising off the hot chips, Gabriel felt more relaxed than he had done for months. Running his own business, and wining and dining prospective clients wasn't nearly as much fun as blowing stuff up. Or even just going a few rounds in the ring with "Sarge", the ex-Paras guy who ran the gym he visited when time commitments permitted.

After demolishing his plate of food, Don put his knife and fork down, and looked Gabriel squarely in the eye. Gabriel knew instantly what was coming, and downed tools as well. He leaned back in his chair and prepared himself for the question.

"What really happened at the National Portrait Gallery?" Don asked. "The truth this time, please. You were never one for feeling a bit peaky in the heat. Wouldn't have really suited the job description, would it?"

Gabriel sat a moment, considering what to say in response to his old boss's enquiry. In some ways, saying it out loud would be to shuck off a huge burden he'd been carrying around ever since he'd left the Regiment. But was he ready for what would inevitably follow from that? Or could he stick to his story, tell lies to one of the best men he'd ever known, let alone served under, keep the demons squashed inside that bottle and push down hard on the cork?

Don didn't seem in any hurry for an answer. He just sat, sipping tea and waiting, regarding Gabriel like a headmaster with a favoured prefect who'd committed a minor indiscretion. Behind them, Gabriel heard the waiters clinking plates and cutlery together as they cleared the table from a group of half a dozen officers who'd been laughing loudly about one of their number's failings as a cricket player. Now, the mess was empty, apart from him and Don. He drew a breath and felt his throat thicken up. *Please, don't start crying now. Get it out there, but save the waterworks for later.*

"Do you remember my last mission in Mozambique? The search and destroy against Abel N'Tolo?"

"Went bad, didn't it?" Don said, putting his emptied mug down on the table and leaning forward, steepling his fingers under his chin.

"Depends who you talk to. We got the plans that put a stop to N'Tolo's evil little band of murderers and rapists, but we lost Smudge. *I* lost Smudge. I sent him back for the plans, and he took a round in the head. We couldn't even retrieve his body – they were about to take us all out. The last thing I saw was Smudge, pinned to a tree by machetes through his hands."

"You blamed yourself. That's why you came to me with your resignation so soon afterwards."

"Of course I blamed myself. I *do* blame myself, still. I sent him back in. I got him killed."

"Look, I'm not going to patronise you and tell you what you already know about the burdens of command. Though from what I heard, Smudge was already halfway back before you even gave the order. But we both know what's going on here, don't we? Flashbacks? Panic Attacks? Insomnia? Hitting the old bottle a little too much? Anger problems?"

This was it. This was the moment. Tell the truth. Or back out and repeat the lie again. *Just felt a little off colour. Must have been something I ate.* No. Time to come clean. Who else would understand better than Don Webster – the man who'd given Gabriel his own orders? He drew in a shuddering breath, then let it out again in a hiss, clasping his hands together between his knees.

"I've . . . I've been having a few problems. Seeing Smudge. In cars. Lifts. On a plane once. That business in the States? I saw more corpses in a week than I did in my last year in the Regiment. Then in the gallery, one of the photos was of the boss of the Hells Angels I had to deal with. It just, I don't know, it triggered something. I turned away and there was Smudge, sitting in one of those hard chairs in a rent-a-cop uniform with his jaw gone and his head split open. After that I just fancied running screaming into the street to get mown down by a van driver on the wrong side of the road."

Don pursed his lips, looked at Gabriel, grey eyes unblinking under a lined brow. "You and I both know this is PTSD, don't we? I assume you're not in denial about it?"

Gabriel looked down at his interlaced fingers, almost bloodless from the pressure.

"No. No I'm not. But when job centre staff who get shouted at are signed off from work with it, you know, it kind of cheapens the currency."

"Never mind what other people are doing. This is about you. Now, nothing you've said makes me doubt in any way your competence to work with me and my team on this mission of ours, but I do want you to call this person."

Don reached into his jacket pocket and pulled out a business card. Extended his hand across the table and gave it to Gabriel.

Gabriel took it and read the details on the front, below the white and blue NHS logo.

"Fariyah Crace, PhD, FRCPsych. Consultant Psychiatrist. What, 'Did you wet the bed? Tell me all about your mother', that kind of thing?"

Don smiled.

"She's not like that at all. But she's helped a lot of guys get through some bad stuff. You'd like her. Think about it. For me, OK?"

Gabriel tucked the card into his wallet.

"OK, fine. I'll think about the good Doctor Crace."

"Good. Tell her secretary I sent you. It'll help. Now, if you'll forgive me, I have a report to write and believe me, I'd rather spend an hour talking to Fariyah about my childhood than pounding away on a keyboard. But with great power comes great paperwork, as they say."

The two men got up and walked back to the office block. The sun was out and it warmed Gabriel's skin. He felt good. Better than he had done for a while. He turned to face Don. They shook hands.

"Good to have you on my team again," Don said.

* * *

On the way home, Gabriel thought about what Don had said, hardly noticing the road, the unspooling countryside or the other vehicles around him. Not the mission – that was all fairly clear-cut. But about his health problem. He knew PTSD was nothing to be ashamed about. In fact, sometimes it seemed the whole bloody world was bleating on about mental health. It was virtually fashionable. But he had so many skeletons in his closet, he sometimes felt if he were to open the door, even a crack, he'd be submerged in a tumbling cavalcade of bones, rattling and splintering till he screamed.

"Do you want to spend the rest of your life plagued by zombies, then?" he asked out loud, pulling into the outside lane to surge past a procession of articulated lorries labouring up a long incline. "Maybe Smudge will be joined by Davis Meeks and the other Angels. Hey, they could set up a little zombie clubhouse in the sitting room. And who needs sleep anyway? You could just carry on snatching a few hours here and there, dodging nightmares. That would be fun for another forty or fifty years, yes?" *No. No. It wouldn't. Holding stress in is supposed to give you cancer. Best avoid that if at all possible.* He was suddenly tired and opened his mouth in a yawn so wide he felt the hinges of his jaw pop. Coffee. And a phone call.

CHAPTER 20

Gabriel drove on for another few miles until he saw a sign for a service station. He signalled left and pulled across two lanes of traffic to get to the slip road, earning an angry honk from a sales rep in a BMW 3 Series, jacket dangling from a hook in the rear window. He pulled over and let the car coast round the bend into the car park.

Inside, the place was abuzz with families and management types milling around, buying sweets, queueing for the outlets offering sustenance in the food court, arguing, texting, and devouring what the manager of the place would no doubt refer to as a wide selection of freshly home-cooked foods and beverages. He ordered a cappuccino from a girl who looked barely old enough for a driving licence.

"OK, brilliant!" she said. "Anything to eat with that?"

"Yes, please. A blueberry muffin."

"Fantastic!" she said, in a tone of breathless admiration for his choice.

"And could you stick an extra shot in the coffee, please?"

"No problem!" she chirped. "What name please?"

"Wolfe," he said, deadpanning.

"Ooh, scary," she said, widening her kohl-rimmed eyes. "Don't bite me." Then she called out his order to the baristas and moved on to serve the next customer, a burly guy in a cheap suit, huffing and puffing with impatience.

Gabriel took the coffee and muffin outside and found an empty table in a landscaped garden that wouldn't have looked out of place in the grounds of a stately home. Surrounded by softly undulating grassed mounds was a huge pond, half-choked with yellow and blue irises. Somehow the architect, or garden designer, had managed to deaden most of the vehicle noise from the six lanes of traffic thundering along barely two hundred yards away, and Gabriel found he could distinguish birds singing, crickets chirping and even the splishing of an ornamental fountain on one side of the pond.

He pulled out his wallet and extracted the card Don had given him. Then he retrieved his phone. Placed them next to each other on the table. All he had to do was touch the screen eleven times, and he could open a door that might lead away from all the ghosts. He sat with the tip of his right index finger poised over the slick glass screen, unable to push it down those last few millimetres, unwilling to withdraw it. He could feel a thin film of sweat forming on his forehead, which had nothing to do with the warm weather.

Come on, this is silly. It's a phone call to a doctor, nothing more.
(the skeletons)
She's not going to psychoanalyse you on the spot; that would be
(lying in piles)
silly. Plus, Don said you'd like her. So that would be
(with bullet holes in their skulls)
fun. Wouldn't it?

He swallowed, trying to shift the lump that felt like a golf ball stuck halfway down his throat. Then, just as he decided to man up and make the call, a woman's scream pierced the calm of the picnic area. All around him, people were looking up, scanning left and right like meerkats on guard against predators. He stood, trying to locate the source of the sound. Nothing looked out of place, and within seconds everyone but him had gone back to their devices, heads down again, looking for mentions, or updates, likes or new followers. He got up from his table and headed for the pond. The sound had come from there. He began a clockwise circuit, and had to detour where a thick grove of bamboo screened the view beyond. There was another scream, but it was cut short as soon as it had begun. And a man's voice.

"Shut up, you fucking Paki bitch!"

Then another voice. Hard. Unforgiving. A woman this time.

"Yeah, shut the fuck up, bitch. You can't come over here and start giving us white people lip. We live here, don't we? Who the fuck do you think you are?"

There was the sharp, flat crack of a punch, then crying, low and whimpery.

Gabriel rounded the stand of bamboo. In front of him, grouped like an awkward composition of models for a painting, three people froze as they saw him.

In the centre of the group was a slim, brown-skinned woman in a black business suit. Her burgundy leather briefcase lay behind her on the ground. Pinioning her arms by her sides was, no other word for him, a skinhead. A real old-school thug with shaved head, tight jeans, red braces over white T-shirt and tall, oxblood Doctor Martens. In front of her, hand clamped across her face to stifle her screams, was a woman of maybe thirty, hair scraped back revealing a high, shining forehead and huge, gold hoops dangling from her ears.

The businesswoman widened her eyes as she saw Gabriel and began bucking against her captor's grip.

"Let her go," Gabriel said, quietly.

"Or what, fuckface?" the woman said, turning to speak but leaving her palm muffling the woman's renewed efforts to sound the alarm.

"Yeah," the skinhead said. "Fuck off back there with the others. This ain't got nothing to do with you."

Maybe inspired by the arrival of a witness or better yet a rescuer, the businesswoman kicked out, then back, and managed to rake the side of one high-heeled shoe down the skinhead's left shin, before jamming the point of her heel into the top of his foot.

"Fuck, you broke my fucking toe!" he yelled. But he stepped back all the same, releasing his grip to clutch his leg before tripping over a tussock of grass and falling into the pond, splashing through the skim of duckweed on the surface.

Gabriel had closed in on the woman while this was happening. Grabbing her by both wrists, he pulled her off her captive, maintaining a vice-like grip so she couldn't hit out.

"Go," he said to the businesswoman. "Call the police. Get the manager of this place. You'll need witnesses."

She looked at him, mouth downturned.

"I'm sorry. Thanks for helping but I have a meeting to go to. Massive new client. I can't afford to be late. Thanks. Thanks so much."

She swept her long hair back behind her ears, stooped to pick up her briefcase then ran back towards the seating area.

The skinhead had got to his feet and waded out of the shallow water, dripping with pond slime.

"You're going to pay for that, you cunt."

He lunged for Gabriel, who was still holding the skinhead's girlfriend, swinging a fist weighted with wide, silver rings.

It was too easy, dealing with untrained sluggers like these. In one quick movement, Gabriel tripped the woman onto her back, sidestepped the incoming punch and elbowed the man hard in the throat. As he went down, coughing and clutching his windpipe, Gabriel punched him on the back of the neck, speeding his fall so his head hit the turf fast enough to disorientate him. The woman was struggling to her feet but Gabriel just pointed at her and looked her straight in the eye.

"Stay down," he said. "Or I'll put you down."

Without turning away from her, he stretched out his left hand and grabbed her companion by the front of his T-shirt, hauling him over so the two of them were lying head to head and looking up at him. Their expressions had changed from naked aggression – all bared, bad teeth and wrinkled snouts – to panting, wide-eyed fear.

Gabriel leaned over them until he could smell them: a mixture of bad breath and muddy pond water from the man and heavy perfume from the woman. He was deliberately breathing slowly, and spoke in a quiet voice, forcing them to crane upwards to catch his words.

"What gives you the right to treat a stranger like that?"

The man glared at Gabriel as he spoke, cords standing out in his neck as he drew his lips back from his teeth once more.

"She pushed in front of me, didn't she? In the queue. Told her to get back in line where she belonged and the bitch just ignored me. Me! A white man. What's been here, like, for ever. And she's just a fuckin Paki immigrant."

Gabriel backhanded the man across the face. Not hard. Not enough to produce a sound that would carry. But hard enough to shut him up.

"She didn't sound Pakistani. She sounded like she came from London. I want you to listen to me. And you," he said, eyeing the woman who had subsided into a kind of trance. "I don't have the time to call the police, but I really don't like people like you."

"Please," the man said, eyes pleading, perhaps realising just how far out of his depth he was. "Don't do nothing else. You can't. You're white, like us."

"Give me your car keys. I assume you drove here." Gabriel sat back on his heels and held out his right hand, palm upwards.

"Why? What you going to do with them?" the woman said. "Don't stab him or nothing."

Gabriel twitched his flattened fingers upwards impatiently.

With a scowl, the man stuck his hand down into the front pocket of his water-tightened jeans and pulled out a set of house and car keys. The black plastic fob, for a BMW, was clipped onto a split-ring alongside a rectangle of thin rubber printed with the flag of St George. He dropped them into Gabriel's palm.

Gabriel stood, pushing up from his heels in one smooth, fast movement that caused the two supine bullies to flatten themselves back into the grass. With an easy underhand action, he lobbed the jingling keys into the centre of the pond, where they disappeared between the sword-like leaves of the irises, making the barest of splashes as they found the water.

He marched off, back to his table, listening for the sounds of onrushing feet, ready to turn and strike. But none came. Just the sound of muted swearing and more splashing, heavier this time, as the man and woman waded around among the flowers.

If he'd been expecting applause, or admiration, he was to be disappointed. Displaying a mixture of British reserve, caution and an engrossing interest in their phones and tablets, the people at the café tables barely looked up as he emerged from the vegetation shielding them from the scene of his most recent encounter with wickedness. *Not even a video? Nobody wanted to put that little fracas on Facebook? Wonders will never cease.* He reached his table and, still standing, took a swig of the coffee. Stone-cold. He grimaced. Not the relaxing rest stop he'd planned.

CHAPTER 21

By the time Gabriel climbed out of the car and squeezed the little green button on his garage door closer, he'd made a decision. Yes, he would call the psychiatrist. He'd also spent the last twenty minutes of the drive, as he thrashed along an arrow-straight three-mile stretch of the A30, drafting a letter in his head that he would type up, edit and send to the CEO of Dreyer Pharma, James Bryant. Asked to form an impression of the man from his name alone, Gabriel would have guessed white, forty-five, nice suit, good grooming, well spoken, could be an army brat, private schools and a decent redbrick university. Plus an MBA from somewhere in the US. Harvard Business School or maybe Stanford.

He went inside and headed upstairs for a shower.

As the scalding water beat down on his shoulders, he stood, eyes closed, reviewing the intelligence he'd gathered. One: Tom Ainsley, the pilot, had told him he suspected there was something up with the experimental drug they were developing at Dreyer Pharma. Two: it was fine on the ground and even on low-altitude flights, but take your plane up higher, and something happened to cause hallucinations and blindness. Three: there'd been some sort of internal investigation, and they claimed to have fixed the problem. This was either a lie or a mistake – Tom's accident had happened the day after the two-week MOD investigation concluded. Four: all along, some shadowy Government department headed by his old commanding officer was already investigating Dreyer and wanted him to help. Five: to complete the recipe for chaos, add in a dash of Chechen separatists, and a big pinch of skullduggery involving a Russian oligarch, and some international under-the-table drug-dealing. Should be interesting, he thought as he towelled himself dry. He dressed in an old pair of Levi's and a white T-shirt, slipped on a pair of beaten up navy-blue boat shoes and went downstairs. He was hungry.

Sometimes you want to fiddle around with vegetables, slicing and dicing. And sometimes what you really want is a thick slice of red meat. Today was the second kind of time. He wanted a steak, rare, with chips; and a decent bottle of wine. Something hefty. A Barolo, perhaps, or an Aussie Shiraz. Both were to hand, in the village pub: The Angel Inn. He pulled on a soft, caramel-coloured leather jacket and headed out.

Inside, the pub was busy with midweek drinkers, and families having dinner together. The noise was cheerful, rather than oppressive. Over a quiet lunchtime pint one day, the landlady had confessed to Gabriel that she didn't really go for all that "bloody mood music the bosses insist we play", preferring instead either the chat of contented customers or the occasional raucous gig from a bunch of middle-aged, middle-class rockers who called themselves The Deadbeat Dads and played blues, rock and roll, and the odd funk cover. "They're about as rock and roll as I am," she cawed as she pulled pints. "The singer's a bloody management consultant, and the guitarist works for an insurance company."

The landlady was working tonight and flashed him a smile as he approached the bar.

"All right, my lovely?" she said, tucking her hair behind her ears with both hands, a gesture that lifted her considerable breasts and pushed them out towards him.

"Can I order some food please, Steph? Rib-eye, rare, chips and a bottle of the Barolo."

"Building yourself up are you?" she said, squeezing his right bicep across the bar. "Not that you need to."

He grinned at her. "You think? You'd have me on the ground in seconds if we were fighting."

Her eyes were twinkling in the light from the soft lamps above the bar. "Chance would be a fine thing. Now, leave me alone so I can get chef onto your dinner. I need to serve these other poor sods who've been waiting for their drinks while you've been flirting with me."

With that unanswerable rejoinder floating between them, she flounced away with a twitch of her hips.

There was a small table free in a corner where the light wasn't so bright. Gabriel settled in to wait for his steak and thanked the young waitress who brought him the wine a few moments later, registering six separate pieces of decorative metal inserted into her otherwise satin-smooth face. As he took an appreciative mouthful of the full-bodied red, he started reworking the letter to Bryant in his head.

His thought process was interrupted by the waitress returning with a circular white platter dominated by a slab of steak that was virtually falling off the rim. The bottoms of the thick-cut chips, which smelt deliciously of hot goose fat, were turning pink as they soaked up the juices that were oozing out from underneath the steak. Gabriel thanked the young woman and bent to his meal. The steak fell apart under the swift slices of his razor-sharp serrated knife, and for a few minutes, his questioning inner self fell silent. Then it piped up again with one final thought. *Maybe this is what you can talk to Fariyah Crace about. Now shut up and eat your dinner.* That sounded like the best advice he'd heard in a long while, so he took it.

The combination of the wine, the massive chunk of beef, and his eight hours of driving, not to mention the altercation at the motorway services, overwhelmed him in a sudden rush of fatigue. He shook his head and leant back in his chair. Felt his eyes closing again. A voice close to his ear startled him. He realised he'd been on the point of sleep.

"Everything all right, my love?" It was Steph.

Gabriel got to his feet, swaying a little as his balance deserted him momentarily.

"I need to go, Steph. Sorry, not feeling myself tonight."

The cool evening air partially revived him as he stepped out from the pub's warm interior. It was only a ten-minute walk to his cottage, but each step seemed to drag energy from him that he couldn't replace. He made it to his front door and was asleep fifteen minutes later.

* * *

Shooting. Lots of it. The gunfire was coming from his back garden. This was no countryman's shotgun, either. The rate of fire alone marked it out as an automatic weapon, and the noise was deafening. Had to be an assault rifle at least. An AK? Maybe. Could be an LMG. No. Light machine guns didn't sound angry like this one. This one was shouting with each round that exploded in the breech. "Gotcha! Gotcha! Gotcha! Gotcha! GOTCHA!"

Gabriel leapt out of bed and rushed to the window. Shit! He was still in his dress uniform, medals and all. They'd see him a mile off. And his weapon was missing. Where was his M16? He pulled the curtain back to make a viewing slit and crouched before peering through. The garden was full of dark-skinned fighters. Lean men with ropy muscles, wearing gold-framed Ray-Ban Aviators and Adidas T-shirts. All bombed-up with Kalashnikovs, Glocks, Uzis, grenades, machetes and, yes, there at the back, a wild-eyed dude with two-foot-long dreadlocks tied back with a skull and crossbones bandanna, swinging a Heckler & Koch MG4 light machinegun from side to side, his finger crooked round tight on the trigger, spraying 5.56mm rounds that were decapitating the blooms in Gabriel's flower beds. No. Not blooms. Those were bodies. British soldiers: Guards, Royal Engineers, SAS – buried up to their waists in the sludgy red soil. Their heads leapt upwards in welters of blood as the explosive rounds blew their necks apart. They were calling out to him as they rose in arcs before thumping down into the grass. "Don't leave us, Boss. We want to get back for Nathalie's birthday." All the heads had the same face. A deep brown face with a shattered jaw.

Gabriel tried to shout down to them. "I'm coming Smudge. I'm coming to get you." But he could only croak out nonsense. "Your flight leaves in an hour. Please do not leave personal items behind you."

The rebel soldiers had reached the back of the cottage and looked up at him. They knew he was there, cowering behind the curtain, and they laughed at him, showing rows of big, white teeth, filed to sharp points.

"We're coming to get you, Boss," the leading soldier whispered. Then he started walking up the wall, perpendicular to the old brickwork, his AK-47 pointed straight at Gabriel's face. "Then it's crucifixion time for you."

Gabriel looked back to the lawn. There was Smudge, his old patrol number two in the Motorised Troop, a good soldier whose life he'd saved back on the last day of stage one training. Only now he was impaled through his palms by machetes, pinned to a cross-shaped tree. Smudge strained to release himself, but only succeeded in tearing deep gashes in his hands from which horizontal rivers of bright blood flowed outwards to each side of the garden.

"Look out, Boss!" he cried, sending teeth spinning from his broken mouth.

Gabriel looked down. An enemy fighter was standing on the wall just below the window. The muzzle of his AK was pointed straight at Gabriel's face, separated by a few inches of air and a quarter-inch of glass. The man's face was gone, replaced by a death's head: a shining, white skull with blood-filled sockets and those hideous pointed teeth champing up and down. Gabriel tried to move out of the line of fire but couldn't. His hands were pinioned to the wooden windowsill by his own cook's knives, their stainless steel blades rocking back and forth, driving themselves deeper into in the wood under his bleeding flesh, which smelled of rare steak.

In front of him now, the soldier reached through the glass and opened the curtains all the way. "Fariyah Crace says you've been a very bad man," he said. Then he pulled the trigger.

As the rounds slammed into his torso and head, Gabriel shrieked and fell back into a deep pool of his own blood, tumbling down through the murk and landing with a crash on his kitchen floor.

* * *

He staggered to his feet, clutching the back of a chair, and looked at the clock on the cooker.

03.00.

His pulse was drumming in his ears, and his whole body was slick with sweat.

Shaking, he lurched to the door and the downstairs cloakroom beyond. An acrid surge of red wine and half-digested meat raced into his throat and he threw up into the lavatory, gripping the cold, white sides of the commode as if to stop himself disappearing into the sewer below.

Fuck. You're in deep trouble, Boss.

CHAPTER 22

Sitting in his office over the garage the following morning, he placed the NHS business card Don had given him on the desk in front of him and called the number.

"Dr Crace?" he blurted, as soon as the call was answered.

"No, this is Valerie Pearce. I am *Professor* Crace's secretary. How may I help you?"

"Sorry. I need, I mean, if it's possible to see Doc— Professor Crace? Talk I mean. Not about me. To find out more." Aware he was gabbling, Gabriel took a deep breath, let it out again and started again. "My name is Gabriel Wolfe. Don Webster gave me Professor Crace's card. He said she might be able to help me."

At the mention of Don's name, the secretary's starchy manner softened.

"I'm sure she can. Now. Give me your name again and I'll see if she's free. She's teaching today, but I know she has some gaps in her schedule."

"Wolfe. Gabriel," he said, and nearly added his rank and service number.

"Well, Wolfe Gabriel, just hold on for a sec while I track her down."

He heard the phone at the other end click as Valerie put him on hold. No Vivaldi, thankfully. Or recorded message telling him about new NHS services for the psychologically disturbed.

A minute later, she came back on the line, her voice warm and friendly. He could picture a motherly type, smiling as she spoke.

"I'm putting you through now Mr Wolfe. She doesn't have much time, but she said any friend of Don's, etcetera."

Gabriel readied himself to say something he'd spent years avoiding. He heard a click as Valerie put him through to another phone.

"Hello Gabriel, I'm Fariyah Crace. You know Don?"

"He was my old CO. He gave me your card."

She laughed. A lovely trilling sound that made Gabriel's heart leap. "He gives them out like confetti. I ought to put him on commission. Now, I don't know if Valerie explained, but I have a lecture to give in ten minutes, but I wanted to have a quick chat with you now. So why don't you give me the bare bones of it and let's see where we can go from there."

Where to start? Gabriel ran his hand through his hair, digging the tips of his fingers into his scalp.

"I think I may be having some . . . psychological problems."

"Well, that would certainly be my field of expertise. If you'd sprained your ankle, I'm not sure I'd be of much use to you. What kind of psychological problems have you been having?"

"If I tell you, I know what you'll say."

"Maybe you can just tell me and we'll see if I agree with you."

She was patient, he gave her that. But the clock was ticking.

"Where shall I start? I keep seeing someone who's dead. And I have nightmares. Bad ones. And sometimes I feel like I'm going to die. I mean, I am, I know that. We all are. But die right now. In a coffee shop. Or an airport lounge."

"Without putting a label on it, that doesn't sound pleasant. And for a man with your background, I'm sorry to say it doesn't sound uncommon, either. Can I suggest something?"

"Please do. I'm not really in my comfort zone at the moment."

"Don't worry, I'm not going to start psychoanalysing you down the phone. I want to ask you whether you have experienced any of the following symptoms since leaving the Army. Just say 'yes' or 'no' to each one. Hold on a second. I just need to find the document."

Gabriel held on, listening to his pulse beating in his ears with a dull achy throb. Then Fariyah came back on the line.

"OK, I have it. Are you ready?"

"As I'll ever be."

"Good. Yes or no, remember?"

"I remember."

"Repeated disturbing memories, thoughts or images of a stressful experience from the past."

"Yes."

"Repeated disturbing dreams of a stressful experience from the past."

"Yes."

"Suddenly acting or feeling as if a stressful experience were happening again."

"Yes."

"Feeling very upset when something reminded you of a stressful experience from the past."

"Yes."

"Having a physical reaction such as your heart pounding or trouble breathing when something reminded you of a stressful experience from the past."

"Yes."

She paused and Gabriel could hear her put a sheet of paper down. Somehow he'd imagined she'd be reading it from a screen.

"I'm going to stop there," she said. "I think it would do no harm for you to come and see me. Just for an exploratory chat. I don't like to give diagnoses over the phone, but I think we both know that what you're experiencing has a name, and more to the point, a treatment. I'm going to transfer you back to Valerie. She'll help you make an appointment."

"Can I just ask about your fees? I have money and I do want to get this sorted, but I'd like to know what I'd be looking at. Financially, I mean."

"My consulting fee for private patients is three hundred pounds an hour. However, you can see me via Audley Grange; they'll pick up the cost for you. All you need to do is get a letter of recommendation from one of the doctors. Have you seen anyone there?"

Gabriel thought of Dr Norton. "Yes, there's someone I can call."

"Very good. Now I'm afraid you'll have to excuse me. My lecture starts shortly. I'm looking forward to seeing you, Gabriel."

"Me too. You, I mean. Sorry. Bye."

He waited while the line clicked and chattered, then he heard Valerie's voice again.

"Hello Gabriel. Professor Crace has an appointment free next Monday at eleven in the morning. Would that suit you?"

He could picture her, manicured nail hovering over the mouse, ready to click his life into another phase. But what would it look like? Would he have to spill his guts in some shrink's office for years to come? Would he end up weeping as he described his childhood? He inhaled deeply, opened his mouth and began to speak. He realised he didn't know which answer would emerge from his trembling lips.

"Yes. That would be fine."

Valerie's fingernails clicking on her keyboard sounded like the rattle of distant small-arms fire. Only this sound promised fighting of an altogether different kind. Today was Wednesday. That gave him five days to prepare himself. Before then, though, he had to secure an opening with Dreyer Pharma's CEO. That meant writing and posting the letter today. He needed to clear his head, so he changed into running clothes and headed out.

CHAPTER 23

Coming in after his run, Gabriel saw a bulky brown A4 envelope on the mat. He picked it up and turned it over. On the front was a white label with a crisply rendered logo in a soft grey and gold colour combination: Lainey Evencroft. His name and address were written in exquisite calligraphy, by one of the Jennifers, presumably. He took it through to the kitchen and placed it dead-centre on the table.

He grabbed some cold roast beef, very rare, from the fridge, along with gherkins and English mustard. From the pea-green earthenware bread crock by the toaster, he lifted out a rough-crusted rye loaf. He liked to bake his own bread. It was a form of meditation: weighing, mixing, kneading and shaping. He sawed off two thick slices, slathered them with butter, added a swipe of the fiery yellow mustard to both buttered surfaces, then layered a few pieces of the bloody beef to one of them.

As he munched the sandwich, pausing occasionally to wipe away the meat juices that squirted from his mouth and ran down his chin, he read the dossier that Cressida Pennard-Johnston had prepared for him. He knew the Jennifer's real name because she'd added it, again in beautiful handwriting, to the compliment slip paper-clipped to the front page. *Hope this is useful, Gabriel,* she'd written. *Massive fan.* He had no idea what she was a massive fan of – maybe Annie had been bugling his achievements. He'd have to ask her next time he saw her.

It became clear as he read that Dreyer Pharma wasn't in the best of health. Since the founding partners had cashed out, the company had made only lacklustre profits. Its drug development pipeline was currently more of a trickle than a gush, placing huge pressure on James Bryant to deliver on Project Gulliver. Then Gabriel came to a section that brought him up short. Under "Executive Remuneration" there were concise notes explaining how the board of directors were due a huge payout, but only if they could meet certain financial targets. Bryant himself stood to collect £20 million – if he steered the business safely into the financial harbour the investors had planned for it. If he hit the rocks instead, he'd be down by a whopping amount of money and probably out of the business. *No pressure there, then, eh, James?* Suddenly, Gabriel felt a lot more confident that his missive would yield a request for a meeting. If there was outside interference with Project Gulliver that could damage the drug's development, or stall it altogether, then here was a CEO who would bite the hand off anyone who offered his services as a troubleshooter.

Now, he sat at his desk, the silver sliver of his MacBook Air beckoning his fingertips to begin a letter that would lead him into the depths of a possible terrorist plot to kill British fighter pilots. He flicked through the dossier to the profile of Bryant himself. Would he match Gabriel's knee-jerk character sketch or not?

It turned out Gabriel was right in places and off in others. Bryant was born in 1970, so he'd nailed his age. As far as being an army brat, Gabriel was one hundred and eighty degrees wrong: Bryant was the son of Philip, a postman, and Molly, an office cleaner. Like many working-class children before him, he'd used education as a trampoline to bounce right out of the path that life, fate or the British class system had mapped out for him. King Edward VI School, Stratford-upon-Avon; then a first-class degree in chemistry and a PhD in pharmacology, both from Cambridge; and finally an MBA from Harvard Business School. One for three, Gabriel thought.

Bryant had spent his entire career in the pharmaceutical industry and was now the boss.

"So, James Bryant," Gabriel said to the thin screen of his laptop, "how shall I pique your interest and get some time with you face to face?"

He paused, then bent his head and started typing. An hour later, after a few false starts, and a lot of deleting, retyping and cut-and-pasting, he was finished. He pressed 'Print' and waited as the laser printer to his right hummed its digital tune while delivering a crisply rendered letter in 12-point Times Roman type on some expensive cream stationery.

* * *

Dear Mr Bryant,

I was a disappointment to my father.

He hoped I would follow him into the Diplomatic Service. Instead, I joined the Parachute Regiment. Then I applied for, and was badged into, the SAS.

More than how to fight, what I learned in the Army was how to communicate.

With the men I commanded. With terrified civilians. With terrorists. With captured enemy fighters who at best possessed only rudimentary English.

I also learned how to negotiate, to compromise and to persuade. These skills helped me in the advertising industry, where I found a berth after leaving the Army. Now I work with senior executives as a troubleshooter.

I'm sure Dreyer Pharma runs smoothly for ninety-five per cent of the time. And when things are going your way, you'd have no need of a man like me. But for the other five per cent, when union officials are giving you sleepless nights, or competitors are playing dirty, or regulators are winding you up tighter than a clockwork toy, perhaps someone with my talents might be of service. I am very good at listening, so you might find me an asset in situations ranging from hostile takeovers to litigation, where a confidential sounding board could help you try out different approaches.

Would it be too forward of me to suggest that I might be of help to you from time to time? If you could find forty-five minutes in your schedule, I would be delighted to come and see you.

Yours sincerely,
Gabriel Wolfe, MC.

* * *

Gabriel picked up his fountain pen – an old black and silver Parker he'd inherited from his father, whom, in the end he had pleased rather than disappointed – and signed the letter. He folded the sheet into precise thirds, then slid it into a matching envelope, feeling the subtle ridging of the paper under his fingertips as he sealed it. Finally, he hand-wrote James Bryant's name and address, added a first-class stamp and then headed out to the village postbox.

The following day, at 11.48 a.m., his phone rang. He was in the middle of some woods near his house walking with a friend, Julia, and her Irish terrier, Scout.

"Sorry, I have to take this," he said.

She widened her eyes and nodded vigorously. "Go on then, it could be a new client."

"Gabriel Wolfe."

"Hello. This is James Bryant. I got your letter this morning and, er, well your timing was spookily good. As it happens I would like to talk to you."

There was something in the man's voice that triggered Gabriel's antennae. A tightness that flattened out his intonation, as though he was being forced to talk.

"Name a time. Your office is about a ninety-minute drive from here."

"Could you come tomorrow? It's a rare free day for me. And there is a potential . . . project . . . where I need some outside help."

CHAPTER 24

For the meeting with James Bryant, Gabriel selected a navy two-piece suit with a thin strip of his crisply ironed handkerchief showing above the top pocket. A white button-down shirt, maroon silk tie with matching cotton socks, and a pair of black, monk strap shoes completed the outfit.

On the drive up to the business park in Reading, Gabriel planned his strategy. Start with the usual chitchat about family and careers, then ask Bryant how things were going. Or maybe what was top of his "most-hated" list at the moment. Those were the questions that got people talking. Julia had once called them his "oyster cracker" questions after a dinner party inquiry of a successful but reticent policewoman had yielded a flood of embarrassed and then hilarious anecdotes from the thirty-something detective inspector. What he'd said was, "Did you ever steal money from your parents when you were growing up?" Here, he wouldn't let on that he knew something was amiss with Gulliver. Far better to get close enough to Bryant for him to volunteer the information. Then he could report back to Don and they could decide what to do next.

Planning meetings in his head was something Gabriel did out of duty rather than desire, so once he'd rehearsed a couple of oyster-crackers, he switched on the radio. It was 10.00 a.m. and the Radio 4 "pips" were on their last, elongated bleep. After a few items about wars in the Middle East and strikes in the West Midlands, the newsreader introduced a short item about the Farnborough Airshow.

"Britain will be showing off the Eurofighter Typhoon at this year's Farnborough Airshow. A Royal Air Force spokesperson promised 'something a little out of the ordinary' that would really show off the jet's spectacular capabilities."

"Huh!" Gabriel grunted. "Spectacular would just about cover it, if the pilot tripped out and flew into the crowd."

He changed from radio to the Aux setting and told his phone to "play Jazz playlist". After a few seconds, while the digital circuits in the Maserati engaged their counterparts inside the phone in conversation, Ella Fitzgerald's yearning tones burst from the car's speakers. Every drawing of breath as she sang was audible, and Gabriel leaned back into the cushioning embrace of the leather sports seat, rolled his head from side to side, then swept past a convoy of lorries with a broad smile on his face.

He arrived on the perimeter of the business park at 10.45 a.m. It wasn't the first he'd visited, and he felt sure it wouldn't be the last. Whoever designed these places – 'campuses' they liked to call them – seemed to have a love affair with Mediterranean planting. Gravel paths curved between neat beds of spiky grasses with sword-shaped leaves, nodding cobalt blue agapanthus, red hot pokers and lots of lavenders. Less maintenance, he supposed. But always looking like they should be in Barcelona or Aix en Provence, rather than the commuter-belt towns of Southern England.

He followed the road round to the car park for Dreyer Pharma plc. The huge, cuboid building was hard to miss. Its exterior was encased in sheets of bronze-tinted glass that reflected the sun in a blaze of burnt-orange light. Each side of the building was branded with the company's logo, a Moebius strip rendered in green, yellow and black, its eternal twisting form seeming to move restlessly in the sunlight. He parked in one of the visitor spots thoughtfully provided close to the main doors, and clicked the switch to release the Maserati's boot. The sun was warm on his back as he pulled his battered, tan leather briefcase from the boot then walked into the reception area.

Inside, the air was cool and scented faintly with vanilla. The reception desk was situated right in the middle of the creamy marble floor. Above him, nothing but a glass roof several storeys up, with banana palms and black-stemmed bamboo twenty feet high growing right through the middle. He walked up to the desk, smiling at the two receptionists, one male, one female. The woman was on the phone and so, although she returned his smile, he approached the man to her left, thirtyish, blond, handsome, muscular build under a plain back suit.

Looking up at Gabriel over the wood and glass plinth topping the reception desk, the man was all business efficiency.

"Yes, sir. How can I help you today?"

"I have an appointment with James Bryant."

The mention of the top dog's name clearly impressed the receptionist. He sat a little straighter and smiled a little wider.

"Yes, of course. May I take your name and ask you to sign in?" He pushed a leather-bound visitors' book towards Gabriel, who scribbled his registration and name on the next free line.

"Gabriel Wolfe, of Wolfe and Cunningham." His company was a one-man-band. But he'd named it in memory of a man he'd worked with in the US.

"Very good, Mr Wolfe. Thank you. I'll let Mr Bryant's secretary know you're here." He looked over at a set of leather sofas and armchairs against one wall. "Please take a seat. Would you like tea or coffee or a water while you wait?"

"No thanks, I'm good."

Gabriel picked up his briefcase and wandered over to the seating area. Selecting an armchair and pulling the Financial Times off the mahogany table in the centre of the seats, he settled in to wait. A wall-mounted plasma TV was tuned to Sky News. The presenter, long golden hair, bright-blue eyes, pouting carmine lips, was as beautiful as a model.

The click of high heels alerted him to the approach of another

Dreyer functionary. It was the female receptionist.

"Mr Wolfe? Mr Bryant is waiting for you. Please take the lift to the fifth floor. His secretary will meet you and take you through."

By the time the lift reached the fifth floor, it was empty apart from Gabriel. A robotic female voice announced the floor and the doors whispered open. Facing him across the carpeted corridor was a solidly built woman wearing a tweed skirt and cream silk blouse. She was in early middle age, he estimated, and clearly chosen for her business smarts; in the looks department she couldn't compete with the male and female eye-candy on the ground floor.

"Gabriel," she said, real warmth in her voice. "I'm so pleased to meet you. Come this way, please."

She walked off down the corridor, her sensible flat shoes silent on the thick woollen carpet, a custom job with repeating Dreyer logos woven into the pattern. She half-turned to him as they neared a door and stopped before they reached it. Her forehead furrowed and the muscles around the eyes tightened.

"Please help him, Gabriel," she whispered. "I've worked with James for over five years and I know when he's keeping something from me. He's resilient, that's what the HR bunnies call it. He's a fighter, too. But he's really frightened, I can tell."

She did something surprising then. She took his hands in hers and squeezed them. Then she knocked on the door, waited a beat, and pushed them open. The bottom edges of the solid timber doors brushed across more of the branded carpet.

"Gabriel Wolfe is here to see you, James," she said, then left, drawing the door closed behind her.

Gabriel looked around. The room was vast. At least thirty feet square. Bryant had full glass walls on two sides, the fabled corner office. The glass stretched from floor to ceiling, but by luck, or because Bryant was the first to sign a lease with the business park's developers, his view was unimpeded by any other buildings. It stretched to the horizon over unbroken farmland. Hanging on one of the two solid walls was a large painting of a molecule of some kind. Gabriel was no chemist, but he recognised the complex assemblage of coloured spheres and rods. He guessed it was the drug that had made Dreyer's founders rich. The space under the painting was taken up by a pair of saddle-brown leather sofas facing each other across a low table. Bryant's desk was itself a singularly impressive piece of furniture, a thick slab of frosted glass supported by a delicate geometric scaffolding of brushed aluminium. Through the glass, Gabriel could see shallow aluminium drawers apparently suspended in space.

Unlike many of the CEOs Gabriel had met since forming his own company, Bryant had resisted the urge to dump an ugly PC onto his workspace, cables snaking every which way. Instead, a folded laptop sat discreetly to one side. Other than that, the desk held nothing but a silver-framed photo, its back to the visitor.

Bryant came out from behind the desk to greet Gabriel. He was smiling, but it was a social expression only. He was conservatively dressed in a charcoal grey two-piece suit, white shirt with buttoned, not French, cuffs, and a navy tie patterned with small, white polka dots. His blond hair was cut short and parted. Was there a factory that turned out these handsome, trim men to order? *Oh, yes. Harvard Business School.*

"Hi Gabriel, I'm James," he said, shaking hands. *Firm, but damp.* "Pleased to meet you. Thanks for coming at such short notice."

Gabriel returned Bryant's pressure, adding a genuine smile of his own. "It's a pleasure. Dreyer Pharma would be a very welcome addition to our client list."

Bryant returned to his side of the desk; Gabriel took one of the chairs opposite him, lying his briefcase flat on the floor. The two men looked at each other across the modernist desktop. Gabriel waited for Bryant to speak. He'd noticed that Bryant's right knee was bobbing up and down under the glass.

"Thanks for coming to see me. Oh, didn't I just say that? Sorry. I'm just not sure where to begin."

Then he did a surprising thing. He began sobbing. Gabriel was totally and utterly unprepared for this. He'd sat in front of marketing directors as an advertising account manager and suffered their spit-flecked rants about the work he'd presented. He'd been dressed down as an officer-in-training by burly sergeants who'd threatened to pull his bollocks off and make him use them for ping pong balls, sir! He'd faced suspicious tribal leaders toting Kalashnikovs and toking reefers the size of Cuban cigars. But a well-dressed CEO crying in his own office? No. That was a first.

It was a first in his business career, but Gabriel had comforted enough crying soldiers in his life to know what to do. He sat quietly, not moving, not saying anything, waiting until the other man's tears exhausted themselves and disappeared as suddenly as they had arrived. Then he drew the spotless, white handkerchief from the top pocket of his suit and proffered it across the expanse of glass that separated them.

Bryant stretched out a hand and took it, wiped his eyes and then half-offered it to Gabriel, his hand hovering in No Man's Land, the white square now limp.

Gabriel smiled his warmest smile and softened his voice to a soothing, low-toned murmur. "It's OK, James. Keep it. I have plenty more."

"God, I am so sorry about that. How embarrassing. For both of us."

"I said on the phone my services are confidential. That extends to everything that passes between me and my clients. But it seems like we just skipped the small-talk stage of our relationship."

Bryant laughed at this, swiping at his reddened eyes with the handkerchief.

"Yes, I think you could say that. Look, I'll be honest with you. I know who you are and what you've done in your life. That's why you're here. After I got your letter, I did a little bit of research." He nodded towards the folded computer. "You're a war hero. The Military Cross. SAS: 'Who Dares Wins'. Then advertising. Now you work as an independent corporate troubleshooter. I was impressed. I daresay you did the same sort of thing with me. Nothing so glamorous, I'm afraid."

"Nothing glamorous about any of it," Gabriel said, looking down, then back up at Bryant. "The Army was a job. A great job, by the way, but a job all the same. Great bunch of lads doing something incredibly exciting or else sitting around playing cards or writing poetry. And advertising? Please! You know the score there. I was a salesman, nothing more, nothing less."

"Nonetheless, I checked you out. And on your website you mentioned you handle, I quote, 'sensitive matters'."

Now we get to it.

"And you have a 'sensitive matter' of your own to contend with?"

"Oh, oh . . . fuck, yes I do!"

Bryant was twisting and interlacing his fingers then untwining them and running them over his face and through his hair. Gabriel doubted he was even aware he was doing it.

"Look, whatever it is, and I'm going to stick my neck out and say I don't think it's a problem with your next investor presentation, why don't you tell me? Put it on the desk between us and let's have a look at it together."

Bryant's lips were working soundlessly, compressing and releasing. Gabriel waited. Bryant's eyes flicked down to the photograph. Gabriel noticed. And realised what the problem was. Just like that. A flash of insight. It was an ability that had kept him alive on more than one occasion as an SAS patrol leader. The whispery click of a twig snapping out of his eyeline, or a path through a village that looked a little too straight and easy. The guerrilla hiding in a pile of leaves died, while he lived. The bomb disposal team detonated the IED while he and his three men found another route through. He spoke.

"Has something happened to your family?"

Bryant looked up in shock, eyes wide, mouth open.

"How did you know?"

"I wasn't sure. Now I am. Tell me, please. Are they being threatened?"

Bryant leaned across the desk and fixed Gabriel with a wild stare, his hands closed into fists, knuckles white and shining, reflected in the pale mist of the glass.

"Threatened? No, it's gone way beyond that. They've been . . . Oh, Jesus, they've been kidnapped. Weeks ago. I don't know how I've kept going, I'm so worried. And don't say 'call the police' because they said not to, and I have . . . they're barbaric . . . I have it here. Proof, I mean. They're evil. It's a man, at least one. But there have to be more, right? I mean it's a gang of some kind."

Bryant was free-associating and Gabriel needed him to calm down. He stood and moved round the desk to stand at Bryant's left shoulder. Put a hand on the man's back, which was taut with nervous tension, the muscles stiff beneath the suit jacket.

Bryant looked up at him. "What is it?"

"Come and sit with me over there," Gabriel said, pointing at the sofas. "And do you think your secretary could bring us some tea?"

"Yes, of course. Good idea."

Bryant depressed a button on the slim, grey intercom unit sitting on a bookshelf to his right. "Jill, could you bring us some tea, please."

The secretary's tinny vice crackled back, "And biscuits? Of course. Won't be long."

"I hate to sound like a therapist," Gabriel said, prompting a rueful smile from Bryant, "but why don't you tell me how it started?"

CHAPTER 25

Bryant had the look of a man who had finally been told he could drop the sack of rocks he'd been carrying. His shoulders slumped and he leaned forward, palms pressed together between his knees.

"My wife and daughter have been kidnapped. They were on holiday in Stockholm. I got a call about six weeks ago from a man who said he was a Chechen. He said they'd keep them safe but I had to mislead an MOD inquiry and keep quiet about the kidnap, or . . ."

"Or harm would come to your wife and daughter," Gabriel said, leaning forward to mirror the other man's pose. "Tell me their names. Please." He knew them already, from the dossier, but it would help establish a closer rapport with Bryant.

"My wife's name is Sarah. My daughter's is Chloe. She's only twenty-five. How did this happen? Sweden is safe, isn't it? It's hardly Mexico or the Congo." He looked beseechingly into Gabriel's eyes, mouth downturned. "They should have been safe, shouldn't they?"

"Yes, they should. But if these Chechens wanted to get power over you, they would have found a way wherever Sarah and Chloe were. Have they made any other demands or communicated with you again?"

Bryant looked at the ceiling. Then back at Gabriel. "They sent me two packages. One had a video cassette in it, a micro one. The other . . . it didn't."

Bryant levered himself up from the soft leather cushions of the sofa and went to his desk. He slid open one of the slim silvery drawers and extracted two small, white boxes. Brought them back over to Gabriel.

"They sent this one first."

He placed the pads of his fingers on the box's lid and slid it towards Gabriel. Gabriel lifted the lid and placed it beside the open box. Inside was a small tape cassette and a silver earring, crusted with dark brown flecks of what Gabriel realised was blood.

"Then this one."

He repeated the oddly precise movement with the second box. Gabriel opened it and drew in an involuntary gasp. Centred on a square of white cotton was a human earlobe, sliced off by a craft knife or some equally sharp blade. Piercing it at the fattest part was the twin of the ear-ring in the first box.

Bryant was crying again, silent sobs that heaved his shoulders up and down as he hung his head down to his knees.

Gabriel replaced the lids on both the boxes, picked them up and walked over to the desk, where he placed them inside his briefcase and pushed the lid closed with a damped click. When he returned, he sat next to Bryant, who looked up, eyes red and puffy.

"Listen to me, James. We're going to get Sarah and Chloe back safely. I promise." *I don't promise any such thing, but I have to get you right-side up emotionally, at least for now.* "I have friends I can call on to do some intelligence gathering, and I'm pretty handy in that area myself. But now I want you to tell me about what's happening here. At Dreyer."

Bryant heaved a huge sigh, then looked round his office as he spoke. "They're messing around with a drug we have in development for the RAF. It's called Gulliver. It gives pilots a cognitive boost, helps them fly the new Typhoon fighter jets better. They've screwed around with it and now two pilots are dead."

One, actually; I've spoken to the survivor.

"Screwed around with it how?"

"Do you know much about chemistry?"

Gabriel smiled. "I wasn't exactly academically gifted. I scraped a GCSE in chemistry but that was a long time ago."

"I'll try to make it simple then. In its original form, Gulliver used a Benzedrine-based amphetamine coupled with a mild antidepressant called paroxetine to speed up reaction times. Paroxetine retards the bloodstream's reabsorption of serotonin, which is essentially a happy chemical we manufacture in our gut. More of it drip feeds into the brain and promotes feelings of wellbeing. We engineered Gulliver to reward pilots who executed tricky manoeuvres with a little extra squirt of serotonin into the reward circuits of their brains."

"I'm still with you, just. Go on."

"I think the new guys have stuck on an additional chemical from the methyl group. It affects solubility of the original active compound in the brain's fat cells. That turned the Benzedrine into an inhibitor of its own uptake."

Gabriel's brow puckered in concentration.

"You lost me there."

"Sorry. In the new version of Gulliver, because of the additional methylated molecules, the amphetamine works initially, but then actually reduces alertness and slows down reaction times. Like giving Ritalin to kids with attention deficit hyperactivity disorder. ADHD, heard of that?"

Gabriel nodded.

"They bolt on lysergic acid diethylamide - LSD - to create the hallucinations, and use an oxyphilic . . ." Gabriel frowned again. ". . . an oxygen-loving coating round its molecules using a modified amino acid called gamma-butyl-amylase. As the pilot flies higher, the oxygen concentration in his air supply, coupled with the change in cabin pressure, activates the LSD."

"But what about the blindness? I've heard of moonshine causing temporary sight-loss. Could that be involved as well?"

Bryant scrunched his knuckles against his eyes, then looked blearily at Gabriel.

"To be absolutely honest? I have absolutely no fucking idea. I used to know every last detail of the pharmacology side of things, but these days I'm more of an administrator than a scientist. I'm supposed to let them carry on and deflect a MOD investigation. I've got half my corporate affairs team on it – I've promised them double bonuses, threatened them with the sack, whatever it's taken. The Typhoons have to fly at Farnborough or Sarah and Chloe, they'll . . . and I can't carry on. There's too much pressure. Our investors would be happy to see my head on a spike as it is."

"I understand." Gabriel stopped. He'd had a sudden idea that might, just, get round the problem. "Tell me, is your whole research and development department working on Gulliver?"

"No. I mean, half of it is. Under a guy my head of R&D recruited."

"What's his name?"

"Dr Solmin Tarbosy. He checks out. He's eminent; that's what the scientific lot call it when you're a hotshot."

Gabriel fished a slim black notebook from his jacket and made a note.

"Obviously, we can't let any more pilots take Tarbosy's version of the drug. Can you whisk up a new batch?"

The crass representation of the pharmaceutical manufacturing process was a calculated attempt to pump some air into Bryant's deflated ego. It worked. A wry smile curved his mouth.

"Could we 'whisk up' some more? It's a little more complex than that. But, yes, we could. I'd have to keep it away from Tarbosy and his team. I assume they're reporting in to the man I spoke to on the phone."

"I'm sure they are. And any changes in the way your R&D department operates will be picked up and relayed back to the kidnappers. Could you outsource it?"

Bryant frowned, thinking for a few seconds, his eyes roving the ceiling as if checking for hidden microphones.

"We'd need a couple of our senior scientists to run the process, but with the data and a cooperative lab, I think it would be possible. Why though?"

"Because we need to keep things stable here while I find your wife and daughter. The Typhoons will fly and the pilots will have the drug. But they'll have our version in their bloodstreams, not Tarbosy's."

"But if the pilots don't crash, they'll know. The kidnappers, I mean. Then they'll . . . harm Chloe and Sarah."

Gabriel paused. "I'll have them back in England before then. We'll round up Tarbosy and his gang of eggheads, and other people will chase down the kidnappers."

"You can do that? We don't even know where they are, and Farnborough's only a few weeks away."

The man was pleading for certainty in a world where it was in increasingly short supply. And Gabriel hated making promises he wasn't certain he could keep. However . . .

"You know my background. I give you my word. I will bring them back."

I just hope we're not sitting here in a couple of weeks' time with your right arm wrapped in a black band.

CHAPTER 26

The following morning, after leaving his bags at a hotel near Waterloo Station, Gabriel was sitting next to Don Webster in a sparsely furnished room deep within the corridors of the MI6 building on London's Albert Embankment. The contrast between this taxpayer-funded office and the one enjoyed – if that was the right word – by James Bryant was stark. The desk was surfaced with cheap veneer, stained to resemble mahogany, or so the manufacturers had obviously hoped. Repeated trips around the building had resulted in numerous scars and wounds, and the veneer had disappeared altogether from the corners, revealing chipboard beneath. There were two chairs, steel-framed and padded with scratchy grey cushions, stained by countless spillages of coffee and tea. Apart from a battleship-grey, four-drawer, steel filing cabinet, the room was empty.

Gabriel and Don were staring at the open screen of Don's official MOD laptop, a creaking, black thing. An MI6 tech had transferred the video Gabriel had brought with him onto Don's hard drive, and now they were watching and re-watching the video of Sarah and Chloe Bryant.

Don cued up the video again.

"Listen to how Chloe speaks and watch her eyes. God, she's a clever girl," he said.

Gabriel leaned forward on the hard chair and watched Chloe intently, frowning with concentration and pulling on his lower lip. She was frozen in a stare of defiance mixed with fear.

Don clicked on Play, and Chloe began to speak.

"Every nation should be free to govern itself. Its people should have the same basic human rights as all other peoples. This is true for Chechnya. This is true for the Chechen people. Think back, Mr Bryant..."

Don clicked paused the video.

"Notice anything?" he said.

"No. I mean, not really. She just looks a bit scared, wide-eyed."

"Look again. When she says, 'Think back'."

Don rewound the video and hit Play again.

"Think back," video-Chloe said.

Gabriel's eyes narrowed.

"She just pushed the 'k' sound a little harder than she should have. Stressed it."

"Yes, she did," Don said. "And that's not all. Look how her upper eyelid retracts just a tiny bit."

"Yes, I see it. You get a flash of white above the iris. Just a tiny line."

"So. She's sending us a message inside the one the kidnappers have her reading out. Now, keep watching."

He clicked Play for the third time and let the recording run until video-Chloe said, "We intend to free our country from Russia's stranglehold. But to do that..."

Gabriel jabbed his finger at the screen.

"Stop!" he said. "She does it again. On 'Russia's stranglehold'."

"Good boy," Don said. "So that's a 'k' and an 's' she's signalled us. Right, on to number three." He clicked Play.

"You will hire them directly, bypassing your HR department."

"See it?" Don said.

"Yes. Clear as day. Once you know what you're looking for it's easy, isn't it? The 'm' in 'them' is where she does it."

Don closed the lid of the laptop.

"So, she's given us three letters. K.S.M. If you run the rest of the message, she pulls the same trick again, on 'project', 'safe' and 'involvement'. Trouble is, we've searched through every database available: MI5, MI6, Europol, Interpol, FBI, CIA, plus a good old poke about on the dark web. Nothing. No criminal gangs, militias, organised crime syndicates, terrorist groups or freedom fighters go by those initials. I was hoping you might be able to play around with them using your linguist's mind."

"OK. Can I have a copy of the video?"

"Here," Don said, handing Gabriel a USB stick.

Looking down at it, Gabriel laughed.

"It's got an MI6 logo!"

"I know. Hardly James Bond is it? Apparently too many spooks have left laptops on trains so they're trying to shame people into taking better care of the Firm's IT."

"Well, I promise I won't lose it."

"Good. I'm going to set a couple of the brainiacs here on it after you go. They've got all sorts of clever toys they love to play with. We'll see whether there's anything else on the video that could be useful. Now, lunch, I think. My club, my treat. You can brief me on what happened with Mr Bryant yesterday."

Outside, Don flagged down a black cab and gave the driver an address in St James's, home to the bespoke gentlemen's outfitters of Savile Row and dozens of members-only clubs. Don's club was a comfortable-if-stuffy establishment in which they were attended by decrepit men in frock coats who looked as if they had served the Duke of Wellington in their boyhood. Over pink-fleshed lamb chops, Gabriel filled Don in on the conversation with Bryant.

"I suggested they start parallel manufacturing of Gulliver. That way the flyboys – and girls – can do their thing in the Typhoons at Farnborough. In the meantime, I can track down Chloe and Sarah, exfiltrate them, then you can put some men on the ground to mop up after me."

"Ah yes, mopping up, the job of an old soldier," Don said with a rueful smile. "So while Bryant's real people are turning out a safe batch of Gulliver, Tarbosy and his gang will carry on regardless."

"Do you think it will work?"

"It'll have to, won't it?"

After lunch, the two men shook hands with an agreement to speak by phone the moment Gabriel figured anything out – even a wild theory would be acceptable according to Don.

Later that day, in his hotel room, Gabriel booted up his laptop and loaded the video. With a bottle of chilled Burgundy by his right elbow, and a half-full glass in his hand, he clicked Play on the video and leaned forward.

He watched and listened as Chloe Bryant read out the speech prepared for her by the kidnappers. It was a very clever trick. The eye-widening and vocal emphasis on the 'k', 's' and 'm' was subtle enough to be missed by a kidnapper looking through a camcorder's viewfinder or LCD screen. The fact she'd done it twice spoke of courage and determination. He'd seen the results of failed kidnap rescues in Afghanistan. In one village, the remains of two American oilmen were found in a cellar beneath a dusty, greyish-white concrete hut. The Taliban had removed their eyes, crudely, to judge from the jagged tears around the empty sockets, and their genitals. Their stomachs were painted with the Arabic word 'Infidel' in their own blood. He doubted the people holding Sarah and Chloe Bryant were as bloodthirsty or as unconcerned about human life as the Taliban, but it still took guts to risk your life when your captors were filming you up close and personal.

Taking a long swallow of the wine, he pushed the laptop away and picked up a pencil. He scribbled the letters on a sheet of the hotel's notepaper, first in lower case, then in upper case.

k s m

K S M

Then he rewrote them in different orders.

k m s
  s m k
  m k s
  m s k
  s k m

Nothing. He closed his eyes and pinched the bridge of his nose, leaning back in his chair and letting his head flop back. "Come on, Gabriel," he said to the ceiling. "She's trying to tell you something."

He got up from the desk and went to the window. Across the street, a row of cheap restaurants and takeaway joints competed for the custom of the passing commuters and tourists. Each outlet, whether selling pizza, falafel, fried chicken or burgers, advertised itself with a gaudy plastic sign. The concept of branding had clearly passed these restaurateurs by, since their signs were a random mixture of bright colours and typefaces. The lack of consistency amused Gabriel, and a smile crept over his face as he spotted spelling errors, wonky typography and other mistakes repeated from shop to shop. Clearly one enterprising shop-fitting firm had cleaned up, winning the business of each place on the little strip.

Our Customer Always Come First, read one slogan.
  You're burger, you're way, said another.
  OlyMpiC ChiCkeN, another.
  Pizza, spahgetti, lasagne, a fourth.

. . .

Something clicked in Gabriel's brain. He tracked back along the row of orange, yellow and red plastic signs.

OlyMpiC ChiCkeN

He rushed back to the desk, knocking into the standard lamp on his way. He shot out a hand and steadied it without breaking step.

He fell into the chair and wrote out the three letters again.

K S M

It wasn't an acronym at all. No wonder Don Webster hadn't found a gang called the Knights of Strife and Murder, or the Kenya Street Mechanics. It was an abbreviation. Just the consonants of a word.

He wrote them out like a half-solved crossword clue.

K_S_M

Now, what are you? He repeated the word dozens of times, using different combinations of vowels, but quickly realised he was going nowhere. Time for a different approach.

"Kessem," he said aloud. "Kossam, kissem, kuzzum . . . chasm."

On the last try he stopped. Smiled. Took another sip of the burgundy, now approaching room temperature.

"Not chasm. Qasim. Is that who you are?"

He wrote it down then picked up his phone and called Don, tapping his teeth with his pencil and making a quiet ticking sound as he waited for the call to connect. Don answered.

"What do you have for me?"

"I think I know who has the Bryants."

"That's my boy. So enlighten me."

"It was the letters. KSM. It's not a group: it's a name. An Arabic name. Qasim. Sometimes it's spelt with a Q, sometimes a K. So I think we're looking for a guy called Kasym." He spelled it out. "It's a European variant of the Arabic spelling. It feels more likely somehow, given they were picked up in Stockholm."

"Fantastic work, Gabriel. OK. Get some dinner or go for a walk. I'll have some people run another search."

CHAPTER 27

Somehow, among all the preparations for a search-and-rescue mission to Scandinavia, Gabriel had committed himself to seeing a psychiatrist. Fariyah Crace sounded friendly enough, but that was probably headshrinker voodoo. He, himself, was moderately adept at hypnosis, and therefore distrustful of anyone who claimed a direct line to the unconscious.

He walked from his hotel in Waterloo to a private hospital – The Ravenswood – in the heart of Mayfair. This was where Valerie the secretary had told him to present himself. "Professor Crace runs her private practice there. Her NHS work is on a peripatetic basis." Fancy word for 'travelling', Gabriel had thought at the time, but then Valerie seemed to delight in obscuring anything about her boss that might make her seem merely mortal.

If he'd ever wondered where the rich came to play in London, he found his answer in the neat geometry of the streets bounded on the south by Piccadilly, the west by Park Lane, the east by Regent Street and the north by Oxford Street. With the exception of sandwich bars and traditional, family-owned Italian *trattorie*, the commercial properties seemed to divide equally between art galleries, boutiques, jewellers and luxury car showrooms. All, regardless of the merchandise they purveyed, were staffed by thin, beautiful women.

They stood, like models, balanced atop four-inch-high stilettos, dressed in severe but beautifully cut clothes and turning on smiles like flashbulbs whenever a potential customer approached.

The streets were lined with expensive cars. On the ten-minute walk through the district that almost confirmed the old image of London's streets being paved with gold, Gabriel lost count of the Mercedes S-Classes, BMW 7 Series and Audi A8s. These were just filler, the rides, chauffeured or otherwise, of business-types. The jewels in the German setting were British or Italian. Gabriel counted three Maseratis like his own on Albemarle Street alone. Sleek Ferrari 458s cosied up to the back bumpers of barge-like Rolls Royces. A vintage lime-green Lamborghini Miura, surely no more than three feet tall from tyre-treads to roof-line, dominated a street of grey, silver and black execmobiles. Best – or worst – of all, a Bugatti Veyron, its squat, bug-like bodywork wrapped in what was essentially red flock, the type of stuff you'd find gracing the walls of old-style tandoori restaurants in every city in the world. Gabriel saw the sign for The Ravenswood ahead of him, and quickened his step. Looking up at the midnight-blue and white signboard, he collided with a young woman with long, silky, black hair and olive skin emerging from a dress shop, a multicoloured clutch of glossy paper bags looped over her wrists by their twisted, silken handles. He apologised, but she ignored him, blipping a plastic key fob in her right hand and striding across the pavement to a powder-blue Lamborghini Aventador.

The quarter of a million pound hypercar – all angled planes and sharp points – hunkered down at the side of the road, about the same height as the cropped waist of her leather jacket. The woman, hardly more than a girl, dumped her purchases onto the passenger seat and moments later, roared away from the kerb, causing a black cab coming up behind her to screech to a halt. The driver leaned on the horn, but the prolonged parp seemed comedic compared to the feral growl of the Lamborghini.

Inside The Ravenswood, all was calm, unlike the NHS hospitals Gabriel had seen. More like a corporate headquarters or one of the upmarket art galleries nestling alongside it. Behind a reception desk constructed from translucent green glass blocks, a brightly smiling woman in nurse's whites looked up at him, eyebrows raised in enquiry.

"Yes, Sir. How may I help you?"

"My name's Wolfe. I have an appointment . . ."

"With Professor Crace. Yes. Here we are. You're a little early. Please take a seat, and I'll let her know you're here."

Impressed with her knowledge of what he assumed were many doctors' appointments, Gabriel had one more question to ask.

"Will you call me or something, when she's ready? I've never been here before."

"Oh no," she said. "Professor Crace will come and collect you."

Gabriel found an empty chair in a quiet waiting area supplied with current copies of *Vogue, The Economist, Car* and *The English Garden* – a far cry from the tatty celebrity magazines that littered the waiting rooms of dentists, doctors' surgeries and A&E departments. His neighbours were sipping cappuccinos and herbal teas, procured, he saw, from a low table stocked like an airport lounge. He was just considering whether he could be bothered to decipher the pictograms on the coffee machine when a tall, dark-skinned woman wearing tailored cream trousers, high heels and a rose-pink hijab came towards him, a white and deep-blue identity card on a matching blue lanyard bouncing against her chest.

"Gabriel?" she said, as she stopped in front of him.

The other waiting patients looked up briefly then returned to their magazines.

"Yes. You must be Professor Crace."

"I am, but please, Fariyah is fine. Only my parents, my students and my secretary call me 'Professor'. It makes me sound like some crusty old Oxford don, which, as you can see, I am most decidedly not. Come with me."

He took an instant liking to this woman. She radiated energy, from the glinting deep brown eyes to the firm pressure of her warm, dry hand as they shook. They walked down a corridor lined with tasteful, inoffensive paintings and prints – they were mostly landscapes and still lives, no abstracts. Too unsettling for people who need help making sense of the world, he thought. Fariyah stopped outside a plain door made of the pale, satiny wood. Her name and title were rendered in elegant, white capitals on a midnight-blue strip of plastic slotted between aluminium runners.

"This is me," she said, brightly, swiping her ID card against a flat, plastic rectangle set into the wall to the right of the door.

Gabriel had seen the inside of hundreds of offices, from his time in military service, to advertising, and now his own business as a security consultant. Military, corporate, public sector, government, each had its owner's personality stamped on top of the generic flavour determined by budgets, brands and ideology. He took the comfortable leather-upholstered chair she offered, then, from his side of the desk, cast his eye over the furnishings and decorations as Fariyah assembled a toolkit of clipboard, sheets of paper from a filing cabinet, and a generic, black fineliner pen.

That she was an observant Muslim called for no Holmesian levels of observation; her hijab was enough for that. A painting of a butterfly, executed in bright, garish oils, reinforced the impression she'd created that she was a woman who wanted to make a mark on the world. The desk was clear apart from a computer screen, keyboard and mouse, and a photo frame turned away from him. Someone important. He checked out her left hand – a ring of intertwined strands of white, yellow and rose gold encircled her fourth finger. Husband then. Or perhaps husband and children.

She sat next to, rather than behind, the desk and crossed her legs at the knee. Gabriel shifted to his right in his own chair to face her, momentarily surprised that she had not chosen to sit behind the desk. The lack of any physical barrier between them created an intimacy that discomfited him. Surely, not the effect the manoeuvre was intended to produce.

"Have you ever visited a psychiatrist before, Gabriel?" she asked him now, her eyes watchful.

"To be honest, no. No therapists or counsellors of any kind, I'm afraid. If it counts, in the SAS, they had trick-cyclists train us to resist interrogation." He blushed. "Sorry. Not 'trick-cyclists', psychiatrists. Army slang, old habit."

She smiled, resting the top of the pen against her lower lip. "If we're going to work together, and I have a strong feeling that we are, then let's establish a quick ground rule: we'll save our outrage for things that are truly outrageous. I've been called a lot of things by my patients over the years, from 'sadistic Arab bint' to 'Mummy'. Calling me a trick-cyclist didn't even move the needle. Is that all right with you?"

That dispelled the tension. Gabriel laughed. "Fine. Agreed."

"Good," she said. "I know Don referred you. Do you want to tell me why?"

He ran a hand through his hair from front to back and clamped it around the back of his neck. Took a breath and let it out slowly.

"I've been having . . . moments, where, I don't think I'm where I am, really. Sorry, that was rubbish. Look, Don thinks it's PTSD. He didn't say it but I know that's why he gave me your card."

"How did Don come back into your life? You left the Army some years ago, I think."

"I was involved in an accident."

"What kind of accident?" Fariyah wasn't writing anything. She cocked her head to one side and waited.

Gabriel heaved a huge sigh. Rubbed his neck again. "I ran into the road outside the National Portrait Gallery and got hit by a lorry. Which was on the wrong side of the road, by the way. Ended up in Audley Grange."

"Did you forget to look both ways, then?" she said, face impassive, not even a hint of irony in her tone. "Listen, I think something must have happened to shake you up. It's not easy for everyone to talk about these things, so rather than you struggling to decide how much of your story to tell me, I'm going to take charge and ask you some questions. How would that be?"

"Yes," he sighed. "That would be much better."

Fariyah uncapped her pen and held it poised over the clipboard. She asked Gabriel a series of questions, beginning with innocuous facts about his birthplace and date ("Kingston, Surrey, 1980"), childhood homes ("King's Norton, Surrey, Hong Kong"), number of siblings ("none"), parents' occupations ("diplomat, private tutor"), schooling ("chucked out of loads of schools, private tutor"), hobbies ("nature"), friendships ("no memorable ones") and religion ("basically Church of England"). Then she asked more intimate questions, from the age he lost his virginity ("sixteen") to how he would describe his sexuality.

In answer to the last question, Gabriel said, "ninety-nine per cent straight". When Fariyah frowned and repeated the percentage, Gabriel said, "I'm completely heterosexual but I thought you lot all think people are on a spectrum, so if I said a hundred you'd think I was hiding something."

Fariyah laughed. "Well that's a first. A straight man claiming to be a little bit gay to fit someone's expectations. Normally it's the other way round. You can be one hundred percent straight; it's fine by me."

This exchange finally broke whatever lingering ice lay between them. Gabriel felt he could trust this attractive Muslim woman, and decided at that moment to be as honest with her as he could manage. As she questioned him, listened and made notes, he told her about the bungled mission in Mozambique. He told her about his nightmares. He told her about his flashbacks and his sudden urges to take his Maserati up to its top speed and just keep it there until fate or a sharp bend in the road intervened. He told her everything.

After he had spoken for about twenty minutes without pausing, Fariyah held up a hand, palm outwards.

"Let me stop you just for a moment, Gabriel. What I'd like to do is administer a standardised, seventeen-question checklist for post-traumatic stress disorder. Try to answer each question as honestly as you can OK?"

Gabriel nodded, "OK."

After she had finished asking the questions about moods, behaviours, beliefs and emotions, she laid her clipboard to one side and uncrossed her legs.

"This is the point where you've told me your story and now I try to build a narrative about you and tell you what I think," she said. "Based on your answers, yes, you have PTSD, and I think it's fair to say you are suffering from it as well. Not to the point where you can't function, but I can see it's affecting your ability to enjoy life, if nothing else. You use alcohol, and work, to cope, but they're not working very well any more. In this session, I don't want to go any further, and I'm not going to reach for my prescription pad. But I do want you to see a colleague of mine. His name is Richard Austin. He is a very experienced therapist and he works a lot with veterans of conflict. He uses a technique called EMDR. Have you heard of it?"

Gabriel shook his head. She smiled and continued.

"It stands for Eye Movement Desensitisation and Reprocessing. It's been credited with some amazing results among PTSD sufferers. I'm going to write to him and ask him to call you. Then the two of you can arrange a set of appointments."

Gabriel frowned, thinking of his imminent trip to Stockholm. "How many appointments? And how soon do I have to start?"

"Well, you've managed this far without EMDR, so the urgency I'll leave up to you. Typically, people need between three and six sessions. It's very effective, so don't think you'll be in analysis for years or any of that Freudian bullshit."

Gabriel's eyes popped open at the profanity. He'd heard – and spoken – far worse, but somehow, coming from her lips in this setting it seemed far more transgressive than any amount of effing and blinding on the battlefield or in the Sergeants' Mess.

"Did I shock you?" she asked. "A good Muslim woman using bad language like that?"

"No," he lied. "It's just ... you're a ... Actually, yes. Because of that. The hijab and everything."

"Relax," she said, smiling and leaning over to pat his knee. "I still say my prayers and I don't eat pork."

She looked at her watch. "That's our session over, I'm afraid. Make an appointment with Richard and see how you get on. Come back for another session with me in, what? A month's time? We'll have a chat about the therapy and maybe at that meeting, we'll discuss whether any drug therapy would be helpful to you."

She stood and held out her hand. Gabriel took it.

"Your husband is a lucky man," he said.

"I know," she said, dropping her voice to a husky, seductive whisper. "That's what I keep telling him."

* * *

Five minutes later, Gabriel was outside The Ravenswood, heading back to his hotel. He felt elated, and strode along the streets feeling, finally, that someone other than him was carrying at least part of his burden of guilt.

CHAPTER 28

Deep within the Senate Building in the Kremlin, the former KGB officer who now ruled Russia sat behind his mahogany desk, reading a defence briefing on air force capabilities in the seven countries judged the biggest threat to his own.

There was a brief double-knock at the door, and his new secretary, a young woman fresh from Moscow State University, entered the office.

"Mr President, Oleg Abramov is here to see you, sir." She was smartly dressed in the western style tailored suit, sheer stockings, high-heeled shoes, minimal make-up, blonde hair cut in a sharp-edged bob that emphasised her long, slender neck.

"Thank you, Valentina. Keep him waiting for another hour, then show him in."

The president returned to the document before him. He underlined passages here and there with precise, arrow-straight lines of blue ink that he drew freehand.

Exactly sixty minutes later, Valentina returned, accompanied by a tall, smooth-faced man in an expensive suit, procured from a London tailor to judge by the cut and the fabric, his white hair cut short and brushed straight back from his forehead.

The president stood and came round the desk. He walked straight up to Abramov, grasped him by both shoulders and kissed him three times on the cheek: left, right, left.

He pulled back from the embrace and gestured to a chair.

"Please, my friend, sit, sit."

Valentina turned on her heel and was gone, drawing the double doors closed behind her like a courtier.

Back behind the desk, the president looked at the man facing him, who did not appear to be nervous. In fact, from his posture, leaning back, one ankle resting on the other knee, anyone would think he was relaxed. That annoyed him. Had his power brought him no more than the professional respect anyone would pay to a run-of-the-mill CEO or party functionary? There had been times, in his KGB days, when merely to appear in the same room as a detainee would cause the man, or, more rarely, woman, to void their bladder, if not their bowels. That fetid, meaty stink made him smile then, as the memory did now. It spoke of the stark terror he inspired in people. Often, his reputation alone had sufficed to loosen their tongues, but he was more than happy to demonstrate his skill with a wide variety of implements whose designers had never, in their worst nightmares, imagined would be put to their current purpose. He spoke.

"Oleg Vasilievich – I hope you don't mind my using your patronymic, Abramov sounds too Jewish to these simple Russian ears – I was speaking to our air marshal this morning. He leaves for a tour of our air bases tomorrow. I reassured him that he would be perfectly within his rights to preempt our official announcement and tell our pilots that they would soon be flying higher, faster and with more agility thanks to our forthcoming acquisition of the Gulliver drug." He paused for a moment. "I hope I did the right thing."

He watched the other man swallow, the lump of his Adam's apple disappearing and reappearing above his shirt collar.

"Of course, sir," Abramov said, running a finger around the inside of his shirt collar. "The Farnborough Airshow is just a couple of weeks away. It is the final proving ground and demonstration of the drug's capabilities. After the show, I shall be meeting the British Secretary of State for Defence and some of her senior advisers, along with the Secretary of State for Trade, and a procurement consultant from McKinsey and Company. They are the world's leading management consultancy firm."

"Yes, yes, I know that," the president snapped, his face darkening with a scowl. "Do you think I am some provincial *durak* who has never studied *biznes*?"

"A fool? Of course not! Never. My apologies."

Good. Now I can see a few beads of sweat on your face and your hands have clenched. Not so relaxed now, are you, my billionaire friend? "Continue, please."

"We will conclude the deal that we have been negotiating for many months now. Gulliver will be licensed to one of my companies, a pharmaceuticals manufacturer in Germany named AbraPharm. The British believe I am selling it to Ukraine to help them resist the embrace of Mother Russia. You and I know whose pilots will eventually benefit."

"Yes, we do, Oleg Vasilievich. And we know who else will benefit from this deal, to the tune of one hundred and seventy five million US dollars."

"Of course, Mr President, that is true. But, as you said yourself, you understand *biznes*. My company profits at the same time as Mother Russia. And what is money compared to the resurgent glory of our military in a world dominated by the Americans, and even the Chinese?"

The president smiled and watched as Abramov relaxed again, believing his rhetoric had won the day.

"Of course," he said. "There is always more money, after all, but respect for our country is an altogether more precious commodity." His smile widened though the lips remained pressed together and the cold, grey-blue eyes remained flat and expressionless. "Let me show you something," he said, pulling open a drawer in the desk.

He leaned over and picked up a small cylindrical object, and positioned it exactly halfway between them on the expanse of walnut.

"Do you know what that is?" he asked.

Abramov glanced at the object, twitched his lips, then looked back at the president, who was smiling good-naturedly.

"A bullet?"

"Exactly. Although technically, one would call it a round. Specifically, it is a nine-by-eighteen millimetre Makarov round. Steel cartridge, cupronickel ball. It costs about forty-eight rubles. Now, how about this?"

This time the president's hand, when it reappeared from under the desk, held a pistol, dark-grey steel with a ridged brown plastic grip. He placed it next to the round with a soft clunk.

Abramov's eyes flicked down to the pistol. He wiped his top lip with his forefinger.

"That is a gun. A pistol, I mean."

"Very good. Again, to be specific, it is a Makarov semi-automatic pistol. *My* Makarov semi-automatic pistol. It costs us about six thousand rubles to manufacture. And do you know the most interesting thing about these two objects that sit between us?"

"What is that, Sir?"

"Simply this, Oleg Vasilievich. If I take this little round here," he plucked the cartridge from the desk, "and push it in here," he thumbed it into the magazine that he'd dropped from the pistol butt by depressing a knurled metal lever, "then push this home here," he slotted the box magazine back into the pistol grip, "I have a weapon system just as capable of stealing a man's life from him as one of those twelve-and-a-half-billion-ruble Typhoons. Imagine," he said, pointing the muzzle of the weapon at Abramov's chest, "how many Makarovs we could buy for the price of the Gulliver technology."

Abramov swallowed. Beads of sweat rolled freely down his forehead and into his eyes, making him blink.

"Not much prestige in bullets, Mr President," he choked out.

The president had his index finger curled round the Makarov's trigger.

He paused for a few seconds, enjoying the older man's discomfiture. Then he laughed and thunked the pistol down onto the desk, making Abramov startle and rear back in his chair.

"Of course, you are right. We can't frighten NATO, or the Ukrainians, or those fucking black-asses to the south with bullets. For that, we need air superiority. So . . ." he leaned across the desk. "Just make sure we have it, yes?"

He stood and leant across the desk, offering a hand. Abramov followed suit, and the two men, each powerful in his own way, shook hands briefly, though only one had rivulets of sweat trickling from his armpits, dampening his shirt.

Once Abramov had left the room, closing the doors behind him as the young secretary had done, the president picked up the pistol, aimed at the door and mimed a shot.

CHAPTER 29

Gabriel was on the website of the City of Stockholm, cross-checking a list of hotels to find those close to the centre without being bang in the middle of the tourist areas. Preferably somewhere cheap and unflashy. A Holiday Inn or an ibis hotel, where he could blend in, coming and going with the minimum of attention from uniformed flunkeys.

His phone rang; it was Don.

"Hi Don, got something for me I hope?"

"I do indeed. One of those bright young things who wasted their teenaged years playing *Call of Duty* has had his finger in our pie since we last spoke, and he pulled out a plum. Did you notice the window was open behind Chloe in the video?"

"Yes. Her hair kept blowing across her face. Why?"

"Tell me. What comes in through open windows besides air?"

"I don't know, smell? Sound? Wait. Did you get some audio?"

Don chuckled. "That we did, Old Sport. That we did. Church bells. They were muffled by the wind in the trees, but he did all kinds of jiggery-pokery, the technical description of which I must confess I have totally forgotten, isolated them, and cleaned them up. In fact they're not just church bells, they're cathedral bells. A carillon, know what that is?"

Gabriel felt he was back in the classroom, eager to please his instructor. "It's like a tune isn't it? A pattern of chimes."

"Exactly. But it's no carillon you'll hear in Stockholm. I had one of our analysts here confirm it. We know Sarah and Chloe Bryant were taken from there. But where would Chechen kidnappers take them after that?"

"Out of Scandinavia," Gabriel replied at once, beginning to assess the kidnap as an operation. "They'd probably travel by boat. Much lower visibility, more places to land the hostages. Not south – why risk German or Polish border security? So east, then. The Baltics, probably; Russia's the enemy if you're a Chechen." He Googled 'Baltic States' and pulled up a map of the region. "My best guess? Estonia. Although Lithuania or Latvia would still be possible destinations."

"Give him a medal," Don said. "That's what I thought, too. I contacted our field offices in Vilnius, Tallinn and Riga, and played them the recording of the carillon. The young woman in Tallinn took precisely no seconds to identify it. It's St Mary's Cathedral. Now, it was faint on the video, so they weren't central. Our boy in the basement did some maths and estimated that for that volume level, the safe house was within a two-mile radius of the cathedral."

Gabriel did a little quick maths of his own. "So that's, what, somewhere over twelve-and-a-half square miles?"

"About that, yes. Twelve-point-five-five-six to three decimal places. Not great, but better than just flying to Stockholm and asking around."

"I know. It's brilliant. Give that tech a pay rise."

Don grunted. "Huh! You think people like me have any say over the money? It's all those smartarses in their designer suits and BMWs. We're the same as we always were, my boy. The action men. Well, you are, anyway. Now, get yourself over to Tallinn and start sniffing around. Any thoughts on your line of attack?"

"I have. We've got a minimum of four targets, I'm thinking. A driver, two heavies and a boss. It's the optimum ratio of kidnappers to hostages, too. Four Chechens are going to draw attention in a place like Tallinn. They'll want to be under the radar, so they'll be staying somewhere cheap and bland. No penthouses or underground lairs in volcanoes."

Don laughed. "They'd be lucky. I think the highest mountain in Estonia's only about a foot taller than you are."

"Plus, they'll have bought guns, cars maybe. Or booze, or drugs. The kidnapping has a specific purpose, but people like that always have other stuff going on to raise funds or to further the cause."

"So ..."

"So I'm going to head for the places where the action is. The docks, the railway stations, the third-rate nightclubs. If I find the strippers and the lap-dancers, I'll find people who know who's new in town. Maybe who's causing trouble for the local mob."

"Right. That sounds good. Get yourself a hotel room. Text me. I'll have someone drop you off a shooter. Any preferences? You used to be a dead shot with that SIG Sauer of yours. Never could persuade you to use anything official, could I?"

"True, but you didn't have any complaints either, did you?" *Even when I fucked up so royally in Mozambique, you stood by me, Don.* "Yes, for choice, a P226 would be great. With an SWR Trident-9 suppressor, please. And a couple of hundred rounds."

"A couple of hundred? What are you planning, World War Three?" Don's gruff chuckle sounded down the line again. "Sure. Anything else?"

"I'll pick up some stuff over there. I have a feeling that where I'm headed, there'll be a couple of obliging pawnshop owners who can kit me out with a few little extras."

"OK, good. Listen, I have to go. Bloody budget meeting with the Queen's Own Versace Rifles. Keep in touch. And call me if you need me. Day or night. That's an order, Captain Wolfe."

Under the playacting, Gabriel sensed genuine affection from his old boss. He'd been a good commander. Willing to lead from the front and get his hands dirty. Now he was tethered to a desk and leaving the fight to others. Not Don's style at all. *I'll make you proud Don. Don't worry.*

* * *

What do you pack for a hunting trip when your quarry is a group of Chechen separatists hiding out in the arse-end of Tallinn? No suits, that's for sure. Gabriel had been shopping for one item especially. Folded on top of his other clothes in a black nylon holdall was a dark red and duck-egg-blue West Ham replica team shirt. The fabric was slick and shiny, and the colour was so intense it seemed to bleed out of the design. Just right for his cover – an ex-soldier looking for spare cash while bumming round Europe.

Under the football shirt were two pairs of jeans, old and faded, and another two pairs of black chinos. T-shirts – white, black, navy blue – were rolled and packed on top. A black zip-up hoodie and a navy fleece went on top. He rolled underwear and socks and stuffed them inside a pair of rugged, black work boots with thickly ribbed treads. Next to them, he packed an old pair of running shoes – he had no idea if he'd be able to find a gym in Tallinn, not that he expected to have much free time, but there was always time for a run. Washing and shaving gear, and a battered paperback copy of *Crime and Punishment*, completed his kit. He zipped the bag closed and rubbed his thumb along the three combination wheels of the lock to pin the zip-pulls together.

In his wallet, he had five hundred euros, a hundred in sterling and two hundred in US dollars. When it came to money "better safe than sorry" was his motto. And he'd often found that dollars bought answers from people who clammed up in the presence of other currencies.

Six hours later, after a one-hour stop in Helsinki, the Finnair Airbus A320 he was flying in touched down on the runway at Lennart Meri Airport Tallinn. The tyres screeched in protest at the rough landing, then all sound in the cabin was drowned out by the surge of the engines on reverse thrust as the pilot brought the plane to taxiing speed.

The girl on the immigration desk scrutinised his passport, switching her gaze from the grainy image on the page to the human face that looked back at her with a tired smile. She couldn't have been more than twenty-two or twenty-three, but she had none of the gaucheness of the young when asked to wield power over their elders. She slid the passport under the scanner, and Gabriel followed her right hand down to her hip, where she absent-mindedly stroked the grip of her semi-automatic pistol, a 9mm Heckler & Koch USP. The leather holster was highly polished; it looked sexy on her. Like an accessory. She seemed more than comfortable wearing a high-powered weapon. It appeared to inspire confidence, to judge from her relaxed pose. She looked up at him again and smiled, a dazzling expression that momentarily distracted him from the tedium of getting landside.

"You are here for a holiday, Mr Wolfe?" she asked, in an accent coloured with an American twang.

Did you learn by watching MTV? Or did you do a student exchange in the land of the free?

"A trip, yes. Looking up a couple of friends."

"Are you staying in Tallinn or moving on?"

"Not sure," he said, keeping the tone of his voice light and unconcerned. "What would you recommend?"

"Oh, you should stay here for sure. The countryside is pretty, but there is countryside everywhere, isn't there? Tallinn is a beautiful city. So," another smile, blue eyes twinkling, "enjoy your stay."

Then her eyes were on the next man in line and Gabriel was forgotten. Good. That was how he liked it.

* * *

He checked into a chain hotel an hour later. The room was functional. Designed to a budget. White-painted woodchip wallpaper, orange and brown curtains, wood flooring. He supposed it was an attempt at a pared-down Scandinavian look. If it was, it failed. They'd pared away until nothing was left except the bed – comfortable, he was pleased to note – a small, flat-screen TV set into the wall, and a hard chair positioned under what the hotel would probably call a desk, and he would call an extended windowsill. It didn't matter; it was a base, nothing more. The window gave onto a flat roof punctuated by an array of stainless steel ventilation shaft hoods, set, for no reason he could fathom, in small square beds of gravel. He tried it. A locking bar prevented its opening more than six inches, but a good hard shove would snap the feeble screws holding it into the frame. That was good; it was a second exit route from the room.

He changed into a pair of jeans, the football shirt and the hoodie, and prepared to head out. Time was in short supply, and he needed to start tracking the Chechens and their hostages. First, he needed to text Don the address. Two minutes later, a reply caused the phone to buzz in his hand.

I'll have your toys delivered within 24 hours. If you're not in, he'll wait.

CHAPTER 30

Finding the area of Tallinn he wanted was easy. He flipped through the traveller's guide to Estonia until he reached the section on Tallinn and skimmed it, looking for a particular heading.

Staying Safe.

On the whole, Tallinn is a safe city, no different from any other European capital. Common sense and keeping your eyes open will usually be enough to ensure your stay isn't interrupted by an unpleasant encounter with a small-time thief – the most likely variety of crime you'll encounter. The tourist areas in and around the Old Town are always busy with people, but there's no need to worry. We recommend that you avoid the badlands around the streets of Viru and the aptly-named Sauna; this is the nearest thing Tallinn has to a red-light district and is crammed with dubious clubs and bars.

"Thank you," he said out loud. "I'll start there, then."

The fifteen-minute walk from the hotel to Viru gave Gabriel time to sink into his adopted persona. He was Terry Fox, ex-infantry sergeant, dishonourable discharge from the London Regiment for hitting an officer. Served two tours in Iraq, one in Afghanistan. Looking for bar work, on the door. He adopted a bouncing walk, coming up on the balls of his feet, arms hanging at his sides. The replica shirt itched; he used the irritation to feed a sense of grievance, of entitlement. *How come I do my bit for Queen an' Country then get fucked over by the brass just for popping some Rupert in an argument over a late return to camp?* He kicked an empty drinks can off the pavement with venom, swearing at it under his breath and baring his teeth. A couple coming towards him moved over as he approached, glancing at him with compressed lips and furrowed foreheads, then looking away as he met their gaze.

Arriving in the 'badlands', he slowed down and began appraising likely targets for an informal, in-person job application. One in particular looked promising. It was called Jonny Rocketz, and had violet and acid-green neon cocktail glasses flicking from side to side in the blacked out window. The big man outside was kitted out in standard-issue doorman rig: black trousers, black dinner jacket (not matching the trousers, ripped on one shoulder), close-cropped hair, curly-wire ear-piece, scowl. His deltoids and biceps were so massively overdeveloped that his arms dangled away from his sides, giving him a simian appearance, accentuated by the jutting jaw and small, close-set eyes.

Gabriel approached. Monkey-man straightened up, leaned forward, and looked down at Gabriel as he stood toe-to toe with the bouncer.

"I fancy a few bevvies. You gonna let me in, big fella?" Gabriel said with a wink, knowing his rapid colloquial English would unsettle and hopefully irritate the bouncer.

The giant looked down at him. "No sportswear. This upmarket club."

"Sportswear? This is West Ham, mate. The Hammers. The old claret and blue." he put a little slur into his voice and swayed as he spoke.

"No sportswear. Fuck off and find other club."

Gabriel shrugged, half-turned, then whirled back and drove his bunched fist straight into the man's throat. He collapsed, gasping and gurgling, hands clasping his windpipe, only to meet Gabriel's knee travelling upwards. The contact between knee and jaw was solid. All the force was transmitted into the man's skull, throwing his brain forward where it crashed into the inside of the frontal bone and immediately shut down. A few passing punters looked over at the commotion, then turned away, laughing. Just another fun night out in Viru.

Gabriel stepped over the body of the doorman and pushed through the door into the buzzing crowd of drinkers. Not taking too much care whose drinks he spilled on his journey to the bar, he reached his destination and put both elbows on the rolled sheet of zinc. If this was an upmarket bar, he'd hate to see a downmarket one. Slopped beer and soggy cocktail napkins littered the bar, the music was a blare of eighties techno, and the clientele could charitably be described as looking relaxed. He caught the barman's eye and beckoned him with a twenty-euro note between the first and middle fingers of his right hand.

"Your boss around?" Gabriel said.

The barman looked at the blue banknote hovering in front of his face.

"Who are you?"

"I'm looking for work. You need a new doorman. Thought I could fit right in."

The barman, twenty-four or twenty-five, frowned. He pulled on his earlobe, hooking the tip of his index finger through a white plastic grommet the size of a two-pound coin.

"Teet is on the door tonight."

"Tit?" Gabriel widened his eyes as he crowed the word. "That's about right, mate. He's looking a complete tit at the moment. Sleeping on the job. Look, be a good boy, take this and then fuck off and fetch the manager."

Sensing trouble, the barman nodded, plucked the note from

Gabriel's fingers and disappeared through a door between two rows of optics. Gabriel turned away from the bar, pushed his elbows behind him to rest them on the bar and surveyed the room. It was a useful act to show his confidence, but it also allowed him to assess any potential threats, not least Teet. He should be out for a while yet, but he was big and strong and you never really knew how long an opponent was going to stay down for. Not unless you killed them.

The patrons were a mix of young clubbers, yelling into each other's ears or texting, and a rougher looking type of drinker, lining the room at the sparse tables and nursing big mugs of beer. A couple of these gave Gabriel hard stares, but he outstared them until they shifted their attention back to their drinks. A hand on his shoulder made him turn back to the bar.

He was expecting to be facing a blinged-up Estonian heavy, all thick, gold chains, prison tats and cheap aftershave. Instead, the person looking at him was female. She was about five-five or six, slim, hair bleached white, and wearing a white vest that showed off her muscular arms. She had two tattoos he could see: a horseshoe on the inside of her right forearm and a diamond on her left shoulder with "Eternity" inscribed across its facets on a ribbon. He couldn't read much in her face, which was devoid of expression. Her dark eyes were smudged with smoky make-up that made them look huge in the dim light of the bar. Her lips were a slash of vivid scarlet.

"You're looking for a job? We already got a doorman. I'm surprised he let you in wearing that." She pointed at his shirt.

"That's my point exactly," Gabriel said, starting to enjoy this pugnacious persona he'd adopted. "Your man Tit is asleep on the job. Go and have a look if you don't believe me."

She raised a hatch at the end of the bar and stalked through the customers and pulled the door open. When she withdrew her head and turned back to him, her face was easier to read. She was pissed off.

"What the fuck are you playing at?" she spat at him, as soon as she'd reached his station at the bar again.

"Listen, love. A place like this has to be ready for anything. All kinds of rough sorts are gonna want to drink in here. Stands to reason your man on the door has to be able to cope with 'em, doesn't it? Consider it a sales demo."

"What the fuck are you talking about?"

"Simple. He's rubbish; I'm not. Give me Tit's job, and I'll keep out the undesirables. You know, people who don't dress proper." He winked at her and plucked at the nylon of his shirt, which was sticking to his chest and back with sweat.

She paused before answering, her eyes travelling all the way from his head down to his feet and back up again to meet his eyes again.

"Come through to the back. My office. You want a drink?"

"Jesus! I thought you'd never ask. A beer. Whatever's good."

She turned to the barman, who was hovering, ready to do his mistress's bidding.

"Marek, get him a Saku Rock."

Gabriel carried the glass of pale lager through to the woman's office beyond the bar. It was a poky room, no more than eight feet square, most of which was taken up by a broad-topped, black desk. It was swathed in paperwork and scattered with pens, pencils and a silver paperknife with a handle made of coloured glass. An aged, black tower PC stood to one side. There was only one picture on the wall, a shocking abstract in yellow and black. It looked like what would happen if a giant wasp smashed itself to pieces on a windowpane. He hated it.

The woman motioned him to sit and turned sideways to squeeze between a filing cabinet and the edge of her desk, before she, too, sat.

"What is your name?"

"Terry Fox. What's yours?"

"I am Silvi Tamm. I run this place. You did that to Teet?"

"Needed to get your attention, didn't I?" Gabriel took a long pull on the beer, which was gassy and insipid, and leaned towards her across the desk, belching loudly. "I need a job. I've done security work all over. Army before that."

"British Army?"

"Of course British! What did you think, Russian?"

At the mention of Estonia's giant neighbour, the woman stiffened.

"Be very careful how you talk about Russia in here, friend. You know who owns it?"

"Surprise me," he said, leaning back and putting his hands behind his head.

"Never mind. You're not very big to work door, are you?"

"No," he said, lowering his voice and drawing her towards him. "But I tell you what I am." He slammed his left hand down on the desk with a bang. She jumped back, eyes wide, and when she looked at him again, he had the paperknife in his right hand, pointing at her chest. "Fast. And very, very good at putting people in their place." He waited for a beat. "Ask Tit if you don't believe me."

She looked up at the ceiling, then back at him.

"Say I take you on. You start right now. Pay is ten euros an hour. Hours eight till three. Think you can handle that, tough guy?"

Gabriel let his lips drift upwards in a lazy, smug smile. "Let's find out, shall we?"

"OK. Trial period. Three nights. You fuck up, you fuck off. I'll square it with Teet, and you can get a spare suit from the staff room next door. You get a staff meal at one a.m."

Gabriel got to his feet and stuck his hand out across the desk to her.

"Thanks, Silvi. You won't regret it."

She took his hand and squeezed, hard. He'd underestimated women before, to his cost, and he'd done it again. She had his knuckles lined up before he could settle his grip and she ground them together like ball-bearings in a sock.

"I'd better not." She smiled for the first time, showing even little teeth, pointed like a cat's.

* * *

That night, he didn't learn anything of direct relevance to finding the Bryant women, but he hadn't expected to. He did scope out a couple of the other places trying to wheedle the punters through their doors as he stood outside Jonny Rocketz, though. There was a club directly opposite called Nitro. He wandered across the cobbled street at about two, during a lull in the comings and goings from his own bar, and got talking to the two goons on the door. They were manning a tatty, twisted red velvet rope supported on four battered brass stands. He felt like a pygmy standing next to them. Both were well over six feet tall, one edging up towards seven, and built, as Terry Fox would say, "like a brick shithouse".

"Listen," he said, looking up at the bigger man's slab of a face after the introductory banter had petered out, "I've been away from home a long time. I fancy a bit of English pussy to cure my homesickness. You ever see any British girls down here?"

He watched carefully as he asked his question, not so much interested in the answer as whether the reference to "English" or "British" would elicit any kind of response." It was a good hunch. As each of the words slid from his mouth, the larger man's eyes closed as if to shut out the reference.

"No English girls. Russian. Latvian. Lithuanian. Estonian. Is all you get in Tallinn."

"What about Chechen girls? I've heard they're up for it."

Once more, on 'Chechen', the man's eyes blinked.

"No Chechen girls."

"What about pimps? You ever hear of a bloke called Kasym round here? I heard he could fix a bloke up if he knew who to ask."

The man's impassive face hardened.

"No Chechen. No pimp. No Kasym."

"Ah well, no harm in asking, is there?" Gabriel winked at the pair, feinted a punch at the ogre's stomach and sauntered back to his post.

* * *

Back in his hotel room after the end of his shift, Gabriel lay on the bed, arms folded behind his head. He was tired and energised at the same time. Back in action. Gathering intelligence. Doing some good again. The last job he'd undertaken had been strictly money-work, protecting a fat New York banker while he took a trip to Mexico City to negotiate the acquisition of a failing baby food manufacturer. Lauren had sold him in to the bank as a "British security expert, very discreet, very experienced, ex-SAS". He'd had the feeling from the word go that it was the "British" in that profile that had won him the gig rather than the other, more relevant words.

Those rich idiots loved to boast of the credentials of their staff, and having a "Brit" was like holding four aces. The only high point in an otherwise mundane three-day trip happened in a restaurant where they'd gone out for dinner on the day they arrived. Four loud – and loudly dressed – young men had burst into the steakhouse, causing a group of young women sitting two tables away to scream. The banker had nearly wet himself until it became clear that the men were members of a local boy band. Nonetheless, Gabriel's hand had strayed under the table and unsnapped the catch on the holster carrying his SIG. Once it became clear that the worst he could expect was to drown in a tide of female hormones, the banker's shoulders slumped from the position adjacent to his ears where he'd jacked them, and he resumed his monologue about the pressures he lived under "twenny-four-seven".

This mission was altogether more exciting, but the downside was also weightier. The world could probably stand to lose one merchant banker, but two kidnapped English women guilty of nothing more than taking a city break together to strengthen the bonds between them were a different story. Gabriel's mind was still alert and spinning after his shift, so he poured himself a stiff drink – he'd bought a bottle of Scotch from the club at staff rates – and took a hefty swallow, wincing as the fiery spirit hit the back of his throat.

The following day, after waking, groggy, at noon, Gabriel went shopping. He'd scoped out the perfect street on his walk home from the bar. It was a wide, tree-lined avenue, cars parked haphazardly along both sides and down a central strip painted with white zigzags. Most of the retailers plying their trade there were selling goods aimed at the everyday residents of Tallinn: clothes, household goods, books and electrical appliances. However, as he walked eastwards, the style and character of the shops changed. It was a subtle transformation, the kind that could creep up on perfectly happy tourists and have them clutching their purses and wallets tight inside their jackets, or moving their bags round so they could clamp them against their waists. The shops at this end of the street were functional rather than aspirational. There were cheap grocery stores, their frontages cluttered with random assortments of knobbly fruit and vegetables, stacks of plastic storage crates and displays of household cleaning materials, their windows obscured by brightly coloured posters for cheap overseas calling cards. Squeezed into spaces barely wide enough for their own front doors and maybe one small side window were cheque-cashing joints and Western Union outlets.

Down an alley opening out between a gaudily lit sex shop and a takeaway, its window filled with a slowly revolving column of obscenely glistening, greyish-brown meat, was a pawnbrokers-cum-junkshop. Gabriel stopped outside and reviewed the goods on show in the big plate-glass window. To the left and right were shelves of glittering, over-decorated watches and scuffed smartphones. Between them sat a pair of crossed Samurai swords, their handles wrapped in black and gold tape. The *katanas* formed an arch beneath which the shopkeeper had arranged a tableau of martial arts gear on a ruffled pool of emerald-green silk.

The weapons were all familiar to Gabriel from his time in Hong Kong where, as an initially unruly teenager, he had been educated by Zhao Xi, a close friend of his parents. Displayed like a cluster of exotic metal starfish were four- and five-pointed throwing stars, known popularly as *shuriken*, though Master Zhao would have pursed his lips and corrected anyone who called them that. "*Shuriken* is any small-bladed, handheld weapon. If they are designed to be thrown you should properly call them *shaken*".

Propped up behind the flat steel stars were a pair of pale, inch-thick wooden staves joined by a short chromed chain – *nunchucks*. Completing the display was an ornate dagger, its blade chased with a design of dragons, its hilt protected by a curling brass cross-guard.

Gabriel turned to his left and pushed the door. It opened with a grudging shudder before the top edge flipped a bell attached to a curved strip of sprung steel. The interior was lit by a harsh fluorescent strip light that flickered from time to time, and buzzed when it wasn't flickering. Gabriel swung his head left and right but saw nobody. Knock-off musical instruments, including a cherry-red "Finder" electric guitar, jostled for space with games consoles and exercise bikes. A whole shelving unit was devoted to digital cameras, DVD players and camcorders, their technological charms obviously having worn off on, or worn out, their former owners. More, and gaudier, watches and gold chains winked in the light from the intermittently firing neon tube overhead.

Ahead of Gabriel was a doorway screened by a curtain of red, white, yellow and blue plastic strips. A crude hand-lettered sign was taped above the lintel:

ADULT ONLY - XXX VIDEO, POPPERS

He pushed through the plastic ribbons, and was confronted by a rack of garish DVDs and magazines, the covers of which featured drugged-looking women in the throes of simulated sexual passion. Behind a small counter of thickly varnished plywood stood a short, balding, scrawny man wearing a stained, white vest. He was scratching his left armpit and regarding Gabriel with interest through gold wire-framed glasses.

"All here, man, whatever you want," he said in a parodic American accent, his watery blue eyes blinking. "Oral, anal, group, teens, bondage. Take a look around. Other stuff for special customers." He leered. "Just ask, man. You want it, I got it."

Gabriel turned away from the display of glossy, pneumatic flesh and walked over to the man.

"I need some stuff. Not that," he said, waving his arm at the racks of porn. "Training supplies. Martial arts. Like in the window."

"OK, man, fine, whatever. You need *katana*, *nunchucks*, what?"

"I need a knife. A good one, none of that ninja shit you got. Hunting, military, special forces, yeah?"

The man stood for a moment. Gabriel had squared his shoulders before speaking and leant over the counter fractionally, invading the other's domain. Now he planted his hands flat on the shiny wood. "I ain't got all day. You going to help me out or not?"

The man appeared to be calculating. His eyes flicked upwards and he scratched the ginger stubble on his chin. Then his eyes found Gabriel's again.

"Yes, I got knife you might like. What else?"

"OK, that's more like it. I need a knuckleduster."

The man looked at him. No comprehension visible on his face.

"Brass knuckles, yeah?"

Nothing.

"Fine. Speak Russian, do you? *Russkiy*?"

"Yes, of course, Russian."

"*Kastet*. Get me now?"

The man looked at Gabriel with a more searching expression this time. He, Gabriel, knew what was running through his mind. You might actually need a hunting knife for hunting. Or for displaying. But *kastet*? That was strictly for fighting. For head-breaking. *And none of your Marquis of Queensbury shit, either*, as Terry Fox would say. *We're talking gashed cheeks, broken teeth, cracked skulls. Heavy, heavy stuff.*

"*Kastet*. Sure. Not cheap."

"Never mind about the money. Why don't you go and get your stuff, and we can take a look. If it's good, I'll pay."

The man left through a white-painted door behind the counter. While the man was gone, Gabriel felt his phone vibrate in his pocket. He checked it: a text from Don.

Man in reception. Tall. Suit. Carrier bag.

·   ·   ·

Good, he thought. That's the firepower to go with the brawling kit. He sent a one-word text back.

Thx

The shop owner reappeared in front of him. He carried a cardboard box, the top flaps interleaved, the sides sagging outwards. It clinked as he lifted it onto the counter.

Without talking, he undid the top and began displaying the contents across the counter. The knives came out first: an oversized hunting knife with a polished rosewood and brass handle; a battered tactical knife, double-edged with a spear-point; a couple of switchblades with horn and silver handles; and then the prize, a US Marine Corps KA-BAR. According to legend, it was modelled on a knife found on the frozen body of a Canadian trapper. He'd scratched "Killed A Bear" on the hilt, and some of the letters had worn away.

The KA-BAR's brown leather grip had been dyed almost black with sweat and grime from its previous owners' hands. Gabriel tested the seven-inch carbon steel blade against the ball of his thumb. Still sharp, through some whetting on an oilstone would bring the razor-edge back. He put it to one side.

"I'll have that," he said. Then he picked up one of the switchblades, thumbed the silver button and smiled as the five-inch stiletto blade snapped out of the handle and locked with a soft *snick*. "This one, too."

The man smiled back at him, perhaps sensing that here was his best deal of the day, or possibly the week.

"*Kastet* now," the man said, reaching into the carton and pulling out a handful of different knuckledusters, arraying them in a row behind the knives like a jeweller offering engagement rings to a groom-to-be.

Two of the fearsome hand-to-hand combat weapons were made from brass, one from cast iron, and one from blued steel. They all shared the same basic design: four linked rings for the fingers, and a palm piece to absorb and spread the counter-impact force. Gabriel tried all four for size and fit before selecting the steel model. The striking surfaces were milled to a precise edge and would cause more damage than the rounded angles of the brass and iron versions.

"Right then," Gabriel said, pushing his three purchases together into a tight group on the counter. "How about a nice all-inclusive price for cash?"

"Always is cash here, buddy," the man said, grinning to reveal a mouthful of twisted and chipped teeth. "Cash is king." He laughed and a gust of foul breath flew across the two feet of air between them. Gabriel reeled back from the stink as the man finished his speech. "You give me five hundred euros."

"Fuck off! A monkey for that lot? Tell you what, sunshine, I've got a hundred and fifty dollars here. I'll give you that for the merchandise and another fifty for an answer to a question."

The man shook his head. "Not enough, man. Four hundred euros."

"Let's see, I *could* pay you four hundred. Or I could just call the cops and let them know what kind of merchandise you're knocking out back here. I'm sure they'd be interested. Now. Two hundred dollars, like I said. OK?"

He pulled the roll of green banknotes from his hip pocket, snapped off the rubber band, and let them spring apart into an untidy scatter in a clear space among the assorted head-breakers, skin-unzippers and gut-puncturers. Sighing, the man went to pick up the notes but Gabriel's own hand darted out and seized his wrist, holding it down and pulling the man towards him.

"OK, OK," the man said. "Two hundred dollars and I answer question."

"Nice one," he said, releasing the wrist, which its owner rubbed as if he'd been unlocked from handcuffs. "Here we go then, and listen carefully. I'm going to make this nice and simple for you." The man frowned with theatrical concentration, cupping his chin in one hand. "I want to know if you've sold gear like this to any Chechens in the last month. Or if you have any mates in the trade who might have done."

The man's eyes closed tight as Gabriel uttered the word "Chechen", then reopened slowly as if he were worried the people so designated might appear in his shop, summoned by their name.

"No Chechens. Not here, man. Russians, yes. Estonians, yes. No Chechens."

Gabriel suddenly pointed to a spot high above the man's eyeline. "What's that up there?" he asked.

The man obliged by looking upwards. If he heard the click of the switchblade he gave no indication. When he looked back it was at its point. He went cross-eyed as he tried to focus on it.

"Shall we try that one again?" Gabriel said with a smile, then tapped the blade on the guy's nose. "Have you sold . . ."

Tap

". . . any gear like this . . ."

Tap

". . . to Chechens recently?"

Tap

Once again the man's eyes closed on "Chechens". Gabriel had his answer.

"How many?"

The eyes shifted left and right. Then down at his hands. He placed four outstretched fingers on the counter.

"OK, one more question, then you get your money and I'm out of your life for ever. Ready?"

The man nodded several times in quick succession. "Ready."

"Where are they living?"

"I don't know."

Gabriel moved the tip of the switchblade a centimetre inside the man's left nostril.

"I said, where are they living?"

"Seriously, man. I don't know. I'd tell you. I promise. Please don't cut me."

Gabriel believed him. "You know what? I just thought of another question. These Chechens. Was one of them called Kasym?"

The man swallowed. Waited for a heartbeat. Then he nodded.

"Thanks, buddy," Gabriel said. He withdrew the knife, closed it, then gathered up his purchases, stuffed them into the pockets of his windcheater and left through the ratty plastic curtain.

CHAPTER 31

Hands shoved deep into his pockets to stop his newly acquired arsenal from clanking too loudly, Gabriel made his way back to his hotel. The streets were full of shoppers, women walking with children dressed in school uniforms – home-time he supposed – and the random assortment of tourists, strollers and office workers you'd find in any European capital city. As he walked, he kept to the outside of the pavement, just inside the kerb. It was an old habit, staying away from buildings, and alleys in particular, that assailants could use for cover.

His eyes were never still, checking each and every oncoming pedestrian from six or seven feet out, assessing them as a potential threat. The only thing he saw, and it was a phenomenon that always amazed him, was the apparent oblivion in which many people seemed to exist. Thousand-pound digital SLR cameras slung from one shoulder; soft, brightly coloured leather handbags hanging open from a hand; fat wallets stuffed carelessly into a back pocket. They might as well walk around wearing a sign declaring, "I am rich and stupid, please rob me". He was also, vainly, he knew, hoping he might see someone who would trigger his internal early-warning system.

He reached his hotel having seen nobody who looked like a mugger or a Chechen kidnapper, though he did find an old-fashioned ironmonger who sold him a whetstone. Pushing through the revolving door, he headed for the reception desk.

"I'm expecting a guest. Has anyone called to see me?"

The redheaded woman on reception nodded with a smile. "Yes, Mr Wolfe. Your brother has come to see you." She pointed past his right shoulder to a small seating area.

He turned and walked in the direction she'd indicated. A lean-looking man, six-two or three and wearing a dark grey, two-piece suit, stood up to greet him. He was tanned and had white squint-lines around his eyes – a recent trip to somewhere hot then. Somewhere sandy, maybe. Somewhere Her Majesty might have need of tough-looking men whose muscles weren't always concealed in discreetly expensive tailoring?

The man beamed at him, arms wide.

"Hello Shorty!" he said, enfolding Gabriel in a bear-hug and clapping him on the back.

"Hello yourself!" Gabriel said returning the stranger's smile with a wide grin of his own. "How's Dad?"

"The Don? He's just fine. He asked me to bring this for you as you were in the neighbourhood. One of Mum's cakes."

He bent to pick up a supermarket carrier bag that bulged and sagged where the outlines of a square box of some kind distorted the thin plastic. Gabriel took it from him.

"Thanks. Hope it's as tasty as the last one."

"Tasty? You know Mum. This one packs a real wallop."

"You remember I asked you about those lady friends of mine I was looking for?"

"Chloe and Sarah, you mean? How could I forget?"

"You wouldn't know where they're staying, would you? It would save me a lot of time."

"Sorry. Maybe they're avoiding you. Must have been something you said. *Cherchez la femme*, mate. Now I've got to run. The minister wants me back in the office pronto."

They shook hands and then Gabriel's "brother" left through the revolving door without a backward glance. Gabriel walked back to the desk to collect his key. The receptionist smiled at him again.

"He is handsome, your brother."

"You think? We always used to call him beanpole at school."

She handed him his room key, which dangled from a thick brass disc the size of his palm, and wished him a good evening.

Back in his room, Gabriel put the carrier bag on the desk, the box inside clunking against the wooden surface. Then he emptied his pockets. He lined up the switchblade, KA-BAR, whetstone and knuckleduster to one side, and turned his attention to Mum's cake. He lifted the box out of the carrier-bag. It was made of plain, pressed steel and felt reassuringly heavy, seven pounds at least. The lid was hinged and secured with a small snap. He unclipped it and lifted the lid back to reveal the contents. As the Army would have put it,

Weapon, personal, Wolfe, Gabriel for the use of:-

Pistol, one, SIG-Sauer P226 semi-automatic, modified barrel with stainless steel thread mount

Suppressor, one, SWR Trident-9

Oil, gun, one bottle, 100 ml

He lifted the pistol out and placed it next to the knuckleduster. Below the box the pistol came in were three square cardboard cartons, about six inches to a side and an inch and a half deep. He slit the adhesive tape on one of the lids and flipped it off to reveal the blunt, copper-jacketed noses of one hundred 9 x 19mm Parabellum rounds. *Just like Don to up the ammunition by fifty percent.*

First things first. He stripped and oiled the SIG Sauer, then reassembled it. He pushed fifteen rounds into the magazine, and pushed it home into the butt. He marvelled once more at the fanatical attention to detail that the Swiss manufacturers, or to be more exact, their engineers, paid when producing these weapons. The two screws holding the grips onto the chassis of the butt had their heads perfectly aligned on their vertical axes. Even the SIG Sauer logo on the barrel was engraved in crisply edged type.

Between his haul from the pawnbroker, the firearm, and his own hands and feet, Gabriel felt he had all the *matériel* he needed to mount a hostage rescue. What he lacked right now was intelligence. He knew there were four Chechens in town, including the one called Kasym, or four *at least*, he corrected himself, and he knew they'd be patronising the same high-class quartermaster's that he had. But he didn't have names, faces or locations beyond a twelve-and-a-half-square-mile circle centred on St Mary's Cathedral.

* * *

That evening, Gabriel was manning his post outside the club at eight. It was still light, and he didn't have much to do beyond standing at the door and barring the way to any obviously pissed customers. The street was crowded with a noisy bunch of under-dressed women and their leery boyfriends, plus single-sex groups holding bottles of beer by the necks or swigging from bottles of clear spirits. He'd read how the Baltic capitals had marketed themselves enthusiastically as destinations for stag and hen weekends, but he wondered if the city fathers had realised what they were letting themselves in for.

A group of eight or ten English twenty-somethings came swaying down the street, singing Madonna's *Like a Virgin* loudly and in about five different keys. Clearly, they'd ignored the warning in the tourist guide, or used it as a recommendation. The women seemed to be competing for two different prizes: "highest heels" and "skimpiest dress". One girl in particular was having trouble in the latter category. Her stretchy scarlet dress was so short in the hem that she kept twitching it down to cover her knickers, only to risk falling out of the top, whereupon she repeated the movement in reverse. Her eyes, bright in clouds of panda-ish make-up, darted from side to side, and her brow had three or four furrows grooved into her matte skin. Not as happy as her singing suggested. The boys were swaggering. Cheap suits in pale grey, burgundy and powder blue, with narrow trousers and sleeves tight around their biceps.

They stumbled to a stop outside Jonny Rocketz, bunching around Gabriel as he folded his arms and stepped towards the leading girl. She was wearing a neon pink mini-skirt, stockings and suspenders, and a white vest to which an "L"-plate was pinned. A bride's veil rigged out of toilet paper trailed down her back to the ground.

A sudden inspiration flooded his mind. "Sorry ladies and gentlemen, club's full. You'll have to find somewhere else to do your celebrating."

"Fuckin' 'ell," the girl shrieked, turning to her posse of mates. "He's English."

She turned back to him and pouted, turning her sticky lips into a caricature of a movie-star's kissy face. "Come on, darling, don't be like that. We all just joined up for a bit of a laugh."

A couple of the boys she was with shouldered their way to the front and bookended her. One spoke.

"Yeah, mate, like, don't be a dick. We only want to have a little fun."

Gabriel paused, as if considering the merits of this entreaty, then shrugged.

"OK," he said. "But no trouble, all right? Or I'll come in there and sort you all out."

"Fine, whatever," the bride-to-be said, tossing her teased and ringleted locks. "Come on, we're in."

Gabriel stood aside as they crowded into the bar through the narrow door. Then waited.

Sure enough, after five minutes or so, a scream cut through the booming music. Then the sound he'd been waiting for: glass smashing. He counted to ten – slowly – then pushed through the door.

The English boys were engaged in a sloppy brawl with a bunch of locals. Who knew what had sparked it – a jogged elbow, a misjudged glance at a girl's chest or pair of long, fake-tanned legs. Who cared? The women had joined in too, though they kept to strict, gender-based contests, pulling hair, gouging long painted nails at equally colourful faces, and kicking with their towering platform shoes. He marched into the centre of the mêlée, grabbed the largest English boy by the scruff of his neck and threw him against a wall. One down. Then he whirled round, ducking to avoid a chair thrown by the guy's girlfriend, and straight-armed the second-biggest boy with the heel of his hand. The blow caught him on the nose, which spurted blood like a showerhead. Two down. All around him, the screaming and swearing continued, overlaid by the insistent pulse of the music.

A third guy, jacket off, displaying muscular arms, pulled Gabriel round by his shoulder then stepped back a pace and brought his hands up, left in a fist, right in a stiff blade.

"I'm going to fucking do you. I'm a cage fighter."

"No. What you are," Gabriel said, "is a pedigree cunt."

Teeth bared, the man leaned back, lifting his right foot in a Thai kickboxing move. Gabriel closed in fast, kicked the guy's left ankle, hard, and kneed him in the face as he fell sideways. His head bounced on the floor and he was still. Three down.

A glaring face loomed into his own, and its owner's hands closed on the lapels of Gabriel's dinner jacket.

"You fucker!" the boy screamed into his face. "You should be fucking protecting us, not beating us up." Then he reared back for a head butt. The move was too obvious and too well telegraphed to trouble Gabriel. As the guy exposed his throat, Gabriel simply stabbed his four straightened fingers into the soft flesh under the Adam's apple. With a hollow choking sound, the boy doubled over, falling to his hands and knees. Gabriel delivered a kick to his stomach, hard enough to keep him down but not to cause any damage to the internal organs.

"That's enough! Stand still!" he shouted, just as the music died, mid-track. Everyone stopped, rooted to the spot as his bark of command. He pointed at the remaining members of the joint stag-and-hen party who were clutching each other, make-up smeared by fists or tears, suits torn or spattered with blood from busted noses or cut cheeks. "You lot. Out!" He pointed to the door. Nobody moved. "Now!" he bellowed. "Before I get seriously pissed off."

A couple of the English boys looked as though they still had some fight left in them and they were exchanging killer glares with some of the local men. As they grudgingly made their way to the door, supporting their walking wounded, Silvi appeared from her office and pushed her way through the crowd. She planted herself, legs akimbo, arms crossed over her breasts, in front of the girl with the "L"-plate on her own chest and jabbed her finger at it.

"Yes, you are a learner. You're still learning to behave like a civilised human being. So you can leave my club now and take your disgusting friends with you. Tallinn doesn't need people like you. Estonia doesn't need people like you. Get out. *Kao välja!*"

Silvi turned on her heel, but as she stepped away, the woman grabbed her hair and pulled down hard. Silvi's head jerked back, and she had to sink to her knees to lessen the pain. The woman kneed her in the back, but as she was winding up to stamp on Silvi with her viciously thin heel, Gabriel marched over and seized the woman's wrists, spun her to face him and delivered a ringing slap to her left cheek that drew gasps from those people close enough to witness it. She stared at him open-mouthed, and a couple of the now recovered English boys looked like they were weighing up their chances if they re-engaged him. He wagged his finger in her face and then pointed to the door.

"You heard the lady. *Kao välja!*" he said.

They understood his meaning clearly enough, even if they didn't know any Estonian, and this time they did get out, a couple of the stragglers shouting threats over their shoulders as they pushed their way through the still-crowded bar and out of sight through the door. The trouble over – for now – the regular punters resumed their enthusiastic drinking and dancing.

Gabriel followed Silvi to her office, putting his hand onto her shoulder to slow her down.

"You all right?" he said, genuinely concerned.

"I'm fine. Those English bitches are worse than the men. You should see the mess they leave in the toilets. Animals. Thanks for what you did back there, Terry. You're a good man. Get Astrid to pour you a drink. On the house. Tell her I sent you. I'll put someone else on the door."

Then she was gone, fleeing the scene of the fracas towards the security of her office. He walked over to the bar and signalled to the raven-haired girl pouring drinks. She finished the round then came over.

"You speak English?" he said.

"Of course! We all do, pretty much a condition of working down here. Some slick moves you got, Terry. Thirsty?"

"Yeah. Silvi said . . ."

"On the house? Sure. What do you want?"

"A beer, but not that fucking awful stuff I had last time, what was it called? Saku Rock? Yeah, that was it."

"Don't worry, I'll get you something better."

She came back a few minutes later with a tall, waisted glass of dark beer crowned by a thick, creamy head.

He took a long swig of the beer. It was good – deep, earthy flavours and a lemony aftertaste. He wiped his mouth with the back of his hand and put the glass down on the zinc.

"That's better," he said, grinning. "Always like to wet my whistle after a little scrap. Listen, what time do you get off tonight?"

"Same as you. Three. Why?" She was looking straight at him, green, almond-shaped eyes twinkling in the lights reflecting off the shiny metal bar top.

"Thought you might want to grab breakfast."

She put her head on one side and touched the tips of her fingers to the little notch between her collarbones. Then she nodded. "Sure. Why not? There's a good place up the street where we sometimes go."

The rest of the night passed quickly. No further trouble, but plenty of people to check over, sometimes for weapons if they looked dodgy, and either let in or turn away, politely, with suggestions for other establishments that would be more than happy to cater to their needs.

After the last customers had left, staggering home or onwards to another club, Gabriel went inside to change into his own clothes. When he came out of the walk-in cupboard that doubled as a staff changing room, Astrid was waiting for him. She was skinny, no more than five-two, brought up to five-six on a pair of platform-soled biker boots, the shins ornamented with shiny metal plates. White, over-the-knee socks came to mid-thigh, revealing a strip of fishnet tights that disappeared beneath a black velvet skirt. On top she wore a black T-shirt, ripped artfully just below her small breasts. The words printed across it, in a typeface resembling blood spatters, read, *Gone To Hell.* A dinged-up, black leather biker jacket completed the look.

He pointed at the slogan across her chest. "Beats *I Heart Tallinn.* I suppose."

"Not heard of them, then?"

"Heard of who?"

"Gone To Hell, numbskull. They're a band. My brother plays bass for them. They're awesome."

"OK, that's pretty cool. Come on, let's get something to eat, and you can tell me all about your brother's band. And anything else you think I should know about you."

As the cold air hit them on the street outside, Astrid leaned into him. "Put your arm round me, I'm cold."

He did as she asked, and they walked, hip to hip, up the street towards a crossroads.

"Here we are," she said, as they reached the traffic lights on the corner. The glowing windows of the cafe were steamed up on the inside, but he could see that the place was at least half full.

They went in, and Gabriel inhaled deeply. Coffee, really good coffee, warm bread, pastries, and eggs and sausages frying somewhere towards the back. They ordered cappuccinos, sausage sandwiches, and a couple of Danish pastries thick with icing and dried fruit, then found a table and sat opposite each other, surrounded by a mixture of night-shift workers, clubbers and a couple of uniformed police officers, a man and a woman, wedged in at a corner table.

After their sandwiches arrived, they ate in companionable silence until the thickly cut bread and smoky, garlicky sausages were all gone. Gabriel swallowed the bite of Danish he was chewing, took a sip of the hot coffee, then tried a direct question.

"You ever get any English around here who aren't pissed up and looking for a fight?"

"Sometimes, yes. But mostly it's people like them," she said, nodding in the direction of Jonny Rocketz.

"How about other countries? Germans, Dutch?"

"Sometimes."

"What about Chechens?"

Her eyes widened in surprise. "Chechens? I don't think so. Why?"

"A couple of friends of mine – women friends – are travelling round here. They set off a month or so ago. They emailed and said they'd met up with some Chechens. It seemed really unlikely, you know? Given their reputation. So I'm just trying to find them. Make sure everything's tickety-boo."

She snorted, then started coughing as coffee tried to force its way out of her nose. "Ticket-what?" she said, before blowing her nose with a paper napkin she plucked from a red and chrome dispenser on the table.

"Tickety-boo. You know, it means everything's all right. Kosher. A1. Tip-top. Jesus, don't have a fit."

Astrid was laughing loudly, and people at nearby tables were turning to look, smiling as they caught her mood. She cleared her throat noisily and wiped her eyes with another paper napkin.

"You English and your expressions. You kill me. You'll have to tell Joonas when you meet him. He could put them into a song."

"He's your brother, yeah? The bass player?"

"That's right. They're playing all this weekend at a great little rock club, Darkness. They've got, what do you call it, a residency. Why don't you come on Sunday? The bar's closed, so we both have a day off."

"That would be great. I could do with some company. Gets a bit lonely travelling around on your own."

"Great!" she bestowed a wide smile on him. "Do you want to come to mine a little before on Sunday night? Say seven-thirty? I'll make you something good and filling. Proper Estonian food. You're probably living on pizza and McDonald's, yes?"

She wasn't far from the truth. "Sounds good to me."

"So, then. Drink up and you can walk me home. Then I want to find out if you fuck as well as you fight."

Gabriel thought of Annie. How would she feel about his having a new friend with benefits? Somehow, he imagined she'd not be best pleased. But she didn't have to know.

"Come on then," he said, getting to his feet and pulling her up to join him. "Let's see if we can find out, shall we?"

CHAPTER 32

Earlier that evening, at the scrapyard in Tartu, Sarah sat opposite Kasym at the table in the cabin that served as kitchen and living accommodation for the Chechens and their hostages. Chloe had retreated to her music in their bedroom, and the other three Chechens had gone out for a meal. A half-empty bottle of wine stood between them.

"Tell me, Kasym. Do you have children?" Sarah asked.

Kasym drained his glass and set it down on the table. He rubbed his face from eyes to chin with his palm. Then he began speaking in a quiet voice.

"My wife and I were childhood sweethearts. Our families owned neighbouring farms. Nothing big, just smallholdings with a few goats, maybe a pig or a cow from time to time, ducks, chickens, rabbits sometimes. Anja and I would play together all the time. Before school, after chores, any time we could get away. There was a stream running through our families' land, and in the summer, when it warmed up, we used to go swimming there at the weekends. We used to sit on a little stone bridge to dry off and one day, when I was seven and she was six, I asked her to marry me. Not then, of course. But we agreed that we would be married as soon as she was sixteen. Our parents were delighted with the idea. We were both only children, and they could see the two farms merging and becoming a much more substantial enterprise.

"Little Zora came along after one year. We doted on her."

Kasym looked at the ceiling. He could still picture Zora as she was then. Her mother's dark skin and his blue eyes.

"When she was sixteen, she told us she didn't want to work on the farm any more. That she wanted to go to university. Nobody in our family had ever gone to university before, but we were pleased. We encouraged her to study hard and we began to think of how we could support her financially. This was May 1999.

"This was a bad year in Chechnya's history. The Russians decided that independence – freedom – was not something for the Chechen people. They sent in troops. Some little more than boys, no older than my Zora. One Tuesday morning, I was working on a broken harrow in the fields at the back of our house when I heard a sound that chilled me to the bone. It was my wife and daughter screaming together."

Sarah put her wineglass down, frowning with concentration. "Why were they screaming? An accident?"

"No. Not an accident. I dropped my tools and ran back towards the house. Their screaming was pitiful – they were crying, 'No, no' over and over again. I came round the corner of the house to see the worst sight of my entire life, before or since. There were six Russian soldiers standing with rifles in a group, smoking and laughing. In the centre of the circle, two more, with their trousers round their ankles, were raping my wife and daughter."

Sarah's hand flew to her mouth. "What did you do," she asked through her fingers.

"I yelled at them to stop and they just laughed harder. Two of the bastards grabbed me by the arms and held me between them, forced me to watch. They took turns with them and when they were all finished, they shot them, simple as that."

Kasym paused and drained his glass. He looked away from Sarah while he wiped his eyes.

"You don't have to go on, you know," she said, "if it's too painful."

He shook his head.

"One of these men spat at me and called us Chechen pigs. Said we were animals, not humans, and I should be grateful Mother Russia was rounding us all up again. After they left, I had two choices. I could give in, collapse, and shoot myself, or I could become a real man. I chose to be a man. I buried my Anja and Zora. Then I fetched my hunting rifle and began to track the Russia soldiers. They were an advance party, with no support. I found them inside two days with the help of our neighbours. They had murdered another family – hadn't even moved the bodies – and were sitting round a fire in their yard, roasting a goat and drinking plum brandy."

Kasym's voice took on a rougher, harder edge. He picked up the cook's knife he'd used and began turning it in the light.

Sarah's eyes flicked to the blade and back to Kasym. "What did you do?"

"I was the best shot in our neighbourhood. I could put a bullet through a squirrel's eye at a hundred metres. Their eyes were much bigger than a squirrel's. From my hide, fifty metres out, it was like a fairground shooting gallery. You know? Hit five soldiers and win a prize? I lined up my first target in my sights and shot him through the head. Before he fell off the log he sat on, I had killed two more. The other five were scrambling around for weapons, but that was not to be. I took two more with body shots, and the other three with shots to the legs.

"I walked into the farmyard. It smelled of the brandy and the charring goat. And Russian blood. I have smelt a lot of it since. The three men I'd wounded were pathetic. Crawling around clutching themselves, praying to their stupid saints, calling for their mothers. My blood was rushing in my ears – it sounded like the high wind through the forest in midwinter. I pulled my skinning knife and killed two of them cleanly, stabs to the heart. The eighth man was bleeding badly. I had clipped his femoral artery. You know, the big one inside the thigh? I tied a tourniquet round his leg, up high, to stop the blood. He tried to thank me but I shushed him." Kasym put his fingers to Sarah's lips in an oddly gentle gesture that she did not resist. "Until I started shooting, I had never killed a man before, you see, and now I was shaking. Trembling all over. This man had raped and killed my wife and my daughter and I wanted revenge. I wanted him to know what he had done. But he was drunk on the brandy, weeping and pleading with me to spare his life. All manner of tortures and slow deaths rushed through my mind, but in the end, he made me feel sick with his begging. I just untied the tourniquet and left him there to bleed out. I walked back to my farm, packed a bag, locked the doors, and never went back."

Kasym swiped at his eyes with the balls of his thumbs and refilled their glasses. He noticed that Sarah's eyes were frosted with tears that glistened on her fair eyelashes like dew on spiders' webs. He cleared his throat and refocused on her face, bringing it into sharp clarity.

"You poor man," she said.

"Forgive me, others' tragedies make poor entertainment."

"No, I understand. If anything happened to Chloe, I'd want to kill the man who did it. I hope you know that."

CHAPTER 33

Astrid's flat was on the top floor of a tower block that stood, sentinel-like, on the edge of a park. The block itself was built with at least half an eye on how it looked for its residents and those passing in its shadow. Between the flats, square steel panels in bright blues, greens and yellows gave the building a festive feel, at odds with much of the Soviet-era architecture elsewhere in Tallinn. Once the lift doors closed on them, Astrid turned to Gabriel, placed her hands on his cheeks to turn him to face her, then stretched up and kissed him. Her lips were soft and warm, and as he kissed her back, she opened them a little. They stood, locked together in an embrace as the lift ascended without stopping to the eleventh floor. He could taste the sweetness of the pastry on her and inhaled her heavy, musky perfume, and felt himself growing hard under the insistent pressure of her hips grinding against his own.

When the lift doors opened, they stumbled out, separating and laughing as Astrid drew her front door key out from her T-shirt on a looped leather thong. Gabriel reached around her as she pushed the key into the lock, cupping her breasts and nuzzling the back of her neck where her piled-up hair exposed the skin.

Inside, she pulled him by the hands into her bedroom, walking backwards and locking eyes with him.

"Take your clothes off," she said, hands on hips. "Come on, soldier boy, I haven't got all night."

Gabriel undressed, folding each garment and placing them in a pile on a chair next to the wardrobe. When he was naked, he stood still in front of her, letting her look him up and down. He was in good shape from the gym and the physical nature of some of his work, but he still felt vulnerable as the fully-dressed woman scrutinised him.

"Turn around," she said.

He complied, then turned again to face her.

"Now undress me, and don't be rough."

He came up close to her and pushed the biker jacket off her shoulders, and dropped it behind her onto the chair. Astrid lifted her arms up above her head, never once taking her eyes off his, letting him pull the hem of the T-shirt up and over until it came free with a whisper as a few strands of her hair escaped from their bonds and stuck to the material with static. He drew a breath in and groaned as she placed her fingers around his penis and squeezed him gently there before letting go again.

"Keep going," she whispered.

He reached around her and unclipped her bra – plain, black cotton, designed for support not seduction – and let it fall to the floor. Then he knelt in front of her, pausing to kiss her neat little navel before unzipping the skirt and pulling it down to the ground for her to step out of. The boots, knee socks and tights all followed. Finally he hooked his thumbs into the waistband of her tiny, black knickers and drew them down over the firm contours of her thighs. He stood and let her lead him to the bed, a giant iron-framed antique, dressed with a candy-striped pink and white sheet, antique lace throws and a voluminous duvet covered in black and pink skull-print fabric.

"On your back," she said, swinging one muscular leg over his hips to straddle him. She settled down onto him with a sigh of pleasure, closing her eyes and rocking her hips to and fro in a steady rhythm. Gabriel held her around the waist and looked up at her. She was biting her lower lip, pulling it between her teeth as she ground and swayed on him. He reached up to her breasts, letting his hands cover them and enjoying the feeling of her hard nipples under the skin of his palms.

Astrid began to move more urgently, pushing down onto him and leaning forward to place her hands on his chest. Her hair had come unpinned, and as she fucked him, the long, black coils trailed across his eyes. He moved under her, matching her pace and then, with a small cry like a wounded animal, she came. The contractions around him were enough for Gabriel to reach his own climax, and moments later, they were lying in each other's arms, panting, sweaty, and laughing.

"Are you this friendly with all the staff then?" he asked, when his breathing had settled.

"Fuck you!" she said, slapping his chest before snuggling back against him. "You're cute, and you seem to like being around people, at least when you're not beating the crap out of them. And your accent's really hot."

"Really? I never thought of it like that before. I mean, Yanks love it, but I didn't know it played well this side of the pond."

"Well it does."

She levered herself up onto one elbow and ran her hand over his torso, from his flat, muscular belly up to his collarbones.

"How come no bullet holes? I thought that's what all you soldier boys came back with."

"Disappointed, are you?"

"No," she said, with a smile. "But, you know, it's kind of sexy when a guy has a few scars."

"That your thing is it? I got this one," he said, taking her index finger and tracing a line from his eyebrow to his left cheekbone. "Bayonet. You know what one of those is right?"

"Did it hurt?"

"No. Not at the time. You're too pumped up with adrenaline. Hurt like fuck later, though."

She ran her finger up his thigh, then stopped as her nail snagged on a puckered ridge of skin on the inside, near his groin. She kicked the duvet off and bent to peer at the white scar.

"This?"

"That was a bloke who should have known better. Did it with a hunting knife but he missed the artery."

Her eyes widened as she turned to him. "What did you do?"

"I delivered The Queen's message, didn't I?"

Her brow crinkled. "What do you mean?"

"I mean, I'm walking around up here, fucking a beautiful Estonian girl, and he's walking around down there," he said, pointing at the floor, "getting red-hot pitchforks shoved up his arse."

"I have a scar," she said, rolling onto her stomach. "Look."

He scanned her pale skin in the weak dawn light coming in through the window.

"I can't see anything."

"My last boyfriend stabbed me in the back; two-timed me with my best friend."

"Those wounds always take longer to heal."

He rubbed her smooth skin, feeling the knobbles of her spine from the nape of her neck all the way down to the little dimples each side of her tailbone. As he stroked her skin, a faded bruise on her right tricep caught his eye, little more than a pale yellowish-green blob. He looked more closely. The bruise was actually four small bruises. There was a matching set on her left arm. He rolled her back to face him, holding her gently by the shoulders.

There were two more bruises, on her biceps, roughly opposite those he'd seen first.

"Who did this to you?" Gabriel said.

Astrid looked away. "It's nothing. Forget it."

"No it isn't. Someone gripped you hard enough to leave bruises. A man?"

"I said it's nothing!" she snapped, whirling back to face him. Her eyes were hard points in the dawn light.

"Not a customer. They couldn't reach you. And I'm fairly sure you don't have a boyfriend. Who then? Silvi?"

"Not Silvi. She's a good friend."

Gabriel placed his fingertips against the bruises, measuring the spacing. "No, not a woman." Then he cupped her cheeks in his hands and looked deeply into her eyes. "Who did this to you, Astrid? Tell me."

"Who do you think? A man who thinks he owns the staff as well as the bar."

"Yuri?"

She lowered her eyelids. Gabriel pulled her into him and held her against his chest.

"Please don't do anything, Terry. I need this job. Yuri owns all the places round here, or he protects them. And he knows everything that happens in the rest of Tallinn – I'd never get another job if you hurt him. It was just one of those things. I'm fine."

Gabriel looked across the room over the top of Astrid's head, stroking her hair. Enemies everywhere. The old-fashioned alarm clock read four-fifteen. He felt his eyes closing.

* * *

"Chechens!" Gabriel cried out as he jerked awake, startling Astrid and almost pushing her out of bed in his struggle to get out from the bedclothes twisted round him.

She grabbed hold of the duvet to prevent herself from falling to the floorboards and pulled herself back to Gabriel. He was trembling and bathed in sweat. The clock on her old-fashioned, white-painted dresser said it was ten-thirty. Sunlight was streaming in through the window. Hexagonal rainbows refracted through a crystal pendant hanging from the frame and crawled across the rose-print wallpaper.

"What the fuck?" she said. "Are you all right? Wow, I mean that was some nightmare. Look at you. You're soaked."

Gabriel was heaving great oxygenating sighs as he struggled to get himself free of the nightmare vision of two Englishwomen lying dead in a pool of blood. Astrid wasn't done with her interrogation.

"Also, why were you shouting about Chechens?"

"OK, look," he said, drying his chest on the duvet cover. "I need to trust someone in this city, and I sense you're not exactly an establishment figure."

She sat straighter, not bothering to cover her breasts, and placed her hands on his shoulders.

"If you're about to tell me you're on the run or something, I'm not interested. And what happened to your voice? You sound different."

Gabriel realised that in the aftermath of the nightmare his voice had lost Terry Fox's East London roughness and resumed his own careful diction.

"I'm not on the run." He paused. How he phrased his next utterance could be the difference between closing in on the Bryants and leaving Tallinn empty-handed. "And I'm not Terry Fox either. I am looking for a mother and daughter from England, though. But they've been kidnapped, by Chechen separatists, and we believe they're here, in Tallinn."

"Really? What are you? Some kind of secret agent? Oh, my God, this is so cool. I mean, like, I'm your way in, aren't I?" She frowned, her brows knitting and her plump lips compressing in a moue of suspicion. "Hey, was all that," she poked his groin through the bedclothes, "just to get information out of me?"

He laughed, her obvious enjoyment of the moment dispelling the last tenebrous shreds of his nightmare. "No, it really wasn't. I think you're very pretty and I wanted to ask you to breakfast. Plus it was you who practically pulled me into bed, or had you forgotten?"

The frown softened, then disappeared, and Astrid smiled. "It's just, you know, a girl's got some self-respect, that's all."

He took her hand and pulled her towards him for a kiss. He stayed close, looking into her eyes. "I could use a friend in Tallinn. I need to find out if anyone knows if there are Chechens operating here. They may still be here, or they may have moved their hostages, but I need to find them, and quickly too."

"I know who would know," Astrid said, getting out of bed and fishing clean underwear out of the top drawer of the dresser. "Yuri."

"You said he's a big Russian player here, when he's not beating up his female employees. Owns half the clubs in Tallinn?"

Astrid nodded. "I heard rumours he runs girls too – you know, prostitutes. Russians and Chechens, they don't get on so well. So you need to get to see Yuri."

Gabriel felt as if he were taking a massive step closer to finding the Bryants. He swung his legs round and got out of bed, dressing and talking at the same time.

"What his surname?"

"Volkov. Talk to Silvi. Maybe she can get you an introduction. After last night, I guess she feels she owes you."

"That's what I'll do, then. I'll ask Silvi. And Astrid?"

"What?"

"Thanks. For the company. For last night. For being so clever. I owe you."

She smiled. "That's OK. You're a good guy. And now . . . Terry . . . if that's even your real name ... you need to go home. I've got stuff to do. But we're still going to see Joonas's band on Sunday, yes?"

Gabriel looked up at her as he tied the laces of his boots.

"My name is Gabriel. And wild horses . . ." he said. As she frowned, he pulled open the door and slipped out into the corridor.

CHAPTER 34

On his one-mile walk to the bar, Gabriel ran through different angles that might lead to a meeting with Yuri Volkov. *I need more shifts. I want to work in a different market – hotels, maybe, or casinos. I'm looking to travel round Russia for a bit and need some work contacts.* The last option was the best – there was no way Silvi could provide that herself. As it turned out, he could have saved himself the effort.

The bar didn't open until seven, and that was really only to provide a few die-hard boozers with their fix and a sandwich. Gabriel arrived at half-past and was heading in to change when Silvi popped out of her office like a punky Jill-in-a-box and waylaid him in the dingy corridor.

"Hey, got a minute?" She crooked her finger at him.

"Sure, Silvi. What can I do you for?" he said, turning and followed her back into her office.

"You'll find out."

Inside, her paper-stuffed quarters were hot and humid, the air smelling of recycled breath and sweat from the bar area beyond her door, combined with a harsh bleachy aroma that made his nose tingle.

She sat on the edge of the big desk, hands planted to each side of her, gripping the edge, feet swinging, four inches clear of the floor.

"I want to thank you for last night," she said. "That bitch would have had my hair out by its roots."

He shrugged. "No big deal. It's what you pay me for, isn't it?"

"Yes. And you're good. You pass your trial. What do they say, 'with flying colours'?"

"Yeah, about that," he said, preparing to ask her about Yuri.

She held up a hand. "And a pay raise, yes? No problem, I was going to offer you one anyway. Twelve Euros instead of ten. It's worth it to keep the place happy so people spend more. There's another thing though."

"What? Don't tell me those stupid Brits filed a complaint with the police."

She laughed and crossed her arms over her chest. "No, I pay the right people. They'd get booted out of Tallinn if they went to the cops." She leaned forward and looked him in the eye. "I said Jonny's is owned by a Russian, yes?"

"Yes. Told me to watch my mouth about him as a matter of fact."

"Yes, well, you should. But anyway, our boss wants to meet you. His name is Yuri Volkov."

Even though the prize had just fallen into his lap, Gabriel didn't want to appear too eager. "Why does he want to meet me?" Gabriel matched her body language, folding his arms and altering his stance to move his feet further apart. He frowned, trying to look suspicious.

"I told him about your . . . performance. How you kicked them out and pulled that bitch off me. He likes to know what's happening in all his clubs. So now he wants to meet you. He told me he might want to move you. Which, obviously, I would be sad about. Astrid, too, from what I hear."

"Fine. I don't mind meeting anyone. When and where?"

Silvi reached behind her and pulled a scrap of paper from the middle of a pile near the PC. "Here. And tonight. You got the evening off till you come back."

"Really?" he said, frowning. "I can't afford to lose the wages, though. I need that dosh."

"It's fine. You're meeting the boss. The big boss. Time off, with pay, all right?"

"Cool. So I'll go now?"

"Sure. You can change when you get back."

* * *

Twenty minutes later, Gabriel was standing outside a grey stone building of six floors at number 205, Viru. It looked like serviced offices. Through the spotless plate glass of the door, he could see a security guard behind a desk watching a small black-and-white monitor. To the left of the door was a brass plate housing a dozen plastic rectangles about half an inch by two, covering printed company names and logos. He pressed the button at the bottom of the plate. The guard looked up and reached under the desk. Gabriel waited for the harsh metallic rattle from the latch and pushed hard on the door.

Once inside, he showed the guard the company name on the paper Silvi had given him, tapping it twice.

"I'm here to see Medved Investments."

The guard held the card close to his eyes, squinting at the tiny, black type, then repeated the name. "Medved. Yes. OK. You stand there."

He levered his frame out of the swivel chair and came round the desk to stand in front of Gabriel, lifted his own arms in a crucifixion position, then nodded at Gabriel. Gabriel raised his arms to shoulder height, straight out. As he did so, locking eyes with the guard, he let his left hand skim the man's side. It ran over a hard, bulky object under the waist of the man's suit jacket. The guard noticed nothing and subjected him to a thorough, and very professional search: chest, stomach, back, armpits, groin, buttocks, thighs, down the shins and calves, check the ankles, run the hands down the arms from shoulder to wrist, finally a thick finger round the inside of the T-shirt neck. Gabriel was impressed. The man's expression never flickered from its impassive stare, the pressure was firm enough to root out the thinnest concealed blade without hurting, and the whole process was over in less than thirty seconds.

"I call Medved," were his only words.

Gabriel stood while the man picked up his phone and punched a couple of buttons. With someone on the other end, the guard rattled off a couple of sentences in thickly accented Russian. Not a Muscovite, Gabriel concluded, but I can still get the gist. *English guy to see you. Small. No threat. Not carrying.*

The guard clicked the receiver back into its cradle and pointed to a narrow-doored lift. "Six floor. They meet you."

When the door slid open on the sixth floor, Gabriel was confronted by two more specimens of what he referred to privately as *Homo sapiens giganticus*. Seemingly constructed rather than grown, these men either were or had been soldiers. Their bearing gave them away. None of the swagger of the amateur bodyguard, none of the flab. Just a quiet confidence and a certain watchfulness in the gaze. Both heads were shaved, revealing a diverse array of lumps, nicks, scars and, visible at the back when the lead man turned, small smudgy tattoos. Soldiers who'd done time – these were Russian prison tats, with their own intricate code for offences, years served, fights won and gang affiliations. Gabriel didn't know the code, but he'd fought against men with similar inking.

He walked between them, feeling like the meat in a very rough and ready sandwich, towards a plain, wooden door. The lead man knocked twice, then opened the door and preceded Gabriel across the threshold. Volkov stood up and came around the desk to greet Gabriel. He motioned the two guards away, and they both left the office, closing the door silently behind them.

"So you are the fearless Fox?" he said, striding across the expanse of cream carpet and grasping Gabriel's hand in his own, then covering it with his other hand and shaking vigorously. "You proved yourself very capable last night, so I hear. Come, sit down."

He gestured for Gabriel to take one of two armchairs facing each other across a low table.

"Would you like a drink? I have excellent vodka, if that isn't too much of a cliché for you?"

"Vodka's fine by me. How come you talk like you grew up in London instead of Moscow? If you don't mind me asking?"

"I am a businessman. You have to learn English to do business, yes? So, I hired a tutor in the US. Very expensive, two hundred dollars an hour."

"Fuck me! I hope you learned the whole language for that kind of money."

Volkov laughed and walked over to a mini-bar with a glass door, selected a bottle with a red-and-gold label, and cracked the seal on the metal cap. He poured a couple of fingers into two cut-glass tumblers, added a fistful of ice cubes, and brought them back to the table where he clanked them down onto the polished wooden surface. Gabriel picked his up, and they clinked and drank.

"So, my friend," Volkov said, "Silvi is my favourite employee. She is like a daughter to me. I owe you a favour for last night. Ask me anything." He smiled, spreading his arm along the back of his chair.

Your favourite? Unlike Astrid, then?

"OK then. Look, I've been asked to do a little bit of freelance private detective work. I got this friend, and his mum and sister have gone missing. He told me they were here, in Tallinn, on holiday. They're not answering calls or texts, not posting on Facebook. Just gone. I only got one thing to go on."

Volkov leaned forward, hands hanging down between his knees. "Tell me, Terry. What can I do to help?"

"I got this tip from an old mate of mine. He works in security for an oil company in the Caucasus. Told me if they was kidnapped, it'd most likely be Chechens. That's their MO, he reckons, taking Western hostages for ransom. So, I was wondering, you're obviously a big man in Tallinn, you must know a few people. Maybe you've heard of something I could use."

Volkov's face had remained expressionless until Gabriel mentioned Chechens. Then his eyes blazed, his nostrils flared, and he glowered at Gabriel, his mouth compressing into a thin line so tight his lips disappeared. Breathing heavily through his nose, he spoke.

"Chechens! They are *tarakany*. Cockroaches. Worse than animals. What they do to innocent Russians, schoolchildren and their teachers, or people going out for the evening. Yes, my friend, we have an infestation here in Tallinn, and I can tell you all about them."

The older man got to his feet and poured two more huge vodkas, added ice and brought the drinks back to the table, and carried on talking.

"There is a gang led by a man called Kasym Drezna."

Gabriel finally had the hard evidence he needed. His hunch was replaced with certainty. A grim smile flitted across his face, to be replaced with a bland stare a second later.

"Funny sort of name," he said.

"No my friend. There is nothing funny about it. Or Drezna. He has three close associates: a woman and two men. They are all veterans of the Chechen wars, and Drezna even fought for us against the Mujahideen. They are running protection rackets, trying to muscle in on my clubs, and they have insulted me personally by ruining a very valuable car."

"No love lost there, then?" Gabriel said.

"Love? Ha! If . . . when . . . I find Drezna, he will learn why nobody who crossed Yuri Volkov still walks the Earth. There is a man you should talk to. His name is Ferdinand Tarvas. He sold them a truck. Maybe they had cargo they needed to transport out of Tallinn. Here . . ." Volkov pulled a sleek, black Mont Blanc fountain pen from his pocket, uncapped it and scribbled a phone number and an address on the back of a stiff cream business card. "Take this. Everybody calls him Ferdy Motors. Phone him and say you're working for me. You'll find he is most willing to cooperate. Maybe you find the registration plate of the truck or a description and we track it, yes? I have a couple of people in the council on my payroll. We can access CCTV records, but I have a strong feeling I know where Drezna and his pack of rats are heading."

Gabriel took a pull on the vodka, feeling the smooth heat all the way from his lips to the pit of his stomach. "Where's that?"

"Drezna bought a scrapyard over in the southeast about a year ago, just after he moved over here. Near a town called Tartu. I've never had it checked out, but now maybe I think we should."

"We?" Gabriel said, putting his tumbler back down. "I'm kind of a solo operator, if you know what I mean. No offence, but I'm not much of a team player these days."

Volkov put his own drink down and smiled, showing a lot of expensively restored teeth – no Russian could have a mouthful as white as that without help from an American dentist. "Listen. You are my employee anyway. You're doing some freelance work for your friend on the side. Fine. Now you can freelance for me, too. Plus I will pay you. Erik and Konstantin will go with you. They are ex-Spetsnaz – you know, Russian Special Forces. I will give you a hundred fifty thousand Euros between the three of you when you bring me proof the Chechens are dead. There! You can be the white knight and rescue your friend's womenfolk, and get rich doing it."

"Sounds like a lot of money just for slotting four people. I've been offered much less than that in my time."

Volkov smiled a humourless smile. The mouth curved up, but the eyes were cold. "I don't doubt it. If they were Russians, or Estonians, I'd give you five thousand euros a head and you'd be grateful to have it. But they aren't Russians or Estonians. They breed them different down there. Savagery from the nursery onwards. Even three against four is not good odds. So take my offer and remember my words while you're earning your money."

"All right, fine. But it's my party, yes? You're the boss of us, but I'm the boss of your boys Erik and Konstantin. Deal?" he said, extending his hand across the table.

Volkov spat into his palm and slapped it into Gabriel's hand. They shook. "Deal," Volkov said, not smiling now. "But remember, the hundred fifty thousand is for proof. Photos can be faked, videos too. You know what I want?"

"I think so. Something in the way of physical evidence, yes?"

Volkov nodded twice, slowly, his eyes never leaving Gabriel's. "Now go. Call Ferdy. Find out about the truck. I will brief Erik and Konstantin and put together a vehicle and some equipment. You are ex-Army, I think?"

"I think you already know that I am," Gabriel said.

"Clever fellow, yes I do. You know your way around weapons. Good. I will be your quartermaster. What do you need?"

Jesus! All that funny business with my "brother" and now I have the Russian mafia offering to go shopping for me anyway.

"You know a word I like, Yuri? Overkill. Can you source three assault rifles? M16s, for choice. And a sniper rifle. Best you can find, please, equipped with a telescopic sight, zeroed for seven hundred and fifty yards. Plus pistols, decent make. Glocks, Berettas, SIGs, something like that. Plenty of ammunition. Maybe add in a few grenades, teargas and smoke. Then we ought to think about explosives. A little bit of *plastique* wouldn't go amiss. That should do it, unless they've got tanks. Mainly what we're going to turn up with is the element of surprise. Oh, and better throw in some night-vision binoculars."

Volkov laughed. "This I like, Terry. You are planning a military campaign. I will have a vehicle fully stocked and ready to go in the car park behind my building this time tomorrow. You have a preference for what you drive?"

"Something fast and anonymous. Maybe a secondhand Volvo estate with a decent motor, something like that. Boring colour, too, dark-blue or green."

"Fine. Consider it done. Now, give me your number and I swap with mine."

After the exchange of numbers, Volkov stood. The interview was over. It couldn't have gone much better. Gabriel had weapons, a couple of seriously experienced Russian veterans in support, a tactical vehicle, a rich, discreet and unscrupulous backer, and, best of all, a solid lead on both the kidnappers' vehicle and their likely destination.

CHAPTER 35

The Chechens had begun allowing Sarah and Chloe to walk, escorted, around the scrapyard and the derelict land beyond the piles of wrecked vehicles and household appliances. They had to take turns: one woman in the morning, one in the afternoon. It was 11.00 a.m., and Sarah's turn for some fresh air and exercise.

"See you later, darling," she said to Chloe, before leaving with Kasym.

Kasym had already given his orders to Dukka, who was "saddled" with guard duty.

"Don't get up to any mischief, Dukka. Just sit and read the paper until we're back. I told Elsbeta and Makhmad to fetch some of those cakes you like from the shops.

That Dukka could read was a fiction the two men maintained between them to save Dukka's face in front of others. In fact, Dukka was quite happy to sit doing nothing but singing old folk songs, or just staring off into space, day-dreaming about the ducks and geese he would raise on the farm he intended to buy once the fighting was over.

* * *

With her mother gone for at least an hour, and only one of the Chechens in the building, Chloe put the plan she'd been formulating into action. First, she took one of the wooden spindles out of the back of the chair in the corner of the cabin she shared with her mother. She'd loosened it the first night they'd stayed at the scrapyard. Wrapping it in a few turns of blanket, she placed it on the floor with one end propped up on a book. With her pillow placed over the entire assembly to act as further sound insulation, she drew her right knee up then stamped down hard on the approximate centre of the spindle. There was a muffled crack.

She bent and unwrapped the bundle, frowning with concentration.

"Yes!" she whispered.

The spindle had fractured, leaving two six-inch-long pieces, each tipped with a dagger-point where the wood had split apart. She selected the piece with the stronger-looking tip and slid it beneath the pillow, which she'd replaced on the bed. The second piece she secreted in her holdall.

Her pulse throbbed uncomfortably in her throat, and her ears filled with a rushing noise as she undid the button on her jeans and pulled them off. Then she took off her sweatshirt. The T-shirt she'd picked to wear that morning had a scooped neck. She tried leaning towards her reflection in the mirror hanging from a nail in the wall and was gratified to see plenty of cleavage.

She heaved a deep breath, let it out again, smiled brightly in the mirror, followed it with what she hoped was a seductive pout, then walked through the door into the kitchen area.

The fat Chechen, whom she had identified as being mentally slow, was sitting at the table, staring at the scrubbed wooden surface. He looked up with a start as Chloe came into the room. Then he grinned, as he took in her lack of clothes. The T-shirt was only just long enough to cover her knickers, leaving her long, coltish legs exposed. She sidled over to him, heart pounding, and nudged his shoulder with her left hip.

"I'm bored," she said.

The Chechen said something in his own language, then reached out a hand and squeezed her buttock. She smiled at him and leaned down to whisper in his ear.

"Why don't you come into my bedroom?"

He clearly caught her meaning, because he nodded rapidly and leered at her, before getting to his feet.

"Two minutes," she said, then smiled again and held up two fingers before tapping her watch.

He nodded again and spoke in English. "Two. Yes. I wait."

With her stomach fluttering, Chloe walked back into her cabin, hoping the dim Chechen would give her enough time. With the door shut she grabbed the sharpened piece of wood and stood with her back pressed against the wall on the hinge side, gripping the makeshift dagger so hard it drove all the blood out of her fingers, leaving her knuckles yellow and waxy. Outside the door she could hear the Chechen pacing up and down. Either he couldn't count or his patience had evaporated, but after just thirty seconds, she saw the door handle move down.

Her breathing was fast and shallow, and she made an effort to slow it down before the excess oxygen made her pass out. The door opened wide as the Chechen squeezed his body through the narrow gap. He had taken off his shirt and was looking down, yanking at his belt buckle. He took a couple more steps and then stopped as he saw the empty bed. Peeping around the edge of the door and staring at his broad, hairy back, Chloe knew she had to time, and aim, her strike to perfection.

A big blood vessel pulsed beneath the skin on the left side of his bull-neck. There! That was the target.

In a single, silent step she closed the distance between her and the Chechen, the makeshift dagger in her fist gripped for a stab.

Time seemed to slow down for her as the sharp point of the spindle descended towards the vein, or artery. She could see individual pulses swelling the thick tube in his neck and imagined the next few moments as a welter of horror-film blood, splashing out and covering her face.

Then there was a shout from the kitchen.

"Dukka!"

The Chechen turned his head towards the sound just as her blow landed. He yelled in pain as the force of the thrust drove the splintered wood an inch deep into the muscles of his neck and whirled around, felling Chloe with a massive backhanded blow before snatching the bloodied wood from his neck.

Kasym burst into the room and restrained his friend before he could kill Chloe, which he was clearly preparing to do.

"Outside, now!" Kasym shouted at him.

Dukka complied, his hand clapped to the wound on his neck, blood leaking out between his stubby fingers.

Sarah rushed into the room behind Kasym, and her mouth dropped open when she took in the sight of her daughter, half-naked, with a spray of blood across the front of her T-shirt.

"Oh, my God darling! What were you thinking?"

"Never mind that," Kasym barked. Then, to Chloe, "Get dressed. No food or water for you for the next twenty-four hours. Try anything like that again and we'll take both your ears off."

He stormed back out of the cabin and slammed the door. The women heard the sound of a key turning in the cheap aluminium lock.

"Oh, Chloe," Sarah exclaimed, as her daughter broke down in sobs and shook in her arms. "That was such a stupid thing to do. He would have raped you. Maybe even killed you."

"I just had to do something, Mum," Chloe said, through the snot and tears. "They're not our friends. I don't think they care if we live or die."

CHAPTER 36

When Gabriel awoke, seven hours had passed. It was midday. Beyond the curtains, the sun was baking Tallinn's pavements, warming the backs of tourists. If they had detoured to an industrial estate north of the Old Town, they would have witnessed two burly men with shaved heads taking a series of canvas-wrapped bundles out of a pickup truck and loading them into the back of a grey estate car. The bundles were long and slim, and tied with green canvas tapes. A red-and-yellow sports bag followed them, bulging with uneven corners and angles where the contents forced the material outwards.

Gabriel shaved and showered, taking his time under the water jets to assess the situation. The disposition of forces was asymmetric, and in the enemy's favour: four to three. Plus, the men Volkov had assigned him were an unknown quantity. They were loyal to Volkov, not to him, and presumably only to Volkov because he was the paymaster. When push came to shove, literally, hired muscle was still hired. That meant it was always available to someone with more money – or power – to offer. They also decreased his chances of mounting an operation by stealth. Counterbalancing these problems, he reflected, having a couple of Special Forces veterans of Russia's many wars and "police actions" would undeniably come in handy if things kicked off with Drezna and his associates.

Then there was the weaponry. They had enough firepower to take out anything short of an armoured vehicle, plus personal equipment including, in Gabriel's case, the KA-BAR, switchblade and knuckleduster. He assumed the two Russians would be similarly well-equipped. However many rounds you start off with in a firefight, there's always a point when the ammunition simply runs out. One moment you're putting down fire, the next you have a very expensive club. At that point, short of fixing bayonets, which Gabriel had once been ordered to do on a jungle mission in Latin America, your next best option was handheld weapons, either issued or improvised. In his last year in the SAS, one of the favourite stories doing the rounds was of a patrol fighting their way out of a house in a remote village in Afghanistan armed with kitchen knives and an iron cooking pot.

Ranged against them were four Chechen separatists. Even allowing for Volkov's visceral hatred for them, his broad assessment was spot on. Chechens weren't exactly known for their timidity in battle. Whether it was a full-on firefight – the smell of burnt cordite and hot brass stinging your nostrils, and the crack-thump of rifle rounds all around you – or the desperate eye-gouging, gut-stabbing, throat-slicing and groin-kicking of hand-to-hand combat, nobody who had seen Chechens in full fury would ever forget it. Gabriel had, and he never would.

Dressed in jeans, T-shirt and windcheater, plus the combat boots, he let himself out of the room, deposited the key with the perpetually smiling receptionist and headed out for some food. Two hundred yards along the street, in the direction off the Old Town, was a café. He'd eaten there once already, and the fat old couple running it had taken an instant liking to him. Today, the woman was running the show, and when he entered, she bustled over, wiping her reddened hands on a flowered and frilled apron, beaming a gap-toothed smile at him.

"Mr Terry! Come, sit," she said in heavily accented English, her voice loud above the chatter of the other customers, the hissing of the Gaggia machine and the intermittent shouting from the kitchen.

She showed him to a table by the window, and he took the seat facing the door. He didn't need a menu. "Beef stew and dumplings like last time, please, Marta," he said in the passable Estonian he'd learned from a phrasebook and a teach-yourself app on his phone. He had no idea where his talent for languages had come from. His parents both spoke Mandarin, Cantonese and English, but he'd not studied languages as a boy, so the rest was down to natural aptitude or a quirk of his DNA. "Some bread too, and a coffee. Large. Thank you."

While he waited for his order, he made a call to Ferdinand Tarvas AKA Ferdy Motors. The ringing phone at the other end sounded a long way away, though Gabriel knew his quarry had business premises right here in Tallinn. Just a street or two away from Jonny Rocketz, as it happened. He held on, half-expecting to get voicemail. What would it say? *Hi, this is Ferdy Motors. I'm out nicking a getaway car for the Russian Mafia at the moment, but if you leave your name and number and a brief description of the knocked-off wheels you want, I'll get back to you?*

"Hello?" The speaker managed to pack enough suspicion into those two everyday syllables to fuel a whole police station. He'd clearly had been engaged in a lifelong love affair with high-tar cigarettes.

"Hi. That Ferdy?" Gabriel stuck to Estonian.

"Who wants to know?"

"Terry Fox. Yuri told you I wanted a word?"

"Oh, yes, OK. Can you come here this afternoon?"

"Fine. I'm not far. I'll be there about two o'clock."

The phone clicked. Ferdy had hung up. His timing was unwittingly excellent: Marta approached, bearing a shallow, steaming bowl. She squeezed her elephantine hips between two chairs, knocking each diner forwards into their respective tables, and placed the food in front of Gabriel with a mother's twinkle in her eye.

"Eat!" she said. "You are too much skinny." She pinched his cheek as she put his mug of coffee next to the plate before swinging around and heading back towards the kitchen.

The stew was delicious: earthy, garlicky and gamey, with a

generous dollop of red wine in the gravy. The dumplings were the approximate size and shape of cricket balls, chewy but not dense, and flavoured with herbs. Gabriel worked on his meal, washing down the heavy food with mouthfuls of the hot coffee. Every now and then, he'd flick his gaze to different points around the room, but there was no threat. It was a homely place full of office workers, builders and tourists filling their bellies before an afternoon of paper-pushing, wall-building or pavement-pounding. He felt sure he was the only person stoking the fires in preparation for a hostage rescue mission in the east of the country.

He signalled Marta for the bill, which came to sixteen euros, left a twenty-euro note under his empty mug, and headed out. Ferdy Motors was a ten-minute walk away.

He found the place easily enough; it was on a street he'd walked down on his way home from Jonny Rocketz. He pushed the button by the door and waited. The interlude was lightning-fast compared to the wait before Ferdy had answered his phone. Any friend of Yuri's . . . Gabriel thought, as bolts scraped on the other side of the door.

The man facing Gabriel was about his height, but carrying an additional twenty or thirty pounds, mostly around his middle. His sallow complexion was pockmarked from childhood acne and his nose had been recently broken, to judge from his black eyes and the crude bandaging and sticking plaster in the centre of his face.

"This way," he lisped.

Gabriel followed Ferdy down a narrow gap between a couple of dark-grey Škoda estates, their windows blacked out on the sides and back. In the centre of the yard, a heavyset boy of maybe sixteen or seventeen was kneeling by an old Jaguar saloon, one of the big V12 executive models, welding a steel plate onto the moth-eaten rear wheel arch, which had been ground back to the bare metal. Or appearing to. He didn't have a welding rod in his hand and was just going through the motions. A crowbar lay by his side. Gabriel ignored him. He hadn't come to cause trouble, and if having a wingman, even a skinny adolescent like this one, made Ferdy more comfortable, that could work for both of them.

Ferdy turned to face Gabriel, thumbs hooked into his jeans pockets. "Yuri said to give you information. Ask what you want, I have nothing to hide."

"You sold a ride – a truck. Who to?" Gabriel already knew the answer but he wanted to gauge how much he could trust Ferdy Motors.

Ferdy's eyes flicked up and to the right – a sure sign a lie was coming, according to an FBI interrogator Gabriel had once sat next to on a flight. "A man called Kasym Drezna. A Chechen."

Good for you, Ferdy, you told the truth. That's going to make this a much shorter and more pleasant conversation. "You know what he wanted it for?"

"He didn't say." The eyes flickered towards the roof again.

"You sure about that? Not even a hint or a little joke?"

Ferdy looked down, then back at Gabriel. "You're making me write my own suicide note. If Kasym finds out I talked to you, he'll kill me. Or worse, set that deranged bitch onto me."

"And if you don't talk to me, guess what? Yuri's going to kill you. The difference is, Kasym might never find out you talked. Yuri definitely will if you don't."

Ferdy sighed. He'd been outmanoeuvred, outgunned and outplayed. "Fine. But I beg you, if Kasym finds out? Come back here and kill me yourself. With a bullet. It will be a mercy. He told me he had some cargo to transport. That's one of his code words. When he's moving people about – you know, girls, migrants . . . bodies – he calls them 'cargo'."

"There, that wasn't too hard, was it? Next question. I need an ID on the truck. Make, model, colour, registration plate."

Ferdy's eyes flashed in surprise for a split second. "Registration? What do you think this is, Avis? Truck didn't have no plates. Kasym probably went out and ripped off a set from some commuter here in Tallinn, or had some he brought in from that bastard country he calls home."

"All right, then, just the vehicle details."

"Brown. Volkswagen. Three-tonne."

"That's it? No other details I can use?"

Ferdy's eyes did their up-down and sideways dance again. "Oh Jesus, he'll make me eat my own cock. On the roof. He never checked. It has a big Kodak advertisement stuck on there. A woman in a bikini holding a camera. It was old, from a factory. I didn't have time to get it off, some stupid fucking superglue shit they must have used."

Gabriel leaned forward and patted Ferdy on the shoulder, noticing as he did so how the boy with the welding rig stood up and took half a pace towards him.

"Thanks Ferdy, you're a star. We'll just have to hope Drezna doesn't figure who ratted him out, won't we?" Then he snapped round to face the boy, who had turned the control knob on the torch to extend the jet into a roaring blue and violet spear-point of flame. "Watch yourself with that," he said. "You could give yourself a nasty burn."

Then he was gone, back between the Škodas, through the steel door and out into the sunshine. He had a few hours until he needed to be back at Volkov's office building. He didn't feel like sightseeing and apart from Astrid, he didn't know anyone in Tallinn he'd care to spend time with. But there *were* people he cared about, and who cared about him. He made his way to Toom Park, to the west of the Old Town, and a body of water called Snelli Pond. The sun was still out, and he found a quiet spot in the shade of a lime tree and sat with his back to the trunk. The grass was dotted with picnickers and students sitting in groups of five or six, strumming acoustic guitars or working on laptops, and there was a noisy group of winos way over to the south of him, but he had the tree and its immediate environs to himself.

He called Don.

"What news, Old Sport?"

"They're in a brown, three-tonne, VW panel van. It's an old Kodak delivery truck, I think. There's a girl in a bikini on the roof."

"A real one?"

Gabriel smiled. "A photo. And I think they're heading for a scrapyard in Tartu."

"OK, that's fantastic. I'll relay it to our eyes in the sky. See if they can't pick it up. We've got thermal imaging off a US satellite coming down the pipe in an hour or so. I'll call you with login details."

"Thanks. I'll call you if there's anything new."

He ended the call then scrolled through his contacts list to F, and tapped the first name in the list.

CHAPTER 37

"Hey you! How are you? And where are you?" Britta said.

"I'm good. I'm in Tallinn. I thought I was going to be blowing through Stockholm. I was going to look you up."

"You wouldn't have found me. I'm still in the UK. That temporary job I had with our friends in London? They've asked me to stay on for another six months."

Gabriel knew Britta was talking about her extended secondment to MI5 from Swedish Special Forces, and was enjoying their little game of 'disguise the spook talk'.

"So they liked your style with our little adventure in Wiltshire, then?"

"I got a commendation, as a matter of fact. Had to go to this fancy ceremony. I needed to get my dress uniform couriered over from Stockholm. What are you up to in Tallinn?"

"I'm doing my Sir Lancelot act – rescuing two damsels in distress. How about you. What are you up to?"

"Animal rights. I've joined an offshoot of PETA. You know them?"

"People for Eating Tasty Animals?"

Britta laughed, thrilling Gabriel even over the hundreds of miles that separated them. "*Ja, det är korrekt!*" she said, lapsing into Swedish, then laughing again. "Or maybe People for the Ethical Treatment of Animals."

"Eating animals can be ethical, if you cook them properly."

"Stop it, Wolfe, you're impossible. Anyway, so I am getting to know the guy in charge. He says animals have the same rights as humans only more because they haven't fucked up the planet."

Suddenly, Gabriel knew she was sleeping with the leader of the splinter group. Because that's what he'd ask her to do if he was running the mission. What he was doing with Astrid. Pillow talk: the oldest form of espionage in the world. And he felt a tightening in his stomach.

"If you get time off from saving the planet, do you fancy getting together when I'm back? Dinner or something. I could come to you this time."

"I would love that. I can return the favour. I'll be ready for a big, juicy steak too, I tell you. They eat so many beans they've turned farting into an Olympic sport."

"Jesus, Falskog, you Swedes and your humour. Not very ladylike, is it?"

"No, it is not! And nor is rifle-shooting, but I do that too when needed, remember?"

"Good point. I'll call you, then. When I'm back."

Gabriel got to his feet and headed across the park back to the hotel, texting Volkov with the details of the truck's unusual roof decoration. He needed to collect his gear then get over to Volkov's building to pick up the car. Why was it that he didn't see Britta Falskog for months, maybe even years, at a time, and then when he did, he felt such a pull towards her deep in the pit of his stomach? And why the jealousy? He'd been sleeping with Annie Frears for a couple of months when they were both free and in the mood, and hadn't he let Astrid seduce him – there was no other word for it – the other night? He couldn't formulate an answer that didn't make him sound like a hypocrite, even in this internal dialogue, so he decided to leave it alone. For now.

CHAPTER 38

"Hey, Ivar. Nice new car I saw you arrive in this morning," Eva Kallas said to her colleague in the Tallinn Police traffic monitoring and control department.

The pudgy, fortyish man smiled and touched his bald spot as he answered.

"It is nice, isn't it? Maybe you'd like to come for a drive some time."

She touched her throat and blushed.

"Maybe I would. What are you up to?"

"Reviewing some footage from yesterday. Some big guy in CID is hot on the trail of some villain or other. You know, usual story."

He turned back to his work. He didn't want to cut Eva off; she was nice, always had a smile for him and sometimes brought him homemade cakes. But his client, who'd called him moments earlier, had been most insistent that he needed confirmation on the target vehicle immediately. And although he wasn't in CID, he knew plenty about criminal investigations. He'd also paid for Ivar's new, well, nearly new, BMW 3 Series.

Ivar set the playback to fast-forward, running the digital video at sixteen times normal speed. He had feeds from cameras on all four of the main routes out of Tallinn tiled on his screen: the E20 heading east towards Rakvere; the E263, southeast towards Tartu; the E67, southwest to Pärnu; and the E265, west to Paldiski.

His practised eye darted from one quadrant to the next in a random sequence. It helped that he had a detailed description of the vehicle he was looking for, and after all, there couldn't be that many three-tonne trucks leaving Tallinn with a ten-foot, bikini-clad babe reclining on the roof, now could there?

Eva delivered a coffee to his desk after thirty minutes but Ivar was too engrossed in his work to do more than grunt his thanks.

Then, just as his eyes were beginning to tire, and a break would be necessary, he spotted it. Unmistakable.

"Yes!" he shouted. Then he looked around in embarrassment. Jubilation was more of a squad-room kind of emotion, after a big collar. It was certainly not experienced in the library-like quiet of the CCTV monitoring room. Once his colleagues had turned back to their own screens, he grabbed a screenshot of the target vehicle and emailed it to his client along with a short message:

Miss Estonia was travelling on the E263 – towards Tartu.

CHAPTER 39

Gabriel packed a bag with a change of clothes, toothbrush and razor, then laid out his personal weapons and, one by one, packed them amongst his clothes.

The KA-BAR, which had come complete with its original tan leather sheath, he rolled inside a spare pair of jeans. He stuffed the knuckleduster into a pair of socks. The switchblade went into a jacket pocket. That left the SIG Sauer. The magazine was full, the chamber empty. He screwed on the suppressor and put the remaining rounds in their boxes in a nylon rucksack he'd bought in one of the many down-at-heel general stores that lined the back streets of Tallinn.

He considered sticking the pistol into the back of his waistband, then changed his mind and buried it in his bag. He still remembered fondly the story told by a grizzled former sergeant of his. "Tiny" Tim McDonagh, an eighteen-stone, six-foot-five Glasgow protestant, had been on a tour of duty in Belfast in the late 1990s. He'd walked into a supermarket in a staunchly Catholic part of Belfast to buy beer and crisps for a boys' night in with a few videos, wearing civilian clothes and carrying a concealed sidearm under a tweed overcoat.

"Aye, so I'm walkin up and down the aisles choosing the scran, you know? And I'm gettin the funny look left right and fuckin centre. So I get to the checkout and when I reach to get ma wallet from my back pocket, I realise what the problem is. Ma coat's hooked up over the fuckin pistol. I was walkin roond Sainsbury's like Jesse-Fuckin-James!"

The far-off laughter in the Sergeants' Mess echoed down through the years as he left the hotel.

Gabriel flagged down a minicab within seconds of exiting the lobby. He immediately wrinkled his nose as the combined aromas of artificial pine and rancid, spice-tainted sweat assailed his nostrils. He sat back and stared out of the window as the car dipped and swerved through the late afternoon traffic. Leaving the Old Town, the architecture lost its distinctive character and blurred into a boring mixture of steel, glass and concrete. Arabic pop music crackled from the tinny speakers in the front of the cab as the driver – a migrant or refugee from some war-torn state in the Middle East – jousted with other vehicles to gain a few yards here and there. He clearly took the same approach to personal hygiene as he did to lane discipline, and the tree-shaped air freshener swinging from the rear-view mirror had no chance.

The same guard was on duty at Volkov's building, but he didn't bother frisking Gabriel this time. *Orders from Volkov, probably, but you missed out on the search of the century, my friend.* Instead he picked up the desk phone and called Volkov. He glanced up at Gabriel a couple of times and nodded, then replaced the receiver.

"You wait. He come," the guard said, turning back to his monitor and impressing Gabriel with his combination of taciturnity, disdain and signal-to-noise ratio.

"Sure," Gabriel said, slipping into Terry Fox's laid-back style and smiling broadly. "I wait, Yuri comes. And you sit on your arse, you lazy bastard, eh?"

Five minutes passed. Then the lift doors opened, and Volkov strode out to greet Gabriel, hand extended, white teeth showing. Erik and Konstantin came out after him, both dressed in jeans and T-shirts that revealed their thickly muscled arms.

"Ready for a little drive up country, my friend? Come, I'll show you what I've assembled for your hunting trip."

Gabriel followed Volkov through a service door beyond the reception area. Whatever attention the architects and interior designers had felt it necessary to lavish on the public areas of the building, it was immediately clear that their eye for detail had closed here. The corridor was little more than a concrete tunnel, lit with the cheapest industrial strip-lights. Cracked and peeling white gloss paint covered the walls. With Erik and Konstantin close behind, they made their way past a trio of scuffed grey plastic rubbish bins to another door. This one had a steel push-bar across it. Volkov struck it with the heels of both hands and it swung open and back on itself to hit the outer wall with a rattle and a clang.

They were in a car park. Waiting for them directly in front of the security door was a brand new Mercedes estate. It was a dark, metallic grey – gunmetal – and all the windows apart from the windscreen were blacked out. The car sat low on massive alloy wheels, through which Gabriel could see bright-red brake callipers. As they rounded the back of the car, the chrome badging told the full story: E63 S on the left, AMG on the right. A 5.5-litre V8 engine, hand-built by a single engineer so proud of his – or her – work that they signed their name on it. Or, to put it another way, a way Terry Fox would probably use, "a fuck of a fast motor".

"You like it?" Volkov said, thumbing the boot release button on the black plastic key fob and standing back as the tailgate swung open to the whirr of electric motors.

"I love it. But it's not quite as anonymous as I was thinking."

"It's grey! How much more anonymous can you get?"

"Good job I didn't ask you for anything flash, then, isn't it?"

Volkov laughed and clapped Gabriel on the back. "You English. Always so worried about what other people think. It doesn't matter. You have my best two men with you. And listen, my man in the Police Department reviewed the CCTV tapes. Those *tarakany* were headed towards Tartu. You go after them, you squash them, you rescue your friend's women, you come back, you collect your money. Everybody's happy."

Gabriel stowed his gear in the boot to the side of the canvas-wrapped bundles.

"You get everything I asked for, then?" he asked Volkov.

"Of course. Three M16s, three hundred rounds apiece. One Dragunov sniper rifle, with telescopic sight, one hundred rounds. Three Glock 19 semi-automatic pistols, one-fifty rounds apiece. You have twenty grenades: half teargas, half smoke. And a kilo of C-4 with wiring kit, timers and detonators, including a couple of radio-controlled units."

"That ought to do it. So I reckon we get to Tartu, scope out the local scrappies . . ."

Volkov frowned. "Scrappies?"

"Sorry, scrapyards. Anyway, we track the Chechens to whichever one is theirs, go in hot and heavy, get the women and then get out. Your boys Erik and Konstantin, they on board taking orders from a Brit?"

Volkov turned to the two big men and asked, in Russian, "The little man wants to know if you will do what he orders?"

All three men laughed and then Konstantin, taller and broader than Erik, answered. "As long as he's ordering your orders, we're happy if he thinks he's in charge."

Volkov turned round to face Gabriel again. "They're fine."

I bet they are. The question is, what exactly are your orders?

"Good," Gabriel said. "We'd better be going then. Got a lot of driving ahead of us."

"On you go then, my friend. I wish you success. We will share some good vodka when you return with your friend's womenfolk, yes?"

Gabriel climbed into the big German estate's driver's seat, breathed in the new-car smell – all leather conditioner and chemically treated airflow – pushed the key fob into its receiving slot, and thumbed the starter button set into the top of the gear selector. The big V8 didn't so much erupt into life as come out of hibernation like a bear. All the aggression and power was there, on tap, but the car had no need to shout about it the moment it woke up. Instead the combined engine and exhaust notes formed a drowsy grumble just audible inside the cabin. Gabriel adjusted the little chromed levers in the shape of a seat until he was comfortable. Konstantin squeezed his bulky frame in beside him, knocking his right elbow as he clicked his seatbelt home. Erik took the backseat, filling most of it. Gabriel buzzed his seat forward a few inches to alleviate the pressure where the big Russian's knee was jammed into the back of his seat.

Next stop, Tartu.

* * *

Getting out of Tallinn at six o'clock in the evening was not the smooth journey Gabriel had hoped for. Within minutes of leaving Volkov's car park, they were mired in traffic, most of which consisted of cars fitted with weapons-grade air horns. That was the impression created by the sonic assault that belaboured Gabriel's ears the one time he tried driving with his window down. Estonians were obviously as in love with driving – and as fond of improvising road rules – as their counterparts further to the south in Italy, Rome in particular. Using your indicators was clearly viewed by most of the drivers they shared the roads with as an optional extra, like air-con or iPod connectivity.

Gabriel swung the Merc from lane to lane, spotting gaps and diving into them. The size and power of the car, coupled with the three-pointed star on the bonnet and those chromed letters and numbers on the tailgate, guaranteed him a measure of respect from other drivers. At one set of traffic lights, as he cruised to a stop on the inside of a two-lane stretch of highway, an old, matt-black Toyota Celica coupe drew alongside and blared its air horns. Gabriel looked to his left to see a kid of eighteen or nineteen, grinning wildly at him, exposing his teeth, and pointing forwards with a finger-wagging gesture.

He, the kid, raised his eyebrows at Gabriel. The meaning was clear. Gabriel took in the sticker under the passenger-side window. *Nitrous . . . is a Gas!!!* it read in an acid-green, vaporous typeface. He smiled and shook his head. However, he blipped the throttle a couple of times just to wind the boy racer up. The sound of the German V8 built from a muted throb to a hard-edged roar. Konstantin scowled and muttered about "fucking children", but did nothing else. The kid answered by gunning his own engine. The standard Celica was equipped with a one-point-eight-litre petrol engine – nothing much in the world of high-performance cars. But the kid had obviously been busy tuning his. Gabriel thought he detected the whistle of an aftermarket turbocharger as the Japanese car's revs built to a scream. The big-bore exhaust bellowed then subsided as the kid took his foot off, and the dump valve for the turbocharger huffed out a great breath of unused pressurised air.

The lights turned from red to amber. With a squeal from the rear tyres, the kid was away, leaving two black smears on the road behind him and a drifting cloud of blue smoke. He slewed wildly left to right and back again as the power at the back wheels threatened to overwhelm the steering. Gabriel pulled away smoothly, catching a whiff of burnt rubber even through the Merc's sophisticated air-filtering system.

Half an hour later, the architecture around them changed from classical municipal to contemporary business, and then to who-gives-a-fuck suburban. The city, and the traffic, had thinned out, and finally they reached the E263, which would take them all the way to Tartu. Gabriel flexed his right foot and the Mercedes surged ahead, the acceleration pushing back into the welcoming embrace of the padded and bolstered driving seat. He took it up to ninety-five kilometres per hour and then sat there, watching the road unfold ahead of him in a series of cresting hills and long, swooping curves through the Estonian countryside.

Now they had left the city behind, the traffic had all but disappeared. Konstantin nudged him and jerked his chin towards the open stretch of motorway ahead.

"Faster," he said, in unaccented English.

"Faster?" Gabriel said, keeping his eyes on the road. "All right, Konnie me old mate. You want faster. We'll do faster."

Gabriel stamped down on the throttle pedal, burying it in the thick carpet lining the footwell. The car seemed to hunker down on its haunches for a split second as transmission, engine and steering spoke to each other in a stream of ones and zeroes through the performance control chips. Gabriel could just discern the whine of the two turbochargers as they spooled up, shoving massive amounts of fuel and air into the eight sucking cylinders. But something was wrong. He'd been expecting to get kicked in the back as the Merc's five hundred and fifty-seven horses galloped off towards the horizon, with him hanging onto the reins. Instead, the acceleration, while still impressive, felt subdued somehow.

He held the car at around a hundred and eighty for thirty seconds or so, flicking his eyes upwards to the rear-view mirror and then in front, scanning the horizon for lorries, caravans and, especially, red lights. He had no doubt that the car's brakes were burly enough to cope if he needed to scrub seventy or eighty kilometres an hour off the speed, but he preferred not to attract the wrong sort of attention. These days any indiscretion was likely to end up on YouTube or Facebook way before it ever made it onto a speed camera or police patrol car's dash-cam. Despite the high cruising speed, the interior of the car was sepulchrally quiet, hardly the point of a big engine in Gabriel's opinion, thinking about the yowling cry of his Maserati's power plant under full throttle. But that was the difference between the Italians and the Germans. Flamboyance versus efficiency; "look at me" versus "nothing to see".

Ahead, as the road curved gracefully round to the right and began a long incline, Gabriel could see a couple of container trucks labouring up the hill, dirty puffs of smoke jetting from the upright exhaust pipes mounted directly behind the tractor units. He pulled out to overtake, crossing the white line, and found himself racing at roughly double the speed limit towards an oncoming camper van just a few hundred yards away. The pair of lorries turned out to be a trio; the foremost of the big rigs had been completely hidden by the other two. He had two choices: slam the brakes on and scooch in behind the trailing truck; or put his foot down and chase the gap ahead of the leader.

He looked down.

Konstantin's left hand was gripping the front of the armrest between them.

The knuckles were whitened and bloodless.

The man's face was set in a grim, lipless stare.

His right leg was straining as he pushed his foot down where the brake pedal would be if he were behind the wheel.

Gabriel chose.

As he put his foot down, the E63's engine management computer sensed his intentions and swapped cogs somewhere beneath his right thigh, dropping down two gears. The engine and exhaust notes, finally, broke into wild and unconstrained song as the big estate surged forward. The white speedometer needle swept round the dial to the 265 kph mark, way over into the final quarter of the indicated range and about 160 mph in English money.

Ahead, the camper van was flashing its headlights in hysterical Morse code. The meaning was clear. *Get back! Get over! You're going to kill us all!*

To his right, Konstantin was breathing heavily through his nose and behind him he could hear Erik swearing, a continuous stream of the most obscene Russian cursing he had ever heard.

The distance between the Mercedes and the oncoming camper van was telescoping under their combined closing speed of somewhere around 240 miles an hour. To his right, the leading truck's cab came into view. Out of the corner of his eye he could see a fist being waved at him.

He drew ahead and flicked the steering wheel to the right.

The car fought to keep running in a straight line, as the laws of physics dictated it should want to. But the German engineers were as efficient at designing steering systems as they were engines and transmissions. The car obeyed Gabriel's will and pulled ahead of the truck and its sonorous air horns.

The camper van flew past on his left with a Doppler-shifting blast of its air horns.

The road ahead was empty. Konstantin resumed his normal rate of breathing and his fingers unclenched from the armrest, which bore four deep dents in its white-stitched leather upholstery.

Erik's swearing descended from the frenzied peak of inventively violent oaths to a subterranean mutter before stopping altogether.

Gabriel lifted his right foot and let the car resume its steady southeastwards progress at a more stately, though far from slouch-like, ninety. Now the excitement was over, he felt the backs of his knees aching with adrenaline and his right leg began trembling as the knotted muscles discharged their unspent energy.

After another two hours of driving, the first sign for Tartu appeared. Ten miles further on, the exit sign glowed electric blue in the late evening sunshine streaming right to left across the carriageway. Beyond the sign, silver birches planted in profusion along the grass verge flared white, their leaves translucent in the slanting sun. Gabriel dabbed the brakes and signalled to pull off the motorway.

Following signs for the town centre, it took a little over fifteen minutes to find a hotel. He drove round the block to the underground car park, located a secluded space in the furthest corner from the entry ramp, and killed the engine. All three men left the car at the same time, stretching and bending before gathering at the tailgate.

"We go in, we get rooms," Gabriel said. "Get yourselves dinner. I'm having room service. Tomorrow morning, we have to find Drezna's scrapyard. I'm going to find out how many there are here. Shouldn't be more than a couple."

The Russians nodded. Either they understood enough English to follow his simple instructions, or Volkov's own instructions were to nod whenever the Englishman said anything, then carry on regardless. Gabriel decided to test them.

"You both understand all that, yeah?"

They both nodded, faces revealing nothing of their thoughts.

"Erik. What are we doing now?"

"Now? Get dinner."

"Good lad. Konstantin, your starter for ten. What do we do tomorrow?"

"Find scrapyard. And kill Chechens."

"Yeah, well, let's start with finding the scrapyard."

Gabriel was about to lock the car and was pointing the key fob at the rear window when Konstantin put a hand on his outstretched forearm.

"Wait. The guns. Not good idea leaving them in car."

"What, so you want to check in carrying a fucking arsenal under your arm, do you? 'Here, I say, Comrade Hotel Porter, do you mind lugging this sniper rifle up to my room for me?' I don't think so. They're disguised. This is a secure underground car park. And this fucking Panzer has got better security than Yuri's office. The guns stay here." *I don't know about you, boys, but my own personal weapons are all coming to bed with me.*

Konstantin glared at Gabriel, who noticed with interest how the Russian's biceps were flexing. Not saying anything, but holding the bigger man's gaze, Gabriel let the seconds tick on. To his left Erik seemed content to let Konstantin make the call for both of them. A follower by temperament, if not by position in the pecking order. Konstantin hung on for a count of nine, then glanced away.

"Let's go. I'm starving," Gabriel said. *No need to rub it in.*

Once inside his room, Gabriel placed his bag on the folding rack provided by the hotel and sat on the bed to unlace his boots. His stomach growled, reminding him he hadn't eaten. A call to room service for a burger and fries and a beer sorted that simple problem, then he went into the bathroom, a modular construction seemingly moulded from a single piece of slightly sandy-feeling, off-white plastic, and turned the shower to hot.

He stripped off his clothes, folded and placed them on a chair and stepped under the scalding water. With the back of his head, his neck and his shoulders heated to burning point, he stared at the floor and let rivulets of water course over him, running from the end of his nose, his eyebrows and his fingertips.

After his shower, he put on the white, towelling robe hanging on the back of the bathroom door, and sat on his bed to make a call.

Don picked up on the second ring.

"I'm in Tartu," Gabriel said. "You know I said Drezna has a scrapyard here? I got the lead through a guy called Yuri Volkov. He's your basic Russia mafia, owns clubs, bars – including the one where I was working – runs prostitutes, the works. And he's not a big fan of Chechens."

"Par for the course. I'd say the antipathy is equally intense whichever way round you look it. What else?"

"He's fitted out an AMG Merc estate like an Apache. We have M16s, a Dragunov, Glocks, grenades, C-4 and more ammunition than we'd need to take out an army. And he's billeted a couple of his men on me. They're like a couple of pumped-up undertakers only without the happy-go-lucky demeanour."

"Still, they could come in handy, eh? Even up the odds a little more in your favour?"

Gabriel ran his fingers through his hair, pushing it up into short, black spikes. "True. Although we're a long way from nine to one."

He was referring to the ratio of "us" to "them" favoured by the SAS, a tripling of the balance of forces deemed acceptable in the general Army.

"You have the element of surprise working for you, remember that. Any chance you'll get them out by stealth? There's an order from on high that you can use lethal force, but it's always good to keep the claret to a minimum on friendly soil. I don't want to be hauled in for a tongue-lashing by the Estonian Ambassador."

Gabriel shrugged. "Too early to say. But a scrapyard? I'm thinking dog, or dogs plural, loud rusty gates, razor wire, Christ knows what additional security if it's a holding pen for kidnap victims. I'll do my best."

"I know you will. But the women's lives are your prime and main goal. Anyone gets between you and them, you deliver the Queen's message."

"Understood. My only challenge at this point is pinpointing the scrapyard itself. I'm going to do some research after this and identify how many there are here. Volkov was vague on the details."

"Which is where I can save you some time and effort."

"What do you mean?"

"I had my usual email update this morning from my oppo in Langley. One of their spy planes picked up what she called 'an anomalous mobile signature' in a routine sweep over the Baltics. Some bright spark has been transmitting a military-strength GPS ping every fifteen seconds from a smartphone. No chip apparently, just a signal booster of some kind. Nothing a regular app would ever do. Anyway, this little nugget has been stuck in the bowels of CIA HQ because nobody could find a connection that mattered. Well, it's got one now. We have the coordinates for a location in southeast Estonia. Tartu."

"That's the best piece of news I've had since I arrived in Tallinn." Gabriel leaned over to the side table and grabbed the pocket-sized pad of notepaper and branded pen left there by the hotel. "OK, go ahead."

While Don gave him the precious string of digits, then repeated it, Gabriel wrote neat, upright numbers in a line across the page. He repeated them back to Don.

"That's it," Don said. "Now all you need to do is get tooled up and get our girls out of there. Shouldn't be too difficult."

Gabriel smiled at his former CO's laconic sense of humour. "Walk in the park, Boss." *If only.*

They signed off after this exchange, with a promise from Gabriel to report in as soon as he had the Bryant women safe, or if he had less welcome news. Gabriel launched a geo-location app on his phone and keyed in the map reference. As he watched the screen redraw itself, zooming in from a point somewhere out in the stratosphere to Estonia, then the southeast of the country, then Tartu itself, there was a knock at the door and a call.

"Room service."

He let the uniformed man in, watched in silence as he placed the tray on the low table, then tipped him a couple of Euros and waited for him to leave the room.

The burger, contrary to expectations, was excellent. Dense, lean meat with just enough fat to enhance rather than smother the flavour, white onions fried to crisp brown shreds, and a spicy relish, rich in paprika, spilling out the sides where Gabriel could collect it on the fries. He washed the food down with long draughts of the cold, gassy lager.

As he ate, he looked at the screen of his phone. Now he had a location for the search and rescue. But although the display could tell him a little about the layout of the terrain and the surrounding network of roads, the real intelligence-gathering was still to come. It was clear that they'd have to leave the Merc in Tartu and tab out to the scrapyard cross-country. There was only one road that led from town to the scrapyard, and they couldn't risk being seen making a direct approach. And despite Volkov's jibes about the English love of discretion, Gabriel remained unconvinced that a brand-new, steroidal Mercedes muscle car with a crew of three fit-looking ex-Special Forces soldiers packing assault weapons was exactly unobtrusive.

CHAPTER 40

In the hotel restaurant the following morning, Gabriel and the two Russians didn't stand out as much as he'd feared. They'd all dressed in the same outfit of dark chinos and sweatshirts or hoodies, with high combat boots covered by their trousers. Seven-thirty was obviously the preferred time for the corporate-type guests to be up and doing. Nearly every table was occupied by small groups of men dressed in dark suits, their shirts open at the neck, ties left in rooms to be knotted and cinched into place before the real work began. For now, though, they lined up along the buffet, loading plates with sausages, limp rashers of bacon, grilled tomatoes, and rubbery mountains of scrambled eggs. It was easy to spot the Germans – they always began with a plate of cold meat and cheese.

The room was noisy. Perhaps fearing that the combined bantering and laughter of seventy or eighty engineers, salesmen and management consultants wouldn't be sufficient to create the correct atmosphere, the manager had piped soft-rock through speakers let into the ceiling and screwed to the walls. Combined with the noise of clattering plates, stainless steel serving spoons clanking on dishes, hissing coffee machines and the occasional dropped plate, it served as an effective mask for any conversation containing sensitive information, whether details of a business deal or a paramilitary search-and-rescue mission.

They sat at a corner table, Gabriel having rejected, politely, the table in the centre of the room offered to them by the young Italian hostess. The two Russians sat facing him, working through pyramids of eggs, bacon, grilled tomatoes, hash browns and sausages. Each man had also loaded a side plate with pastries, dinky replicas of full-sized croissants and cinnamon buns. As they pushed the food into their mouths, cheeks bulging as they chewed, he pushed hand-drawn maps of the route from the hotel to the scrapyard towards each man.

"This is where the Chechens are. It's a scrapyard. We go over there very quiet, understand?"

Both men nodded, without raising their eyes from their food.

"On foot."

The men nodded again, chewing rhythmically.

"Split up. Take one side each. North, east, west," he said, pointing first at his own chest, then at Erik, then at Konstantin. "Leave the south – not enough cover from the road side. Observe and make notes. Get back here by eighteen hundred hours. OK?"

Another synchronised nod.

"Erik. Tell me the plan."

Erik put his knife and fork down, finished chewing a huge mouthful of sausage and egg, wiped his mouth with the back of his hand, then spoke.

"We go to scrapyard. Quiet. No car, too much flash. I take east, Konstantin takes west, *zaichik* takes north." Konstantin sniggered at the Russian word, then Erik continued. "Gather intelligence. Meet at hotel at six. *Da?*"

"*Da*. Very good. So what did you call me, then? Zy-what?"

"*Zaichik*. Means 'big boss' in Russian," Erik said, to another snort of laughter from Konstantin.

Gabriel nodded, signalling his approval. So you think I'm a little hare do you? Just remember two things about hares then, tovarishch. They're fast. And they're excellent boxers.

Back in his room after breakfast, Gabriel spread the map of Tartu out on the bed. He found the scrapyard easily enough, tracing his finger along the main access road. Then he spotted something potentially far more useful. Curving around from the southeast was a road marked "Military – disused". It left the E263 and continued for half a mile with no junctions all the way to the perimeter fence.

Happy with his initial intelligence on the scrapyard, Gabriel moved to his weapons. The six-and-a-half-inch-long suppressor made the gun less easy to conceal, but the advantages of the device were overwhelming. He unscrewed it from the SIG's barrel and slipped it into a trouser pocket, covered by a flap closed with a press-stud. Then he selected another thirty rounds from one of the boxes and zipped them, clinking quietly, into the right hand pocket of his windcheater.

Firearm sorted, he strapped the switchblade around his right ankle with tape. No need for the KA-BAR today – or the knuckleduster. As a recon mission, the whole objective was to stay silent and invisible. He grabbed the binoculars, then took the notebook and pen from the nightstand and shoved them into another stud-fastened pocket on his chinos. Time to move out.

The day was foggy, but Gabriel could still feel the sun warm on his chest as he left the hotel. Erik and Konstantin were standing, smoking to the left of the main doors. Konstantin came over.

"Fog. Good for close target recce. This your words, CTR, yes?"

"CTR, yeah."

Konstantin smiled. "Spetsnaz. Me, Erik, five years. Know many things about SAS, Delta, Mossad."

"Special Forces, eh? Well, good for you, mate. Yes, the conditions are perfect. Now go and do your stuff, and we'll meet back here for a debrief later."

* * *

It took Gabriel fifty minutes to reach the scrapyard. He could have done it in less by following the road, but the whole point was to stay out of sight. Instead, he made his way there around fields and through the woods fringing Tartu. He saw nobody on his journey, and was certain nobody had seen him. If there were farmers in this part of Estonia, they were all obviously indoors filling out paperwork to get EU grants because they sure as hell weren't out on their land. The fog was lifting as the sun burned its way through, but there was still plenty of cover for a skilled and determined man to approach a reconnaissance target without being observed.

The site was huge, enclosed by a boundary fence of chain-link topped with coils of razor wire. It resembled a shanty town, only instead of rows of corrugated steel dwellings, there were towering piles of cars, each one squashed into a brick, its cabin flattened so it was level with the bonnet and boot. Lanes and roadways led between the piles, and directly in front of Gabriel's position beyond the wire, where he'd hunkered down in a thick hedge of flowering shrubs, was an orange and white crane, its boom mounted with a circular electromagnet.

The fog inside the yard was thicker than in the open scrubby ground outside the fence. Gabriel peered through the binoculars but couldn't see further than fifty yards. He flicked the switch for the night vision and waited while the electronics whined to life. The image through the eye-pieces changed from the natural colours he could see unaided to a ghostly green and black. If anything, the electronics made things worse, so, cursing, Gabriel switched them off and left them to dangle on his chest.

He lay flat under the bushes for another four hours and thirty minutes, willing the fog to lift. There was the occasional break as a gust of wind split the drifting vapour into strands and wisps that swirled amongst the ruined cars, but for most of the time, it obscured all but the closest details in a sickly, grey blanket.

There was a buzz against his hip from his phone. An email from Don. It contained a URL that began HTTPS and ended with a gov.uk domain. The message was terse.

Login: gwolfe

P/W: tf54£9HHcs7

Gabriel clicked on the URL and waited while his phone launched a browser and served the page. Typical spook site: terrible design, worse English. He tapped in the login and password and fifteen seconds later, found himself looking at . . . himself.

On the phone's screen he could see, rendered in grey, the scrapyard. On one side, there was a man-shaped blob, prone, picked out in shimmering white. As an experiment, he brought his right arm out from his side and flapped it up and down as if making a one-sided snow angel. The tiny figure on his screen followed suit.

He swiped right and left and found Konstantin and then Erik, well separated and also lying flat just outside the wire.

"So, Mr Drezna, where are you and your bloodthirsty band of cutthroats?" he murmured, swiping, pinching and then spreading his index and middle fingers apart as he zoomed in on the small complex of structures at the centre of the parcel of land.

Outside stood two vehicles: a small car, a hatchback of some kind, and a biggish van or small truck with the faint but unmistakable outline of a woman's body on the roof. There they were. Inside the central building, he could make out four separate figures. Two were seated, one was standing by the window and one was walking towards the door. Out it went, into the yard outside, where it came to rest. A flare of bright white told the story: cigarette break. Two smaller blobs closed in on the smoker and merged into one. They moved fast. Guard dogs, maybe.

Best of all, he could see two more blobs in a second building abutting the first. Their silhouettes were full-body, so they were lying rather than sitting or standing. And the heat signatures meant they were alive. But were they OK? Had they been abused or tortured? That, the technology couldn't tell him. He watched for a few minutes longer, but they didn't move, and the only change was that the Chechen smoking finished his cigarette and went back inside. He logged off.

"OK," he murmured. "So we have confirmed sighting of the targets and the hostages. Four of one, two of the other. Time to end this lurk and get back to town."

He pushed his way out from the bushes and stood, brushing the dirt of his front before turning and walking away, back to the hotel.

CHAPTER 41

The following morning, Gabriel and the two Russians drove out of the hotel carpark back to the scrapyard. The three men were dressed virtually identically in black trousers and boots, black T-shirts, and black or dark-grey hoodies. On his CTR, Gabriel had confirmed the presence of a disused road leading from the E263 motorway and right up to the southwestern edge of the scrapyard. He headed towards it now. The exit from the main road was a broad swathe of grey gravel, but the start of the narrow road itself was blocked by two truncated pyramids of white concrete, each of their four sides stencilled in bright green with the words *NO SÕIDUKEID* – 'No Vehicles'. The blocks were about eighteen inches high and twelve to a side. He pulled the Mercedes off the main road and onto the gravel. He pointed to the concrete blocks through the windscreen.

"Think you can shift them?" he said, turning to look at Konstantin, then Erik.

"Those little things?" Konstantin said. "Of course. We take one each. Show you what real men can do, *zaichik*."

Erik and Konstantin got out of the car and walked up to the blocks. They flexed their biceps and performed a few perfunctory stretches from side to side. They exchanged a few muttered words Gabriel didn't catch, then laughed. They put their right hands behind their backs, counted to three in Russian then pulled their hands out. Now he understood. Rock-Paper-Scissors was alive and well, and being used in Mother Russia to settle matters like who would lift a sodding great block of concrete and risk making a fool of himself in front of his comrade. Konstantin's meaty palm was held flat above his friend's fist. He clapped it down to wrap the rock. Erik smiled, then squatted in front of his block. He pulled it towards him then, holding it balanced on the near edge of the base with his left hand, he slipped his right hand underneath it.

Transferring the weight to his right, he repeated the action so that he now held the weight of the block on his hands. With a grunting yell, he bounced a couple of times on his heels then strained and brought the block off the ground and cradled it against his chest. He puffed his cheeks out then straightened, his massive thighs pistoning him upright. He turned to the side of the road and staggered on stiff legs to the edge, then rolled the block of concrete off his hands and into the tangled undergrowth of brambles, long grass and nettles, where it settled in a hidden ditch with a smashing of concealed bottles.

He walked back to Konstantin and, dusting his palms against each other, stood, legs apart as if to say, "Now it's your turn". The bigger man spat on his hands and rubbed them together.

Konstantin stood four or five inches taller than Erik. The man had to be six-seven, easily. His weight was harder to estimate, not least because muscle, which nature and Russian army PT instructors had endowed him with the share normally allotted to two men, is denser than fat. If Gabriel had been forced to guess, he'd have said two-fifty to three hundred pounds. Konstantin took off his hoodie and T-shirt to reveal a vast V-shaped torso, the latissimus dorsi muscles two great, triangular slabs of meat each side of the spine. Spread across the upper half of his back, from shoulder to shoulder and reaching halfway down his spine, was a tattoo of a bear, rearing up, clawed forepaws outstretched towards the viewer, fangs dripping blood. Behind it, the Russian flag fluttered from a spear driven into a pile of skulls. His forearms were striated with longitudinal bands of muscle, but it was the upper arms that really impressed. The biceps, triceps and deltoids were dramatically enlarged and defined from working out, and possibly steroid use, too, Gabriel thought – every swell and pleat of muscular tissue was clearly visible under the pale Russian skin.

The giant squatted behind the lump of concrete, as Erik had done, but he took a different approach to lifting it. He placed the flats of his hands against it, put his legs back as if he were a prop forward in a rugby scrum, then grunted with effort and pushed it right over and onto its square top. With the inverted block in front of him, its sides sloping outwards, he simply wrapped his arms around it in a bear hug and stood up, his feet angled outward like a weightlifter. Then he marched to the edge of the road and jettisoned his burden into the ditch alongside Erik's, before returning to put his T-shirt on again.

Both men swaggered back to the car and climbed in. No safety belts needed now, they lounged in their seats and exchanged compliments in Russian. Konstantin poked Gabriel in the right arm.

"Russian soldiers stronger than British. Better, yes?"

"Yeah, Russian soldiers fucking monsters. You win, Ivan." *For now.*

Seemingly satisfied with Gabriel's capitulation in the face of superior physical prowess, Erik and Konstantin resumed their noisy silence, breathing heavily from their exertions but saying nothing, not even to each other.

The road must have been regularly used at one time – it was metalled and largely free of potholes. Now it was being narrowed by nature, as brambles, nettles, cow parsley and blackthorn threatened to engulf it completely. Gabriel eased the big estate down the centre of the road, but the thorns and spines of the burgeoning greenery still etched their signatures down the shining grey sides of the car with a thin screeching. Tall hedges on both sides prevented Gabriel from seeing the target site. All he could do was to keep moving forward until he reached the dilapidated but still padlocked gates at the end of the track. Above the road, a bird of prey soared in lazy circles on a thermal, too high for Gabriel to identify it. He didn't know which raptors were native to Estonia, but he wanted it to be an eagle, something majestic and free from fear of predation.

Then a tap on his shoulder from Erik brought him back to the present.

"Look," the Russian said, pointing between Gabriel and Konstantin and through the windscreen.

There they were. The rusted and chained steel gates of the scrapyard.

Gabriel slowed the car and pulled over behind an untidy tangle of scrubby thorn bushes. He went to the rear of the car and waited for the tailgate to finish its self-propelled ascent. From the load space, he retrieved a pair of bolt-cutters he'd bought the previous day. He walked up to the gates, slid the jaws of the bolt cutters around the chain, and squeezed the plastic-sheathed handles together. The sensation was like cutting through thick rubber: a steady pressure followed by a sudden yielding, accompanied by a double-chink as the quarter-inch steel links parted and fell to the ground. He pulled the remaining length of chain through the frame of the gate and slung it to one side. But when he tried to open the gates they held stubbornly in place.

"Look," Erik said, pointing at the vertical, black gap where the gate frames butted up against each other. "Weld."

He was right. Someone had gone belt-and-braces on security. To the rear of the join, he could make out a thick, vertical bead of rippled steel: the gates had been welded shut and then chained, presumably to deter casual visitors. Konstantin grunted a confirmatory phrase from the hinge end of the right-hand gate.

"Is welded, also."

"OK," Gabriel said. "We brought C-4. Now we're going to use it."

The Russians' eyes lit up at the mention of C-4. They high-fived like children excited at the prospect of some unexpected destruction of property.

Gabriel returned to the boot and pulled out the shrink-wrapped package of C-4 plastic explosive. Using his switchblade, he slit the thick plastic wrapping, exposing the dull-grey, greasy material within.

It had a smell equal parts hot plastic and window putty. He carved off a thin slice about four inches long, divided this into eight stock cube-sized pieces, and pushed them methodically into the gaps in the centre of the gates, starting at head height and working his way down to ground level.

The *plastique* in place, he unwound a length of twin-core, copper bell-wire from a white cardboard reel, stuck the two exposed ends into the topmost cube of explosive, and then crimped the wire every foot or so and stripped off an inch of the plastic insulation, before pushing a copper V into the remaining lumps. Finally, he unspooled another thirty feet of the bell-wire before cutting it off from the reel, which he stowed back in the Merc's boot. He stripped a half-inch of the insulation from each of the two conjoined wires with his teeth, pulled them apart and clipped them into the firing device. This was a small aluminium box the size of a cigarette packet with a set of red and black terminals protected by knurled plastic dust caps, and a red firing button on the side.

"These will be small bangs," he said to the other men, who had watched him lay the charges with interest and were now crouching on the far side of the Merc. "We're at least a mile and a half from the buildings, so we should be fine. But if we attract some attention, be ready to deal with it, yes?"

Konstantin and Erik both stood, walked round to the Merc's boot and unwrapped three canvas bundles, revealing what appeared to be brand-new, American-made M16s. These were desert warfare models, their hand guards and other furniture painted in black, sand and white camouflage. They sat side by side on the boot lip and began loading magazines, first sliding thirty 5.56mm rounds onto the thin steel stripper clips that gripped them by the grooves at the base of the cartridges, then mounting the clips on the empty magazines with a loading guide, and finally pushing down with their thumbs to slot all thirty rounds home. They worked in silence apart from the ratcheting noises as the rounds were pushed down, zig-zagging their way into the pressed-steel magazines. With six magazines apiece loaded, they slotted one into all three of the M16s, slapping the bases to ensure they were correctly seated and wouldn't come loose in firing. They took a rifle each and resumed their cover positions behind the Merc.

Gabriel looked at them and signalled with the flat of his left hand to keep their heads down. He crouched, counted down from three with the fingers of the same hand, turned away from the gates, and pressed the red fire button.

The six tiny charges blew instantaneously, with a noise like the rockets you'd find in a domestic fireworks set. Out in the open air, with nothing to catch and reflect the shock waves, the sound dissipated quickly. The charges did their work: the gates had been blown apart and off their hinges, and had flown back a few yards to lie on the roadway, their frames buckled, the chain-link infill shredded and torn.

The explosions were loud, but Gabriel hoped the Chechens were too far away to have heard them. Nevertheless, he pulled the P226 out from his waistband, slid out and checked the magazine before reseating it, and screwed on the suppressor.

The men maintained their cover for a full five minutes before moving. Once he was sure they had managed this infiltration without alerting the kidnappers, Gabriel motioned for the other two to get back into the car. He opened the boot with the remote and they stowed the M16s before joining him.

Driving on a feathered throttle so that the engine was barely more than idling, he drove along the access road, crunching over the ruined gates. To their left and right, stacks of flattened cars formed a steel canyon, cutting off the sunlight apart from a narrow strip of sky directly above them. Then, way up ahead, he caught sight of the small cluster of prefabricated buildings that formed the heart of the scrapyard.

He pointed out of the windscreen at the buildings.

"Target acquired, boys," he said. "Out you get."

The three men left the car and went round to the boot. Konstantin and Erik grabbed an M16 each, and shoved a couple of spare magazines into their trouser pockets. They unwrapped the smallest canvas package and took out Glock 19 semi-automatic pistols. The Glocks held nineteen rounds, and they each pocketed two spare magazines. One hundred and forty-seven rounds to a man, across two weapons, making two hundred and ninety-four. Gabriel had forty-five rounds for the SIG, making a grand total of three hundred and thirty-nine rounds. In the heat of battle, an infantryman could expend that amount of ammunition in seconds, but he hoped they could avoid the chaos of a full-blown firefight with the Chechens, not least because he wanted the Bryant women alive and not the victims of trigger-happy Russian mercenaries or the murderous Chechen kidnappers.

And then there was the Dragunov.

Gabriel unwrapped the third canvas package and spread the loose flaps of fabric to the sides of the rifle. Less advanced than the US-manufactured Barrett Light-Fifty or the Accuracy International L96 he'd used in combat, the Dragunov resembled a more conventional weapon. A weapon that members of the general public would probably describe, were they to be prompted, with the word "rifle". It had a combination wooden stock and pistol grip, a two-foot barrel tipped with an iron sight, a ten-shot magazine and a PSO-1 telescopic sight. Despite the rifle's Soviet design, all the usual controls – from the lever safety selector to the magazine latch – were where he expected to find them. Experimental trigger-pulls, once the magazine was ejected and the chamber checked, revealed a weapon that was easy and smooth to fire. Gabriel slotted the magazine back into the receiver, cocked it, then slid on the safety. He doubted he'd have time or opportunity for more than one kill with it, but that would immediately level up the odds to three against three.

Gabriel looked around and up, trying to find the best sniping position. The stacks of cars gave height, but they looked unstable and he didn't want to be stuck somewhere with poor access if he needed to get out in a hurry.

"Take five," he said to the Russians, holding his right hand up, fingers outspread. They seemed to understand him, judging by the speed with which they sat on the ground, fished cigarettes out of their jackets and lit up. "I need to find a firing position. Dragunov, yes?"

Konstantin blew out a cloud of harsh-smelling smoke. "Yes. Sniper nest. Got it, Boss."

Carrying the Dragunov by the hand-guard, Gabriel set off down one of the alleys running perpendicularly off the access road. More piles of cars, missing everything but their bodywork, chassis and running gear. Then he saw it. The perfect spot to set up.

With great care, someone had lined up two rust-red train carriages next to each other, and then piled two further carriages on top of them at right angles. The smashed-in windows and gaping doorways offered plenty of climbing aids, and it was a simple matter to clamber up the outside of this improvised steel-and-iron fortress, and onto the roof of the topmost carriage closest to the scrapyard buildings. There was a hatch let into the roof, and when Gabriel tried it, he found he could open it and pull it back on itself. The hinges permitted it to travel back to an angle of forty-five degrees, where it locked. Now he had a firing position and cover. Bulletproof cover at that.

Gabriel left the Dragunov on the roof and scrambled down like a monkey leaving a fruit tree. He found what he needed in a pile of odd scraps of steel, brass and other metals lying beside a pyramid of crumpled washing machines: a straight piece of aluminium stock, white with leached metal salts, about thirty inches long, one inch wide and a quarter-inch thick. He ripped an electric motor out of the back of one of the washing machines, and used it to hammer a V-shaped dent in the centre of the piece of aluminium. Threading one end into a narrow gap between two of the washing machines, he bent it back on the V and repeated the process for the other end. Now he had a crude bipod: M-shaped but with much longer legs than the central dent. He yanked out half of the wiring loom for the washing machine and stuffed the multicoloured strands into his trouser pocket.

He was concentrating so hard on fabricating the bipod for the Dragunov that the dogs were within eighty yards of him before he picked up the sound of their paws drumming on the road surface. He stood and whirled round, simultaneously reaching for his KA-BAR and threading the fingers of his left hand into the holes of the knuckleduster. Eight seconds later the dogs were on him.

The leading dog leapt up towards his throat, its pulled-back lips exposing long, yellow fangs. Gabriel thought how odd it was that guard dogs should be silent. You'd think half the point of guard dogs was to warn intruders off and let the owners know that they had company. But then, if your dogs were supposed to kill the company, maybe doing it quietly was a good thing.

He braced his right leg against the door of the car behind him, lightly bent his left knee and thrust the KA-BAR, point uppermost, into the dog's abdomen. Its momentum carried it forward against the pressure of the blade, which unzipped its belly from throat to groin. Now it did make a sound, a high-pitched wheezing cry that died out as the hot mass of viscera splashed down onto the ground beneath it.

The other dog leapt up at the same moment, but with the favoured target of the throat obscured by the other animal, it lunged for Gabriel's left forearm. This forearm ended in a fist enveloped in half a kilo of milled steel. With his right hand half-buried in the lead dog's torso, Gabriel punched down with his left hand, catching the second dog a glancing blow on its skull that slit its scalp, a huge flap of its short-haired pelt falling forwards over its eyes. It yelped with pain and fell back, skidding and spinning in the pool of blood surging from its mate's arteries. The dog backed away, growling, unsure whether to run or fight. Gabriel pulled the knife free from the other dog's body and stabbed the second animal in the side, angling the blade so it slid between the ribs and burst the heart. The dog fell sideways with a thump.

Gabriel staggered back against a wrecked car and sat heavily in the hollow steel cage where the passenger seats would normally be, looking at the bright red pool beneath the corpses. He'd killed animals in war before, for food, mostly. But he hated doing it. It felt shameful, somehow. A sudden breeze wafted the coppery smell of the dogs' blood up into his nostrils and reminded him of the mantra Master Zhao had taught him whenever their bow-hunts ended in a kill: "I honour your life".

The harsh buzz of a fat bluebottle jolted him back to the present, and he became aware of his heartbeat knocking in his chest.

He cleaned and sheathed the knife, then dragged the bodies of the dogs away from the road and towards a pile of fridges. Most had their doors removed, but at the back of the pile, he found one that was intact. He lifted the door, gagging at the rank smell of rotted vegetables and soured milk that rolled out, and let it down gently till it rested on the ground. In went the dogs, one by one, and down went the door on top of them, sealing them into their deluxe, five-hundred euro coffin.

There wasn't much to be done about the blood, and he hoped by the time it was noticed, it would be government troops or the local police doing the discovering and not the Chechens. He kicked some debris into the darkening pool, briefly scattering the growing cloud of flies.

Back on top of the rusted carriage, he wired the end of the Dragunov's barrel into the bipod and pulled the assembly tight against the fore-end of the handguard. There was plenty of room to lie down, and Gabriel adjusted the rifle's position until, when he looked through the telescopic sight, he had a clear view of the scrapyard buildings and the rough square of ground they enclosed. According to the curved rangefinder in the sight, the distance to the target was about five hundred yards, two hundred and fifty less than the distance it was zeroed for. An easy-enough compensation to make.

As he watched through the sight, mentally calculating the sighting adjustments, the door to the central cabin opened and a short, fat, barrel-chested man walked off the narrow front step and into the yard. He had several days' growth of stubble, and this, combined with the shaggy mop of dark brown hair, gave him a wild look. He stood still with the pale-grey wall of the cabin behind him, as if he'd been ordered there by a gunnery instructor intent on giving new recruits an easy target.

The man was wearing a dark shirt with white buttons. Gabriel sighted on the man's chest, moving the centre chevron until he had its point stuck to the button just over his sternum. He moved it fractionally to the right, over the heart.

The Dragunov was loaded with Soviet-designed 7N14 rounds tipped with hardened steel-core projectiles, each weighing 9.8 grammes.

At this range, the 7.62mm round would hit the target travelling at roughly nineteen hundred miles per hour. The transfer of kinetic energy on impact would be sufficient to ream out his ribcage, leaving a hole big enough to kick a football through. Or there was the sniper's glory shot: a round to the head. Then the pressure wave generated by the round piercing the skull would explode it like a ripe fruit, transforming eleven pounds of blood, bone and soft tissue into a cloud of wet, red dust.

Later.

For now, Gabriel needed to get back to Erik and Konstantin and lay out the plan of attack. He climbed down from his sniping position, careful to replace the steel hatch in the roof of the carriage, carrying the Dragunov in one hand. Keeping to the shadows cast by one enormous wall of crushed cars, he made his way back to the Mercedes. As he drew closer, he picked up the sound of the two men arguing in Russian. He stopped, turned around and backtracked until he came to a narrow pathway leading off the access road. He followed it for fifty feet then propped the Dragunov against the smashed-in side of an old Nissan saloon and slipped between its rear end and the front bumper of the car behind. Arching and twisting his body, he squeezed himself through a series of tight gaps until he was close enough to the two men to make out exactly what they were arguing about.

It wasn't good news.

CHAPTER 42

"Yuri said he doesn't care about the Englishman, or the women," Erik was saying to Konstantin. "He just wants Drezna and his gang dead, with proof. So I say we waste him now. I'm tired of taking orders from a little prick like him. Do him, use the grenades and the M16s on the Chechens, and then party time with those English cunts!"

"Don't be such an idiot. If you stopped thinking with your dick for two minutes, you'd see what a fucking awful idea that is," Konstantin said. "Number one, he's ex-SAS. That means he's going to be handy in a firefight or if it gets personal. Number two, they're Chechens. Did you forget what those animals are like? Were you not there when we found Andrei hanging upside down from a tree with his cock and balls cut off and stuffed into his mouth? Those were village women who did that to him, Erik. Fucking milkmaids and farm girls and old babushkas. That lot over there are *soldiers*. Drezna himself was in Afghanistan. On our fucking side! So I say we keep him alive for now. That makes it three against four, which are odds I prefer."

Erik sounded sulky now, but he wasn't giving in without at least one more attempt at convincing his partner.

"Listen. Yuri said we could split the money between us. Half-shares, right? So I've got half the share of being in charge as well. Who is this Fox guy anyway? From what I hear, he just turns up in

Tallinn one day, beats the shit out of Teet down at Jonny Rocketz, and all of a sudden he's on a fucking search-and-rescue mission for Yuri. Something's off, Konstantin, I can feel it."

"Yes, and I know what you can feel, you randy bastard. You can feel your dick getting stiff thinking about fucking those women can't you?"

"No harm in it. We always used to do it to the women after a fight, didn't we? Anyway, you agreed. We kill the Chechens, take some souvenirs for Yuri, do the women, and then waste them with the Chechens' weapons. Pin the blame on them, make them look like the savages they are."

"And that is still the plan, my friend. But Fox stays alive until either all the Chechens are dead, or it's clear we're going to fuck them over. Now let that be an end of it. OK?"

A pause.

"OK, fine. But I want the girl first. You can fuck the mother and warm her up for me."

* * *

Gabriel leaned back against the doorframe of the car he was squatting inside. The steel was cold against the back of his neck, adding to the gooseflesh that had broken out all over his body. Shit! Now I really have a problem. Odds of six to one, with two on loan until Konstantin judges I've become surplus to requirements. *He reached round and put his right hand on the grip of his SIG.* So do I off the Russians and take on the Chechens solo? That's what Erik wants to do. Or do I keep them with me, fight the Chechens and then waste them before they try to do the same to me? Konstantin's view. Jesus. Time for clear thinking. What would you do, Don?

Well, Old Sport, I'd put the rate of exchange at one of our chaps to a dozen Russians. But then, as you said, we used to go in nine to one. So, you against four bloodthirsty Chechens doesn't sound too attractive from a tactical point of view. I'd keep the Borises alive for now, but you'd better be ready if they decide they don't need you earlier than expected.

How about you, Britta? Any tactical insight would be great about now.

Me, I'd off them right away. You can't concentrate on what's at your front if you don't trust what's at your back. Remember all those stories from Vietnam? They made us study them in class. An unpopular officer flies in from West Point or some cushy job in Texas counting Jeeps and starts ordering his men into risky situations, playing favourites, maybe, or just being no damn good. So the enlisted men let him get ahead in a rice paddy and toss a fragmentation grenade under his boots. They used to call it "fragging", remember? Lesson number one in warfare: trust your leaders/trust your men. You can't trust those Russians. You got your SIG right there, with a suppressor. Use it!

For once, Gabriel had no instantaneous decision. No gut feel that said "do this" or "do that". He twisted round further to ease a cramp that was threatening to explode in his back and dislodged a door that was leaning against the car he was hiding in. It fell sideways and clanged against the Nissan's neighbour. He heard Erik and Konstantin jump up, swearing. And the ratcheting creak of two M16 bolts being pulled back and released. *Three against four it is, then.*

He swore loudly, then pushed his way out of the Škoda, through another narrow gap between a couple more cars, and staggered into the space in front of the Merc. The Russians were standing there, back to back, faces tense, eyes narrowed, the muzzles of their automatic rifles making rapid, jerking sweeps in front of them, covering a circle.

"Thought I'd surprise you," he said, back into full-on Terry Fox mode. "Give you a bit of a fright. Looks like I succeeded, doesn't it?"

The Russians lowered their weapons, though not before Gabriel noticed the way Erik's M16 swung his way and stopped, pointing straight at his chest, before he de-cocked it and let the muzzle drop.

"Very funny. English joke, yes?" Erik said, giving Gabriel a filthy look before turning to Konstantin and muttering in Russian, "I told you so."

"Listen up," Gabriel said. "I've found a sniping position. It's on top of some old railway carriages." He pointed back the way he'd come with the muzzle of the Dragunov. "Perfect view of the buildings and the yard. Normally, I'd say wait until just before dawn. About oh three hundred hours. Catch them sleeping, maybe one guard, maybe none somewhere this remote. But we can't risk it. They could get bored, change their minds, anything, and waste the women. That ain't going to happen. Not on my watch."

"Agreed. Now is better. What is plan?" Konstantin said, sliding the magazine out from his Glock and then slapping it home again with a clack.

"Plan is, you give me fifteen minutes to get back in position. Then you wait. I put a round into the first one who shows their face outside that door. After that, we're three against three. If they come out the same way, I'll drop them all then we go in and get my mate's family."

"Chechens animals. Not stupid," Erik said. "One down in doorway, others go out back. Come out firing."

"My thinking exactly. So, one down, three to go, you and Konstantin come up on two of the other flanks. Full-auto, waste anything that moves. Maximum firepower. If nobody moves, you chuck smoke and teargas grenades in through the windows, and shoot the fuckers when they come out. Only one rule: you do not harm the English women. Got me?"

"Of course," Erik said, smirking. "English women off limits to dumb Russkies, yes?"

"You better believe it, friend. Now, give me quarter of an hour, then wait for my shot."

This time, Gabriel took one of the M16s himself, alongside the Dragunov. One 30-round magazine in the assault rifle, plus two in press-studded trouser pockets. Ninety 5.56mm NATO rounds. The SIG in his waistband, plus suppressor: fifteen 9mm rounds in the magazine and thirty in his pockets. One-thirty-five rounds. The Dragunov loaded with ten 7.62mm 7N14 body armour-piercing Soviet rounds. One-forty-five. He clinked as he walked away from the Russians. Bombed up.

Ten minutes later, he was approaching the oversized Jenga tower of railway carriages. The smell of the dogs' blood carried on the warm summer breeze blowing through the scrapyard; it nauseated him and he had to breathe through his mouth to avoid gagging. He carried the M16 across his back by its sling of green webbing. It was still an awkward climb up the side of the tower, the Dragunov knocking against his thigh, the SIG's suppressor digging into the small of his back. All this while trying to climb onto the roof of a carriage balanced thirty feet above the ground.

Eventually, he made it onto the roof. The black-painted steel was hot under his belly as he slithered into position by the hatch. He lifted it and let it settle back against its stops, forming a small but effective barricade from which to shoot behind. Domed rivet heads ran along the centre-line of the roof of the carriage, and he squared the feet of the bipod against two of these, giving it some protection against slippage.

Gabriel shuffled back on his belly until he could cradle the Dragunov's hand-guard in his left palm. Then he curled his right hand around the pistol grip and let his index finger find its natural resting position against the side of the trigger guard. As the breeze sighed through the distant conifers and birch trees that fringed the yard, carrying a fresh, sharp scent of pollen and pine needles into his nostrils, he bent his head to the sight, resting his right cheek against the side of the wooden stock.

Through the optically ground lenses of the sight, the door to the central cabin was rendered in such pin-sharp detail that Gabriel could make out the text on the scattering of stickers that dotted its scuffed and fading surface. Most were promotional decals for car component companies: brakes, carburettors, electrics, transmissions, performance parts. He pivoted the rifle to the left, then the right, searching for a gap in the window blinds. Nothing. They were the old-fashioned, wide Venetian slatted type, and the Chechens had pulled the cords to blot out even the slightest hint of light. Nothing to do but wait for the target – any target – to appear.

* * *

Whatever else he'd learned in the Army, he'd learned how to wait. Some soldiers brought the ability with them, perhaps having a contemplative turn of mind. Others had to work at it. All managed it, in the end; it was either that or go mad. Gabriel could remember the feeling well: a squirming of nerves in the stomach mixed with a fevered anticipation to close with the enemy, overlaid with crushing boredom. "Standing by to stand by", that was what they used to call it. A mate of his in the Regiment had spent his downtime writing poetry. Not free verse, either. Tightly controlled sonnets that produced in him a trancelike state from which it was hard to awaken him except by the simple phrase, "Time to go".

As he waited now, Gabriel let his breathing slow, and focused on easing his heartbeat down into the high fifties. Master Zhao had told him stories of Buddhist monks who were so adept that they could reduce their pulse to a mere whisper of pressure, just sufficient to move the blood around their bodies and keep it oxygenated, but slow enough to resemble death to a casual observer.

He'd been in worse combat situations, but he'd also been in better. The two Russians wanted him dead, their point of disagreement, when they'd do it. They wanted him alive to help them defeat the Chechens; he wanted them alive for the very same reason. The only question was, who would decide enough was enough first?

No time to debate that now; the door was opening. It was the barrel-chested man again. Just as before, he walked into the yard and stood in the sun, looking all around, before rootling about in his jacket pocket and extracting a cigarette from a squashed cardboard packet. As he curled his hand around the lighter he was using and blew the first lungful of blue smoke into the air above his head, Gabriel took aim.

In his career as a soldier for Her Majesty, Queen Elizabeth II – fighting wars, spying, conducting covert operations – Gabriel had had occasion to kill men many times.

In the Parachute Regiment, they had exclusively been enemy combatants. Men in uniform, like him. Carrying automatic weapons, like him. Doing their duty as they saw it, like him. He was there, in Africa, Bosnia or the Middle East, to achieve a goal. To the politicians who had ordered him there, that goal might be to reassert British sovereignty or to protect a shaky peace deal. To the generals in charge, it might be to win this particular war. To his boss, it might be to take that particular hill, or liberate that particular town. But to him, and to his mates, it was far, far simpler than that. His goal was to protect each other, do their job, and come home in one piece. Or die trying.

Then, later, in the SAS, the picture had become darker, more patches of grey among the black and white of regular soldiering. The enemy then had included drug lords in Latin America, militia leaders in Africa, terrorists of both persuasions in Northern Ireland, and a ragbag of "legitimate targets" that might include torturers, secret policemen, corrupt officials and child soldiers. Those engagements were harder to square with your conscience. All the targets were doing bad – even evil – things, but they were often unarmed and unsuspecting when they received The Queen's message.

Gabriel had never become used to killing. He was good at it, had won medals because of it, but he had deliberately not allowed himself to lapse into triumphalism. He didn't want to find it easy to take another person's life, easy to let a man's blood out with a slice of a knife, or burst his skull with a rifle round, then laugh at comedy videos back at base.

Was that behind his PTSD? His refusal to take the easy road and dehumanise those he killed? One for Fariyah Crace, he thought.

Gabriel realised he'd dropped his eye from the telescopic sight, so he refocused down the narrow tube crammed with clever optics and electronics that would even register infrared. His heartrate spiked, and a wave of terror washed through him.

Smudge Smith was standing next to the Chechen. He looked over at Gabriel and waved, his teeth bright against his brown skin, his uniform immaculate in the sunshine. Then he spoke. His mouth moved and Gabriel heard Smudge's voice inside his own head.

"Hi Boss. Going to take the shot, then? Should be a doddle for you at that range. How about we make it more interesting?"

Then Smudge stepped in front of the Chechen and turned to face Gabriel head-on. He reached up to his face, hooked his fingers over the bones at the base of his eye sockets and pulled downwards. With a wet scraping sound the whole of Smudge's face came away in his hands. He dropped the rubbery mass of flesh to the ground. Below his expressive brown eyes was a hole where his face had been. No muscle or bone, just a gap through which Gabriel could see the Chechen's own grizzled face, cigarette clamped between his lips. When he exhaled, the jet of blue smoke puffed through Smudge's emptied-out head and dissipated in front of him.

Please Smudge. Leave me alone to take the shot. I'm seeing a shrink to lay you to rest. I promise I'll let you go.

"I believe you, Boss. But come on, a quid says you can do him without touching me."

Gabriel took his right hand off the pistol grip and put the web of soft skin between his thumb and forefinger – his trigger finger – between his teeth. He bit down, hard, drawing blood and grunting with the effort of not crying out. When he looked back, Smudge had disappeared.

He sighted on a point above the Chechen's heart. Centre-mass shots were less risky, but also less certain of an outright kill. With a familiar rifle, he'd have gone for the headshot, but he'd never shot a Dragunov before and knew nothing about how this particular example had been set up, beyond his instruction to have the sight zeroed at 750 yards.

No time for any more delays. He breathed in, let it all the way out, took up first pressure on the trigger and waited.

A heartbeat.

He tightened his finger a little more.

A heartbeat.

He stilled his mind.

A heartbeat.

He squeezed the trigger.

CHAPTER 43

The rifle was unsilenced, and in the still of the late afternoon, the sound as the 7.62mm bullet left the barrel was immense. The man's accomplices inside the cabins would hear it, but he would not.

The round began its fifteen-hundred-foot journey towards its target at a speed of almost three thousand feet per second. Over so short a range, its flight was virtually flat. It arrived, having dropped from its starting elevation of twenty-seven feet to four feet nine – the height of the man's heart, half a second later.

The damage created by the sharp-pointed steel round was catastrophic – it broke three ribs on the way in, collapsed his left lung, burst his heart and sucked half the shredded organs and flesh out through a six-inch-wide exit wound. It travelled on through the thin plywood wall of the cabin before embedding itself in a tatty vinyl-covered sofa inside.

The man died instantly, while his legs were still holding him upright. Gabriel watched for another few seconds, before leaving the Dragunov and sliding his way off the curved carriage roof, and jumping down behind the mound of rolling stock.

He heard the loud hammering of automatic weapons, M16s and Kalashnikovs. The Chechens must have gone out the back, or through an escape passage at one end or another of the complex of buildings, and were engaged in a furious firefight with the Russians. Gabriel unshouldered his own M16, cocked it, and sprinted towards the front of the central cabin.

He was within thirty feet when a bearded man charged at him from fifty yards to his right, long, straggly, black hair flying out behind him. He'd been hiding in the lee of a huge, yellow crane. The man fired from the hip with a Kalashnikov as he ran at Gabriel, spraying rounds with a deafening continuous roar of explosions. Gabriel dropped to one knee, pulled the M16 to his shoulder and squeezed off a three-round burst. Two of the rounds caught the man in the torso, doubling him over so he rolled rather than fell. Before he could retrieve the AK47, Gabriel shot him again: a double-tap to the head.

Crouching low, Gabriel scurried towards the cabin and fetched up against the wall to the left of the still-open door, breathing heavily. Clutching the M16 tightly at his hip, he swung round the doorjamb into the cabin. It was empty. Then, from a closed door to his left, beyond a two-seater orange sofa sprouting foam from a bullet hole, and an untidy tangle of fallen chairs, he heard screams.

"Help us, please! We're in here. Don't shoot for God's sake. Help us!"

He vaulted the chairs and shouted through the door.

"Stand back!"

Then he leaned back and kicked the flimsy aluminium lock assembly with the sole of his right boot. Not a move his mentor would have approved of, but the door cracked off its hinges and toppled backwards into the room beyond.

And there, clutching each other, eyes wide and faces bleached with fear, were Sarah and Chloe Bryant.

"Oh, thank God!" Sarah said. "Please get us out, they were going to kill us. You have to take us away from here."

"I will. But it's not safe. Not yet. Please," he said, as the two women stood and came towards him on shaky legs, "just stay here, under the bed, until I come back for you."

"No!" Chloe Bryant said. "No. You can't. You can't leave us. What if they kill you?"

He looked at the young woman, registering for the first time the ugly, black wound where her right ear lobe had been. "I have to go. Listen to that."

Outside there were shouts, screams of pain, automatic gunfire and the squealing ricochets of bullets bouncing off the steel wreckage of thousands of Estonians' material aspirations.

"I'll come back. I promise."

Then he turned and ran back to the outside door of the cabin. The fighting between the Russians and the two remaining Chechens seemed to be coming from the western side of the scrapyard. There were bursts of automatic fire and the rapid crack-crack-crack of the semi-automatic Glocks.

Gabriel crawled along the front of the cabins, keeping his belly on the ground and the muzzle of his M16 pointed upwards at what would be waist height for anyone he met coming the other way. At the end of the row of buildings, there was another of the car-lined canyons stretching away towards a partially dismantled truck that blocked the end of the path between the stacks of dead autos.

This had turned into street fighting, something he guessed the Chechens were better at than the Russians. He decided to get off the street. Slinging his M16 over his back, he climbed up one of the walls of squashed cars to the top layer. The surface was mainly even, comprising roofs, boots and bonnets, the passenger cells having been flattened by one of the huge machines that stood idle in the yard. He crept to the far edge and slid himself forward on elbows, knees and ankles until he could just peep over and down onto an open space of rough ground between the mountain of cars and the perimeter fence.

Below him, Konstantin and another Chechen – was this Drezna? – circled each other. Behind them lay discarded firearms. The Russian's M16 and Glock, and a Kalashnikov and another semi-auto pistol, presumably dumped by the Chechen. Out of ammo. Gabriel sighted on the Chechen. Then dropped the barrel a fraction. Why not let them kill each other? Two fewer deaths on his hands.

Each man held a knife. The Russian's blade was a monstrous hunting knife half as long as his forearm. God alone knew where he'd been hiding it. It had a wicked point and a deep-bellied blade. The Chechen wielded a long, narrow switchblade, its edge glinting.

Both men were panting. Both appeared to have sustained bullet wounds. The Russian had a bloody patch on the left thigh of his jeans, just above the knee. The denim was dark, and shining wetly. He was favouring that leg, but still putting weight on it – a flesh wound, then, not a broken bone or a severed artery. The Chechen had been shot in the right arm. It dangled by his side, blood dripping from his fingers.

Suddenly, as if weary of the game of feint and counter-feint, Konstantin lunged, the point of his knife angled towards the other man's belly. The Chechen stumbled backwards and half-turned in a fall. It was a ruse. As Konstantin bellowed in triumph, preparing to stab upwards and eviscerate his foe, the Chechen swivelled on his heels, and swept his left arm in a tight arc. The edge of his knife caught Konstantin across the throat and swept on, opening a horrific gash that severed the carotid artery and jugular vein on his right side. Blood flew from his ruined neck in six-foot jets that caught the Chechen full in the face before he ducked and thrust again, this time burying the blade up to the hilt in Konstantin's chest.

The Chechen, shorter by about nine inches than Konstantin, but proportionately more solid, held the Russian as he slipped to his knees before keeling over, blood still coursing from his opened blood vessels and pooling under his body. The victor stood and wiped his knife on his trouser leg. At that moment, Gabriel's rifle barrel slipped on the mangled sheet of rusty steel it was resting on. The scrape wasn't loud, but the Chechen heard it. He looked up. And then he smiled.

CHAPTER 44

"You win," he shouted. "I am out of ammunition. And I don't think I can throw this," he held up the switchblade by the point of its blade, "accurately enough to hit you before you shoot me."

"Are you Kasym Drezna?" Gabriel shouted.

"One and the same," Drezna shouted back, then smiled, though his eyes were screwed up against the pain from his wound. "Enjoy this moment, stranger. You may not have many more left."

Gabriel looked down the barrel of his M16, the iron sights aligned on the man's chest, noticing the subtle change of grip on the knife. *I wish I had more of a reason than logistics to do this.* Then he fired. A three-round burst. And another three.

Drezna staggered under the impact of the rounds as they tore into him. He fell heavily.

Without waiting, Gabriel scrabbled his way down the pile of shattered vehicles, using one hand so he could keep hold of his M16 with the other. He'd almost reached the bottom when Drezna groaned and tried to heave himself up on his elbows. Gabriel ran to the man and kicked him hard in the head, putting him back on the ground. He knelt by his left side and ripped open his windcheater to reveal a khaki-and-black flak jacket, its surface smashed by six bullets. At that range, Drezna's ribs would have been broken by the impact energy of the rounds. Frothy blood was bubbling from his lips. His breath was rasping as he fought for oxygen. In a battle, enemy fighter or no, Gabriel would have called for the medics or radioed for a chopper. But who could he shout for here? The place was empty apart from two frightened kidnap victims and a maximum of two other fighters, neither of whom cared overmuch for Gabriel.

He'd underestimated Drezna's strength, though. In the time it took him to conclude he needed to kill his man, Drezna's heavily muscled left arm swung upwards, switchblade still gripped tightly. Flinching, Gabriel parried the thrust with his right arm and crashed the barrel of the M16 down onto Drezna's chest, drawing a howl of pain. The Chechen was hurt badly, but his will to survive was immense. He grabbed the M16 and pushed it away, screaming with pain as the muscles in his right arm tensed around the bullet wound. He rolled towards Gabriel and, snake-quick, drew his knife hand back and stabbed him in the right bicep. His strength was failing him though, and the blade only penetrated an inch or so into the flesh. Now the two men were locked together in a trial of strength. Grunting with the pain of the knife wound, Gabriel leaned forward and knelt onto Drezna's chest. That drained the last of the Chechen's strength and he fell back, gasping with agony as Gabriel's weight crushed his broken ribs.

Gabriel reared back, trying to free his M16 to deliver the *coup de grace* when Erik burst into the small clearing. His face was red, but this was exertion, not blood. Seeing Konstantin on the ground, bled out, Erik howled and body-slammed Gabriel to one side, causing him to stumble and fall, smacking his head against a rusty engine block. Then Erik turned and fell upon Drezna. He smashed the barrel of his Glock into Drezna's face, shattering his front teeth, then stuck the muzzle into his ruined mouth.

"You scum! You cockroach!" he screamed in Russian. "You killed him. Now you will die yourself. Fuck you and fuck all black-assed Chechens!"

Erik stood, held the Glock in a two-handed grip and started firing.

The bangs were deafening, and Gabriel's ears rang as Erik fired round after round into the Chechen's head.

He went on pulling the trigger, brass cartridge cases tinkling around him, until, with eleven rounds fired, the Glock emitted a rapid series of steely clicks. Then he turned towards Gabriel, who had just staggered to his feet, his head pounding.

"This your fault," he said, pointing at Konstantin's corpse, then ramming another magazine into the butt of the Glock. "All Chechens dead. One was woman. I shoot her over there." He pointed in the direction of the Mercedes. "Now you pay. Pay for Konstantin. Pay for everything. Mission over, Terry."

He levelled the gun, pointing it at Gabriel's head.

Fuck! When did I start trusting you and leave my weapon pointed at the ground?

Gabriel flicked his eyes past Erik's right shoulder. It was the oldest trick in the book, yet it always worked. People were programmed to look where other people looked.

Erik glanced to his right and in that moment, Gabriel brought his M16 up and shot him point-bank in the chest. The three rounds were grouped so tightly, they tore a hole through Erik's body big enough to reach through. Blood and soft tissue spewed from his body cavity in front and behind. He crumpled forwards and fell face down into a pool of his own blood. Before leaving the body, Gabriel patted it down, found what he was looking for, and stuffed it into his jacket pocket among the spare pistol rounds.

So that was it. Four Chechens down. Two Russians down. Two hostages safe. Now for the easy bit. Get them into the car and call Don to arrange an exfiltration. He made his way back towards the cabins, relieved that the bloodshed was over.

* * *

Inside the complex of cabins, Gabriel made his way through to the second building. He stepped into the room where Sarah and Chloe

Bryant were hiding and called, softly.

"Ladies? It's over. You can come out."

Feet-first, the two women shuffled their out from under the double bed. He helped them up and then sat on the bed, his body suddenly a fuel-free zone as the last of the adrenaline from the firefight was metabolised.

"I'm sorry. I didn't introduce myself before. My name is Gabriel Wolfe. I'm working for the British Government."

"Does Dad know we're safe?" Chloe asked.

"No. Not yet. But we can phone him if you like."

Gabriel pulled his phone from an inside pocket and handed it over.

Chloe's thumb danced on the screen, then she pushed the phone against her ear.

They all waited as the invisible packets of data were split, transmitted and reassembled before being sent to a phone sixteen hundred miles away.

Chloe's face broke into a huge grin.

"Daddy? It's Chloe . . . Yes. We're safe. There's a man here called Gabriel. He saved us. He . . ."

The young woman couldn't go on. Her voice thickened in her throat then died. Tears were running freely through the dirt on her face, and she handed the phone to her mother.

"Darling, it's me . . . No, she's fine . . . Yes, I am too. Look, I want to talk and I love you so terribly much, but we have to go. I'll call you again as soon as I can . . . Yes. Bye darling. Bye . . . I love you too. Bye."

Sarah handed the phone back to Gabriel.

"I'm right, aren't I?" she said. "It's not safe here."

"Hmm?" Gabriel said. "What? No. Definitely, one hundred per cent not safe."

He wiped his hand over his face; it came away grimy and dark with sweat and the particles of blood and tissue that had sprayed back when he killed Erik.

Even though their ordeal had been far worse than his, Sarah Bryant immediately began to take care of him.

"Oh, you poor man. At least let's get you cleaned up before we go. Wait there."

She hurried through to a further cabin beyond the living quarters and he heard the sound of a tap running. A few moments later she reappeared carrying a pale-pink washcloth.

"Now then," she said, tipping his head up by lifting his chin, "let's tidy you up so you don't frighten the horses." With brisk but gentle strokes she wiped the muck away with the warm flannel, then smoothed his hair down with her fingers. "There. Much more presentable. Shall we go?"

"Could you take a look at my arm first? I may have a bit of a cut there."

"Of course! How stupid of me to be cleaning your face when you're hurt."

Sarah helped him out of his hoodie and pulled the T-shirt over his head. She winced when she saw the stab wound in his bicep.

"It looks worse than it is, I think. It's still bleeding but it's dark, so no arteries hurt." She caught his quizzical stare. "Qualified first-aider."

She went back to the room she had shared with Chloe, and reappeared a few moments later with a strip of bed sheet in her hand. With deft movements, she wound it tightly around his bicep, and then split the last six inches of the improvised bandage to tie it off. With the bleeding stanched, she helped him back into his clothes.

Gabriel realised he had been sinking into a trance under the woman's ministrations. He stood now, ready to take charge and complete the mission.

"Chloe, Sarah, I have a car here. We're going to walk quickly out of here and turn immediately left. It's about a third of a mile away, but this place is deserted now, so there's no more danger. Whatever you see, ignore it and keep on walking, yes?"

"Yes," they said in unison, mother and daughter ready to go by the look of their faces, which were set in determined frowns. Then Chloe's eyes widened.

"Our stuff," she said. "Can we bring it?"

"Of course. Just be quick."

"Come on, Mum," Chloe said, "I don't want to leave anything here. Not even a sock."

Two minutes later, Gabriel led them out of the nest of cabins, reloaded M16 in the ready position at hip height, finger covering the trigger. Outside, the late-afternoon sun was throwing long shadows across the yard and pushing the narrow gaps between the walls of cars into premature dusk. The yard was totally silent. He walked at a fast marching pace back to the car, rifle barrel moving constantly, left to right, right to left again. Nobody sprang out, blood spouting from a missing eye or cradling their guts in their hands. They had a clear run all the way to the car, which sat exactly where he had left it, with the key in the ignition.

Gabriel opened the tailgate, and Chloe and Sarah pushed their bags in. For a moment, Gabriel debated holding onto the M16, then he turned and hurled it back down the road. He walked to the nearside passenger door and pulled it open.

"Which one of you wants to ride shotgun?" he asked. Chloe answered him by climbing into the rear seat behind the driver.

When they were all seated and belted in, Gabriel pushed the engine start button and the engine growled into life.

"The main gates are locked," Gabriel said. "I'm not going to stop. These cars are solid enough so I'm going to hit them hard and ram our way out. Hold on tight."

He pulled the gear selector into Drive and put his foot down. A thousand yards away lay the access road and after that, a straight run to an extraction point he would set up with Don once they'd left Tartu behind them. There were no obstructions on the roadway leading to the complex of buildings where the Bryants had been held, and nothing beyond.

Grit and gravel spurted from under the massive rear tyres as the Mercedes struggled for grip on the loose surface, then the rubber bit down onto the tarmac beneath and the car surged forward. They passed the cabins doing forty, the right speed to smash through the gates without risking losing control.

Then, halfway between them and the gleaming steel gates in the distance, a figure stepped out into the roadway, carrying a Kalashnikov AK-47 assault rifle.

A figure with long, tangled dirty blonde hair, matted with blood.

CHAPTER 45

"It's Elsbeta," Sarah said, in a dull, defeated tone.

In the few seconds remaining to him Gabriel made his decision.

The Chechen had adopted a markswoman's stance: turned side-on, leaning forward, rifle butt pulled into her shoulder.

Gabriel shouted "Duck!" and pushed down hard on the accelerator pedal. Chloe and Sarah twisted in their seat belts and threw themselves sideways.

He slumped in his seat and braced his arms to keep the steering at the dead-ahead as the Mercedes sensed the change in throttle pressure and leapt forwards, dropping from fourth to second gear in a couple of hundred milliseconds.

Then Elsbeta opened up with the Kalashnikov.

The muzzle flashed as the rounds exploded out towards Gabriel. The roar of the weapon was reduced to a muffled chatter by the expensive sound-deadening of the Mercedes. He flinched reflexively but kept his course.

The AK's rounds should have smashed through the windscreen, shattering it into a million razor-edged fragments. They did not.

Instead, they punched fist-sized craters that blistered inwards in crazed stars. Loud metallic bangs echoed inside the car as rounds hit the bodywork at the front. But the engine kept roaring and the car kept moving.

Gabriel had only time for one thought, which burst from his lips.

"It's armoured."

Then he hit the last Chechen, Elsbeta Daspireva, amidships.

The force of the impact threw her twenty feet into the air, up and over the roof of the Mercedes, the Kalashnikov taking a separate path away from her to clatter into a pile of broken up truck engines. In the rear-view mirror, Gabriel saw the body fall.

He swapped from throttle to brake and brought the Mercedes to a stop, the anti-lock brakes shuddering, before pushing the gear lever to Park.

"Wait here," he said, as he climbed out.

He walked back to where the woman lay on her back, her left leg twisted under her, like a dropped marionette. She was alive; he could see her chest rising and falling as he got closer. Blood was leaking from her ears, nose and mouth. Keeping his SIG aimed at her chest, he stood above her, then crouched beside her head. That was when he noticed the acute triangle of bloodied steel plate protruding from her chest, just to the right of her sternum. She had landed on a piece of scrap left in the roadway.

Her eyes opened and for a moment he was struck by their startling sapphire-blue irises, made even brighter by the blood-filled corneas. In a voice roughened by pain, she whispered, "Come closer. My last wish."

As Gabriel bent, turning his ear to her mouth, he caught a movement at her waist. Her left hand came up gripping a short-bladed knife. But her strength was gone and he simply caught her wrist and twisted the knife from her fingers. He stood back. No medics. No choppers. No chance of an ambulance. But hours more pain for this enemy fighter.

He levelled his SIG, aimed at her forehead, and fired twice.

Then he ran back to the car. This time there would be no more delays. He gunned the engine and tore off towards the gates.

"Hold tight!" he shouted, accelerating up to forty and passing a tower of cars.

He aimed for the centre-line of the gates, where the loop of chain dangled like a necklace. The armoured steel front end of the Mercedes burst the gates open with a bang and the protesting shriek of tearing metal. They were out.

Resisting the urge to floor the accelerator and get away from the scrapyard at top speed, Gabriel kept to forty. No sense in picking up a speeding ticket from local law enforcement and having to answer a whole lot of awkward questions. He drove on for another five miles, listening to the women beside and behind him talking in low yet excited tones about their ordeal, which he could tell was already reshaping itself into anecdotal form. Good for them, he thought.

On a narrow stretch of road through a wood composed of birch and spruce, he found a layby and pulled over.

"I need to call someone."

Gabriel walked a few yards away from the car and called Don. He picked up on the second ring.

"Tell me, Old Sport."

"It's all good. I have Sarah and Chloe. They're both fit and well. Bit grubby, and Chloe's going to need a decent plastic surgeon, but in good spirits. Four Chechens down, and two ex-Spetsnaz Russians too."

"Right. I'll organise a cleanup team. Are you exfiltrated?"

"Five miles from the scrapyard on a bearing roughly north-west from Tartu. Should be plain sailing from here – the Merc's armoured. Took a whole magazine from an AK and didn't even lose a windscreen wiper."

"Extraction point, then. We'll find somewhere suitable. Keep driving, and I'll text you the GPS coordinates."

"OK. We'd better press on. I think we were isolated enough for the firing to go unnoticed but I don't want to get entangled with the Estonian police."

"No. On you go, then. I'll be back in touch."

Gabriel ended the call and turned to Sarah. "Can you open Don's text when it arrives please? He's fixing up your flight home."

"I'll do it," Chloe said.

She reached forward and took the phone then leant back in her seat.

"That was a pretty neat trick you pulled with your own phone," Gabriel said. "How did you do it?"

"Didn't anyone tell you? I'm a genius with electronics. I relax by dicking around with quantum computing."

"Chloe, please!" her mother interrupted.

"Sorry, Mum. I designed a cheeky little circuit that can transmit a super-powerful GPS ping. It was an idea a few of us were working on back at UMIST. Kasym thought he was being clever taking my SIM. But Emmeline works without one."

"Emmeline?"

"After Emmeline Pankhurst. The suffragette leader? We thought it was a cool name for a gizmo designed to let people know where you stand."

"Well, it worked brilliantly. I wouldn't be surprised if you got a tap on the shoulder with a brain like yours."

Now it was Chloe's turn to look puzzled. "A what?"

"When they recruit spooks. Spies, you know? It's what they call it. Shadowy chaps in dark-grey suits and old-school ties loitering around Oxford and Cambridge looking for other chaps they can trust. And chapesses these days."

"Well, they might have to consider slumming it in Manchester if they want to get their hands on Emmeline, then. Oh, your phone buzzed. Here's the text. Hold on. OK: fifty-nine degrees, twenty minutes, zero-point-three-two-six north. Twenty-five degrees, fourteen minutes, forty-eight-point-one-zero-nine seconds east."

"Thanks. Now can you launch an app on there called Recipes?"

"Why? Are you going to cook something for us?"

"Just do it, please. You'll see."

There was a pause while Chloe searched for, found and launched the app.

"Oh, wow, how cool is that? It's some kind of black ops satnav isn't it?"

"Kind of. Just cut and paste the coordinates into the box and then could you hand it to me?"

Another pause, and then Chloe's hand snaked between the front headrests and handed Gabriel the phone. He wedged it into a cupholder, and then his shoulders dropped. He felt the tight steel coils around his chest unwinding until he could breathe deeply again. A glance down told him all he needed to know.

"We have about an hour's driving. I'm going to put my foot down. If you two want to sleep, that's fine by me."

"No thanks," Sarah said. "I'm too excited to sleep. And look at those beautiful trees. I don't want to miss this. After all, I don't think I'll be coming back to Estonia."

Gabriel looked over. The woman was smiling at him.

"When we get back to England, I think I would like to take you out to a very nice restaurant, Gabriel. And your partner, if you have one."

Gabriel wondered if any woman fitted that description. Not Annie Frears. Not Britta Falskog. Not really.

"I'm single. But yes, I would like that very much."

"That's settled then. Though I should probably ask you your surname if we're to become better acquainted."

"It's Wolfe. With an 'e'."

"Well, Gabriel Wolfe-with-an-'e', I shall spend some time thinking where to take you."

With shafts of late-afternoon sunlight arrowing down through the pale-green leaves of the birch trees, Gabriel leaned back against the leather seat, and took the Mercedes up to ninety. There was virtually no traffic as they drove back towards Tallinn, just the odd truck or car, maybe twenty in the entire time they were on the road. Despite her protestations, Sarah had fallen asleep. Gabriel glanced to his right and saw her head was canted over at an awkward angle, her right temple resting on the window. In the rear seat, Chloe snored softly, her face in repose like a child's: unlined, pale complexion showing through the streaks of grime; rounded cheeks, soft, pouting lips. He drove on.

After another three-quarters of an hour, the satnav woke up, and a pleasant female voice told him to turn off the main road. He slowed for the turn and took the sweeping curve of the slip road at a more sensible thirty, before merging onto a single-carriageway country road. It was the end of the mission, and he was exhausted, but he had time and enthusiasm left to admire the countryside: multicoloured fields interspersed with clumps of deep-green woodland. Whether it was pollen or dust blowing off the bone-dry fields, Gabriel couldn't tell, but the hazy sunshine illuminated the air itself and lit up the white trunks of the birches so they glowed. The hedges flashing by on either side bore swags of white flowers amid the glossy leaves shining in the soft, golden light.

Then, in the distance, he saw a familiar object. As the satnav announced he was approaching his destination, the pale blue-and-black signboard confirmed its conclusion.

You are now entering Amari Air Force Base.
   This is a restricted area.
   Please stop at gatehouse.

He turned right onto a wide concrete apron in front of a pair of steel gates topped with razor wire, and got out of the car. A soldier wearing a pale-blue NATO beret and carrying an Israeli-made IMI Galil assault rifle over the crook of his arm came up to the gates from the other side. He had three stripes on his upper arms.

"Yes, sir. How can I help you?" A challenge as much as a request.

"My name is Gabriel Wolfe. I believe you're expecting me?"

The man's face, so watchful a moment or two before, now broke into a wide grin. "Yes, sir. Wait there while I open the gates."

Gabriel climbed back into the car as the young sergeant ran back to the gatehouse. Sarah and Chloe were both awake. A few seconds later, the heavy gates swung back on remote-controlled pistons, and clanked into their open position. Gabriel eased the car through the gap, and watched in the mirror as they swung closed behind him.

"Sarah, Chloe, you're safe."

CHAPTER 46

Sarah and Chloe were taken off for hot showers and a meal by a female Estonian lieutenant who spoke flawless, unaccented English. Gabriel sat with Don Webster in the officers' mess drinking mugs of hot, strong tea.

"Thought I'd pop over and handle things personally, dear boy," Don said, then blew the surface of his tea. "Jesus! What do they use to make this, a nuclear reactor?"

It wasn't a very good joke, but it didn't need to be. Gabriel laughed, relieved that the mission had been a success. Hostages out, unharmed; himself out, also unharmed, more or less. He had an appointment with the base's resident trauma surgeon for some work on the stab wound, which had started to throb.

"How are you getting them home?" he asked.

"We're getting them – and you – home on a chopper across the Gulf of Finland to Stockholm, then you're booked First Class on a scheduled flight to Heathrow. You should be home by midnight. You called Bryant, so he's a very happy man. And," he checked his watch, a battered, silver-faced Timex on a frayed red, white and blue canvas strap, "I would say just about now some very clever, but also very bad Ukrainian scientists are discovering the delights of an MI5 interrogation suite. Gulliver has been temporarily suspended, but we secured the parallel batch of clean pills, so Farnborough's going to be fine. Which just leaves you."

Don leaned back in his chair, careful not to spill any of the irradiated tea, and watched Gabriel over the rim of the mug as he blew on it again. Gabriel looked at the man who had sent him into battle all over the world. Tried to read what was behind those grey, crinkled eyes. Failed.

"Which just leaves me. I know you want me to go back to England straight away . . ."

"But?" The older man waited for Gabriel to speak again.

"But there are a couple of loose ends I need to tie up here. It won't take long. Maybe until tomorrow morning."

"Listen Old Sport, after what you've just accomplished, if you need to kiss a girl goodbye or give someone a hiding, that's your business."

How did you know? We used to joke you were psychic but that was a little too close for comfort.

"Nobody has any further calls on your time. I'll be here until tomorrow, so let me know when you're ready and we'll fly you out pronto."

"Thanks, Don."

"And you'll find, the next time you log on to your bank, there's a rather tidy sum of money sitting there for you that wasn't there when you left England. Your fee from us and a bonus paid personally by James Bryant."

* * *

An hour later, Gabriel was sitting in the Merc on a deserted industrial estate three miles east of Tallinn. He had Erik's phone in his hand. All but one of the outbound calls were to the same contact: Yuri. He tapped the text icon by the number and began the message, the Cyrillic characters on the virtual keyboard no problem whatsoever.

. . .

*Chechens dead. Hostages and Fox dead too. Chechen-style. Have souvenirs.
Out of gas. Rastvallu Business Centre car park. Need ride, bring money.*

Gabriel pressed Send, then waited.

He didn't have to wait long.

Thirty seconds later, the phone vibrated in his hand.

*Good. You did well. There in 30 mins. Next time fill tank BEFORE leaving
the job.*

Gabriel went round to the back of the car and pulled open the
tailgate by the handle, too impatient to wait for the electric motors to
do their work.

He took what was left of the C-4, moulded it into a ball, then got
onto his belly and squeezed under the car. Grunting with the effort,
he wriggled his way between the floor pan and the gritty ground,
wedging the grey lump behind the gearbox above the prop shaft.
Then he pushed the radio detonator supplied by Yuri himself into the
lower surface of the explosive. He flicked the tiny switch to arm it
then crawled backwards to get out, watching the red LED winking its
"ready and waiting" message at him.

With the radio trigger in his hand, he walked away from the Merc,
locking it with the remote as he went. The sunlight was fading fast,
but there was no chance Yuri would see the LED, it was too well
hidden. An alley between two dilapidated factory buildings offered
the perfect place of concealment, and he sat with his back against a
wall, buried in the shadows, with a clear line of sight to the Mercedes.

The dusk faded to night, but there were no streetlamps on the
vast expanse of tarmac to reveal his position. He wiped his palm
across his face, the oily, plastic smell of the C-4 catching in the back
of his throat.

Then, in the distance, a familiar yowling engine note. *Of course, what other car would a Russian gangster drive but a Ferrari?* The white-blue headlamps of the car swept across the deserted space as Volkov drove onto the tarmac and pulled up a hundred yards away from the Mercedes.

Cautious. Even with your own men. Good for you. You sent them to kill the people I was rescuing, and me too. I'd be cautious in your shoes.

There was enough light pollution from Tallinn's streetlamps, pink against a hazy night sky, to reveal the car as a white FF, Ferrari's only four-seater. Volkov emerged. He sauntered towards the Mercedes, no doubt enjoying making his dimwitted lieutenants wait for their lift home, maybe planning a few choice words about efficiency.

Volkov was halfway to the Mercedes. Then he stopped and took his phone out. The phone in Gabriel's pocket buzzed against his hip. He fumbled it out and checked the screen.

Why no lights?

Gabriel's mind raced to come up with an answer. His fingers flew over the screen.

Konstantin asleep. I'm tired, too.

Gabriel watched as Volkov shook his head, pocketed his phone and resumed his march towards the Mercedes. He was within thirty yards now.

Gabriel's thumb flicked the cover from the red 'Fire' button.

Twenty yards.

Gabriel closed the pad of his thumb over the greasy plastic circle.

Ten.

Five.

"This is for Astrid," he whispered.

CHAPTER 47

Gabriel saw the vermillion flash first. Then the crack and boom of the explosion hit him with physical force. He squeezed his eyes shut as what had been a five-tonne armoured Mercedes flew outwards in a hemispherical cloud of shrapnel. The larger pieces of wreckage – doors, body panels, transmission, engine, running gear – travelled hardly at all. Mostly, they were mangled by the blast where they stood. But the windows, the interior and thousands of smaller components, from wires to fuel filters, hurtled upwards before obeying gravity and spattering the ground in a hail of red-hot metal, glass splinters and molten plastic.

Gabriel opened his eyes and looked towards the wreck. A cloud of black smoke rolled around itself as it climbed a hundred or so feet into the air. The remains of the car were burning fiercely, sending flames and showers of multicoloured sparks out as different materials ignited or exploded. He waited, as the harsh, greasy smell of the fire drifted over him on the breeze.

Then with a dull crump, the petrol tank blew, the orange fireball sending green afterimages dancing across Gabriel's retinas.

Gabriel ran over to the burning mess of tangled metal. Of Volkov, there was no sign. Or not precisely no sign. Lying ten feet apart were a pair of blackened Gucci loafers, their snaffle bit decorations distorted into golden pretzels by the intense heat of the blast.

Gabriel smiled grimly and nodded his head.

Knowing that even on an abandoned industrial site like this one, there would be a police and fire presence shortly, Gabriel sprinted for the Ferrari. Thanks to Volkov's instinct for the potential double-cross, it was parked far enough away to be untouched by the explosion. He slid into the scarlet leather seat, turned the key and thumbed the starter button. To his right, lying flat on the passenger seat was a black, crocodile-skin briefcase with gold furniture. He pressed the small circular button beneath the handle. The latches popped open with a muted clack, revealing bricks of green hundred-euro notes encircled by duck-egg-blue paper bands.

He flipped the paddle behind the steering wheel to engage first gear and pulled away, heading back into Tallinn.

Five minutes later, he stopped at a green traffic light to let a screaming convoy of police cars and fire engines shoot across in front of him, on their way to the industrial estate.

His first stop was at his hotel. Ten minutes later, he was packed, checked out and back in the FF. He called Astrid.

"Hello?"

"Hi Astrid, it's Gabriel."

"Hey, where have you been? You were missed, you know."

"Tartu. Are you working tonight?"

"Yes. Till three. You want to get together afterwards?"

"I can't. I'm sorry. I have to leave."

"Leave what? The bar?"

"No. Estonia. I found the women I told you about. I'm leaving tonight. But I have something for you. Maybe it will help Joonas a bit too. I'll see you in fifteen minutes."

* * *

Gabriel parked in a side street and left the keys in the ignition. He grabbed the briefcase from the passenger seat and set off for Jonny Rocketz.

There was a new guy on the door. Silvi had gone back to the tried and tested model: six-five, made out of girders and cement, shaved head, jutting jaw, narrowed eyes. Gabriel nodded at the man and pushed his way into the bar. It was a noisy night. Silvi had installed a karaoke machine, and a paralytically drunk woman of maybe thirty-five or six was staring fixedly at the TV screen in front of her and howling into a metallic blue microphone.

He shouldered his way through the audience and found a space at the bar. Astrid was pouring a pint for a heavily tattooed guy with a huge ginger beard and thick-rimmed, black glasses. She saw him, and then turned back to her customer to take his money and give him change from the till. She came over to Gabriel.

"I knew you were too good to be true," she said. "And I really liked you."

"I'm sorry, Astrid. But work's work, I'm afraid, and my work here is finished. Look, I can't stay but I've got something for you. Meet me at the end of the bar."

Astrid waved a hand to the other bartender, a muscly guy in white T-shirt and bleach-washed jeans.

"Hey, Marek, cover for me for a minute, OK?" she shouted.

He rolled his eyes, then smiled and flapped his hand: "Go! Go!"

Gabriel met Astrid at the end of the bar, and they went through the door to the staff area.

He knelt down and unsnapped the latches in the case. He swivelled it round to face her and lifted the lid.

Her eyes widened and her mouth dropped open.

"What the fuck is this? Did you rob a bank?"

"Not exactly. It's Yuri's. Well, it was. He won't be needing it any more. I want you to have it. You could buy a bigger place maybe, get Joonas's band new gear. I don't care. I don't want it."

She looked up at him, tears running down from the inner corners of her eyes and rolling onto her top lip.

"I said you were too good to be true, you fucker. And now you prove me wrong."

He helped her to her feet and she threw her arms around him and squeezed as if she could drive the breath from him and force him to stay with her. She drew away and kissed him hard on the mouth, searching out his tongue with her own. Finally he eased her away, cupping her damp cheeks in his palms.

"It was fun, knowing you."

"Yeah, you too. Now fuck off and catch your plane. I have a bar full of drunken office workers to serve."

Astrid barged the door open and went back to serving drinks, swiping a forearm across her eyes as she went. Gabriel waited a few more seconds, then followed her. He walked out through the crowded bar without looking back. The cold air hit him as he emerged from the muggy atmosphere of the bar, and he realised Astrid wasn't the only one with wet skin.

He drove to the airport, left the FF in long-term parking with the keys in, and found a room in one of the budget hotels.

* * *

At half-past twelve the following afternoon, Gabriel was climbing the stairs to a British Airways ATR 72 twin turboprop on the apron at Tallinn airport. At the top, he paused while a portly businessman in a wrinkled grey suit rooted around in his jacket pockets for his boarding card.

"It's here somewhere," the man muttered, while the stewardess smiled her professional smile, never letting her immaculately made-up face betray the irritation she must surely be feeling. Finally the card was produced with a flourish from a waistcoat pocket.

"Ta dah!" the man said, as if he'd conjured a dove from a hat instead of a small piece of card from his own pocket.

Gabriel moved forward, holding his own boarding card out ready for inspection. She took it and when her eyes returned to his, her smile widened. "Welcome aboard, Mr Wolfe. Did you have a pleasant stay in Estonia?"

"I may need some time to think about that."

"Well, enjoy the flight. We'll do all we can to make it comfortable for you."

Then he was waiting in the aisle, then sitting, staring out of the tiny plastic oval window, then feeling the familiar tug in the pit of his stomach as the plane parted company with the ground.

He sighed and rubbed his hand over his face, as if he would scrub it away altogether. He was thinking about fixing another session with Fariyah Crace, and about a therapist called Richard Austin and what EMDR might do for him.

"Mr Wolfe?" a voice said.

He looked to his left. The speaker, leaning over the empty seat next to him, was the stewardess. She was holding a plastic tumbler that chuckled with ice cubes, floating in what smelled like a very strong gin and tonic, laced with lime juice, just the way he liked it.

"Let me put this down for you." She put a circular cocktail napkin on his tray table and placed the drink on top of it.

"Thank you. I didn't see the trolley."

"Special service," she said with a wink.

Gabriel picked up the tumbler and took a long pull on the chilled drink. Then he looked down at the napkin. He picked it up, and grinned.

There was a message written on it in blue ballpoint.

"Cheers! You earned it. D."

CHAPTER 48

The Farnborough Air Show's final spectacle took place on a glorious July day. In a VIP stand directly in front of the takeoff zone, a group of very senior Royal Air Force officers drank flutes of champagne.

Their guests included a number of politicians and officials from the Ministry of Defence and the Department of Trade. In the centre of a group of five men, all dressed in virtually identical navy-blue, two-piece suits with white shirts and dark ties, sat a tall, white-haired Russian: Oleg Abramov. They applauded along with the crowds at the end of each display of military hardware.

Two rows further back, Tom Ainsley sat beside Niamh, he in his RAF dress uniform and wearing sunglasses so dark as to be opaque, she in a simple green silk dress. Tom followed the flight path of each aircraft as it performed stunts or low-altitude passes over the airfield.

Finally, the moment the crowd had been waiting for arrived. Over the Tannoy, the announcer explained that they were about to see one of the world's best pilots taking the world's most agile jet fighter to its limits.

Five seconds passed in absolute silence, then with a shriek of combusting aviation fuel and an earsplitting rumble of exhaust gases, an RAF Typhoon, delta wings bristling with missiles and spare fuel nacelles, roared over the airfield, two hundred feet above the heads of the spectators. The thrust from its two screaming Rolls-Royce engines took the plane to nine hundred and ten miles per hour.

The jet pulled up into a vertical climb to fifteen thousand feet, then fell sideways towards Earth, spinning and flickering like a silver sycamore seed.

So focused that she felt she was a part of the Typhoon's avionics systems, the pilot, Flight Lieutenant Shiona Webb, demonstrated to the crowd the incredible acrobatic abilities of her plane, and to the officials and Air Force officers the stunning cognitive enhancements made possible by Gulliver.

Niamh leant closer to Tom and kissed his cheek as he tracked his fellow pilot's rolling, tumbling, looping flight through the crystalline blue sky above the Hampshire countryside.

As the display came to an end, and the Typhoon disappeared over the horizon on its way back to its home base at RAF Lossiemouth in Scotland, Abramov smiled. But then the smug expression on his face changed, as the men sitting to his immediate left and right stood, together.

The man to his right put his hand on Abramov's shoulder and bent to speak into his ear. The Russian frowned and shook his head. The man spoke again and lifted his jacket away from his shirt, showing Abramov something concealed inside. Abramov stood, clearly reluctant, and together with the two men, made his way along the row of seats.

At the back of the VIP seating area, Don Webster waited. He had identified Abramov's true business partner. And now he wanted to talk to him about international dealings in British Government-licensed pharmaceuticals technology. It would be a long conversation.

The End

Read on for the first chapter of the next book in the Gabriel Wolfe series: *Condor* ...

GOD'S TEARS

THE NINETEEN-YEAR-OLD GIRL formerly known as Eloise Alice Virginia Payne, and now simply as Child Eloise, stood in front of the older woman, naked but for a pair of white, cotton briefs and a much-washed, plain, white bra, the thin straps frayed at the point they crossed her bony shoulders. They'd given her an extra cup of the sacrament that morning, and now she was blinking rapidly and couldn't stop clenching her jaw. She was thin, and her skin was so pale the blue of her veins showed clearly on the insides of her thighs and down her neck onto her breastbone. The insides of her forearms were laddered with fine, white scars. The room in which she was standing was on the top floor of a sand-coloured, terraced house on a crescent flanking London Zoo. It was flooded with pale September sunlight that caught the fine, blonde hairs on Child Eloise's arms and legs.

"Will it hurt, Auntie?" she asked.

The short, silver-haired woman took the dressmaking pins from between her thin lips to answer, first pushing her glasses higher up on her beaky nose.

"No, child. You will feel God's breath on you, that is all, just as Père Christophe taught you. Then you will be with the Creator, safe and sound. Now, hold still while I finish your raiment."

The young woman stood, trying to be still, but the muscles in her legs quivered in a relentless beat. She tried to imagine what it would be like. A flash of light and heat, and then some sort of awakening in Heaven. Would God actually be there to meet her? What if he was busy? But Père Christophe was clear on this point of doctrine. She was doing His will by serving Père Christophe, and of course He would be aware of that and would be there, ready to receive her.

As she shuddered and quivered, frowning with the effort of standing still, her Auntie pulled the cotton garment over her head and down her narrow torso. It had no sleeves, nor collar. It did have a series of ten sagging pockets that circled her chest like something a hunter or a fisherman would have on his jacket, each three inches wide, three deep and nine from top to bottom.

With a few deft stitches, her Auntie sewed a narrow strip of cotton from front to back between the young woman's legs, forming a crude leotard.

"There!" Auntie said, standing back to admire her handiwork. "All finished. Now we just need to fill those pockets and you're ready for your glorification."

Three miles away, Harry Barnes was getting ready for another day's sightseeing. He was a trim sixty-three, and liked to keep in shape playing golf and the odd game of tennis. He had a year-round tan, and he thought it set off his close-set, pale-blue eyes just fine. Since the divorce had come through, he'd been enjoying "every Goddamned minute" of his life, as he'd put it to a fellow he'd met in a pub the previous night, over a couple of pints of that weird, flat British beer. That included this no-expense-spared, two-week vacation to the UK.

The day looked like it was going to be fine, but Harry was from Reno, Nevada, where he managed a casino, and counted anything below seventy as dangerously chilly. He shrugged on his fawn windcheater over the sweater, and the Tattersall check shirt and undershirt he'd already tucked into his grey pants, or what did the Brits call them? "Trousers?" Funny word.

He sauntered down the short path from his hotel to the street, pausing on the edge of the black-and-white-chequered tiles to admire the park and its trees opposite the hotel. Back where Harry came from, there wasn't a whole lot of greenery. Bayswater was full of other tourists, folks heading to work, even a party of kids, all wearing plum and grey school uniforms, and matching caps or floppy felt bonnets, like something out of Masterpiece Theatre. They were being led in a crocodile by a pretty young redhead in a lime-green dress with patent leather pumps on her feet. She reminded him of his daughter.

No bus in sight, but Harry didn't mind. Linda had been the one who was always in such a hurry. Well, now she'd rushed off with half his money and her skiing instructor, so fuck her. Harry liked waiting. Gave a man time to think.

* * *

Gabriel Wolfe sat at a small, circular, brushed aluminium table outside an Italian café on the northern end of Regent Street. From his vantage point on Biaggi's pocket handkerchief-sized terrace, he looked south to Oxford Circus, a throbbing crossroads where pedestrians swarmed around the junction, pushed and jostled their way down into the tube station beneath the pavement, or darted across the road in front of hooting taxis and buses groaning with passengers.

He sipped his flat white, savouring the smooth, strong coffee beneath the creamy milk, and took a mouthful of the delicately lemon-flavoured cake. It had been brought to him a few minutes earlier by the owner, a scrawny old guy who still spoke in a strong Italian accent despite having lived in London, as he told Gabriel, "since the sixties. Swingin' London an' all that, innit?"

The day was bright, and the bite in the air was counterbalanced by the warmth of the sunshine on his face. It was "a real Indian summer" as his father would have declared it, before finishing his tea and toast, folding his newspaper under his arm, ruffling his son's straight, black hair, and heading off to his job as a diplomat in Hong Kong.

Gabriel's three-piece Glen plaid suit in a lightweight grey wool was perfectly suited to the air temperature. Today, he'd paired it with a pale-lavender shirt, a knitted, black silk tie, and a pair of highly polished, black brogues. He was on his way to meet a prospective client: the CEO of a firm that offered close protection to foreign celebrities and VIPs visiting London. She wanted help training her operatives, as she called them. Firearms, unarmed combat, defensive driving. Bread and butter for Gabriel, and very well-paid bread and butter at that. Early for the meeting, he'd stopped for breakfast on this wide boulevard, only a hundred yards or so from the streaming crowds of London's main east-west thoroughfare, but as quiet as a village high street in comparison.

With a clatter from its diesel engine, a very high-mileage example to judge from the grey smoke rolling out from its exhaust pipe, a car drew up at the kerb, blocking his view across the street. Nothing fancy, a silver Ford Mondeo estate, one of millions like it on Britain's roads, with the rear windows blacked out with plastic film. A common-enough modification these days, when every suburban middle manager wanted to look like a drug dealer. From the rear seat, a young woman got out. Her hair was blonde and cut short. Nothing stylish – in fact, it looked like someone had done it for her at home using kitchen scissors. Her shoulders were hunched inside a black, padded jacket, and the muscles around her pale-blue eyes were tight. She kept grimacing as if she had just tasted something unpleasant; her mouth kept stretching wide then releasing again. He caught a glimpse of a middle-aged woman ushering her from her seat, gold-framed glasses glinting as a shaft of sunlight penetrated the gloomy interior of the car.

Without looking back, the young woman shuffled down the street towards Oxford Circus.

* * *

Harry was enjoying himself. He'd caught his bus, a 94, after ten minutes' wait, and was sitting on the top deck chatting to a new friend. Her name was Vivienne. She was a little younger than Harry, fifty-eight or nine, maybe. No wedding ring. She was a looker all right, and Harry told her so after a few minutes' idle conversation about the weather.

"My ex-wife would kill for hair like yours," he said. "Real natural blonde, none of that peroxide stuff. It kills the shine, and probably the planet too, for all I know."

"Aren't you the Sir Galahad," Vivienne had replied, patting her hair and smiling. Her lips were a pale pink, and seemed to shimmer in the light coming through the grimy window of the bus. Harry was close enough to see the way traces of lipstick had worked their way along thin creases that ran over the edge of her upper lip.

"Hey, at my age, we call it like we see it. Am I right? Plus, we got taught good manners, which in my book includes complimenting a beautiful woman on her looks."

He really hoped he hadn't just overdone it, but Vivienne seemed happy enough with this gentle flirting. Her figure was just what Harry liked, too: round in all the right places – none of that bony, sucked-in look so many of his ex-wife's friends paid so much to achieve. "Why wouldn't a woman want to look like a woman?" Harry had asked Linda one day when they were still talking.

"Jesus, Harry, you're such a fucking dinosaur," had been her baffling reply, leaving Harry none the wiser but one tick closer to hiring a divorce lawyer.

As the bus lumbered along the start of Oxford Street, they stared down at the tacky tourist shops. Displays of T-shirts emblazoned with union jacks jostled for pavement space with circular racks of sunglasses and displays of miniature red telephone boxes, bear-skinned soldiers in sentry boxes and teddy bears dressed like Yeomen of the Guard. Just in front of them, a bright-yellow metal fitting was vibrating in time with the big diesel engine some ten feet below them. The buzz was loud enough to make Harry have to raise his voice.

"This could be a mite forward of me," Harry said, after clearing his throat, "but would you have some time this morning to see a couple of sights with an American on his first trip to the United Kingdom of Great Britain?"

He held his breath as he watched Vivienne. She checked her watch. Rolex Perpetual Oyster Lady Day-Date, Harry noted with a professional's glance, a nice model. You could tell a lot about a punter by their choice of watch. Then she looked at him. And smiled.

"You know what, Harry? I think I might."

Harry smiled right back.

* * *

Something about the young woman had troubled Gabriel. Now, his antennae were flickering and twitching, and a thin blade of fear was lying on its edge inside his stomach. She'd looked anxious, but so did lots of people. She was so tense she couldn't walk easily. Her coltish legs looked uncoordinated, as if she had only learned how to use them a few hours earlier. A job interview? The clothes didn't look right. Black jeans, black quilted jacket. And no make-up. Which would have been a good idea, as her eyes were red from crying. She'd looked skinny. The jeans were narrow cut, and her thighs didn't even fill them. Her wrists looked bony too. Yet her body looked bulbous, bulky somehow, even allowing for the stuffing of the jacket.

No, it wasn't the woman herself. It was her ride. After she'd left the car, the driver had executed a rapid U-turn in the street, tyres screeching on full lock as their treads scraped across the tarmac, forcing a taxi to slam its brakes on, and the cabbie to curse, loudly and fluently, from his open window. Acrid, blue rubber-smoke drifted across towards Gabriel's table.

* * *

Child Eloise waited at the bus-stop on Oxford Street. She looked behind her at the shop window. It was filled with a display of what she had initially taken to be fruit or perhaps cakes, but which, on closer inspection, turned out to be handmade soaps, things called 'roulades' and 'bath bombs'. Funny name. Her neighbours in the queue were all busy with their phones, swiping, scrolling and tapping. The women wore bright clothes and high-heeled shoes, and they were slathered in make-up. Painted like whores. Sinful. The men ogled the women, peering at their breasts or eyeing their stockinged legs. Lascivious. All seemed more interested in the little slivers of plastic and glass in their hands than in God's creation around them, even if it was mostly concrete and steel here. Decadent.

Despite her quilted nylon jacket, she couldn't stop shivering. She grunted involuntarily from time to time and her tongue kept poking out between her lips, causing one or two people around her to smirk before looking away. Auntie had told her not to be afraid and had given her a sweetie, "to bring you a little calmness as you do God's work, child", but she felt frightened all the same.

Under her jacket, the cotton leotard was packed with seven pounds of homemade explosive, a mixture of diesel oil, bleach, wax and potassium chloride from a health foods website. Each of the ten pockets was packed with a sausage of it; she had helped Uncle and Auntie mould them herself, rolling the sticky, greyish stuff between her palms and inserting a blasting cap and a length of detonator wire into the tops. Around the sausages lay the shiny steel spheres Uncle called, "God's tears".

The ball bearings were twenty-one millimetres across. Uncle had been most specific on that point when ordering them from the factory. He said the number was significant because it was the product of the seven deadly sins and the Holy Trinity. Together, they'd dropped twenty-five into each of the ten pockets, where they nestled against the yielding surface of the explosives.

The woman looked around again. Her phone wasn't as shiny as these others. It didn't even have a camera. Not that she could have reached it to take a picture, in any case. It, too, was sewn into her vest, in a channel sitting right over her heart. The wires from the explosives ended in a control box soldered onto the phone's battery charger socket.

* * *

Harry and Vivienne's bus pulled up outside a shop selling soaps and bath products. Through the narrow windows on the top deck, wafts of scent – tropical, spicy, lemony – insinuated themselves, causing Harry to smile without realising why. He was happy. Happy Harry.

Vivienne's thigh was pressed against his, and even though he knew it was just an accident caused by the stingy seating arrangements, he felt a prickle of desire. And it had been a long time since that had happened. Linda had stopped putting out for him years ago, and he'd never been a guy to go off looking for pleasure in a cat house or a strip club. Not that he'd have had time, the hours he put in.

"Look at her," Vivienne said, prodding the glass on her left and looking down. "Poor thing looks so miserable. And on a beautiful day like today. You'd think she'd manage a smile."

Harry leaned across, taking the opportunity to glance down the front of Vivienne's blouse. *Great rack!*

"Who? Her? The skinny one in the puffy jacket? Yeah, she does look kind of sad."

* * *

Gabriel finished his coffee, dabbed a wet fingertip into the yellow crumbs dusting his plate, sucked them into his mouth, and then stood. His meeting was in an office on a side street leading east from Regent Street. He took one final glance towards Oxford Circus, then picked up his battered Hartman briefcase and strode off towards Great Portland Street.

His phone rang. He saw the small circle enclosing a face he knew and smiled. He swiped his thumb to the right to answer the call.

"Hi, Britta, how are you? *Where* are you?"

"Hey, Gabriel. I'm good. I'm at my place in Chiswick, actually, painting my nails. My boss pretty well ordered me to take some leave. Been burning the midnight oil at both ends."

Gabriel laughed. However good her English was, Britta Falskog hadn't quite mastered all the subtleties of British idiom. On the other hand, he liked her very much; always had. They'd run joint ops for a while, back in the day, she in Swedish Special Forces, he in the SAS. And there had been the odd overnight stay. Now, since she'd been seconded to MI5, working out of their Vauxhall offices, maybe there was something in the air between them.

"So, do you want to meet up?" he said. "I'm in town, too. Going to see a new client."

"I would like that. Do you want to get dinner?"

"Sure. Then I'm heading back to Salisbury."

"Oh, OK. Well, you know, I do have a few days to kill, so maybe ..."

"A trip to the countryside? Sounds like a lovely idea."

While they bantered, Gabriel made his way along the uncrowded roads to the north of Oxford Street, heading for the offices of Faulds & Vambrace (VIP Protection) Ltd.

* * *

Eloise Payne slid her Oyster card over the scuffed magnetic reader and made her way to the stairs of the bus, which she climbed, gripping the handrail tightly. There was one free seat, about halfway back, behind a couple who were chatting away about museums and art galleries. The man reminded her of Uncle. He had the same short, white hair. Only this man spoke with an American accent.

She took the seat, next to a black woman in her thirties who was chatting into her phone and admiring her fingernails, which she extended in front of her in a fan. There seemed to be yellow flecks, like gold, floating in the orange varnish, and the tips were white.

* * *

Standing by the drawing room window in the elegant terraced house where Eloise Payne had so recently been stitched into the garment that was to become her shroud, a grey-haired man named Robert Slater, known to the Children as "Uncle Robert", looked out at the oaks, beeches and hornbeams dotting Regent's Park. He was six foot, slim, and wearing a white shirt and white trousers. He wore wire-rimmed glasses that magnified his eyes. In the distance, he could make out the long, dappled necks of a pair of giraffes grazing in their enclosure in the zoo. Through the open window, he could smell burning leaves from a bonfire somewhere in the park.

In his hand, he held a smartphone, a number keyed in and ready to be called. Beside him, Irene Stevens, Eloise Payne's Auntie and a former manager of a dressmaking business, spoke.

"Père Christophe will be pleased."

"Yes. We have proved our worthiness."

Then he tapped the green phone icon.

* * *

Inside the neat, stitched channel covering Eloise Payne's heart, the phone's circuitry woke up as the incoming call was beamed in from a cell tower on top of an office block two hundred yards to the north.

The electric current it generated was tiny. Just enough to cause a glimmer from a Christmas tree light. Or to cause a child's toy robot to take a buzzing half-step across a polished tabletop. But also enough to excite the atoms in ten, foot-long pieces of copper wire. The wave of energy travelled along the wires at the speed of light until it reached the fat cylinders of explosive corseting their wearer.

There, something curious happened. The energy of that tiny electrical charge multiplied itself billions of times as the chemical reaction it initiated gathered pace, and violence.

Exactly seventy-three milliseconds later, the atoms comprising the charges became unstable and, searching for equilibrium, set off a chain reaction that released all their pent up energy into the surrounding space.

* * *

Gabriel had just turned into the side street where his client was based. He and Britta were fixing the details of a pre-dinner drink.

"So meet at six-thirty at the French House." Britta was saying. "Shall I book the restaurant?"

"Yes, please. Anywhere we can get a decent burgundy. And I hope you …"

Gabriel didn't finish his sentence. A roaring, shattering boom cut him off.

He recognised the sound. It sounded like a truck bomb. There was a second or two of total silence, then distant screaming.

"Call you back!" he said. He stuffed the phone in his pocket, then spun round and ran back towards the main road. He turned left at the junction and sprinted towards Oxford Circus. And hell.

ORDER CONDOR FROM AMAZON

ACKNOWLEDGMENTS

Every writer should have a mentor - someone who will start off with the good news when reading that shaky first draft before suggesting, you know, a few little 'improvements' here and there. I am fortunate enough to have as both a good friend and constructive critic Katherine Wildman. Mine's a Nurotini! My first readers offered brilliant advice and criticism that helped me sharpen up my writing, and the action: my particular thanks go to Giles Elliott, Merryn Henderson and Nicky Parker.

For his invaluable guidance on the lore, language and tactics of soldiers, I need to say a big thank-you to my friend, and ex-Irish Guard, Giles Bassett. For his generosity in briefing me on the best weapons for particular jobs, I must also thank Colonel Mike Dempsey.

The Gulliver drug was my own idea, but for helping me understand a little more about pharmacology, particularly its use by the military, I am indebted to Rod Flower, Professor of Biochemical Pharmacology at Barts and The London School of Medicine and Dentistry, and to Doctor Sian Lewis for referring me to his work.

To Anouchka Askew, a special thank-you for a great little piece of Anglo-Saxon. And to Alexander Avazashvili, thanks for helping out with the Russian transliteration.

As with my first novel, *Trigger Point*, I relied for their professional publishing skills, insights and expertise on a small team of incredibly talented people. Tom Bromley did a superb job of editing the final manuscript. He is also a very good teacher. My good friend and design partner Darren Bennett designed and illustrated the cover.

Kin Ho took the author photograph for the print edition. Michelle Lowery, my proofreader, did a superb job and also offered invaluable advice on US Navy/Air Force ranks, and other military/intelligence matters.

Finally, I thank my family: Jo, Rory and Jacob. Your patience, support and love sustain me each time I embark on another book. And the rest of the time too.

All of you helped make this book far better than it would have been had I gone it alone. The responsibility for any and all errors, glitches and infelicities remains my own.

Andy Maslen
Salisbury, 2016

ALSO BY ANDY MASLEN
THE GABRIEL WOLFE SERIES

Trigger Point

Reversal of Fortune (short story)

Blind Impact

Condor

First Casualty

Fury

Rattlesnake

Minefield (novella)

No Further

Torpedo

Three Kingdoms

Ivory Nation (coming soon)

The DI Stella Cole series

Hit and Run

Hit Back Harder

Hit and Done

Let the Bones be Charred

Other fiction

Blood Loss - a Vampire Story

Non-fiction

Write to Sell

100 Great Copywriting Ideas

The Copywriting Sourcebook

Write Copy, Make Money

Persuasive Copywriting

ABOUT THE AUTHOR

Andy Maslen was born in Nottingham, in the UK, home of legendary bowman Robin Hood. Andy once won a medal for archery, although he has never been locked up by the sheriff.

He has worked in a record shop, as a barman, as a door-to-door DIY products salesman and a cook in an Italian restaurant.

As well as the Stella Cole and Gabriel Wolfe thrillers, Andy has published five works of non-fiction, on copywriting and freelancing, with Marshall Cavendish and Kogan Page. They are all available online and in bookshops.

He lives in Wiltshire with his wife, two sons and a whippet named Merlin.